A
GUSHING
FOUNTAIN

A
GUSHING
FOUNTAIN

A Novel by

Martin Walser

Translated from the German by

David Dollenmayer

Arcade Publishing • New York

First English-language Edition

Originally published in German under the title *Ein springender Brunnen* by Suhrkamp Verlag

This is a work of fiction. Names, places, characters, and incidents are either the products of the author's imagination or are used fictitiously.

Arcade Publishing books may be purchased in bulk at special discounts for sales promotion, corporate gifts, fund-raising, or educational purposes. Special editions can also be created to specifications. For details, contact the Special Sales Department, Arcade Publishing, 307 West 36th Street, 11th Floor, New York, NY 10018 or arcade@skyhorsepublishing.com.

Arcade Publishing® is a registered trademark of Skyhorse Publishing, Inc.®, a Delaware corporation.

Visit our website at www.arcadepub.com.

10 9 8 7 6 5 4 3 2 1

Library of Congress Cataloging-in-Publication Data

Walser, Martin, 1927–
 [Springender Brunnen. English]
 A gushing fountain : a novel / Martin Walser ; translated by David Dollenmayer.
   pages cm
  ISBN 978-1-62872-424-0 (hardback); ISBN 978-1-62872-544-5 (ebook)
 1. Schoolboys—Fiction. 2. Villages—Fiction. 3. National socialism—Fiction. 4. Germany—History—1933–1945—Fiction. 5. Coming of age—Fiction. I. Dollenmayer, David B. II. Title.
 PT2685.A48S6513 2015
 833'.914—dc23   2014045336

Cover design by Brian Peterson
Cover photo of Martin Walser as a boy, courtesy of the author

Printed in the United States of America

Contents

Part Three
Harvest

PART ONE

Mother Joins the Party

CHAPTER ONE

The Past as Present

As LONG AS SOMETHING IS, it isn't what it will have been. When something is past, you are no longer the person it happened to, but you're closer to him than to others. Although the past did not exist when it was present, it now obtrudes as if it had been as it now presents itself. But as long as something is, it isn't what it will have been. When something is past, you are no longer the person it happened to. When things were that we now say used to be, we didn't know they were. Now we say it used to be thus and so, although back when it was, we knew nothing about what we say now.

We can stroll around in the past we all have in common, as in a museum. One's own past is not walkable. All we have of it is what it surrenders of its own accord, even if that be no clearer than a dream. The more we could leave the past alone, the more it would become present in its own way. We destroy dreams, too, by asking them what they mean. A dream dragged into the light of another language reveals only what we ask of it. Like the victim of torture, it says anything we want to hear, but nothing of itself. As does the past.

The moment the last train of the day stops in W., you start grabbing for your bags. You have more than you can pick up all at once. All right then—concentrate—one after another. But hurry, because the train doesn't stop in Wasserburg forever. Each time you get your fingers on one bag, another you thought you had a good hold on slips from your grasp. Should you leave two or three or even four bags in the train?

Impossible. So one more time, with both hands, grab as many bags as you can. But then the train starts rolling again. It's too late.

Where do dreams come from? Telling what things were like means building a house of dreams. You've dreamed long enough, now build. When you build a house of dreams, it's not an act of will that leads to something wished for. You accept. Be prepared.

The two men who carried Father out the front door on a stretcher wore uniforms and Red Cross armbands. Big Elsa the waitress and little Mina the cook held open the swinging doors, whose upper half was of rippled glass. The front door was already open. Johann was watching it all from the kitchen door. Since the front door opened east, he was staring into a fiery streak as the men carried Father across the terrace and turned toward the ambulance. The sun was about to rise above Mount Pfänder. Ice-cold air streamed in through the open door. Early March. Father must have survived that time. The word that Johann, who hadn't started school yet, then had to spell for him was *pleurisy*. One of Father's favorite pastimes was having Johann sound out long words that at first glance seemed illegible, even though at three, four, and five years he had already learned all the letters from his older brother: *Popocatépetl, Bhagavad Gita, Rabindranath Tagore, Swedenborg, Bharatanatyam*. Words you couldn't automatically complete after hearing just the first three or four letters, like *Hindenburg, flagpole*, or *marriage*. When Johann asked what one of the hard words meant, Father would say: Let's put it in our word tree and take a look.

When a guest on the second floor pressed a button, his room number fell into the corresponding glass-fronted square in the bell box that hung in the central hallway, next to the kitchen door. Warm water then had to be taken up to that room at once so the guest could shave. Next to the bell box and also behind glass: tennis players on the deck of the SS *Bremen* from North German Lloyd. Mixed doubles, the men in long white pants, the women in pleated skirts with caps on their heads so that all you could see of their bobbed hair were the bangs. Bruggers' Adolf always called them pangs. Adolf was his best friend, and Johann was too embarrassed to tell him that the word was *bangs*.

As soon as Herr Schlegel spied Helmer Gierer's Hermine approaching, he would call out: My respects, dear Lady! then step aside and nod his huge head. It wasn't just anybody he favored with My respects. He could bear right down on you in all his height and bulk, take hold of you by the shoulders—although his right hand still held a cane (which, however, compared to Herr Schlegel's body mass, was a mere swagger stick)—and demand: Where is Manila? If you didn't answer: In the Philippines! at once, Herr Schlegel would either scold or laugh at you, whichever he felt like at the moment. When he was in a good mood, he would grasp the elegantly curved handle of his cane and draw out a sword, slash it this way and that, and cry: A personal gift from Frederick the Great after the Battle of Leuthen. Then he sheathed it back in the cane. Sometimes, however, Herr Schlegel could hardly lift that ponderous head, heavy as a Chinese lion's. If his reddened gaze happened to fall on you then, he would grate out harshly: Up against the red wall and shoot him! Since Herr Schlegel sat at the regulars' table every day drinking his lake wine, Johann had blundered into that sentence more than once: Up against the red wall and . . . (a slight pause, and then in the same growl) . . . shoot him. Johann liked it better when Herr Schlegel, upon catching sight of him, cried: Pernambuco! If you answered: Seventy-seven hours and thirty minutes! he'd let you pass. If Herr Schlegel demanded: Lakehurst to Friedrichshafen? and you answered: Fifty-five hours, he'd take you by the shoulders and shake you until . . . and twenty-three minutes! popped out. Why did the gigantic builder never let Gierer's Hermine go by without a My respects, dear Lady? Perhaps because Helmer, Hermine's aged father, who had passed away long ago, had bequeathed him a sentence for lack of which not a week would have gone by without his being unable to say—at least once—what needed saying. And that sentence was: *Die Bescht ischt nuaz.* He could not utter that sentence in the kitchen of the Station Restaurant without being furiously corrected by the Princess who stood at the sink washing dishes and detested dialect of any kind: *Die Beste ist nichts*—Even the best woman is nothing. It annoyed the hulking builder to be corrected like that. Faster than you'd think possible, he would whirl around to face the Princess at her sink and ask in a High German every bit as good as hers: Where is Manila? and the Princess would sing out: In the Philippines!! My respects, dear Lady, said Herr Schlegel, drew his sword, declined it toward the Princess, and like a ship leaving port, departed the kitchen for the men's room, which is where he was headed in the first place when he rose from the regulars' table. On the other hand, the builder was also capable of giving in. When he encountered Helmer Gierer's Hermine in the street and asked her the Pernambuco question, she answered in her most haughty High German: Beneath my notice! and he, quite impressed, said: My respects, dear Lady. And once, just to be mischievous, she gave him the brush-off in dialect: *Wenn i it ma, isch as grad as wenn i it ka.* And he, more or less adopting her idiom in return, remarked: Aha*, wenn du nicht magst, ist es gerade, wie wenn du nicht kannst.* If you don't want to, it's the same as if you can't.

The two of them never passed each other without at least a bit of banter.

"Helmer Gierer's Hermine cleans the villas of the summer people," said Father, "without demeaning herself in the least." Without Helmer Gierer's Hermine, one never would have known what went on in those villas dozing by the lakeshore. From Easter to All Saints the motorboat of a manufacturer from Reutlingen lay at anchor between the path along the lake and the steamship landing. The name SUROTMA was on its lofty prow for all to read, but no one knew what it meant. When Johann first saw the word, he was immediately compelled to sound it out. But Adolf, whom he intended to impress with this skill, already knew from his father, who'd heard it from Helmer Gierer's Hermine, that SUROTMA was derived from the first syllables of the names of the Reutlingen manufacturer's children: Susanne, Ursula, Otto, and Martin. Now he knew that and repeated it to himself down by the lake, watching the SUROTMA with its thundering motor almost lift itself out of the water and leave in its wake two foaming white walls worthy of the thunder. Helmer Gierer's Hermine: a source of news. Frau Fürst: her diametrical opposite. Herr Schlegel also stepped aside for Frau Fürst. That heaviest of all bodies in the village—and thus in the world—bowed before her and uttered his My respects, dear Lady. And Frau Fürst said nothing. And Herr Schlegel knew she wouldn't. He would never have thought of asking her the Manila question, the Pernambuco question, or the Lakehurst question. From Frau Fürst you learned nothing, or as Helmer's Hermine put it, everything was beneath her notice. Her lips looked like they were stitched shut. And yet, since she delivered the paper, she entered more houses than Helmer Gierer's Hermine. No one expected even a hello from her. No one—not even the priest (but she was probably a Lutheran anyway), nor the mayor—could claim that she had ever taken any notice of them at all, much less said hello. She always carried her head as if to let the sun shine in under her chin. Frau Häckelsmiller, on the other hand, went around as if to let the sun shine on the back of her neck. How could the village have been a world if it didn't contain not just everything, but everything and its opposite! The only path Frau Häckelsmiller trod, bent over as she was, was from her little cottage to the church and from the church back to her cottage, but she was perpetually on that path through the meadows known as the Moos. When the grass was tall, all you saw of her was the little hump of her back. Not even Helmer Gierer's Hermine could have told you anything about Frau Häckelsmiller's—presumably tiny—face. On the other hand, Hermine would tell anyone who was new to the village and wondering about the expression on Frau Fürst's face, that it had been like that ever since they had brought the news to Frau Fürst that in Memmingen, just as he was about to climb into Herr Mehltreter's automobile, which was being driven by Hans Schmied, her husband had collapsed and died, at the age of thirty-four, on his way to sell the floor wax Herr Mehltreter manufactured according to his own top-secret recipe in the former stable of the restaurant. But before that, Herr Fürst had vulcanized tires in the basement of Herr Schlegel's house. But before that, he had tried his hand at selling radios in a gloomy town called Dortmund. Hermine had it from him, and the village heard it from her, that whenever it hadn't rained for a spell in Dortmund, you couldn't open your mouth without its filling up with the taste of soot that crunched between your teeth. But before that, he'd been in the war—an officer, in fact, and an excellent one, too. Helmer Gierer's Hermine always wound up her story of the Fürsts by remarking that Frau Fürst and her two children now lived in the same subterranean rooms where tires used to be vulcanized and had never once failed to pay Herr Schlegel the rent on time. Then Helmer Gierer's Hermine would say: My respects, while her right index finger—which always ticked back and forth to accompany what she was saying—suddenly stood bolt upright and still. *Subterranean* was one of many words Helmer Gierer's Hermine imported into the village from the villas she cleaned without demeaning herself in the least: *subterranean, kleptomania, migraine, tabula rasa, psychology, gentleman*, etc.

The village blossoms beneath the ground. Or should one say that autumn lays its many-colored hand on our borrowed green? Then the snow assumes the role of conservator. An edging of snow on all the branches. The snow provides silence, isolates certain sounds, and so passes them on. The lake glitters like armor on the body of winter.

We live on, not as those we once were, but as those we have become after we were. After it is past. It still exists, although it is past. Is there more past or more present, now, in being past?

CHAPTER TWO

Johann Makes a Mistake He Doesn't Regret

WHEN THE BARBER WAS FINISHED, he squeezed the red rubber bulb while waving the nozzle around, spraying a generous dose of perfume onto the head he had just been applying himself to, and announced that now Johann was at least presentable again. Then he whisked away the blue sheet like a magician, but of course it was only Johann who emerged and had to try standing on his own two feet again and nod his head vigorously enough that the barber and everyone waiting on the bench could measure the extent of Johann's gratitude and how mindful he was that it was only thanks to the tonsorial skills of Herr Häfele that he was presentable at all. Johann's gratitude had to be so vigorously demonstrated mainly because he had to conceal what a bad feeling this haircut was giving him. Basically, his whole head shaved bald, only a few hairs from the middle of his head to the front permitted to be left standing. Too short to part. "My best to your family," Herr Häfele called after him, "and tell your grandfather I'll be there on Saturday as usual." Johann was always on hand in the office—where his grandfather almost never appeared during the week—when the old man sat on Johann's father's desk chair and had Herr Häfele tie on the blue sheet, lather him up, and give him a shave. Then he permitted Herr Häfele to trim his thick mustache and apply his shears to the dense growth on his head. At such times his grandfather always seemed to him like a king. Grandfather liked it when Johann sat and watched. Johann could sense it.

Every time Johann walked out of the barbershop and into the corridor, he felt miserable. Right across the hall from the barber was Göser Marie's shop, where he was headed next. Without even thinking about it he pushed down the door handle. The bell made a hellish racket—although you hadn't intended to steal anything, you jumped at the noise like a thief caught in the act—and Göser Marie was out of her parlor and behind the counter before he even got that far. He bought ten pfennigs' worth of raspberry drops. He'd spent fifty pfennigs of the mark he had with him on the haircut. By the time he got home, his mother would probably forget to ask where the other fifty pfennigs were. And even if she didn't, she would OK ten pfennigs for raspberry drops. He hoped she would. He wasn't sure. Sometimes his mother groaned while sitting at his father's desk in the office, adding and subtracting something in her head. When she finished, she wrote down the result. Her lips moved a little whenever she added and subtracted like that. Anyone who didn't know what she was doing might have thought she was praying. But then, the soft but still audible groaning wouldn't have fit with praying. What it meant was, Oh dear, oh dear. Which in Mother's dialect was *Aahne, aahne*.

"Now you look like something again, Johann," said Göser Marie. Johann nodded vigorously so that here too, it wouldn't come out how dissatisfied he was with his haircut. If Göser Marie had guessed that Johann didn't like the haircut, after he was gone she would have scurried across the hall to the barber and announced that Herr Häfele's haircut was obviously not good enough for Johann from the Station Restaurant. And the next time Herr Häfele came to the restaurant and took his place at the regulars' table, he would have called over to Johann's mother behind the bar: Augusta, I don't seem to be able to cut your son's hair to his liking anymore. And there was nothing worse than customers, especially regular customers, complaining to their mother about Josef or Johann. That was the cardinal rule of deportment: always behave so as not to give anyone in the village cause to complain to Mother, who would immediately fetch the one against whom a complaint had been lodged and give him a proper dressing-down right there in front of the injured party. The express purpose of every reprimand was to show that you were incorrigible. That's what the injured party expected. But if his mother scolded, she was also desperate. She worked, struggled day and night, to keep the family from ruin, despite the fact that his father—half from illness, half from other incapacities—kept repeatedly steering both family and business toward a predictable calamity with his catastrophically bad ideas. Every time so far, she'd preserved the family and the business from disaster through sheer hard work and determination, but then her own children go and insult the very people on whose good will they all depended. These outbursts always ended with a sigh from deep down inside her: *Aahne, aahne*, where will it all end. In her dialect, it was a sequence of sounds that expressed—even intoned—the inmost depths of her utter tribulation, a sequence in which individual words were no longer distinguishable. His mother never uttered a word of High German. His father, although he'd been born in Hengnau not even two miles as the crow flies from Mother's birthplace in Kümmertsweiler, used dialect words only as a joke. He had learned a different way of speaking at the Royal Bavarian Middle School in Lindau, and yet another during his commercial apprenticeship in Lausanne. And another still, quite different, during the war.

Johann nodded to Göser Marie as if he considered himself fortunate to have Herr Häfele do such a lovely job on such a head as his. But really, he was thinking enviously of his brother, Josef. Josef had persuaded them to leave some hair standing at the back, beyond the top of his skull. It was still short, but long enough to part. Josef was already going to school. Johann's mother said that when he started school he could have a part too. He should be glad he could comb his hair so nicely toward the front. "Take a look at your friends," she said, "Ludwig, Adolf, Paul, Guido, Helmut, and the other Helmut. Do any of them have a part? No. But more than one has his head completely shaved." She was right. Johann couldn't complain. It was just that he knew that Irmgard, Gretel, Trudl, and Leni liked longer hair. In the barn he'd given Irmgard the cologne that had been a present from Mina ("That's for you, Johannle, to make you smell nice," Mina had said), and two days later Irmgard had Trudl tell him to come to the barn on Saturday at four thirty. He did, and in front of the same witnesses who'd seen him give her the cologne, she gave him a little comb in its own slipcase. That could only mean that he should let his hair grow longer, because for what grew on his head now, his fingers sufficed.

Johann popped a raspberry drop in his mouth and quickly descended the sandstone steps to the girl's bicycle he had ridden here. They had two bikes, one with a crossbar that only his father rode, and the girl's bike that Mina used to go grocery shopping for the restaurant, and Josef and Johann were allowed to use it too. It was unimaginable that his mother would ever ride a bicycle. She was too great or too powerful or too exalted or too fearful. One couldn't imagine her using something she might fall off of.

Johann liked the pressure of the serrated pedals against the soles of his feet. By the end of September his soles were so tough from going barefoot all summer that the pressure of the pedals, which still hurt in April, just felt pleasant. He rode up the main street, savoring the sharp sweetness of the raspberry drop and greeting every man and woman so loudly he was afraid he might frighten them and would be called on to stop before he had gotten past the high red sandstone wall that screened the Villa Primbs and its gardens from the street. This wall was so high that even now, at midday, it cast a shadow. In that shadow, there was a man coming toward Johann and gesturing in a way that made him brake. The man had already been looking at him from a long way off. Then he made a brief, unmistakable gesture with a small baton-sized thing that looked like a folding umbrella, the kind that pops open. The man was a stranger. He didn't take the cigarette out of his mouth, not even when he started speaking to Johann. His cigarette bobbed up and down when he talked, just like Jutz the organist's, who also gave Josef piano lessons. The man remarked that Johann must have just been at the barber's. Johann nodded. He was pleased that the stranger noticed right away. The stranger said he was a photographer and had just found a wonderful subject, but needed a living person in the picture, too. "Come on, and I'll show you," and he walked up the main street beside Johann to where the red wall took a sharp turn uphill to the right. The stranger also turned right and Johann followed. When they were almost at the top, where the path continued on to the garden gate of the Hoppe-Seylers' villa, the stranger stopped and said, "Here." He wanted Johann to stand in the middle of the path with both hands on the handlebar of his bicycle. A great big mat of ivy hung over the high red wall, and behind Johann two huge redwoods—he knew they were there and saw them later in the photo—rose skyward from Hoppe-Seylers' garden. They were the tallest trees in the world. People said Professor Hoppe-Seyler had brought them home from California and planted them there. From California or Sumatra. Johann had never seen the professor. The professor's daughter—Johann guessed she must be a hundred years old—lived alone in the old house on the lake. Fräulein Hoppe-Seyler was one of their coal customers. From time to time Niklaus, Josef, Father, and Johann would cart ten or twelve hundredweights of briquettes up from the street below, past the gigantic trees, to the cellar window. Then Father and Niklaus heaved one sack after another off the handcart and together emptied them through the window into the coal cellar. The professor's ancient daughter stood inside and urged them plaintively to "Slow down, slow down. Not so fast." The faster they emptied the sacks, the faster the briquettes tumbled out, the more easily they crumbled, and the more coal dust there was in the cellar. Since Johann and Josef weren't big enough to carry anything yet, they came along only to help push the handcart when they made these small deliveries. The slope of the entire village from the lake up to the Lausbichel was very uneven. When they went back down the hill, all four of them sat together in the handcart, padded with the empty sacks, and of course it was Josef who got to hold the cart shaft between his feet and steer.

Like a magician, the stranger produced a tripod out of his baton, screwed his camera onto it, and started giving Johann orders in a voice that reminded him of the tiger tamer from the Sarrasani Circus. He kept shifting Johann just a few inches. He'd barely move a fraction to the right before he'd have to move back again, but not too far. OK, let's try again. The photographer kept looking up at the tops of the redwoods. Of course they had to be in the picture. Johann would have liked to explain to the photographer that Professor Hoppe-Seyler had brought them back from California or Sumatra, probably from Sumatra—no, definitely from Sumatra. He had it from the only person in town who would know: Helmer's Hermine. Queen Hermine, that's what his father called her when he talked about Helmer's Hermine. Helmer Gierer's Hermine. There were so many Gierers in town that if you wanted to refer to a particular Gierer, you had to add the name of their house or their job. Same with the Zürns and the Schnells and Hagens and Stadlers. "Without demeaning herself in the least," said his father, "she cleans the villas of the summer people." The only reason he didn't mention that she spoke excellent High German was probably that he spoke High German himself. One time Fräulein Hoppe-Seyler wasn't at home when they delivered briquettes. Instead of the black triangle that reached to the floor, topped by a tremulous white head, it was Helmer's Hermine who opened the door. Thin, with pinched cheeks and a prominent, longish wart next to her nose. She unlatched the cellar window and cautioned them to empty the sacks carefully, just like the professor's daughter. But instead of saying *sachte, sachte* like Fräulein Hoppe-Seyler, she said *hofele, hofele*, which also means careful but doesn't sound so High German. As she escorted the coalmen back out the gate, she said that Fräulein Hoppe-Seyler claimed she didn't give a hoot where the professor had brought the redwoods back from—yes, that's just how she put it: she didn't give a hoot where they were from. But Hermine informed them that the professor had brought them from Sumatra. Just consider the bamboo hedge the professor had grown by the lakeshore wall. "In my world view," said Hermine, "bamboo goes better with Sumatra than California. You're the only person I've told, no one else, just so you know." And she tapped Father's forehead with her finger. As they rattled back down the main street, Father shouted, "In my world view, bamboo goes better with Sumatra than California," and he ticked his index finger back and forth like Helmer's Hermine. Actually a gesture of negation, for Helmer's Hermine it excluded the slightest possibility of contradiction. And in this town, being right was important.

Helmer's Hermine wouldn't talk to just any old person on her way home from the villas to the upper village, where she lived with her brother beneath a roof that sloped down almost to the top of their manure pile. In contrast to the *höfe*—the more imposing farmsteads—such small premises that hardly dared peek out from under their overhanging roofs were referred to with the diminutive *höfle*. Hermine's brother Franz, who worked Helmer's *höfle*, went barefoot almost all year round. And if he did put on shoes on the coldest day of the year, he never ever wore socks or wrapped his feet.

When Father pronounced Helmer's Hermine a queen, Johann immediately sensed that her queenliness was expressed by the prominent, longish wart to the left of her nose.

Johann had lost all feeling in his feet from having to shuffle back and forth so much when the stranger finally called out, "OK! Now how about a smile?" Johann gave the best grin he could muster, and the stranger pressed the shutter release. He took down Johann's name and address, and then Johann was allowed to go—or rather, ride—home.

When he got home, he carried the bicycle up the back stairs into the house and left it leaning against the wall of the narrow hallway that led in from the back door. It was shortly before twelve, and what with the season and the nice weather, there were already guests—they called them tourists—sitting on the front terrace perusing the menu. That's why he had to use the back stairs.

He went into the kitchen and said, "I had my picture taken."

"Don't tell me," said his mother, who was just lifting a spoonful of red cabbage to her lips to see if it needed more juniper or bay leaves or a little vinegar. Johann told what had happened. His mother said, "For God's sake, Johann, an itinerant photographer!" When she said that, and by the way she said it, Johann knew he should have refused. Spat on the ground and taken to his heels, that's what he should have done. "An itinerant photographer!" His mother repeated the words.

But Mina, who cooked with Mother and actually was more in charge of the cooking than Mother—Mina said, "But you should be glad someone took his picture, ma'am."

"What's it going to set me back?" asked his mother.

"I'd like a picture of Johann no matter what it costs," said Mina, whereupon his mother glared silently her. "You don't have to look at me that way, ma'am," said Mina.

Mother nodded and said, "There you go again, Mina."

"But it's true," said Mina. The Princess said nothing but did glance over her shoulder. Then she returned to her dirty dishes. Johann said everything extra loud in her presence because, since her accident, the Princess didn't hear so well. It was important to him that she understand everything he said.

On his way home, Johann had already thought this business of getting his picture taken might have unpleasant consequences. He felt a little queasy about it. Mother had put it into words at once: itinerant photographer and What's it going to set me back. Johann had never been photographed by himself before. No one in the whole family had ever been photographed alone except for Father, twice, during the war. Up to now there had been five photographs: two pictures of Father as a soldier; then the oldest of all, Grandfather and Grandmother and beside them Johann's father, maybe nine years old (Josef and Johann could see that the picture had been taken long ago, since the nine-year-old had on pants that went down below his knees); in the fourth picture, his father and mother on their wedding day, Mother all encased in a white veil and Father like a young statesman. While Father looked at you cheerfully, Mother looked like she was peering into a light that was too bright. She was squinting a little and her mouth was puckered, too, and her hands clutched a little white purse as if someone was coming to snatch it away from her. Mother stood there in white, rather on the defensive. In the fifth picture: Father and Mother between Johann's grandfather and his great-uncle from the Allgäu—whom they called Cousin—and Josef and Johann in front of the adults. Josef and Johann in white. Josef was holding Johann's hand as if he'd had to pull his little brother into the picture. Josef's feet were side by side. The toes of Johann's shoes touched and the heels were far apart. The photographer had posed the family on the steep, stony ramp behind the restaurant, where the beer wagons drove down and came to a stop just in time in front of the cellar door. This ramp, which was always full of ruts from the rainstorms, was also where the coal wagon came rattling down, pulled by two horses and filled with coal freshly unloaded from a railroad car, and Johann was always amazed at how Herr Weibel walked backwards, holding the bridles of his two massive dray horses to get them to transfer their weight and strength to their hind legs and brace themselves against the load of coal bearing down behind them. The overfilled wagon had to be brought to a full stop by the time it reached the two stalls the coal would be shoveled into.

Cousin Anselm, the great uncle from the Allgäu, had brought the photographer with him and obviously insisted that everyone put on their best for the picture: Mother in a black velvet dress that Johann never saw her wear again. Sometimes he paid a visit to this dress in the wardrobe where it hung and stroked it. He felt a desire to take it out, slip it on, and look at himself in the oval mirror on the wardrobe door. A V-neck, almost no sleeves, but not sleeveless. Why didn't she wear the dress anymore? Father had put on one of his long suit coats. All Father's suit coats hung almost to his knees. A tie emerged from under his white collar. Cousin Anselm wore a tie that was almost a bow; his grandfather, no tie at all. He hadn't even put on a collar. And his collarless shirt was open. And the jacket and pants he had on showed that he had not heeded the sartorial directives of the great-uncle they called Cousin. His grandfather, who almost always walked and stood with a stoop, gazed out from the picture as if from under his eyebrows. You could see he wasn't happy about being photographed. There'd been an argument. The following day Frau Biermann, who'd come to live with them in the middle of the war shortly after Grandmother's death, had moved out forever, back to Munich. She had expected to be included in the photo. It was said that she'd hoped to marry the widower. She was a cook, they said, who had cooked in an entirely different class of restaurant.

When she didn't get Grandfather, they said, she set her cap for his son. And then he went and married the peasant girl from Kümmertsweiler. And then Frau Biermann didn't even get to be in the photograph. She slammed her door, packed her things, and left. Back to the big city. So Frau Biermann was missing in this picture. Johann didn't miss her. He liked looking at himself most of all, then at the others. The great-uncle they called Cousin was worth looking at. His open suit coat revealed a vest sporting a fine watch chain. This cousin was always a welcome visitor, for his Ford car if for nothing else. The wheels of the car had spokes like a thicket. And you didn't have to start it with a crank, like Father's truck. Cousin pushed a button, the car emitted a gentle gurgle, and the motor started running. It was typical of this great-uncle they called Cousin, who had founded a dairy in the Allgäu by the name of Alpine Bee, that he arrived with a photographer in tow and had everyone get dressed up for the photo, the only picture that showed the entire family. And now Johann comes along and lets some itinerant photographer take his picture! A picture in which he would be the only person! The two pictures from France with his father by himself—on both pictures, a big, dense, black beard and mustache surrounded his mouth—were necessary because Father had been decorated, first with the Bavarian Order of Merit and then with the Iron Cross. But just like that, for no reason! And by an itinerant photographer, yet! And now he could charge them whatever he liked! Johann had guessed it would be like this—guessed it, feared it, known it. And yet he'd let himself be photographed anyway! He wanted to tell his mother that at least once a month, his friend Adolf dragged him over to look at the Bruggers' photo album. He would open it and with his index finger led Johann to every photo that had been added since the last time. Herr Brugger had a camera of his own. Herr Brugger went to Friedrichshafen once with Adolf and took a picture of him in front of a Zeppelin that was about to take off. Adolf was prouder of that photo than of any other. Herr Brugger had already taken two pictures of Johann and Adolf together. And both photos would now be on display in Bruggers' photo album for all time to come. When his index finger arrived at these photos,

Adolf had said, "Whadd'ya think of 'em?" Johann had felt Adolf looking at him and that he should return Adolf's gaze, that it was the kind of moment when in the old days two friends would open their veins and let their blood mix together. He and Adolf together in the same picture. Twice, in fact: once on the landing where a steamer was just docking and once with the church in the background. Johann hadn't been able to look at Adolf. But he'd reached over with his hand and touched Adolf. "It's all right," Adolf had said.

When Mother looked and looked at Mina without a word just to make her realize how ridiculous what she said was, Mina (who was from the Allgäu) said, "*Dös kenna br. Der sell hot g'seit, as ging schu, abr as gaoht it.*" And the Princess, irritated by the dialect, called over from her dishpan in a loud voice, "*Das kennen wir. Derselbige hat gesagt, es ginge schon, aber es geht nicht.*" —We know what that's like. The man said it was all right, but it isn't all right. She overlooked dialect only when Mother spoke it.

His mother asked, "Did you get a look when you passed Schnitzlers' and the Linden Tree?"

In the excitement of being photographed he'd forgotten to. Mother had especially reminded him to do it on his way home. He'd done it often enough already, pedaling slowly past and counting how many guests were in the Linden Tree's garden. In view of the anticipated costs of being photographed, it would have been especially important today to see if there were more guests in the garden of the competition than on their own terrace. When Josef came home from school later, he would report how many people had been sitting in the Lakeshore Café and how many in the garden of the Crown. They couldn't compete with the Lakeshore or the Crown, but they ought to be able to compete with the Linden Tree and Café Schnitzler. Johann carried the bicycle back downstairs and out the back door, pedaled down into the village, counted seven people in the Linden Tree garden and five at Schnitzlers', returned, and reported the results. "Elsa," Mother asked the waitress, "how many do we have?" Elsa added them up in her head and said, "Six on the terrace." Mother nodded as if that confirmed her worst fears. "And inside?" Elsa screwed up her face again, pictured all the tables to herself, totaled them up sotto voce, said "Nine," and added, "but it's only twelve thirty."

Mother turned to Johann and told him his father had called from Oberstaufen to say he wouldn't be coming home until seven thirty, on the workers' train. But his trip to Oberstaufen had probably been a waste of time. "What has that Schulz got to his name?" she said to Mina. "A health food store nobody wants."

"Health food isn't bad," said Mina. And after Mother gave her a look, " . . . for people who can afford it."

"In Oberstaufen!" said his mother. "Health food in Oberstaufen, Mina! He guaranteed a loan of 7,500 marks when we're in debt ourselves for . . ." She didn't finish the sentence.

"Two beef roulades with red cabbage and purée," said Elsa and stuck the order on the nail behind the door.

A man with a briefcase entered the kitchen right behind her and expressed his thanks for the excellent brisket. As long as the Station Restaurant in Wasserburg could serve a brisket like that, he wasn't worried about its future. "Chin up, dear lady," he said. He shook Mother's hand and said, "And best regards to your husband. Just don't lose your nerve! If you could see the sort of places I've been in these days and the furniture I had to repossess, dear lady—it's the elite. The elite are having a tough time of it these days. But you'll pull through, I can feel it. I've been a bailiff of the court since 1911. I learned the trade under the authority of his majesty the king, dear lady, and I can tell the wheat from the chaff. You don't belong to the chaff, no ma'am! Just plug up the little holes for now and you can negotiate the big ones later. Who's better at that than you!"

The whole time he was speaking, the gentleman held Mother's hand. He'd clamped his briefcase between his knees in order to take her hand in both of his. All at once he had to sneeze. He let go of her hand, turned away, and immediately produced a gigantic yellow handkerchief with white flowers and applied it to his equally gigantic and very misshapen nose. Mother and Mina sang out simultaneously, "Gesundheit, Herr Bailiff!" He thanked them, took the briefcase he'd still held clamped between his knees while he sneezed, and departed. It was as if there was nothing left to say after that explosive sneeze.

When he was gone, Mother said, "The worst thing is the electricity. Everybody can see we have to put in a mark for every little bit of current." Mina said she should feed the meter when no one was in the hallway. Hardly anyone noticed the meter because it was right next to the bell box. She was right. Before, when everything was still in good working order, the room number would fall into the corresponding slot when a guest pushed the bell in his room upstairs. His father told him that that's how you knew it was time to bring the member of the Imperial Railway Board the warm water for his shave.

Mina said she thought it would be much worse if they repossessed the gramophone. Mother shook her head as though she'd given up on Mina once and for all. If she'd had anything to say about it, she said, the gramophone would never have gotten into the house in the first place. "No gramophone, no restaurant," said the Princess from her place at the sink, thereby proving once again that her hearing wasn't so bad after all. Johann was glad that the Princess didn't turn around every time she contributed to the conversation. He just couldn't get used to her glass eye. It was never in the place you expected it to be. At least it wasn't in the place you expected a left eye to be, symmetrical with the right one. It was noticeably lower, sitting at the lower edge of her eye socket, right on top of her cheek bone. When she had first introduced herself, she said she was thirty-one, a princess, and had two children, the second one by a seventeen-year-old, the first one by a swindler who turned over a borrowed car with her in it, which is how she came by her injuries.

When Josef threw his school bag onto the bench in the kitchen and reported eleven guests in the Crown and four in the Lakeside Café, Mina said that meant they were keeping abreast of the places on the lake. Mother took a long look at Mina again and said, "What it means, Mina, is that it's not just us who aren't making any money, it's the places on the lake, too." His mother had directed the last part of her sentence toward Johann. Johann knew she meant to remind him who their competition was: the Crown and the Lakeshore Café were run by outsiders, Lutherans. And Herr Michaelsen, the owner of the Lakeshore Café, had not just been a major but was also married to an Englishwoman. Go see if you can compete with powerful people like that.

"Oh, ma'am," said Mina, "*dr sell hot g'seit, wenn d'Henn guat huckt, scherrat se so lang, bis se schleaht huckt.*"

The Princess called out furiously, "*Wenn die Henne gut hockt, scharrt sie so lange, bis sie schlecht hockt.*"—When the hen's nicely settled, she'll scratch till she's badly settled.

Johann had sensed right away that he shouldn't have allowed himself to be photographed. He began to wonder why he had no regrets at all about making this mistake that he could never make up for. He had been photographed. There would be no one to be seen in the picture but him. No one else. It was clear that no one but him knew what that meant. None of them would be in this picture. How would they know what it means to be in a picture all by yourself? Just him in front of the giant redwoods the professor had brought back from—yes, definitely—from Sumatra, as confirmed by Helmer's Hermine's index finger ticking back and forth. Johann could feel it: he wasn't the same person anymore that he had been before the photographer took his picture. And it made almost no difference to him at all now that it was an itinerant photographer. That's how shameless he'd become. Now he was the boy who had been photographed. And he would be that boy from now on.

"What's wrong with him?" said Josef. "Is he running a fever?"

CHAPTER THREE

Suspended Payments

WHEN JOHANN GOT HOME from playing dodge ball, he heard Josef practicing the piano. Josef was playing scales. Next year when Johann started school, he would begin piano lessons too, if only to please his father, who often said it would have been terrible to be born before there were pianos.

As soon as dinnertime approached, Mother sent Johann into the extra room where his father was playing or Josef was practicing scales to tell them that patrons were already being seated. Only a flimsy folding partition separated the dining room from the extra room. Johann went to stand beside his father, whose hands immediately froze in mid-phrase. He nodded, let them drop, closed the piano, then patted his knee and said, "Sit up here." Then Johann sat on his knee while Father finished what he had just been playing by singing it quietly into Johann's ear. His father was a singer, too, second tenor in the choral society. Josef and Johann's room was directly above the extra room, where the choral society rehearsed on Thursday evenings, and Johann always listened to see if he could pick out his father's voice from the others. There were two voices he could clearly make out: the limpid, silvery voice of Herr Grübel, rising effortlessly to any height, and Herr Späth's voice, which made a strained impression while striving for the same notes. When Johann encountered Herr Grübel or Herr Späth in town, he greeted Herr Grübel with respect and Herr Späth with sympathy. Herr Späth was a mason who worked amid sand, cement, and dust. Herr Grübel lived in the center of town in a little old wooden house that huddled beneath its roof, and he was always occupied with his silken-backed cows, with round red and yellow apples, smooth cherries, freshly mown grass, and fragrant hay. Johann imagined that must be good for Herr Grübel's voice. As often as he could, Herr Späth came to the restaurant straight from his dusty work, drank beer or lake wine at the regulars' table, and always smoked a stogie. Herr Grübel almost never came to the regulars' table. It was unimaginable that he had ever smoked. Herr Grübel walked beside his team of oxen as they pulled a cartful of grass or hay into town, moving so slowly it seemed they would never get there. The only sound was the clop of the oxen's resilient hooves on the freshly tarred street. And whenever Johann greeted Herr Grübel, he would reply, "Good day to you, Johann!" It sounded like something from the Benedictus, in which he soared above the choir and made everything in the church seem to float, so that Johann no longer felt the uneven hardness of the kneeler.

The moment Johann appeared at the kitchen door, he knew that his mother would say, "Go tell them there are already guests on the terrace and in the dining room." Johann took off running, but not before he heard the Princess say, "That's his favorite thing, chasing Josef from the piano." It was true that Johann couldn't understand how you could practice scales for hours on end. When he learned the piano, it would be by playing melodies.

In the extra room he stood beside Josef and lowered the fallboard none too slowly. "Not yet!" cried Josef. "People are starting to complain," said Johann. Josef stopped at once. And since he looked so alarmed, Johann conceded, "Not yet, but they will soon." Josef jumped up and began a small wrestling match, which Johann—being two years younger, two years smaller, and two years weaker—lost. But he didn't give up until he was lying on the oiled parquet with Josef kneeling on his biceps. That's how all their fights ended. It didn't hurt to lose to Josef. It was enough that Josef was sweating. As he lay on his back looking up into Josef's face, he saw no intent to humiliate him. Adolf's face beamed with joy when they played dodgeball and Johann was standing where he was guaranteed to be hit. Adolf cocked his arm, made as if to throw, Johann dodged to the right, but Adolf didn't throw. He waited half a second until Johann straightened back up but wasn't ready to dodge again (you weren't allow to move from your spot), and then he threw much harder than necessary from so short a distance and hit Johann right on the neck. It hurt. It hurt Adolf too when he hit Johann so hard, but only after he'd hit him. You could tell. Johann knew for sure that Josef would always protect him. Against anybody. At home, of course, Johann had to do what Josef said. But in the world outside, Josef was his protector.

Johann beat a retreat. He had heard the scratch of his grandfather's rake outside on the gravel. Grandfather was raking up the first fallen chestnut leaves. Grandfather was forever straightening, sweeping, and raking. He moved slowly and breathed heavily. Whenever he passed the boxes of geraniums that crowned the waist-high terrace wall with flowers, he would discover a withered leaf, a faded blossom, or something else that absolutely had to be removed. Nor was he able to pass between the planters of ivy flanking the exit to the train station without plucking off something that had turned yellow in those walls of green. Although he couldn't bend over very well anymore, he still stooped down for anything lying on the ground. He was incapable of passing the least scrap of paper or cigarette butt without bending down to pick it up. Johann always rushed over when Grandfather bent down because it always looked like he wouldn't be able to straighten back up but would fall forward and never get up again. Grandfather sat in the restaurant every evening, but never at the regulars' table. He sat next to the door at the table beneath the clock. He drank nothing, ate nothing, just read the paper. Since he practically never turned the page, you couldn't be sure he was reading at all. In the morning and at night, Johann helped Grandfather put on and take off his shoes. Grandfather couldn't reach the laces by himself anymore.

When Johann emerged from the house, the graveled yard beneath the two chestnuts on the station side of the restaurant had already been raked clean of anything that didn't belong there. His grandfather had even swept the worn wooden planks of the truck scale. It was important to Grandfather that the scale be kept ready for action at any moment. They had a truck scale at the Linden Tree, too, a roofed-over one, in fact. That's why some farmers preferred to drive their wagons full of windfalls or straw onto the Linden Tree's scale. At the Station Restaurant they tared the scale before every weighing so the customer could see that the pointer stopped next to the zero. But some people just didn't get that and chose the covered scale at the Linden Tree instead, especially when it was raining or snowing. That amazing catch of bream last year in April, for instance, when three carts full of fish got weighed on the Linden's scale and it was in the newspaper: The Miraculous Catch—the three carts and the Linden Tree scale. Johann wished he could do the weighing, but he couldn't yet manage to turn the big crank that raised the scale bed. When the crank handle was at the top of its travel, it was out of reach over his head.

Whenever he lost a fight with Josef, Johann sought out his grandfather. Grandfather put his rake and shovel into the wheelbarrow, and Johann wheeled it behind the house and down to the compost pile in the courtyard. Grandfather had followed and now stood under the apple trees, checking to see if the branches sagging under their heavy burden of fruit were properly supported. He called over Niklaus, who had positioned the props. When he wasn't otherwise occupied, Niklaus filled hundredweight sacks with coal and lined them up under the overhanging roof of the carriage house so that if a customer wanted a hundredweight of hard coal or briquettes, it was all ready to go. Grandfather told Niklaus to bring him more props. The Welschisner tree had a particularly heavy harvest this year and needed more support all around so the branches wouldn't break. Johann picked up a fallen Gravenstein from the ground and bit into it. Grandfather said Johann could get a basket and gather the drops for tomorrow's applesauce. Johann fetched a basket from the second floor of the carriage house, where everything they didn't need but might eventually need lay around, and he picked up the fallen fruit under all eight apple trees. There was no one's bidding Johann did more readily than his grandfather's.

He especially didn't like Josef giving him orders. They were mostly chores Josef should have done himself but passed on to Johann when he didn't feel like doing them. And if Johann refused, a wrestling match would ensue that Johann lost and then he had to do what Josef told him. When Grandfather gave you a job, you had the feeling he would rather have done it himself but couldn't anymore. Grandfather was a giant, but a stooped one.

Johann had carried the basket up the back stairs and set it down by the door to the porch when Mina came running through the courtyard and up the stairs. She dashed past Johann into the house, loudly wailing and crying "Noooo!" and "It can't be!" Johann ran after her. In the kitchen she collapsed on the bench next to the door, which was actually Johann's place. But whereas he always slid down the long bench into the corner under the boiler, Mina stayed right at the end of the bench, set her elbows on the rutted tabletop, and wailed and yelled and wailed. Mother, Grandfather, and Elsa clustered around her at once, and the Princess didn't just look over her shoulder from her place at the sink but turned her whole body. Mother and Elsa implored, "Come on, Mina, what's the matter? Come on, tell us what happened!" Mina had planned to withdraw twenty marks from the branch of the Bank of Commerce and Agriculture in Glatthars' house because the Lindau harvest fair was coming up soon, but she'd come back empty-handed. The door had been closed. A posted notice announced that the bank was forced to suspend payments temporarily. A meeting of creditors was being convened. Judicial proceedings had been initiated to avoid bankruptcy. The directors of the bank asked their honored clientele for their continued trust. Only trust could now prevent the worst, namely, bankruptcy. Mina recited all these sentences through her tears in the best High German they had ever heard her speak. She'd deposited years of earnings in the bank—everything she'd earned in that very bank. She hadn't kept a thing for herself, and Alfred had put his savings in the bank too, the same bank. They were going to get married next year or the year after that. And now it was all gone, gone, gone.

Grandfather said it still wasn't clear that everything was gone for good. Big, heavy Elsa was also gazing down at skinny little Mina crying her eyes out and obviously couldn't stand it that Mina was getting all the attention. So she just started in about how when she was in Baienfurt, where she worked before coming here, she picked up the food from a counter window right between the kitchen and the dining room, but here she had to run to the kitchen, pick up the food, run back down the corridor fifteen or twenty feet at least, then turn left and push open the door with her elbow, and only then was she in the dining room. It was even farther to the guests on the terrace: a good twenty feet from the kitchen door to the swinging door, from there another seven feet to the front door, "down two steps and you're on the terrace, but it's still quite a ways to the tables. I'm tellin ya, my first week here, I thought I was gonna eat my own feet." Big, heavy Elsa from Einöd near Homburg depicted her weary trips as though every step was torture. She must not have known that Grandfather had designed and built the building. She probably meant to say that she had it even harder than Mina. Elsa looked forever run ragged. Her considerable lower lip always hung down and showed a good amount of gum and in her glassy stare you could see what a torture it was to wait on tables. To wait on tables in this restaurant. From her place at the sink the Princess said, "If everybody's going to say what they don't like, I've got a few things to say myself." Mina looked only at Mother, Mother only at Mina. Mina stood up. Compared to Elsa and Mother she was really tiny. She said, "Here," and handed Johann her small, dark red passbook. When she came back from the bank, Mina had always handed Johann her passbook and said, "Put it away for me." She knew how much Johann liked to open and close the heavy door of the safe in the front office.

It was time for Johann to fetch the milk. On his way, he saw people standing and reading the notice from which Mina had learned what happened to her money. When he had filled his six-liter milk can in the cellar of the dairy, he hung it onto the railing where other, smaller cans were already hanging and joined the game of hide-and-seek that took place around the dairy each evening. The main thing for Johann was being in the same hiding place as Gretel, Trudl, or Irmgard and until he was found, staying so close to Gretel, Trudl, or Irmgard that he could touch them in a way that seemed more accidental than intentional. And if those touches elicited a response that also seemed more accidental than intentional, Johann felt like he was in a storm. Naturally, then, you didn't want to be it in the next round and have to lean against the wall hiding your face in your arm and counting to ten and then have to look for the others who had hidden themselves in the meantime. When he was it, he was tormented by the idea that Adolf, Ludwig, Paul, Guido, Helmut One, or Helmut Two were touching Irmgard just as unintentionally or intentionally as he had. What darkness you plunged into when running between the dairy and Glatthars' house! Out in front was street, sunlit square, everything bright and clear. In the back: another time of day, another world, a dark confusion of more than one shed, and all under the cover of dense foliage that shut out the light, and beneath the trees, tall grasses that reached to the lowest branches and just beyond that, the shrubbery on the banks of the Oeschbach. Nowhere else in the village was it so easy to disappear. And nowhere else was the early evening twilight as dark as in Bichelmaier's hay barn. In this darkness the sought-after contact seemed both more accidental and more intentional and radiated much more power than the touches one managed to steal when every movement was visible.

Today Johann was the first to have to go home. But behind the dairy in Glatthars' shed he'd managed to get closer to Irmgard than ever before. In the shed, which was tiny to begin with, Irmgard and he had hidden in a bin. Because the bin was really small, they had to press against each other. Johann had the feeling that both of them, he and Irmgard, had ceased to breathe as long as they were so jammed together, he behind her and she in front of him. They would probably never have had to breathe again. They were quickly found—by Adolf, of course—but then Johann, in a positively frantic burst of speed unleashed by the storm of contact, had caught up with Adolf and beaten him to the base. He tagged it and yelled, "In free—and Irmgard, too!" Although that was against the rules, he said it so forcefully that Adolf couldn't object and immediately ran off behind the house to look for the others.

Johann took the lidless six-liter can and swung it so fast in big circles that the milk remained in its container. He relished the weight of the wheeling can, which almost pulled him over every time it reached the bottom of its arc. The fragrance of Irmgard's hair was still in his nose. He was taller than Irmgard, and in their cramped hiding place, he'd had his nose practically in her hair. But when they squatted down and then kneeled to make themselves even more invisible, he was able to do something he'd never managed to do before—to touch Irmgard near the spot where it was strictly forbidden to touch her. He wasn't quite sure how close he'd come. Involuntarily he started to sniff his index finger; maybe it still smelled of the spot. But before he got the finger to his nose, he snatched it away again. There were still people standing in a half circle in front of Glatthars' house, and now Helmer's Hermine stood beside the notice and people were listening to her. Johann didn't understand what she was saying, but he saw her index finger ticking back and forth. And Hermine would have seen him sniffing at his index finger. And she would know at once what had led him to sniff his finger. She must be telling her listeners what they should do in the face of this announcement from the Bank of Commerce and Agriculture, but that wouldn't keep her from catching Johann at his sniffing if he sniffed his index finger. Luckily, Hermine's own index finger ticking back and forth had made him instantly aware of the danger.

Back home, as soon as he had put the milk in the icebox in the hallway he dashed straight up to his room where at last he could sniff his index finger for traces of Irmgard's spot. They called boys who ran after girls skirt-chasers. Johann knew he was a skirt-chaser, but if anyone called him that he would hotly deny it. Not to mention that when he hid in a tight place with Adolf, he would have liked to touch him just as much as Irmgard.

He had to get to the station to meet his father returning from Oberstaufen by the workers' train. They hadn't planned it ahead, but Johann knew his father counted on being met by him. Although Father often tarried for whole minutes at a time behind Josef as he played his scales, Johann thought he was closer to his father. For instance, Johann had never seen his father giving Josef an Eskimo kiss. But he greeted Johann every day by rubbing the tip of his nose against the tip of Johann's. He told him that was how Eskimos greeted each other.

In the hallway he encountered Mina again. She ran her hand over his head as he passed, something she'd never done before. It must have to do with the money the bank had taken from her. Mother came out of the kitchen and said Father had called. He wouldn't be on the workers' train. He would catch the late train.

Back to the dairy again? No, he couldn't, he just couldn't. Irmgard must have gone home by now. He hoped so. And Irmgard would be the only reason to go back. Often, he would pass Irmgard's house without so much as turning his head to see if anyone happened to be looking out or just standing in the doorway. Whenever he did, he had the feeling Irmgard was watching him walk past. And that walking past, observed by Irmgard, filled every step he took with enormous significance.

Johann went into the dining room and sat down next to his grandfather. He was sitting with a guest who never sat at the regulars' table either but always with Grandfather under the clock: Herr Loser from Unterbechtersweiler, the only person who rode a bicycle with only one pedal. The other pedal was uncoupled and served as a footrest for the clunky wooden foot he'd had since the war. He had no trouble making forward progress on the bike, even though there wasn't an inch of level ground between Unterbechtersweiler and Wasserburg; it was up and down all the way.

"Well, Gebhard," Grandfather was just saying as Johann sat down, and he laid one of his hands on the hands of Loser's Gebhard. Usually it was a guest who would put a hand on Grandfather's blue hands. Elsa set a fresh glass of beer in front of Loser's Gebhard and a shot of fruit schnapps to go with it. Herr Deuerling, who always let them know by the way he said Get goin', get along with ya! that he'd been born on the Bavarian side of the Lech River, had taught them that little shot glasses were called *stamperl*. But Johann noticed that the word didn't sound right in the mouth of anyone from around here. Herr Seehahn, however (who never let on where he was from but said that after the revolution he'd fetched up in Munich as a "revulooshunery seaman, ret.")—Herr Seehahn could say *stamperl* so it didn't sound funny. But then, Herr Seehahn was one of those people at home in many languages.

Johann knew Loser's Gebhard even though he didn't come to the restaurant every week. Once, when Loser's Gebhard was sitting at the table, Grandfather told about how when he was twenty-five he, Grandfather, had sold the family house in Hengnau to their neighbor, Dorn. Dorn tore it down, and the lumber and bricks were carted off to Unterbechtersweiler because Loser's house in Unterbrechtersweiler had just burned down. Loser's Gebhard's father had rebuilt his house and barn with that material.

Loser's Gebhard downed the fruit schnapps in one swallow and said, "There you go, Elsa."

"Well, Gebhard," said Grandfather, "you never know. You think it's the end of the world, and then it turns out all right." Loser's Gebhard banged his fist on the table and said, "Seventy-five percent disability, Josef." Grandfather nodded the way you nod when you know exactly what the other's going to say. And Loser's Gebhard talked the way you talk when you've told the same story many times before, and to the same person. You're not telling it to him, you're reproaching him with it. On October 21 in '17, three miles north of Ypres, his foot blown off. Seventy-five percent disabled. Ten years later, his hip starts to go. Grandfather nodded. Dr. Moser sends Loser's Gebhard to the hospital in Hoyren. They treat the hip with high-voltage current. The hip luxates. Grandfather nods as if he knew what that meant. And since Loser's Gebhard had lost so much mobility, when he falls while getting the hay into the barn, he can't get up again and gets gored by the ox. A broken rib. Hematoma in his lung. Grandfather nods. "Time to sell, my wife says," said Loser's Gebhard. "We got to have a smaller place." So they sell and buy Krenkels' Karl's place, only six acres with a mortgage of seven thousand marks on the appreciated value, but from selling their old place they have twenty-three earning interest at the Bank of Commerce and Agriculture. Grandfather nods. So even if the hops should fail again, nothing can happen to them. Then, after Hindenburg's third emergency decree, it's announced that the Dresdner Bank has suspended payments and the stock exchange is closed. Loser's Gebhard goes right into town and asks if the Bank of Commerce and Agriculture is starting to wobble, too. No, it's not in the least wobbly. But Loser's Gebhard insists on hearing it from Herr Kommerzienrat Sting himself, who tells him, "Nothing but rumors, Herr Loser, not a storm cloud in sight." If there were any threat, the Herr Kommerzienrat promised Herr Loser he would be the first to be notified and get his money. That was day before yesterday. And today the teller's window is closed. The money's gone. So he goes to a lawyer, who laughs. A bank director was the last person to ask if his bank was wobbly. Can't make a case for criminal negligence according to the lawyer. "Gone is gone, Josef."

"Oh, Gebhard," says Grandfather, and nods.

In the meantime Herr Brugger, wearing a green suit as always, had come over from the regulars' table and was sitting next to Loser's Gebhard. He removed the toothpick from the corner of his mouth— Adolf had told Johann the toothpick his father always had in the corner of his mouth was made of ivory—laid a hand on Loser's Gebhard's shoulder, and said, "Meeting tomorrow night at Köberle's in Bodolz. Why not come along and join up? Hitler's going to get us out of this. Next month Bavaria's going to lift the ban on uniforms, then you'll see some marching, my friends. We'll show these scoundrels and fops we mean business. Enough is enough. No more lies about who started the war! The ones who fired the first shot didn't start it! Down with the Treaty of Versailles! It's a disgrace: a hundred and thirty-two billion! In the last fourteen years we've paid them twenty billion and now we're bled dry! Bankrupt like no country's ever been before! And we're supposed to keep on like that for seventy or eighty more years? Keep paying out for seventy or eighty years? Paying for a war that everybody started together! We just happened to lose it. Tomorrow night at Köberle's in Bodolz, Gebhard. Hitler'll get us out of this. Heil Hitler!" He thrust his right hand straight out and clicked his heels together. Before doing so, he removed the ivory toothpick from the corner of his mouth and stuck it in his breast pocket. From a hook on the wall he took down his hat, shiny in all shades of green and sporting a tuft of goat-hair, said, "Just you wait and see," and left.

Adolf said his father's hat was velour. Adolf claimed it was the only velour hat in Wasserburg. Everyone watched Herr Brugger leave. Grandfather murmured to himself, so only Johann could hear, "Why didn't I go to America." Herr Seehahn, who always sat at the second table on the terrace side of the restaurant, had jumped up when Herr Brugger called out "Heil Hitler" and had thrust out his hand, too. But he hadn't managed to get the cigarette (which he only ever put down when he was eating) out of his mouth in time, so his own "Heil Hitler" was a good deal less impressive. Herr Seehahn rented a small room on the third floor of the restaurant. Because of the slanted eaves along one whole side of the room, Johann would have much preferred to sleep there than in his own high-ceilinged Room 9 with its merely straight walls and four large windows. Herr Seehahn's room had the most interesting smell in the whole building. Herr Seehahn smoked night and day, drank beer, schnapps, and lake wine every night until closing time and beyond, and carried those smells with him to his room. The result affected the third-floor hallway—almost dominated it, in fact. Again and again, Johann would run upstairs to dip his nose once more into that exciting aroma. People mentioned Herr Seehahn with a shudder of admiration whether he happened to be present or not, simply because, despite the life he led, he had never missed a single minute of work as the bookkeeper of the fruit growers' cooperative and had never made a single error as the cooperative's statistician. Herr Seehahn took three meals a day in the restaurant, always at a table where no one else sat, and murmured to himself the whole time. Johann often tried to loiter unobtrusively near Herr Seehahn, setting out fresh beer glass coasters, emptying ashtrays, or even serving a beer or a *stamperl* or a glass of lake wine, just so he could catch a few words of this never-ending stream. But he had to manage it so that neither Elsa nor Mother noticed. Herr Seehahn's soliloquy consisted of nothing but the worst profanity and the dirtiest of dirty words. It sounded like Herr Seehahn was constantly full to bursting and needed to get rid of what was raging inside him or it would probably have torn him apart or he would have expired some other way from what was eating at him. Johann was, of course, familiar with the words for the private parts of both men and women that Herr Seehahn recited, and now and then he could overhear curses, too, but no one could say these words and curses as softly or as fast as Herr Seehahn. And since he was compelled to talk without ceasing and at tremendous speed, there were never as many words as he needed and he had to repeat them over and over. And since even then, he sometimes ran out of words and the pressure inside him got too great, he would fall into wordless puckering and spitting. Herr Seehahn had false teeth, uppers and lowers, and he concentrated most on not spitting out either his upper or lower denture during his high-pressure cannonades of curses. To that end, he kept his lips as close together as he could while still swearing and cursing, so that only the tip of his tongue would flick out briefly when he said stupid prick or miserable sonofabitch, and then immediately vanish again. And besides all this talking and spitting, Herr Seehahn had to smoke, too. Sometimes, but very seldom, he would hold the cigarette in his thin, white, translucent fingers, but mostly it bobbed up and down in his mouth, echoing everything he said. That Herr Seehahn had some connection to Bavaria was more obvious from his yellowish Tyrolean jacket with the little green stand-up collar and stag-horn buttons than from his dialect. He spoke the High German of educated Bavarians. The softly cursing and swearing Herr Seehahn would not have had such a strong attraction for Johann if he had not always been so friendly during his barrage of dirty words. His eyes smiled while his mouth cursed, smoked, and smiled. Sometimes, when neither swearing nor puckered spitting was possible, Herr Seehahn chewed rapidly on his own lips with the tiniest of movements. He was friendly even then. Johann had the impression that Herr Seehahn didn't mind him getting close enough to catch a few words and fragmentary phrases. Herr Seehahn would even look at Johann and smile with his mouth and eyes while the whispered profanities shot from his mouth at terrific speed: "False serpent, stupid prick, good-for-nothing cunt, lights out knives out three men to stir the blood, miserable twat-fucker, ball-buster, little monster, half-wit, cum-bucket, dirty bum, date mate castrate—bingo, limp dick, pussy-chaser, shrew, blowhard, false serpent, the whole house is shaking what's going on? pants down hands up take it out put it back, if you can do it do it, miserable blockhead, who hasn't had any yet? who wants some more? there once was a brave musketeer got it up only twice a year, scarecrow, jezebel, nympho, false serpent, frozen account, falsehood and swindle rule the world, wacky place shitface, yesterday upon proud steeds now lying fallen in the weeds tomorrow in the cold cold ground, them that has gets more, kick his ass, pow right in the kisser, you must confess the world's a mess a shitty shitty mess, God's bankrupt, sit up and beg, what a laugh, filthy pussy, false serpent, the whole house is shaking what's going on? tumbly bumbly tralala . . ." Johann collected scraps of Seehahn and recited them, silently, but moving his lips. Only when nobody was around, of course. Best of all, in bed before going to sleep, his favorite way to say his prayers. False serpent was Herr Seehahn's most frequent expression, and so it was Johann's, too. He intended to practice until he could recite as softly and amicably and with the same lightning speed as Herr Seehahn.

Since Herr Seehahn remained standing when Herr Brugger was long since gone and still held his hand outstretched (without breaking his verbal stride, however), Elsa shouted, "Sit, Herr Seehahn!" whereupon he sat down, emitting words steadily all the while.

Standing behind the counter, Mother motioned to Johann and left the room. He followed. She told him to bring a rack of bottled beer from the cellar and put the sixteen bottles into the icebox under the bar. Then he was to ride his bike to Gierer the butcher's. Since the shop would be closed already, he should ring at the back door to their apartment and ask Frau Gierer, the butcher's wife, if he could still get a mark's worth of cervelat sausage. Johann wanted to ask why Josef couldn't do it, but he knew that Josef had ridden Father's bicycle to Hemigkofen because Jutz the organist, who always rode to the restaurant and gave Josef his piano lesson in the extra room, had had his bicycle stolen. Johann rode down into the village to the butcher shop, bought eight cervelats with his mark, hung the net shopping bag with the eight sausages onto the handlebar, and headed home. The net bag swung back and forth, and just as he was passing the Linden Tree, it got caught in the front wheel and several sausages were torn up. Back home he delivered the net bag to the kitchen and said, "I had an accident." Mina unpacked the cervelats.

Mother said, "Our profit's down the drain."

Mina said, "We can still use them for sausage salad."

The Princess said, "Schiller dead, and this character still walks the earth."

Johann went to the office and sat down at his father's desk. It was his favorite place. Since it was evening already, he took the rubber date stamp and turned it to the following day. That was his favorite occupation. Poor Mina, he thought, and Loser's Gebhard, too, even worse! Since Loser's Gebhard had to pedal his bike with one foot, Johann pitied him more than Mina. At least Mina was engaged to one of the strongest men in Wasserburg. Alfred ran the whole farming operation at the Linden Tree. He was bigger than all the rest, and the top of his head was a level field of the tiniest blond curls. The sides were shaved bare. Johann imagined that as soon as Mina told him what had happened to her savings, Alfred, who was as friendly as he was large, would pick her up, lift her above his head, and begin to turn in circles until Mina would cry, I'm getting dizzy! Just what I wanted, Alfred would reply, so you get dizzy and finally stop talking about money.

But what about Johann? Could he think about anything else besides money? First he lets himself be photographed, then he lets a mark's worth of cervelat get shredded in his spokes. He didn't care. Defend yourself, man! He was hot. Through and through. Nothing but hot, down to the backs of his knees, down to his feet, heat trickled through him. He had never felt himself so clearly. Saliva pooled in his mouth so he could barely swallow fast enough to keep up with it. His saliva tasted sweet. He had to bend his right arm, make his biceps get big and hard. It couldn't compare to Adolf's muscle. Up to now, when they curled their arms side by side, Adolf always had the bigger, harder muscle. When he was alone in his room, Johann did pushups. Soon he would challenge Adolf to compare. He felt there was nothing he couldn't ask of himself. He felt invulnerable. Money or no money! It seemed to him he could put up with anything. When Johann had run himself a glass of water from the tap at noon while the Princess was washing dishes, she'd called to him, "A drop in my bucket and I'll be with child."

"Adelheid!" Mother had shouted from the stove. Mina laughed. Johann pretended he didn't get it but felt like he was in a storm stirred up just for him.

CHAPTER FOUR

Loan Guarantee

AT HALF-PAST NINE, Johann was waiting at the station. The wooden barrier was painted a light green, and he wanted to be standing there when the locomotive chugged in, released its steam, and came to a stop with a little squeal. The way the railroader's uniform sat on the short but extremely straight-backed Herr Deuerling, it would never occur to a soul to think of him as a senior secretary of the Reichsbahn. Only a retired army captain could wear a railroader's uniform as he did. And not just any captain, but a captain who needed to continually remind people, because they kept forgetting, that he was not from around here. It was true, he'd been born on the banks of the Lech River, but—and this was the crucial thing—on the Bavarian side. Whenever Herr Deuerling crossed the street to fetch his beer from the restaurant, he would suddenly materialize in the kitchen doorway and call out in a commanding voice, "Ten-*shun*! All present and accounted for?" And Mina's little voice would pipe up, "One cook, one dishwasher on duty, one boy doing his spelling!" and snap the fingertips of her right hand to her temple. "As you were!" cried Herr Deuerling. "As you were!" cried Mina. And to Johann he said, "Head up, chest out, suck in your gut!" If Elsa came in, he would try to mix it up with her and crowd his pretend sparring partner up against the nearest wall or behind the stove and then onto the coal bin, which was always kept closed. Elsa was a good two heads taller. Nevertheless, she usually ended up sitting on the coal bin and once there, would pull Herr Deuerling onto her lap and start in with, A farmer went trotting upon his gray mare. Elsa emitted such shrill, penetrating shrieks during these pretend battles that the Princess was compelled to turn around and watch. When Elsa set Herr Deuerling back on his feet, the Princess said, "Schiller dead, and this character still walks the earth." And Herr Deuerling would loudly reply, "Three hours' detention for your fresh mouth. Dismissed!" He bellowed Dismissed! so sharply that the Princess instantly returned to her sinkful of dishes.

Johann always pretended to be completely absorbed by the long words in his picture book, so everything took place as if he weren't there, but he heard it all with his heart in his mouth. No doubt about it, this was life. He was experiencing what life was like. But he wasn't allowed to look. He had to keep staring at the stiff cardboard pages of his picture book. Life was a forbidden thing. The sounds reaching his ears from the other side of the big stovetop intimated that later on, there would be nothing as beautiful as being tossed in the air by the thighs of a powerful woman while singing, A farmer went trotting upon his gray mare. Until not too long ago, Mina had played A farmer went trotting with him, until one day he had declared that it was a stupid game. A farmer went trotting upon his gray mare, bumpety, bumpety, bump! With his daughter behind him so rosy and fair, lumpety, lumpety, lump! A raven cried Croak! and they all tumbled down, bumpety, bumpety, bump! But when Elsa sang it and Herr Deuerling bounced up and down, it wasn't stupid at all. When they did it, it didn't sound cozy, either, as it did with him and Mina. It sounded shrill. Life was evidently a pain you couldn't get enough of.

After Herr Deuerling had raised his signal baton to let the engineer know he could resume his run, he opened the barrier and allowed the few people who had arrived by the late train to leave. Only after he had relieved them of their twice-punched tickets, of course. Johann would have liked to save his father's ticket, a round-trip Wasserburg-Oberstaufen on September 29, 1932. Actually, Johann wanted to save everything. Having to throw anything away was painful. As soon as his father was through the barrier, Johann took his briefcase. Johann knew that they were not going to give each other the Eskimo kiss, tip of nose to tip of nose, out here in public. But Johann had the briefcase. Sometimes, when he knew he wouldn't be observed, Johann took the briefcase out of one of the two giant, dark armoires in the upstairs hall and, holding it in his hand, walked back and forth in front of the big oval mirror in his parents' bedroom. No one else in the whole village had a briefcase to match his father's. The doctor's bag, for instance, didn't have a lock shiny as gold under its handles. It didn't have a reddish sheen like his father's either, but was dark and nondescript. His father's briefcase bulged out more on both sides and had a silken lining and two compartments. Helmer's Hermine might have a similar briefcase, but it was much smaller. Everyone knew that it came from Berlin and had been given to her by the second Frau Professor Bestenhofer, whose house Hermine cleaned. Father had had his briefcase since before the war. He'd brought it back from Lausanne, where he'd gone to learn French and business. Today it was stuffed full but not particularly heavy. It was the teas. Father bought all his teas at his friend Hartmut Schulz's health food store in Oberstaufen. He was an army buddy of Father's, actually, a fellow POW in a French retaliation camp near Chantilly: thirty or forty thousand prisoners out in the open from July to November 1918, all with diarrhea. The weaker ones toppled backwards off the plank over the latrine pit, sank in, and disappeared. Father called the plank that the weakest ones fell off of the latrine plank. Everyone else at the regulars' table called it the thunder board when they talked about the detention camps. Then by train to Tours on the Loire, where they had actual tents and adequate food. But Johann's father and his friend Schulz were already sick and had to be sent home on a medical train in the summer of 1919. They traveled together as far as Kempten. When they had recovered, they exchanged letters. Schulz, ten years younger than Johann's father, planned to be a pastor, became a pastor, but didn't stay a pastor. Instead he opened a health food store in Oberstaufen.

Johann saw that his father was sweating. As soon as Father started perspiring, he got quite pale. They went straight to the office, and Father sat down on one of the chairs. Johann ran to the kitchen, called to Mina—who was standing motionless in the straightened-up kitchen, staring at the stovetop—that his father needed hot water for his maté tea. When he returned to the office, Mother was already unpacking the graham-flour bread that Father had brought home, as well as a tube of vitamin cream. Johann handed her the knife; she spread the cream on the bread and gave it to Father. Grandfather came in, too, and sat down on a straight-backed chair. "Armchairs aren't for me," he would say if someone offered him a seat in one. Mother had closed the door to the office so no one who might come through the hallway could look in. After he had eaten a third piece of bread, Father took off his jacket and rolled up his right sleeve. Mother had already taken the hypodermic needle out of the cabinet. She filled it, soaked a cotton ball in disinfectant from a little bottle, wiped a spot where there weren't any previous needle marks visible, squeezed the skin between her thumb and index finger, pushed the needle in, and pressed the piston until the hypodermic was empty. Wiped the spot again. They did that twice a day.

Father showed them all the things he had brought home. A wreath of figs for Josef and Johann. For Mother there was a bottle of Indian perfume. "Musk," he said, "take a sniff." She turned away brusquely, wanted nothing to do with musk perfume. He looked at her as if asking for something. She looked away. He'd brought teas and a tincture for Grandfather, hawthorn and Korodin drops, and told him, "You'll be surprised how much it clears up your chest, Father."

Mother said, "And what about the loan guarantee?"

"He had to make use of it," said Father. "The bill was due on Saturday."

"So it has to be repaid by Monday," said Mother.

"Yes," said Father. "They say it's been the worst season in Oberstaufen since 1919."

"Same here," said Mother. Father said nothing more. "Seven thousand three hundred," said Mother. Father nodded. "What am I going to do?" said Mother. "We have two outstanding loans of our own, one due October first and one on the fifteenth. The brewery and the savings and loan."

"Savings and loan, too?" said Father in surprise.

"Three thousand four hundred," said Mother, her voice rising, "endorsed by Strohmeyer and Co."

"I see," said Father, "the coal. But we have receivables."

"Three thousand seven hundred ninety-five," said Mother.

"Exactly," said Father.

Mother: "But they won't be paid off by Monday."

"In any case, the brewery can't lodge a complaint about the bill," said Father.

"Oh, yes, they can," said Mother. Father stood up, went over to Mother, and put his hands on her shoulders.

Father was a bit shorter than Mother. Johann thought no one had jackets as beautiful as his father's: green with white flecks, brown with white flecks, a gray one with black pinstripes. And all his jackets were quite long, with two rows of buttons to be fastened. And he never wore a shirt without a collar. Grandfather wore almost nothing but collarless shirts. Grandfather, however, had a grayish-white mustache. Under his nose it was wonderfully dense and full. It narrowed only a bit toward the corners of his mouth, and right at the corners it turned up in two flat curves. Grandfather had a field of stubble on his head, too, a thicket of stiff gray hairs. And so, Johann felt, Grandfather had no need of a collar.

Father paced up and down the office and said he and his friend Hartmut Schulz were planning to take over a silver fox farm in the Allgäu. And here at home, down in the shed, he was going to set up some hutches next week and start raising angora rabbits. There was room in both the pigpen and the old horse stall, now empty and unused. It was ridiculous to keep pigs. But angoras! They didn't smell and brought in ten times as much. There were purebred pairs for sale right now in Lindau-Reutin. In a year you'd have forty to sixty angora rabbits, pounds and pounds of angora fur every week—basically cash in your pocket. Angora fur was bidding fair to crowd cashmere out of the market. Didn't it make sense to raise angoras? And no expenses. You could feed them on kitchen leavings and the grass under the trees. Josef and Johann could see to feeding them and mucking out the hutches; he'd comb the fur. It wouldn't make them rich, but the income would be steady. Of course, the silver fox farm would earn them a lot more. If his friend Hartmut Schulz had to close his health food store in Oberstaufen, it would free him up to run the silver fox farm. Demand for silver fox fur was on the rise as well. A silver fox farm in Ellhofen was for sale. He and his friend Hartmut Schulz were going to Ellhofen in the next few days to have a look at it. Silver foxes! Ellhofen had the ideal climate for raising silver foxes. It was in the Allgäu sure enough, but not in Upper Allgäu. Ideal! And to guarantee success, they would clear out a room in the attic and raise silk worms. Silk was always in demand.

Father stopped pacing. Everyone looked at him. Johann liked listening to his father talk. He had such a lilting voice. By the way, Father said, he was going to Mariabrunn and Neukirch next week, too. There was a farm for sale in Mariabrunn. Mostly orchard, twelve and a half acres, almost no animals—just what he had always been looking for. And in Neukirch there was an inn with a bakery. Right beside the church, that is, vis-à-vis, on the other side of the street. A prime location in Neukirch, an up-and-coming town. If they kept on asphalting the roads at this rate, there'd be an asphalt road from Tettnang to Wangen by the end of the decade, and halfway between: Neukirch. And in the middle of Neukirch: us.

Father was excited by the prospects that were opening up for him and for the entire family. When he fell silent for a moment, all his animation seemed to be gathered in his mouth, his lips. They practically swelled, and his mouth and mustache almost stood out from his face. Johann was sure there was not a father in all the world to equal him. Whether his father spoke or played the piano, it always sounded beautiful. Not to mention his penmanship! The restaurant's books were all written in his wonderful hand with generously large and beautiful loops. Not a letter went unadorned. The initial letters sometimes disappeared entirely in a thicket of spiraling tendrils that sprouted for their sake. Johann rescued all the paper from his father's wastebasket and on the unwritten side practiced making letters like his father's. When he started school next year, he would show off with Father's handwriting. He wanted nothing to do with the clumsy descenders and rigid loops that Josef brought home from school. Josef said that it was German script, Sütterlin script. What Father wrote was italic. Johann would write in italic.

From his bag Father extracted a little black case, fished a tiny key from his wallet, and unlocked the case, whose two equal halves hinged open. In both halves, all sorts of glass components shimmered and glinted from the green felt lining: tubes that ended like trumpets or blossoms or flutes, round parts, wavy parts, small and large spheres, triangles—all made of glass. It was a magnetizing apparatus, the wonderful invention of his friend Hartmut Schulz. Schulz had entrusted it to Father so he could look for someone willing to finance its production. With this apparatus, virtually any illness was curable, since all illnesses arose from a failure of excitation in the nerve fibers. To reawaken that excitation through magnetization was the great, universal cure. Of course, it wasn't Hartmut Schulz's discovery that the entire universe and all of life consisted of the subtlest of fluids, an emission much more delicate than light or sound, a fluid so fine that no one had yet succeeded in measuring it, although one could constantly sense it, experience it, and recognize it. Which was why wise men like the Englishmen Locke and Newton, as well as Kepler, Paracelsus, Franz Anton Mesmer, and Maxwell—each in his own way, but all talking about the same thing—had given us reports of this *coelesti invisibili*. And now, after ten years of labor, his friend Hartmut Schulz had taken what had previously depended on an extraordinary and rare talent, the talent that a hundred and fifty years ago had made Franz Anton Mesmer world-famous and the most sought-after physician of his time in Vienna and Paris—namely, the talent to heal the sick without laying a hand on them, but merely through the emanation of his own power— his friend Hartmut Schulz had captured this talent in his apparatus.

Then Father connected what looked like a glass comb to an electric cord, plugged the other end of the cord into the wall socket, ran over to the little case, and started twirling knobs and pushing down tiny levers until a buzzing noise became audible and a violet light began to flash from the comb's glass handle all the way down to the very last of its teeth.

"Augusta, wait," cried Father, but his mother ran over to the door. "Please, don't!" cried Father. Don't open the door, he meant. "Augusta!" he said again. Luckily, he stressed the first syllable of Augusta. Johann couldn't stand it when people called his mother Au-*gus*ta or even worse, Au-*gus*te. They were people who spoke High German. Father also spoke mostly High German, but he said *Au*-gusta. And that was her name: *Au*gusta. Just like his own name was *Jo*-hann and not Jo-*hann*, for heaven's sake.

"You try it, Johann," said Father. Johann went over, and his father ran the glass comb with its violet flashes over Johann's head and down his neck and back up to his head. Then he turned the machine off. "How was it?" he asked.

"Good," said Johann. "Real tickly like."

"It'll get even better," said Father. "But not a word about it to anyone!" he said as he packed everything back into the little case. They didn't have a patent for it yet, so caution, caution! This apparatus was going to cause a revolution in the field of medicine. And his friend Hartmut Schulz was going to give him a share of the profits. "Then all our troubles will be over," said Father.

Mother turned to Grandfather and said, "Won't you say something to him, Father?" Grandfather lifted his hands a little from his thighs but let them drop again. Mother started talking, her voice pitched higher than Johann had ever heard it before. The Bank of Commerce and Agriculture had closed all its branches, including the one in Glatthars' house. Mina would never see her savings again, and there was nothing left of Loser's Gebhard's twenty-three thousand. Day before yesterday, Kommerzienrat Sting was still saying the bank was flourishing—nothing but rumors, and he was going to take legal action to put a stop to them—and now word had it the farmers weren't being paid for their milk, and that meant the end for sure. Herr Kalteissen, the bailiff, had been in the restaurant that very day. Precautionary garnishment of the safe, cabinet, the icebox in the hall, and the piano. Now they would have to feed coins into the meter next to the bell box to get any electricity. The teller at the savings and loan in Unterreitnau came up twenty-four thousand marks short: arrested. Hartmanns' nursery had applied for a renegotiated loan but was turned down. Now they were going to be liquidated. Merk in Nonnenhorn declared bankruptcy two weeks ago and just got caught trying to steal a bicycle in Tettnang. Suddenly she stopped and said to Grandfather in her normal voice. "So you have nothing to say."

Grandfather addressed Father: "Now there's that new auction hall. We're a member. Every day dealers from out of town buy at least a hundred thousand pounds of fruit. We paid the fee for stall five, but we're not there."

"Right now we don't have the capital to trade in fruit," said Father. "The credit terms are too short. I can't push the BUY button at the auction if I then have to go to the farmer and confess I won't be able to scare up the money for four weeks. You know farmers don't give credit, Father."

"Why didn't I go to America," Johann's grandfather murmured to himself, stood up wearily, and left the room.

Mother said, "Max Brugger says only Hitler can help us now."

Father said, "Hitler means war." Then he said he had to go to bed.

"Yes," said Mother. "All the color's drained out of your face." Father took the little black case with him.

Mother sat down at the desk, rolled a piece of paper into the typewriter, and began typing with the index finger of her right hand. Johann went and stood behind her. He knew all the letters because he had learned them all with Josef, starting the very first day his brother came home from school with his homework. He would certainly have been able to type faster than his mother. In the upper left-hand corner, Mother had written the name Thaddäus Unsicherer. That was

Mother's father. Under the name she wrote, Farmer, and under that, Kümmertsweiler. In the right-hand corner, September 29, 1932, and in the middle, LOAN GUARANTEE. Johann sounded out the words until they put up no more resistance.

Mother used Father's fountain pen to practice a signature. She practiced on pieces of paper from the wastebasket, then crumpled them up and threw them back into the basket. Then she signed Thaddäus Unsicherer under what she'd typed. "This is just between you and me," she said. She needed her father's signature by tomorrow forenoon but couldn't leave the business to run over to Kümmertsweiler and fetch it, so she had to imitate his signature. "So we don't have to declare bankruptcy, Johann," she said, "but it'll be just between the two of us." Johann nodded. Her tone of voice held the echo of everything his father and mother had said in the previous hour.

He went upstairs, down the dark hallway, and saw that there was still a light shining under his father's door. He knocked as quietly as possible and entered the room upon Father's "Come in."

Father was sitting more than lying, propped up on three pillows and reading one of the yellow booklets he got in the mail. Johann sat on the edge of the bed and held out his face the way he did when he wanted an Eskimo kiss from his father. Father still smelled of peppermint. He showed Johann two words in the booklet he had just been reading. "You know these already," he said. "Go ahead and read them." Johann sounded them out: *Rabindranath Tagore*. In the books and pamphlets in his bedside bookcase, Father had a supply of words that were still difficult to pronounce, even after Johann had sounded them out. *Rabindranath Tagore*. And when Johann succeeded, Father said, "You're amazing, Johann." Then he made Johann say the word without looking in the book. "You see," Father said, "at first these words always look unpronounceable, but then they come out of your mouth all by themselves. At first, the words resist, but then they give in. Look here, sound it out!"

Johann tried: "Phil-o-so-phy."

"Good. And now this one!"

"The-os-o-phy."

"Good. Now something easy," said Father. "What's it say on this booklet?"

Johann sounded it out: "The Path to Perfection."

"Johann," said Father, "time for beddy-bye." Almost at once, Father closed his eyes. Johann turned off the light and crept to his own bed on tiptoe because Josef was already asleep.

The streetlight was reflected in the glass of the picture of the guardian angel. It hung at a slight angle from the wall that Johann faced when he lay in bed. And the light always shone right on the part of the picture where the guardian angel, dressed in white, was walking across the bridge without a railing and holding his hand above the child who walked ahead of him. The glass reflected the light so that Johann couldn't see the guardian angel, but he knew that in the place where the light was falling, the guardian angel was depicted and was protecting the child from falling into the dark abyss.

The next day was Thursday, and from eleven to twelve, Herr Witzigmann would be in the storeroom of the savings and loan. Johann and his mother were already coming up the narrow side stairs to the loading dock just as Herr Witzigmann was putting his key into the padlock. He pushed back the heavy sliding door, and they followed him into the storeroom and then into a boarded-off cubicle containing a table, two chairs, and a writing desk. On the table was a shiny green cash box. Fortunately, the stairs to the loading dock were so narrow that Mother couldn't hold Johann by the hand. She was always leading him by the hand. If no one was looking, Johann had nothing against holding her hand, but not in front of other people.

"Have a seat," said Herr Witzigmann. But Johann preferred to stay close to his mother for now. Mother took from her black handbag the loan guarantee on which she had signed "Thaddäus Unsicherer" the previous evening and handed the paper across the table to Herr Witzigmann. Herr Witzigmann took it, read it, and said, "I'm glad, Augusta. I feel sure that in light of this, the executive board will extend the loan. You've come just at the right time; the board meets tonight."

Mother said she was aware of that. Then she stood up. Johann caught a glimpse of Herr Witzigmann opening the cash box and putting into it the paper he had from Mother. As Johann walked back home with his mother along the tracks, Mother held him by the hand again. But here—sheds on their left and the siding and main track on their right—nobody saw Mother holding his hand. As soon as they were past the railroad freight shed, he freed his hand from his mother's. Here he could be seen. He engineered a transition from being led to letting go. Carefully, he pulled his hand out of his mother's but immediately took hold of Mother's wrist with the same hand.

Before they had even reached the terrace, they could hear his father playing the piano. Mother frowned. Elsa came out to meet them and said, "Herr Brugger was just here, ma'am. He drank a small beer in one gulp, slammed his money down on the table, and said over his shoulder on his way out, 'We're gonna pull the plug on that piano player tonight.'" Elsa wanted to know what he meant by that.

"You'll have to ask him," said Mother.

"Herr Brugger is on the executive board of the savings and loan," she said as she gave her handbag to Johann to put in the safe. If there had been such a job as opening and closing the sighing doors of safes all day long, Johann would have chosen it instantly. Mother slipped on her white full-length apron and went into the kitchen. She gave Johann the sign, and as quietly as possible, Johann opened the door from the central hallway into the extra room. He went and stood beside his father, who noticed his presence, stopped playing, took Johann onto his knee, and quietly sang into Johann's ear what he had just been playing. Then he said, "Well, now I think it's time to go over the accounts receivable. Come with me." And he went into the office. Father wrote down numbers from the book in which they recorded everyone who couldn't pay right away for their coal or their wood. He hummed while he wrote the columns of figures. He hummed as if humming was more important than writing down the numbers. Suddenly, he stopped and put the fountain pen into the groove formed by silver leaves that went with the glass cube that held the inkwell. His humming had ceased. From far away, Elsa's voice, calling out even before she reached the kitchen, "Two trout munnair," and then the sharp, long-suffering voice of the Princess: "Meunière!" Johann closed the lid of the inkwell that fitted into the glass cube. The lid was a little dome of silver leaves. Herr Brugger's inkwell had a silver lid in the form of a jockey's cap. When Adolf saw Johann's inkwell for the first time, he said, "What's that supposed to be, cabbage leaves or something?" Johann had asked his father, who asked back, "They're beautiful, aren't they?" Now they always reminded Johann of cabbage leaves. "Aren't they beautiful?" Father had asked. "Yes, they are," Johann had said. And Father: "Art nouveau, Johann, *Jugendstil*. Put it in the word tree." He still always thought of cabbage leaves when he saw the curved lid that Father had called a flat dome, but now the word *Jugendstil* twinkled from the word tree as well; now it was one of the words Father had him spell: *pleurisy, Bhagavadgita, Popocatépetl, theosophy, Rabindranath Tagore, Balaam, philosophy, Swedenborg, Bharatanatyam.* On the wall above the sofa hung a large landscape with red-and-white cattle grazing in a pasture that sloped down to a river and a girl sitting under huge forest trees, wearing a peasant dress that had perhaps never existed in reality. For Johann, this picture belonged to the words he spelled for his father. It was important to Johann that after he was done, his father always said, "You're amazing, Johann."

Father still hadn't stirred from his chair. Johann couldn't leave until his father looked up. It would make it seem like he was trying to sneak away. So he leaned against his father a little. Father put his arm around Johann, pulled him close. Although Johann couldn't see into his father's face as he pulled him in, he knew his father was crying now. So he had to be very careful not to look into his face. If your father's crying, you can't look him in the face. His father took a tiny box from the right-hand desk drawer and opened it. It smelled of peppermint. Father took a small dispenser from its padding, put it under his nose so that the two tiny, green, pointed felt nibs disappeared into his nostrils. When the two nibs dried out and stopped dispensing peppermint aroma, they were dipped into a little bottle labeled Po-Ho-Oil. Father took several deep breaths. Pages covered with numbers lay on the desk. Father took the sheets of paper, crumpled them up, and gave them to Johann, who threw them into the wastebasket. Then he sat quietly on his father's right knee until the office door behind them opened and his mother's voice said, "Supper's ready." And she wanted to know what father thought about the coal dealers' campaign; they should join in, too, didn't he think so? She didn't understand how he could have been sitting there at the desk this whole time and not read the letter she'd left there for him. Nine dealers from the region had already signed the agreement that for the time being, they would only deliver hard coal, coke, and briquettes for cash on delivery. "Sign it," said Mother; they could always still make exceptions. Father signed.

Father ate his steamed vegetables, drank his tea, and made fun of everyone forced to eat the meat concealed under their noodles. But today he couldn't get a rise out of Mother with jokes about the food. She sat with Mina on the other side of the huge stove at a work table whose edges were as thick as they had been thirty years ago but whose center was worn down by the endless cutting and chopping and mincing.

Had he read about the Brems in the paper? asked Mother. Because the Brems still owed them seventy-two marks and nine pfennigs. Father lifted his right hand and pantomimed drilling with his outstretched index finger. This was a reminder of a fight between the Brems. It had started because Frau Brem blamed a hole in the wooden wall of the privy attached to the exterior of their house on a mistake her husband had made with his drill, but he maintained that it was a knothole. And since his wife continued to insist it was his fault, he'd dragged her down to the lake and held her under the water, saying she'd stay there until she admitted it was a knothole and not a mistake with his drill. But even with her head under water, she still stuck her hand up and made a drilling motion with her finger. So carpenter Brem had to give in.

They'd likely never see those seventy-two marks again, said Mother. Clearly, she wasn't in the mood for any of the funny or tragic Brem stories Helmer's Hermine brought up from the lower village and spread

around—not as long as they had to reckon with losing the Brems'
seventy-two marks.

Had he or had he not read it? He had not. "Read it, Josef." Josef
took the newspaper. "Real Estate Auction," said Mother. Josef read
aloud:

> REAL ESTATE AUCTION
>
> At 3:00 p.m. on Monday, November 23, 1932, the house
> no. 9a in Wasserburg am Bodensee (Brem) will be sold by
> the office of the Mayor of Wasserburg at a public auction
> to be held in the extra room of the Station Restaurant. The
> property includes a residential structure with several apart-
> ments, stalls, barn, workshop with wood-working machines,
> farmyard, and large orchard (the latter suitable for building
> lots) and is located on a principal street of the town. It com-
> prises about 25,700 sq. ft. and the structures are in good
> condition. The conditions of the auction will be announced
> on the day of the sale.
>
> Inquiries can be addressed to the undersigned official receiver.
> Lindau-Bodensee, October 30, 1932.
> Noerdlinger, Attorney-at-Law

"And the Capranos," said Mother, her voice quiet again, "are pretty
shaky, too. It's all over with the Hartmanns, and it could happen to
either of the Brodbecks any day now. Glatthars don't know which way
to turn, and we'll be next." Real estate auction, thought Johann, more
words to learn. The harder it was to understand words like that, the
more he wanted to sound them out. Father's answer to what Josef had
read? Angora rabbits, the silver fox farm in Ellwangen, silk worm production in the attic, the inn with a bakery in Neukirch, the small farm
in Mariabrunn. But their best opportunity was his friend Hartmut
Schulz's magnetic apparatus. "Just think," he cried, "he's going to cut
me in!"

Mother said she had got Herr Witzigmann to extend their credit
until November 21. A further extension was out of the question.

Everyone had stopped eating. Father said, "For gold all lust, have it they must. Alas, we're poor." When they all looked at him, he said, "Goethe." But not to worry, he would consult his mantra, and his mantra would tell him where pots of money were to be found. "Don't worry, Augusta, stick with me and you can't fail." Mother said the Lakeshore Café had got a license for live music three times a week.

Father said, "If you call that music!"

Mother said, "It's dance music!" When no one reacted, she said, "The boiler's dripping again." Grandfather and Johann were sitting on the long bench under the hot water boiler. Water dripped onto the bench between them. "After dinner, ride over to Schmitt the tinsmith and tell them to send Fritz," she said. Johann nodded. Mother called over to the Princess, "Adelheid, come to dinner. I'm not going to tell you again." Without turning around, the Princess said, "You might have given me three chances, but since it's you, I'll come now."

Josef was the first to leave the table. He had to practice. Recently, Josef had started to toss his head back even when a tuft of hair wasn't falling into his face. Johann longed to be able to toss his head back the same way. Josef had barely left the room before the scales started up. "There are still guests on the terrace," said Mother. Father was silent. He raised his head and turned so he could hear the scales better. Since he had the biggest ears Johann had ever seen and big round eyes to go with them, Johann thought, Now he looks like a deer again. His mother said, "And the Crown is putting a crown of electric lights onto their facade so everyone driving by or arriving by boat will see nothing but the Crown."

Father said, "What a beautiful attack he has."

CHAPTER FIVE

Blessing the Flag

FATHER AND GRANDFATHER SAT ON their separate chairs as if not in the same room. Although there was hardly enough space in the office to look past each other, they were turned at such an angle that they didn't have to acknowledge each other's presence. Fog outside made even the trees in the courtyard look like ghosts. A foghorn sounded down on the lake, a sound almost like a question. And no answer. The boat blew its horn again—no answer. It sounded like the boat had called out in vain and then called again. And again. But always quite calmly. Johann knew that in the dining room, Herr Seehahn would be getting furiously worked up. Whenever fog horns were heard, Herr Seehahn shouted, "Stop it!" Turned his head toward the lake and cried, "Stop it at once or we shoot, no bleating allowed starting right now, miserable wretch with your idiotic bleating . . ." Herr Seehahn had been in the navy. Whenever a guest he didn't know entered the dining room, he would stand up, raise his hand to his temple like a soldier, say, "Revulooshunery seaman Seehahn, ret." and sit down again. The cigarette never left his mouth the whole time.

The sound of fog horns drifting up from the lake made Johann feel good. Thank goodness the apples are all in the cellar, he thought, and the geraniums, too. For days he had stood on a ladder picking apples. Every year as All Saints' Day approached, Mother was embarrassed that her trees were still full of apples while the trees in front of the next house down the hill had long since been picked, to say nothing of the thousands and thousands of other trees in and around the village. "It upsets our guests," she said, "that apparently we can't find the time to pick our own apples." Josef had homework to do and scales to practice, Father couldn't stand on a ladder that long, Niklaus was too old, and Grandfather even older. Johann said if Niklaus put the ladder up for him, he'd pick the apples. "This is what we've come to," Mother said. Johann definitely couldn't back down now. He promised to hold on tight to a branch with one hand while he picked apples with the other.

"And then the branch will break," Mother said.

"I'll only use big branches," Johann replied. And then for a week he'd stood in the trees. The higher up the ladder he had to go, the louder his heart pounded. But from the second day on, he knew nothing could happen to him. He felt at home in the trees. He picked the shiny red Prince Ludwig apples one after another and slid them carefully, so they wouldn't get bruised, into the picking bag slung over his shoulder. He had even rigged up the bag by himself, just like he'd seen his uncle do in Kümmertsweiler: you put one apple in the corner of the bag and tie it off with a rope, then run the rope up through a hole near the mouth of the bag and then back down to the tied-off apple in the corner. Then you have a double length of rope between the mouth and the bottom. You can slip your head between the rope and the bag and hang it over your shoulder so the mouth is right at the level of your chest and you can slide one apple after another into it. Johann knew he would have more trouble rigging such a thing up than Ludwig or Paul or Adolf, so it was especially important to prove that he could do it, too. Johann enjoyed it when people passing by in the street called up to him to be careful not to fall. He liked it even more when they shouted that he was too little for a job like that. If some time passed without anyone calling to Johann from the street to say that picking apples was something they would never have expected him to be able to do, he realized that he looked forward to hearing it again. Standing so many hours on the ladder and reaching for all those apples and sliding them into the bag so nothing happened to them were things he could do only if people were watching. So he was glad when Herr

Schlegel the builder called to him, "Hold on like a sailor to his girl! My respects!" When Frau Schorer the cobbler's wife called to him, "Your mother must be so proud of you." When Hagens' Fritz shouted that the way down was faster than the way up. When Taubenberger the postman stopped and said more to himself than to Johann that Johann was a devil of a fellow. When Helmer's Hermine called, "One climbs higher for a black cherry than a red." Or when Herr Grübel, walking along beside his cows, called up in his silvery singsong, "Were I a little bird with little wings, I'd fly to you." It was understandable that Frau Fürst, her lips stitched shut by pain and her eyes full of arrested tears, said nothing as she passed. Adolf came by at least once a day, of course, and criticized the varieties Johann was harvesting. Didn't they have a Boskoop tree? he asked. And no Champagne Reinettes either? Not even Cardinal von Galens? No, just Welschisners, Gravensteins, Teuringers, and Prince Ludwigs, Johann replied. Those were his favorite kinds. What he thought was that when his grandfather planted this orchard twenty-five or thirty years ago, he should have remembered to plant some Boskoops, Champagne Reinettes, and Cardinal von Galens, too. When three or four of them hiked to Nonnenhorn through the harvested orchards on a November Saturday to swap Karl May novels with the canon, nobody bothered to raise a finger to pick an overlooked Welschisner, but they would use sticks to knock down a Boskoop. Bruggers had only Boskoops, Champagne Reinettes, and Cardinal von Galens.

Fortunately, the trees were emptied by the time everyone went to church on All Saints' and All Souls' Days. Mother told Johann she was happy now.

Mother had to twist Father's arm to get him to go to church with the veterans' association the following Sunday and march with the group to the war memorial after the service. Grandfather said it was a disgrace for his son not to march along with everyone else for the fifty-year anniversary of the Veterans' and Military Association Grandfather belonged to. And Father himself a member, and a combat veteran, too—a decorated one, in fact. Eighteen seventy-two and 1932—how much more of an occasion did he need, for heaven's sake? And Grandfather to be specially honored that day, too, said Mother. After all, Grandfather had been the association's first flag-bearer, and that Sunday they were consecrating a new flag. The newspaper would probably report that his son hadn't been among the marchers, said Grandfather. "Next thing you know, we'll have to sell the place," said Mother, "and you can stand by the front door with a pistol in your hand like Brem the carpenter to scare off the people who want to have a look at our goods and chattels before they're sold off at auction." Johann liked saying hello to Herr Brem most of all. When Brem the carpenter charged Herr Lachenmeyer fifty pfennigs for sharpening his crosscut saw, Herr Lachenmeyer had said that was too much. Herr Brem took the saw, ran it twice across a big stone, and said, "No charge, then."

Josef stood next to Father, Johann next to Mother. That meant that Josef was also against Father marching. Johann wanted Father to march. He wanted to see Father wearing the Iron Cross and Bavarian Order of Merit with crossed swords. In the winter, Johann sometimes took his father's army things out of the big armoire on the second floor: the bright-as-new 8 mm pistol with magazine, the rusty revolver, the cap with a cockade and gleaming visor, the sergeant's epaulettes, and the gloves now gone a dull white. Johann outfitted himself with these things. He also got out the long, gently curving saber that was almost as tall as he was, together with its glittering pendant, and stood in front of the mirror. His father wanted nothing more to do with military things.

"And he's from the 20th, too," said Grandfather, "like most of our members." Father said he hadn't attended a reunion of the 20th Infantry Regiment since the end of the war.

"But they're going to honor your father," said Mother.

No more was said after that. Elsa came in to say the itinerant photographer was there with the pictures: three pictures, three marks apiece.

Mina came into the office behind Elsa and said, "He must be nuts."

"Pay him and bring me the pictures," said Mother. "Nine marks, Johann. You could have had a new pair of winter boots for that." Mina said she was really sorry she'd lost all her money and now couldn't buy a picture of Johann.

Johann replied at once, "I'll give you one." Everybody laughed. Elsa put the three pictures on the table and everyone bent over to have a look. Right away Johann could see that he hadn't closed his mouth completely. His two incisors were getting bigger every day and they showed. In front of the mirror, he often tried out various ways to hold his lips so those gigantic teeth wouldn't show.

Mina said, "Don't he look sharp standing there! I'm ready for anything, that's how he looks." She liked the way his outstretched arms were holding the handlebar. "As good as any prince," she said. "His bike's his steed! Say something, ma'am, or Johann'll think you don't like the pictures."

His mother nodded and said, "Put them away now."

Johann went over to the highboy but waited until the others had left the office to lower the writing surface, remove the mirror insert, and put the pictures into the secret compartment. To do that, he had to lift the two hinged lids covered in green felt and slide the pictures into the invisible interior. His father had shown him where the secret compartment was. Johann used it mainly for things he needed to keep hidden from Josef. Every time the uncle they called Cousin came to visit from the Allgäu in his Ford, he brought each boy a bar of chocolate. Josef ate his up the same day he got it. For Johann, getting chocolate was at least as marvelous as eating it. Every second or third day he would break off the tiniest little piece and his bar would last for weeks. Unless it fell into Josef's hands. When the shouting of the resultant arguments got to be too loud, Father finally took Johann into the office and showed him how to pull out the mirror insert by the little shiny black columns to the right and left of the mirror. Then you could lift the two hinged, felt-covered lids that concealed the secret compartment. Johann had to promise not to show anyone where the secret compartment was. Not even Adolf, thought Johann, when Father said that. He didn't have to show it to Adolf, but at least he had to tell him that he had a secret compartment now. Whenever Adolf got a present, he couldn't wait to tell Johann about it. Every time, he would come dashing up the hill, rush in calling, Johann, Johann!, grab Johann by the arm, drag him along down the street at a run past the Linden Tree, then a right turn and immediately left again by the fire station to Bruggers' house, in the back door and straight to whatever Adolf had just gotten that he absolutely had to show Johann. Usually he had nothing more to say about it, couldn't even speak for sheer joy and excitement, just hopped around as if the floor was bouncing beneath his feet and whipped his hands through the air so his fingers slapped against each other. Johann knew he was supposed to say something about the wonderful locomotive that was pulling some cars around in a tight circle so fast you were afraid the centrifugal force would hurl it off the track. But that's exactly what didn't happen. It zoomed around and around. You couldn't say anything to Adolf until it came to a stop. Whether it was a new Märklin model train set or just a harmonica (Adolf called it a mouth organ) he'd gotten, he was always bursting with joy. But he needed Johann to make it complete. Of course, Adolf was luckier than Johann: he was an only child and got all the presents himself, and even many more than Johann and Josef put together. Herr Brugger was a livestock dealer, and every week he drove his Mercedes to places as far away as Dornbirn or Kempten or Ravensburg or Stockach, not to mention Lindau, Tettnang, and Friedrichshafen. And he always brought back presents—known in the Brugger household as souvenirs—for Adolf. If it was something to lick or to eat, Adolf shared licks or bites with Johann. Johann just couldn't get over it: he and Adolf would run over to Bruggers' and up to Adolf's room on the third floor. There's an orange on the nightstand, and Adolf peels it with great ceremony and gives Johann half. Not a section less than half. Not once had Johann's family ever had an orange.

So Johann had to at least tell Adolf that he had a secret compartment. It was rare enough for him to have anything Adolf didn't have. Johann led Adolf into the office and said, "I have a secret compartment in that highboy over there." Adolf gave a snort of laughter the way he always did when he knew something better than you. "That's not a highboy," he said. "It's a secretary." And straightaway he made Johann run down the hill with him to Bruggers' and had to show him what a highboy was as well as what a secretary was. At the Bruggers', a highboy was a glass-fronted cabinet with fancy trim on top. Johann felt miserable when he got home. He stood in misery before the red cherry cabinet with its two rather thick, shiny, black-lacquered pillars that framed the entire piece of furniture. At the top, an ornate drawer and then the hinged writing surface behind which was the mirror you could remove by the two small columns, and behind that, the green felt lids under which lay his secret compartment. The removable mirror was his tabernacle.

So the whole thing was only a secretary. But at least Bruggers' secretary was made of dark wood and not as beautiful by a long shot as the one in Johann's office, made of light, gleaming cherry. The one they called a highboy. Every time somebody at home mentioned the highboy, he remembered that it was only a secretary. Adolf had made it clear that a highboy was something more than just a secretary. It had been one of those moments when Johann felt that he needed to defend himself. Put on his armor and defend himself. You couldn't just accept that from one second to the next, a highboy turned out to be just a secretary. Like a prince, Mina had said. He felt the three photographs were his armor. They meant more to him than a new pair of shoes.

Once the photographs were put away, the mirror reinserted, and the writing surface closed, he couldn't bring himself to tell his father that this wasn't a highboy, it was just a secretary.

On Sunday, Grandfather marched in the first rank and Father in the last. He was wearing his two medals. The band marched at the head of the column. Johann, Ludwig, Paul, Guido, Berni, Helmut One, and Helmut Two trotted along beside the band. Adolf wasn't there. He didn't even show up when they marched past Bruggers' house with the music blaring.

Since the band always practiced in the spare room on Friday evenings, Johann knew everything they were playing and sang along under his breath with the march melodies. In the church, the sacristan had placed a coffin draped with a white flag bearing the Iron Cross in front of the high altar. Around the coffin was a miniature military cemetery of moss with many little white crosses and an equal number of little white candles. A man in a tailcoat with a lot of medals on his chest rose from the first pew, walked to the front, and genuflected. Then he turned and gazed composedly at all the flags and people in the church. Although times had never been so bad, he said, there were still twenty-one flags assembled here in honor of the new flag of the Veterans' and Military Association. Ludwig, who was sitting next to Johann in the pew, whispered to him that the man in the tailcoat was his godfather Zürn, a retired senior postal inspector.

"Lives in Lindau," whispered Ludwig. "Writes down everything about the village."

The senior postal inspector, ret., was wearing so many medals it looked like his chest wasn't quite broad enough and he'd had to hang some ribbons and crosses on top of one another. His mouth was topped by a white mustache, and the beard below it tapered almost to a point. Just like Herr Minn, thought Johann, except that the points of the senior postal inspector's mustache turned much farther up into his face than Herr Minn's, even higher than Grandfather's. The points of the retired senior postal inspector's mustache reached almost to the corners of his eyes. And now, announced the senior postal inspector, he would read the speech that Schmid's Thusnelda had delivered back in 1886. In 1886, the association, founded in 1872, had been able to consecrate its first flag, a flag donated by the young unmarried women of the parish's four congregations. It gave him great pleasure to announce that present among them here today were both the very first flag bearer and Schmid's Thusnelda—now the widow of Customs Official Drossbach and a resident of Munich—who had returned to her birthplace especially for the occasion. He pointed to Grandfather on the men's side and to where the former Schmid's Thusnelda, now the widow of Customs Official Drossbach, was sitting on the women's side. Johann didn't need to turn around to know that his grandfather would be sitting there as though he hadn't heard that he was being talked about. You could see how the widow of Customs Official Dross-bach literally swelled up among all the other women and girls around her. The senior postal inspector said that back in 1886, they had fired a fourteen-gun salute in honor of the new flag before a crowd of three thousand. Today, in conformity with the sad state of the times—not even a one-gun salute. He said that Germany today was poor and miserable, as miserable and poor as she had ever been in her entire history. Then he read the speech. Even if Johann was unable to pay attention to every word, he still could feel how beautiful it must have been here in the church and in the whole world back in 1886. Then the new flag bearer with the new flag came down the center aisle. The senior postal inspector, ret., bowed before the flag and returned to his seat. Father Dillmann, dressed in a cope that enveloped him like ceremonial armor, consecrated the new flag with incense, a sprinkling of holy water, and a prayer. The choir sang "Blessed Are the Dead." Then a girl ("Spiegel's Emma from Nonnenhorn," Ludwig whispered to Johann) pinned a ribbon onto the flag and proclaimed in a loud voice, "In the name of the unmarried women and girls." And shoemaker Gierer's Hedwig— Johann knew her, of course, since she lived right across the street from him—pinned another ribbon onto the new flag and said in an even louder voice, "The dedicatory ribbon with the commemorative coins from the wars of 1866, 1870 to '71, and 1914 to 1918." After the blessing of the flag came the Mass. Father Dillmann preached. My soul for God. My body for the Fatherland. My heart for my friend and comrade. Seventy-one sons, brothers, and fathers lost by the parish: seventy-one crosses, seventy-one candles. Again Johann noticed that during a sermon, his thoughts wandered. He began counting to see if there were really seventy-one crosses and candles arranged on the moss around the draped coffin. There were. Sacristan Höscheler hadn't miscounted. In front of the coffin, a Sacred Heart statue. Johann knew what was written on its base and couldn't resist saying it: I shall raise ye from the dead on Judgment Day. He whispered it to Ludwig, who made a face as if he already knew that. Afterwards, they marched to the war memorial, this time with no music except for the drums. The Hitler people in their brown uniforms were already there. In the village, they were known as the Nazi-Sozis. Herr Brugger was the SA leader. They wore caps with chinstraps that made it look like there was a windstorm, and the chinstraps were there to keep the caps from flying off their heads. In their jackboots and stiff, flared breeches, they looked like they could do whatever they wanted to. Next to Herr Brugger stood Herr Minn, the boat builder. Minn's boatyard was way out on the edge of town, almost in Reutenen instead of Wasserburg, but there was no big tip to be expected after you'd pulled the hand-cart with eight or ten hundredweight sacks out to the Minns'. Even so, Herr Minn was the friendliest man Johann knew. As soon as you pulled the handcart up in front of the house, Herr Minn's son emerged from the boatbuilding shed, grabbed the sacks, and carried them into the cellar. He wouldn't allow Johann, Josef, or Niklaus to help. The first time you heard Herr Minn's son speak, you couldn't under-stand a word he was saying. But then you did understand after all, every word, although he covered everything he said with *sh* sounds. The Minns were Lutherans. Herr Minn was the local group leader of the Nazi-Sozi Party. Johann knew every one of the ten or twelve men in brown uniforms: Loser's Gebhard, looking as if he'd already been crying today; Brem the carpenter, with his eyes just barely peeking out over his mustache; Herr Brugger, the ivory toothpick now conspicuously absent from the corner of his mouth; at the end of the brown column, Schulze Max, former escape artist and trum-peter with the Sarrasani Circus and now a fisherman's helper; Herr Häckelsmiller and Fräulein Agnes and Adolf. Herr Häckelsmiller worked as a railroad lineman; Fräulein Agnes was the sacristan and acolyte for the Lutheran services they held in the school building. Her cottage was as small as that of her neighbor Häckelsmiller, and full of cats she had to protect from Dulle, a journeyman carpenter who had washed up in Wasserburg and became a fisherman's helper, though he preferred to chase cats. Fräulein Agnes had been the first to join the new party and pinned her party badge onto what-ever she was wearing, summer and winter. People said it was she who had converted Herr Häckelsmiller. Frau Häckelsmiller, who was even smaller than her husband, never missed Mass and spent several hours every day praying in the church. For her husband, people said. Because he wore that party badge. Standing beside Fräulein Agnes: Adolf. His ski cap, windbreaker, and knickerbockers looked like a uniform too.

The band, the Veterans' Association, and the choral society formed a half circle in front of the war memorial. Since the Brownshirts had already occupied part of the semicircle and stood there as if rooted to the spot, the other groups had to squeeze closer together. Herr Thierheimer from Bodolz stepped forward and said he was speaking as a representative of the Kyffhäuser Bund, but he spoke to every-one present. Too long had discord weakened them, and they owed it to their fallen comrades to unite. "In unity is strength!" he cried. At that moment, the sun broke through the clouds and poured all its light onto Herr Thierheimer. Since the war memorial stands at the narrowest point of the peninsula, the light glittered across from east to west, amplified by the lake. The choral society sang: Once I had a comrade, a loyal friend and true. Side-by-side to battle we marched to the snare drum's rattle, you for me and me for you.

After the church service, Father had left the ranks of the Veterans' Association to join the choral society, where he was needed as second tenor. At the last note of the song, the drums started beating again. Herr Brugger's voice called out, "Ten-*shun!*" The flags were lowered, including the one with the swastika. The Brownshirts stuck out their right arms. Adolf stuck his out too, and his gaze angled upward, like his father's. Johann wanted to catch Adolf's eye to let him know how he admired him. Adolf had said his father was proud that five years ago, he'd already had his only son baptized with the name Adolf. A large framed photograph of Hitler hung in the Bruggers' living room. Hitler was sticking his right arm out as far as he could. Whenever Johann and Adolf entered the living room and Herr Brugger was there, Herr Brugger would say, "Go ahead and salute him, he deserves it." Then Adolf would click his heels together, place one hand on the seam of his trousers and stick out the other like the man in the picture. The eyes and mouth and chin of the man in the picture all worked together, eyes and mouth and chin all focused on the spot toward which the exaggeratedly outstretched hand pointed. Johann tried it out himself, again and again. Then Herr Brugger would laugh and say, "You'll get the hang of it soon enough." Adolf often repeated sentences about this Hitler, and they all sounded like sentences he'd heard from grown-ups, especially his father. And he'd reel them off even when they weren't appropriate. Every day Johann heard sentences from the guests at the regulars' table in the restaurant, but he would never blurt them out when he was playing dodgeball or soccer or any other game. To say nothing of his father's sentences. What his father said to him when they were alone didn't fit in anywhere else than between him and his father. Returning home from church on the narrow path along the lake, Adolf was capable of coming to a sudden halt and proclaiming: Writers bleed ink, they lie and they stink! Or: Show a woman who's boss from day one! Or: Jack of all trades, master of none! Or: Eat a good bit, then have a good shit! Adolf looked like a crowing rooster when he said these sentences. If only he would at least say that he got the sentences from his father! But there were also sentences or expressions that Adolf said, and the next day Guido or Paul or Ludwig would use them as if they weren't from Adolf at all but from whoever was saying them at the moment. So Johann would try and see if he, too, could say about a child who didn't look like its father that Helmer's Franz had helped out; that every broom would find its handle; that such and such a man had put a bun in the oven of such and such a woman. Even if it was the first time you'd heard a sentence like that, you knew instantly what it meant and you looked for an opportunity to use it. Since it was always Adolf who introduced these sayings, he was the most important one in their group. Johann was happy that he and Adolf were best friends. He was sorry when they had to go home at suppertime. He hoped that Adolf was also sorry they had to part. But he couldn't ask him. When he and Adolf had wrestling matches, he had no objection to Adolf putting him in a headlock.

As the various groups marched back to the upper village with music blaring, the Brownshirts fell in so swiftly at Herr Brugger's order that they marched directly behind the band and the other organizations had to follow. At the regulars' table, Herr Brugger had called the Veterans' Association a coffee klatsch club. On the square between the station and the restaurant, the marching column dispersed. The flag bearers rolled up their flags and the restaurant began to fill up.

Ludwig took Johann with him to shoemaker Gierer's house. Even without Ludwig, Johann could go to shoemaker Gierer's any time he wanted. But now, on a Sunday noon, he would not have gone if Ludwig hadn't insisted on it. Ludwig said he wanted him to say hello to his godfather. The senior postal inspector, ret., was a half-brother of the shoemaker and always visited him when he came to the village because he'd grown up in that house. Herr Zürn had been born in the Old Lighthouse in Lindau, but then his mother married shoemaker Gierer's father.

Ludwig and Guido knew everything about everybody, and as soon as someone's name was mentioned, they would tell everything they knew about that person. And not just once, either. If a name happened to be mentioned again the next day, Ludwig and Guido would repeat everything there was to be said about that name. Johann imagined there must be a narrative that continued without interruption in Ludwig's and Guido's houses, one that could not leave unsaid anything that happened in the village. Nothing was insignificant. It's like on a ship, thought Johann. Everything is important to keep the ship from going down, from the smallest thing to the largest. When Ludwig and Guido repeated what they heard at home, one didn't know why they did it. They didn't even know themselves. But it was absolutely certain that what they repeated had to be repeated. In a village, everything is important.

As they stepped through the low front door into the passageway of shoemaker Gierer's house, they learned that the senior postal inspector was still at the Crown having a Sunday morning glass. "With the other dignitaries," said Herr Gierer. Father and Herr Gierer had once started a shoe polish business together that was going to make them rich. But the mixture in the tank had caught fire, the workshop burned down, and they were just able to extinguish the fire before it burned down the house as well. That was the end of the shoe polish business. To recover his losses from that failure, Father soon acquired a consignment of watches at an advantageous price and hired traveling salesmen to peddle them door-to-door. The traveling salesmen, however, had not settled up accounts as they should have. Shoemaker Gierer had once told Johann, "Every scoundrel that comes to town finds his way to your father and exploits him."

By the time the senior postal inspector, ret., and his wife entered the room, Johann was on the point of leaving, because he could see that Frau Gierer was already bringing in the soup tureen. But Ludwig pushed Johann in front of the senior postal inspector and all those medals and Herr Gierer said, "Johann, from the Station Restaurant across the way."

"Well, well," said the senior postal inspector. "We certainly did your grandfather the honors today," and immediately went on: "Born at number 63—Zapfe's—in Hengnau. His father was from number 38—Zitterer's—in Nonnenhorn. Your grandfather sold number 63 in Hengnau to Dorn. Dorn tore it down and some farmers who had draft horses carted it free of charge to Unterbechtersweiler in thirty-nine loads because Loser's had burned down, and with the material from Hengnau they were able to rebuild their whole barn and part of the house."

"Now you know everything you need to know," said the master shoemaker, who also had a white beard but not such a dense, full, protruding one as the senior postal inspector. The most important feature of the senior postal inspector's face was indeed the mustache whose ends turned up toward the corners of his eyes.

The senior postal inspector said that Johann's grandfather had unfortunately disappeared after this morning's inspiring ceremony and hadn't shown up at the Crown for the morning toasts, a fact also remarked upon by Colonel von Reck, the custom official's widow, Father Dillmann, and Herr Heller, the head teacher. But no doubt the good man, who was as modest as he was hard-working, had gone instead to visit the grave of his wife Franziska, from Wielandsweiler, who had passed away of consumption back in 1917.

Ludwig and Johann were dismissed and ran up the path, bordered by espaliered pears, from the shoemaker's house to Bahnhofsstrasse. Beneath the arch of roses at the end of the path, Ludwig said, "Now they're standing at the table but can't say the blessing because I'm not there." But he still had to let Johann know that his godfather Ludwig Zürn was the only man who was an honorary district chairman of two different chapters of the Bavarian Veterans' Association, namely Kempten and Lindau, and an honorary member of the executive committee, too. "And he was born in the Old Lighthouse in Lindau! Can you imagine that, Johann? So long," shouted Ludwig and took off again.

Clearly, Ludwig had learned to say everything associated with someone's name from his godfather Ludwig Zürn, who wrote down every last thing about the village. But it was maybe even more significant that Ludwig was from the Grübel family, just like Guido was a Gierer. Their families had always been here. Neither Johann's grandfather nor his father nor his mother had been born in the village. In Johann's family, it wasn't a matter of course to know everything about the village. They had to learn it.

Over on the other side of the street he saw the men who had finished their Sunday morning wine and were still chatting between the front door and the terrace steps, and it looked like they'd never be finished. How would Johann get past so many talkers when he was supposed to say hello to each one? And woe to him if anyone felt slighted! So instead of going across the terrace and into the house, he'd go around the back, through the gate into the courtyard, and then up the back steps. But just as he was about to turn into the courtyard, Helmer's Hermine intercepted him. "Your grandfather is a frigate," she said. Her index finger ticked back and forth, precluding any contradiction. The longish wart was shining. From her mouth issued not just words, but also an odor Johann recognized: red wine. "Your grandfather's never been a flag bearer in his life," she said. "He's a frigate, Johann, that's what he is. The senior postal inspector, ret., is a nitpicker. A nitpicker without a clue what a frigate is, Johann. There's not much to him, old Hurrah-Zürn. His mother, Zürn's Elisabeth, was unmarried. His father was a Jew by the name of Tänzer, owned a knitting factory in Hohenems. And Elisabeth had barely given birth to her Ludwig in November when she married the first man who came her way, in February, and that was the poor hard-working miller's helper Gierer, Michael Gierer from the Herbolz mill. He was twenty-five when he married Elisabeth and she was thirty-eight. Maybe there was more than just a reward in heaven involved in the deal, and when the first Gierer arrived, his little half-brother Ludwig Zürn was already there to welcome him. You're the only person I've told, Johann, no one else, just so you know." And tapped Johann's forehead with her index finger and resumed her progress in the direction of the station, but before she reached it, she turned left on her way to meet—as Johann knew without having to see it— Frau Gierer from the bank, who walked up and down once a day on the fine gravel beneath the two chestnut trees on the station side of the restaurant, waiting for Helmer's Hermine to give her all the latest news.

They ate at the long table in the kitchen. Johann and Grandfather sat on the bench beneath the boiler that continued to drip, despite several steel bands that had been clamped around it. Josef and Father sat between the table and the stove. Although there would have been plenty of room left for Mother, she almost never ate with them. Had he ever seen her sit down to eat?

Johann told Grandfather that they had been expecting him at the Crown for the Sunday morning glass. Grandfather ran his hand over Johann's head. Before Father ate, he counted out a certain number of drops from various little bottles onto slices of zwieback. No one talked during the meal. Josef had propped a book in front of his plate and read while he ate. Mother called across the stove, "Josef!" Father said, "Let him be." He said it so softly that Mother probably didn't hear it. Josef kept reading. Johann thought about Gierer's Guido and Grübel's Ludwig and their never-ending narratives.

That evening when Josef and Johann were on their way to bed, Father, who was already lying down, called them in and had them sit on the edge of his bed. As always, Father was more sitting than lying. And there were books on his nightstand. He wanted to tell them why he would rather not have marched today, even though it was such a special day for Grandfather. But Grandfather had been too young in 1870 and too old from '14 to '18 and so didn't know what war was like. And the senior postal inspector Zürn with his chest full of peacetime medals didn't know either. Father's last battle was in July '18, near Soissons. He'd been with two other men in a listening post at the head of a trench, one they had dug out perpendicular to the main trench every few hundred yards. At the forward end, the head of the trench, you could often hear the voices of the enemy soldiers at night. Two from the same parish with father: Strodel's Traugott and Helmer's Franz. The sun was blazing down. The enemy's barrage was what they called curtain fire, a curtain of impacts landing behind them. The enemy obviously thought there were more German soldiers than there were in the forward positions. Father had shot off one flare after another, but their own artillery was silent—out of ammunition. The canary they always had with them in a cage, because canaries feel a gas attack before humans do and fall over dead as soon as they breathe it, and then you have time to get your gas mask on—the canary was already dead in its cage, but no trace of gas. The impacts were getting closer and closer. Shells have a melody before they hit the ground, a melody that gets shorter and shorter. Father knew he had to get out of that position. Suddenly, he hears Strodel's Traugott. Father and Helmer's Franz crawl over to him. Strodel's Traugott arches his back and his intestines are writhing out. The two of them stuff them back into his belly. Strodel's Traugott's eyes start open and swivel from side to side, trying to jump out of their sockets. Shoot me! he screams. Shoot me, shoot . . . Father and Helmer's Franz stroke his arms. He screams Shoot me! Shoot . . . my God . . . and screams until he's out of his head.

"That same day they came with tanks and took us prisoner," said Father. "Listening post and the forward trenches. Helmer's Franz played dead and they didn't get him. They put us in a retaliation camp. We had invaded them, destroyed their country one village after another." He opened the drawer of the nightstand and took out a funeral card: Strodel's Traugott. A soldier, spiked helmet, Iron Cross, a beard like Father used to have. Josef read the text under the photograph: Dear Sacred Heart of Jesus, be my love. 300 days indulgence. Sacred Heart of Mary, be my salvation. 300 days indulgence. "Good night," said Father, and returned the card to the drawer.

Just as they were leaving, Mother came into the room, very excited. "Hindenburg was speaking," she said. "On the radio. You could hear him as clear as if he was standing next to you."

Father: "What did he say?"

Mother: "That it can't go on like this. He said Germany won't survive this winter! If Hoover doesn't change course right now and free Germany from reparation payments, it's all over. There'll be a disaster, a catastrophe caused by nothing but hardship and hopelessness."

Father: "The name of the catastrophe is Hitler."

Mother: "He didn't say that."

Father: "But that's what he meant."

"Time for bed, boys," Mother said and pressed her hand against her right side.

Immediately Father said, "Gallbladder?"

Mother sat down on the edge of the bed but stood right back up again and said, "We'll see." Of course, she said it in a different language than Father's. She spoke a different language than he did, after all. Kümmertsweiler German is what she spoke. Father spoke Royal Bavarian Middle School German, even though he was born in Hengnau, and Hengnau is two miles at the most from Kümmertsweiler. As the crow flies. Actually, beyond Hengnau the land climbs fairly steeply, then back down through Atzenbohl woods to Nonnenbach, across the Crooked Bridge and then another very steep climb to the hamlet called Kümmertsweiler.

She said she needed to go back downstairs. But first, the boys had to go to bed.

In bed Johann thought about the cemetery of moss in the church and the seventy-one little white crosses. One of which was for Traugott Strodel. He'd seen old Frau Strodel today, too, even before the blessing of the flag. She was standing by a grave the way you stand when you're praying. Dear Sacred Heart of Jesus . . .

Johann wasn't afraid of war. He really wasn't. He liked to shoot because he liked to hit the mark. When he shot Adolf's air rifle, he didn't pull the trigger until the notch and bead sights were completely lined up and steady. Then he ran over to the target and saw that the little pellet had torn a hole in the ten, or maybe the eleven, and sometimes even the twelve. Then he felt like he had it all under control. Everything. Prince Johann, the king's son. Easy as pie. He looked at the picture of the guardian angel that hung from the wall at a slight angle with the light from the streetlamp reflecting off its glass again. As far as he was concerned, the picture didn't need to be hanging there. My God, what a feeling when he stretched his arms and legs . . . he wished he could tell someone how it felt to stretch like that. But he didn't know who to tell.

CHAPTER SIX

Mother Joins the Party

MOTHER WAS STANDING BY THE STOVE when Herr Minn came into the kitchen to say he wanted to settle his bill before Christmas. She preceded him into the office. Johann followed. After all, hadn't he helped pull the hand cart all the way from here to Reutenen to deliver Herr Minn's eight hundredweights of briquettes? As they walked to the office, they could hear music coming from the spare room and Herr Minn told mother her husband could have been a concert pianist. "*Nehmen Sie doch bitte Platz, Herr Minn*," said Mother. Since Herr Minn wasn't originally from around here, nor even in the parish, Mother invited him to please sit down using the formal *Sie*. Everyone in the village did. And Mother spoke High German with him. For her, High German was dialect forced into a straightjacket of foreign sounds. "Eight hundredweights of briquettes, Johann?" she said. Johann, in the same tone of voice: "Nine fifty-two, plus eighty for the delivery." "We'll leave that off, since it's Christmas," said Mother. "Bless you," said Herr Minn, who was more than a head shorter than Mother. Mother put a piece of carbon paper into the pad of blank bills and asked Johann, "How much was that?" "Nine fifty-two," said Johann. Herr Minn was impressed because he didn't know that, when Mother happened to encounter Johann, she would often show him a number of fingers with her left hand and Johann would have to multiply it by the number of fingers she held up with her right. "You've got to learn it sometime," she told him, "and it might as well be now."

Johann took the twenty-mark bill from Herr Minn, opened the safe, and gave him his change. Mother said she'd heard about the Christmas festivities the new party had organized for children in the spare room of the Crown: a Christmas tree decorated with little swastika flags and a nice speech by Herr Minn that ended with a prayer that God would bless the work of the great Führer, Germany's savior, Adolf Hitler. Herr Minn confirmed that those were his exact words. The crisis had become so severe: more and more people were being killed every day in street fighting in the big cities, the economy on the point of collapse, six million unemployed, the third chancellor this year and he was sure to resign within the month. "Dear lady, the choice is either chaos—meaning conditions like in Russia, i.e., murderous Bolshevism—or Hitler."

As a Lutheran, Herr Minn prayed to the same God as the Catholics, said Mother. She only said it because some people thought joining the new party meant following godless leaders. Just rumors, said Herr Minn. Rumors spread to make the Führer look bad to the faithful, both Lutherans and Catholics. "If I hadn't seen so much evidence of true piety in him, I never would have joined the party, not in a million years." So said Herr Minn. "As you know, I'm on the church council, and I'm actively involved on the building committee, so we don't have to hold Lutheran services in the school anymore. You can't call Mayor Hener a godless person, and he just resigned from the Bavarian People's Party to join the National Socialists, although he's not going around shouting it from the housetops. So did Hartstern the architect. And his wife." People were flocking to the party, people from all walks of life. "And as for religion, take a look at this."

And he took a postcard out of his billfold and handed it to Mother. "A present from me," he said. Mother showed Johann the card as if it was more important for him to see it: Christ on the Cross, and standing before him, a man in a brown shirt with the swastika flag. Next to him another Brownshirt, giving the salute. "Can you read what it says?" asked Mother. Johann spelled it out and then said the whole sentence, "Lord, bless our struggle. Adolf Hitler."

Again, Herr Minn was impressed. Mother put her hand on Johann's head. "Not even in school yet," said Herr Minn, "and he can already read one of the Führer's sayings. Bravo!"

"He gets it from my husband," Mother said.

"And diligent, too," said Herr Minn.

"Maybe he gets that from me," said Mother and ruffled Johann's hair. Johann was glad they thought of him the way he would have liked to be.

His mother said she was interested in joining the party. Herr Minn was delighted. Mother said that then they could hold their meetings at the Station Restaurant. It was already the favorite meeting place for the cycling club, the gymnastics club, the music society, and the choral society. They kept their prizes and trophies on display and even stored some of their flags. "Your mother's a smart woman," said Herr Minn. "But you're right. There's a Brown House in Munich, and just recently in Lindau, too, in the Fischergasse. Here in the village we meet sometimes here, sometimes there." Mother said the spare room could be quickly heated, and there was a telephone, too. "And the tallest flagpole in town," laughed Herr Minn, "except till now you've always flown the wrong flag." Mother made a face that was probably supposed to express the fact that she had nothing to do with what flag was flown.

Herr Minn wished them a blessed Christmas. He'd drop off the application form tomorrow so that her membership could still date from the current year. Membership was still less than a million. Without Adolf Hitler, the country was sure to fall apart next year, so the Führer would definitely take over. It could be that a membership number among the first million would be considered a great honor to have.

They walked Herr Minn to the front door. It had started snowing. In winter, the terrace was empty. Herr Minn retrieved his bicycle from where it was leaning against the wall, and Mother called to him, "Be careful not to fall!" He said something cheery in return and disappeared down the hill. Grandfather was sweeping off the snow that had blown in onto the terrace. "That's enough sweeping now, Dad," said Mother. Grandfather agreed there was no more point to it.

Johann went and stood next to his grandfather. "It's snowing like the devil now," said Grandfather. He laid his hand on Johann's head. His hand was heavier than Mother's.

Since they couldn't do without the piano, they opened their presents in the spare room. That meant that Josef and Johann weren't allowed to go in until Father played "Silent Night" on the piano. The entrance into the spare room took place through two different doors: wine glasses in hand, the four remaining patrons followed Elsa in from the restaurant side: Hanse Luis, Schulze Max, Dulle, and Herr Seehahn. Josef, Johann, Niklaus, and Grandfather entered through the door from the central hallway. Finally Mina, the Princess, and Mother came in from the kitchen.

On Christmas Herr Seehahn always wore on the green lapel of his yellowish Tyrolean jacket the medal he had been awarded by the Holy See. As a sailor during the revolution in Munich, he was supposed to arrest the Papal Nuncio. He'd told him, If you come with me, your Eminence, I'm placing you under arrest. If you take the back door, you've given me the slip.

Dulle was farther from his birthplace than any of the others. Dulle came from a town whose name always sounded to Johann as if someone was making fun of Dulle. Johann would never have dared to utter that name in Dulle's presence: Buxtehude. Dulle talked differently than everyone else in the village. He lived in a shed attached to Frau Siegel's house, north of town in Hochsträss, right next to the freshly tarred road. Dulle was always on the go, day and night, both as a fisherman's helper and a man with a thirst, unless he was chasing Fräulein Agnes's cats. Adolf claimed that the walls and ceiling of Dulle's shed were papered with bills from the inflation. Hundred-thousand-mark bills, bills for millions, billions, trillions. Adolf said that in 1923, a newspaper cost sixteen billion marks. Whenever Johann heard about the inflation, he thought the country must have been running a fever back then—106 or 107 degrees.

Having been in a circus, Schulze Max came from nowhere and everywhere. He slept on a pile of old nets in the attic of the community hall where fishermen's families who had moved to the village from Bavaria were housed.

Compared to where Dulle and Schulze Max spent the night, Niklaus had splendid digs in their attic. Niklaus had a real bed, and he'd arranged old chests around it to make it into a kind of room. Niklaus had attracted Johann's interest when Johann once watched him wrap his feet round and round with rags and then put on his lace-up boots. Last year, Mina had knit Niklaus a pair of socks and put them under the Christmas tree, and he'd just left them there. When Mina tried to hand them to him, he shook his head. Niklaus seldom spoke. He could say what he had to say by nodding, shaking his head, and gesturing with his hands. You could tell he didn't have any kind of speech defect when he reported that Baroness Ereolina von Molkenbuer had ordered three hundredweights of bituminous lignite coal and Fräulein Hoppe-Seyler two hundredweights of anthracite. He just didn't like to talk. Talking was not his thing.

For Josef and Johann there were light gray Norwegian sweaters under the Christmas tree, almost but not quite white—more like silvery gray—with gray-blue, slightly raised stripes. Two different patterns across the chest so that, thank goodness, they wouldn't get them mixed up. Josef put his on right away. Johann would have preferred to put his sweater back under the tree, but everybody said he should try it on too, so he did. When he felt how the sweater hugged his body, he pretended he needed to go to the bathroom, ran out quick, and stood in front of the mirror of the wardrobe in the passageway. He had to have a look at himself. And what he saw were silvery gray, almost bluish, raised stripes and a coat-of-arms in a circle on his chest. The king's son, he thought. As he went back in, he couldn't quite conceal his feelings. Mina could tell. "Looks real good on you," she said.

The sweaters were from the Allgäu, from Anselm, the great-uncle they called Cousin.

Every present was accompanied by a soup plate piled with cookies: S-shaped butter cookies, gingerbread rounds, *Springerle*, cinnamon stars, *Spitzbuben* with marmalade centers, macaroons.

"I could never do that," said Mother to Mina, meaning the cookies. Johann nodded vigorously until Mina noticed him nodding vigorously.

Last year, he'd had a chance to sample the cookies Adolf got. The Bruggers' cookies all tasted the same. With Mina's cookies, each kind had its own particular flavor, but all of them tasted like only Mina's cookies could. This year there was something wrapped in silver paper next to Johann's and Josef's plate of cookies, something longish with a little flag stuck into the silver package that said: "With all my" followed by a red heart. And above that it said: "Merry Christmas from the Princess." Josef was already having a bite by the time Johann got his unwrapped. "Nougat," he said. "Right," said the Princess. "Yummy," said Josef. Johann rewrapped his nougat bar, untouched.

There were silk stockings for Mina and Elsa. Both said Mother and Father shouldn't have. For Mina, there was also a passbook. "And a little seed money," said Mother, "in the District Savings Bank. They're not going to fold." Mina shook her head and said, "God bless you, ma'am!" For the Princess there were several skeins of blue wool under the tree. She picked them up, touched an index finger to her temple in a soldier's casual salute, and said, "Right." Then she turned to Johann and said, "You know what you're in for now." Johann also said, "Right!" and returned her salute. In the evening he always had to stick his hands through the skeins of wool so the Princess could roll them up into a ball from which she could knit. She spent every free minute knitting for her Moritz. She was allowed to visit the one-year-old in Ravensburg once a month but wasn't permitted to be alone with him. The mother of Moritz's seventeen-year-old father sat in the room the whole time the Princess was there. After every visit, the Princess would tell how the mother of the child's father, not even forty years old herself, wouldn't let the Princess out of her sight for a second while she hugged little Moritz. The Princess was said to be thirty-one. Beside everyone's plate she had left her own present, and they all had little heart-flags stuck into them: for Elsa a white linen napkin on which the Princess had embroidered a rearing horse in red yarn; for Mina two potholders, on one a large red A, on the other an M of the same size; for Niklaus she had crocheted a pretty border onto two foot cloths; for Herr Seehahn there was a tiny bottle of egg liqueur; for Mother a tortoise-shell comb; for Father a little sack of lavender blossoms; for Grandfather an ivory snuff box. "Come here, Johann," she said. "Take this to your grandfather and tell him that Ludwig the Second gave it to my great-grandfather because when the king sprained his ankle during a hunt in the Kerschenbaum Forest, he carried him home to the castle on his back." Everybody applauded and the Princess, who had overdone her lipstick for the occasion, bowed in all directions. Johann could have looked at the Princess all night long. That big red mouth went so well with her asymmetrical glass eye. For Niklaus there was again a pair of socks and a pack of stogies under the tree. The socks (it was the pair from last year) were again ignored. He took the stogies, the plate of cookies, and the crocheted foot cloths and put them down by his chair. As he passed the Princess, he said, "You're quite a girl." She saluted and said, "Right!" Then he went back to Father and Mother and thanked them with a handshake. But while shaking hands, he looked neither Father nor Mother in the eye. Even as he stretched out his right hand, which was missing the thumb, he was averting his gaze. It looked almost like he was already turning away, reaching his hand out to the side or even back behind him. You could see he didn't do it out of inattention. He just didn't want to have to look people in the eye who had given him a present. Niklaus sat back down and picked up his glass of beer. He only drank beer from a glass on Christmas, Easter, and St. Nicholas Day, otherwise from the bottle. Johann liked to watch and listen when Niklaus placed a bottle on his lower lip, tipped it up, and emptied it with a sighing sound. How uninteresting drinking from a glass was by comparison. Niklaus also took every bottle that returned from the restaurant, officially empty, to be placed on a rack behind the building and await the truck from the brewery. He put each one to his mouth and drained it dry. He didn't want any to go to waste.

Hanse Luis took out his pocket knife, opened it, and handed it to Niklaus. Niklaus took a stogie from the pack and cut it in half with the blade, which was half-moon-shaped from frequent honing. Like Hanse Luis himself, Niklaus only smoked half stogies. But Niklaus smoked so seldom that the twenty half stogies he got by cutting them in two lasted from one Christmas to the next. Since Hanse Luis constantly had to have a stogie in his mouth, he lit each fresh half stogie from the butt of the preceding one. As Hanse Luis folded up his pocket knife, he said that Hagen's Fritz, who bragged in every tavern that he was only learning tinsmithing so he could make himself a tin wreath to hear the rain falling when he was dead and in the grave—this same tin snipper and Hagen nipper from the Semper house in Wasserburg (who was turning out to have the biggest mouth in the parish) felt it necessary to speak to him, Hanse Luis (in actuality, the dirt farmer Alois Hotz who, because there were already too many Hotzes in the region, had been redubbed with the name of his house: Hans . . . not exactly a name to write home about, and besides, he only came from Hege)—this Semper Hagen's Fritz kid, blond as a sow down to his eyelashes, came up and asked him a stupid question, namely: Why bother slicin' your seegars in two if you're just gonna light the second half with the first one anyways? Don't make no sense. Hanse Luis said he'd coughed out a few ha-has while he was trying to think why he always did stick sliced-off half stogies into his mouth. How should he know? So, saying a quick prayer to Hugo, who as the April Fools' Day saint was in charge of coming up with an answer when you haven't got one—Ha ha ha . . . yes . . . well, it's like this, my little tow-headed tinsmith. See how my nose hangs way out over my kisser and my chin sticks out too, and even turns up a bit? And but my kisser's nothin' but a line way far in the back and more or less tooth-free thanks to Itler the dentist? And this great stuck-out schnoz of mine has never been seen without its glob o' snot. So here's what I'm getting at, you little sow-blond tinsmith: even my world-famous Hanse-Luis-nose don't stick out as far as an uncut stogie, so a drop o' snot would damage my seegar, whereas with a half-stogie there's no cause for concern at all, cause when the glob o' snot has hung there long enough, it finally drops—as is right and proper—down into the abyss, an abyss that yawns before every man and not just Hanse Luis from Hege, parish of Wasserburg.

Got it? Hanse could see right away that the sow-blond apprentice
tinsmith wasn't used to being called to account for his big mouth . . . Did
he say mouth? It was more like a beak the sow-blond tinsmith (and
there wasn't a blonder sow lying around in the pigsty) had on his face.
The upper lip went one way, the lower lip another—but blond as a
sow he was, including his eyelashes. Hanse Luis usually used dialect for
everything he said, but when he switched to High German, as he just
had, every word sounded like he was standing on a pedestal to say it.
And sure enough, just as Hanse Luis finished speaking, another glassy
drop separated from the string that hung from his nose and fell to the
floor past the glowing end of his stogie.

Dulle, Schulze Max, and Herr Seehahn lifted their glasses in a toast
to Hanse Luis. The Princess said, "I couldn't agree more, Luis. If you
were thirty years younger, I'd give you serious consideration."

"Then I'd be thirteen, Mommy dear."

"Just the age I like 'em," cried the Princess.

"That's enough of that now," said Mother.

Father went over to the Christmas tree, picked up a blue package
tied with gold ribbon, and gave it to Mother. She shook her head. He
said, "Just open it, won't you?" It was soap from India. And earrings:
big, shiny black teardrops. She shook her head again, but more slowly
this time. For Grandfather there was a nightshirt under the tree. Johann
wanted to bring it to him, but he said, "Just leave it there." The last to
open his present was Father: a pair of leather gloves—kid gloves, Father
called them. "You could almost play piano with them on," he said to
Josef. And put them on and went over to the piano and favored them
with a quick medley of Christmas carols. Hanse Luis clapped silent
applause with cupped hands because they were so bent and crooked
he couldn't strike his palms together. He said, "Outside music don't
hold a candle to this." He could rest assured that everyone in the room
knew that for Hanse Luis, "outside music" meant the radio. Then he
stood up and said he should get going before he got mixed up in all this
present business too. Mother said it was still snowing, and he should be
careful not to fall. "Don't worry, Augusta," he said. "A good ol' stumbler

almost never falls." He put a crooked index finger to the green, brimless, peaked hunter's cap that he never took off his head, even made a little bow like a dancer, and left. In the doorway, he turned around, held up his hand, and said the only thing that worried him was that he'd be in a fix if it was going to be the fashion now to stick your arm out instead of saying *Grüss Gott*. He had such crooked paws it might look more like those guys who stuck out their fists and yelled *Heil Moscow*! And then, in his own brand of High German, "I foresee calamity, fellow countrymen." And then in his language, "*Der sell hot g'seet: No it hudla, wenn's a's Sterbe goht.*" And with a "G'night everyone," he was out the door before the Princess could give him back what he'd said in her High German: No need to rush things when it's time to die. Elsa ran to unlock the front door for him, and then they heard her screaming, "No, Luis . . . That's enough, Luis . . . Stop it, Luiiiis!" When she came back in, she was laughing. He'd tried to rub snow in her face. Johann was astonished. It was natural that Adolf, Paul, Ludwig, Guido, both Helmuts, and he would rub the girls' faces whenever it snowed; what could be more fun than holding down Irmgard, Trudl, or Gretel in the snow and rubbing a handful in their face? It made the girls squeal like all get out. But how could anybody rub snow in the face of a giant like Elsa! Hanse Luis was a head shorter than her. She was barely back in the room before Hanse Luis popped his head through the door again and said, "*Dr sell hot g'seet, a Wieb schla, isch kui Kunscht, abr a Wieb it schla, deesch a Kunscht.*" And did his little dance and was gone. The Princess shrilled after him, almost in distress, "*Ein Weib schlagen, ist keine Kunst, aber ein Weib nicht schlagen, das ist eine Kunst*"—There's no trick to beating a woman; the real art is not beating her. Dulle from Buxtehude raised his glass and said, "Without you, Princess, I'd think I was in a foreign country."

"My name ain't Schulze Max if I don't see another present lyin' there that hasn't been delivered yet," said Schulze Max and pointed to a bundle of fur. The Princess was sitting nearest the tree and unrolled it: a cat skin.

"Oh, *Du*lle," said Mother.

"Can I help it if they come runnin' after me?" said Dulle. The Princess stroked the tiger-striped fur.

Mina: "Petting a cat means you're in love."

"So who's it for?" asked the Princess.

"Whoever asks," said Dulle.

The Princess: "Oh brother, another fifty-year-old. Forge an ID and then report back to Princess Adelheid, *addio mio vecchio!*"

"Fifty!" shouted Dulle, jumping up. "What're you talkin' about, sweetheart! You hear that, Maxie? She's makin' me into a gramps! Fifty! You gotta promise to take that back." As he said it, Dulle was almost doing a jig, or bending and twisting, at any rate. He still dressed like a journeyman carpenter, but the outfit that once was black had long since ceased to have any color at all. His reddish hair welled out from beneath the carpenter's hat he never took off and fell to his shoulders. And his beard was the same red and stuck out sideways so far from his cheeks that it was almost wider than the brim of the hat. There was very little of his face to be seen. A nose and eyes, and in front of his eyes a pair of glasses with lenses so small and round that his eyes seemed bigger than the glasses. Johann had the feeling that Dulle, who'd never been seen in church, went well with the Christmas tree. Better than anyone else, in fact.

The presents had all been opened and now came the carols. After the first carol, "Oh du fröhliche, oh du selige," Schulze Max said to Mother, "Your two boys could go on stage." Father had taken off his kid gloves and was playing more and more complicated accompaniments. After "Kommet ihr Hirten, ihr Männer und Frau'n," Schulze Max said to Dulle, "We'll drink another glass to the musicians. If you agree." Dulle nodded vigorously. "But then we'll be on our way," said Schulze Max. Dulle nodded again. And vigorously. Schulze Max: "We don't want to start putting down roots here." Dulle shook his head, vigorously. Schulze Max: "Especially not today, right?" Dulle nodded so vigorously that he had to push his glasses back into place. Schulze Max: "Even an innkeeping family needs some private time, right?" Dulle nodded again, but this time, he held onto his glasses so he could nod vigorously enough. Schulze Max: "And when does a family especially want to be by themselves—when do they need some privacy, if not on Christmas Eve, right?" Dulle took off his glasses since he wanted to nod even more vigorously than before. Schulze Max: "And what's today?" Dulle, with an incredibly gentle voice, almost in a whisper: "Christmas Eve." Schulze Max, very serious: "So the logical conclusion, dear and honored hostess, is that the next glass will be—really must be—the last."

Mother refilled their glasses. When you looked over toward Niklaus, you saw that his glass was almost always empty, too. He sat beside Grandfather, not with the guests, because he was part of the family. Just like the others who had presents under the Christmas tree, Niklaus had taken his—the pack of stogies and the plateful of cookies that went with them—back to his chair.

As soon as Herr Seehahn sat down, Elsa brought him his own plate of butter cookies, gingerbread rounds, cinnamon stars, et cetera, leaving no doubt that he, too, belonged in the family circle. Without really bringing his mouth to rest, Herr Seehahn had grinned cheerfully and inserted into his stream of words several repetitions of a clearly audible Peace on Earth, Goodwill to Men, but then continued with his usual text: Out of luck but a good fuck, false serpent, stupid prick . . . Johann probably knew more of this text than the others. Maybe they thought it was just incomprehensible stuff. Johann was interested in every Seehahn-word he could catch. If you were more than a yard away, you couldn't tell if he was talking or just chewing his lips.

Everyone at the table—Dulle, Herr Seehahn, and Schulze Max—demonstrated that the glasses with beer and lake wine were a secondary consideration today. The main thing was the Christmas tree, the burning candles, the glistening red and silver balls that multiplied the light, the glittering tinsel, the hissing sparklers lit by Josef and Johann, and of course the carols they listened to with rapt attention. Schulze Max uttered the compliments for all of them. Johann sang for him. "Lo, How a Rose E're Blooming" was Johann's favorite Christmas carol. He didn't just hear his own voice when he sang it, he saw it, too: a silvery something that glistened and flowed way up high. He would never get as high as his voice was. He would never be that light. His soprano floated above Josef's harmonizing alto and the piano's accompanying ornamentation. When they were done, Schulze Max said, "Johann, if you don't become a famous singer, you'll have only yourself to blame." Johann felt several shivers run down his back. Schulze Max had been a performer himself, both an escape artist and a trumpeter—first trumpet in the Sarrasani Circus! And once or twice a year, whenever somebody had paid in advance for more than ten beers, he would give some samples of his art. He could burst a chain and bite a rope in two. His hair, parted with the accuracy of a straightedge, always looked like it had been painted onto his bare skull. His face one sea of creases and wrinkles. At the war memorial, Johann had thought that the SA cap didn't fit on top of this sea of creases and wrinkles. In the meantime, Johann had learned from Josef—but only after he promised not to tell anyone else and never to let on that he knew— who played Knecht Ruprecht every December 5th, Knecht Ruprecht with his beard-muffled face and jangling bells and rattling chains and terrifying hazel rod with which to punish children who had been bad, striding through the village at the side of Saint Nicholas, who was clad in festive red and white and distributed chocolate Nicholases: it was Schulze Max. You could hear the cowbells' shrill jangle and the rattle of chains as soon as the pair came into view, coming up the street toward their house. Good Saint Nicholas's friendly bell wasn't audible until the two of them were right there in front of you in the kitchen. Till then, getting nearer and nearer and louder and louder was only Knecht Ruprecht's harsh clanging and rattling. When the front door was flung open and both the good Nicholas and the terrible, ferocious Ruprecht came through the double doors into the central hallway, then stopped in the wide corridor, the clanging and rattling grew intolerably loud. The only thing to do was cling to Mother's apron, press your face against her; soon they would burst through the kitchen door, and then . . . Although in the meantime he had learned from Josef that the terrible chain rattler and hazel rod swinger with the terrifying beard was Schulze Max—"you can recognize the chain from his escape-artist tricks in the restaurant"—he was still afraid. There was no conceivable protection from those terrible sounds.

So now, Johann was singing against Knecht Ruprecht. Once and for all. If he praised him like this, he couldn't frighten him anymore. The most terrible threat was that he would stick stubbornly disobedient children into the burlap bag hanging over his shoulder and whisk them off to a kind of immediate hell.

Now they would drink one final glass to Johann, their little Caruso, said Schulze Max. "If you agree; otherwise we won't." Dulle nodded. "Then we really will be going." If there was anything he hated, it was people who said they were about to leave and then didn't. At least they wouldn't be able to accuse him of that. "Nor you neither, if I know you at all." Dulle's nod was slow and generous, almost majestic. Elsa said that midnight Mass was beginning in half an hour. If they didn't leave soon, they wouldn't get a seat. Herr Seehahn stood up, went to pay, was surprised to hear that on Christmas Eve it was on the house. Schulze Max said, "Dulle, if we'd only known!" Dulle said, "Nobody can't know everything." Without taking the cigarette out of his mouth, Herr Seehahn cheerfully requested them to pray for his black soul and went up to his little room.

"Gentlemen," said Elsa, "let me show you the way out."

"Into the snow," said Schulze Max.

"Come to my place," said Dulle, "it never snows in."

"I've still got a swallow of something at my place," said Schulze Max.

"Then you're my man," said Dulle. Elsa went out with them. On the way out, they started to sing, "Silent night, holy night, all is still, I am tight . . ."

Elsa came back in and said, "Valentin's waiting for me."

Mina said, "And Alfred's waiting for me."

"Bon appétit," said the Princess, saluted, and left the spare room before the others. She never went to church anymore. A priest in Ravensburg was responsible for her not being allowed to keep her Moritz.

Grandfather said, "Good night, everybody," and went out. Niklaus nodded and went out. Josef and Johann had started to blow out the candles.

Suddenly Mina cried out, "*Johannle*, look out!" But it was too late. Because he had to pull down one of the top branches to blow out the candle on it, he hadn't noticed that his left arm was too close to a candle that was still burning lower down: a burn hole in the sleeve of his new sweater. Johann took the sweater off at once. He knew he shouldn't have put it on!

Mina examined the burned spot. "I can darn that for you," she said, "so you'd never see it if you didn't know it was there." But I do know it's there, thought Johann. He wanted to cry but didn't dare. But Mina could tell how unhappy he was. She took his face between her two hands, drew him to her, and said in her Niedersonthofen cadence, "An ugly rag's prettier'n a pretty hole." But then she had to go. To her Alfred. She acted as if it was hard for her to leave Johann at a moment like this. Johann felt his eyes getting moist. Mina and Elsa were gone.

Mother pressed her hand against her side and said she couldn't go to church with them. She sat down quickly on the nearest chair, then bent forward as far as she could and stayed that way. Father said, "It's a colic. Come on, lie down and I'll make you some tea and a compress." Mother straightened up and said Father should go to Mass with the boys. Then she stood up, a hand on her right side. She said she'd joined the new party—as good as joined. Herr Minn was bringing the application form tomorrow. Father said nothing. The owners of the Crown, the Linden Tree, and the Pfälzerhof had already joined. Mayor Hener, too.

"I haven't joined," said Father.

"Exactly," said Mother. The church bells began to ring. Now the party meetings would be in the Station Restaurant instead of the Crown, she said.

Father already had on his coat and his new kid gloves. He took them off and said he'd stay with Mother. "You two go ahead," he said. As Johann was lacing up his boots, he thought of the itinerant photographer. Those three pictures were worth more to him than new boots.

It was still snowing outside. As they waded through the freshly fallen snow, he thought about the Norwegian sweater, or rather, about the burn hole in the sleeve. A sweater like the brightest silver, with a pattern of raised blue stripes that formed rings across the chest. And there was something in the blue stripes that glittered, too, a kind of almost-silver. And now, the hole. He couldn't really listen to Josef telling him about how his piano teacher Jutz from Kressbronn was going to play the organ in church tonight. He always rode his bicycle to Wasserburg. How was he going to manage in this snow? Easy for you to talk, Johann thought, you haven't got a hole in your sleeve. When he'd put on the sweater, he sensed that he looked like the knight in *Richard the Lion Heart and his Paladin*. But now—it was all over. Later, when he knelt next to Adolf in church, Adolf would tell him what he got for Christmas, and what could Johann say? He wished he could get into bed and repeat Herr Seehahn's words to himself. But maybe he could say the words when he was still up, too, maybe even in church.

The dark figures emerging from the houses and moving down the hill along with them, saying nothing, didn't bother him. The snow was swallowing every step and every sound anyway. He allowed them all to fall in in his midnight march. He was the Silver Knight, marching through the black night in flurries of snow. The hole in his sleeve proved that life was a struggle.

CHAPTER SEVEN

Meetings

FATHER SAID HE HAD NO OBJECTION if Johann wanted to be there. "You'll hear some familiar words. Look here," he said. "Sound it out." Johann sounded out the capital letters typed on the piece of paper: MEETING TO ORGANIZE A THEOSOPHICAL SOCIETY IN WASSERBURG. "You're amazing, Johann," said Father.

Only one of the two rows of tables in the spare room was occupied, the one along the interior wall that was closest to the stove. Niklaus had already started heating the room around noon. An east wind had been blowing for days. Minus 30 degrees in Silesia. Over in the restaurant, SA men were warming themselves up before starting on their next round through the village. Since early afternoon, ten, twelve, sometimes even fourteen SA men in brown shirts, stiff, flared breeches, and shiny jackboots had been riding through the village on motorcycles. The men on the passenger seats carried swastika flags. They were all wearing their caps with chinstraps again. Again, it looked like a wind storm was imminent. And they also looked stuffed, probably because they were wearing thick sweaters under their brown shirts on account of the cold. The noise of the motorcycles and the flags snapping in the wind brought people to their windows, doors, and into the street. The village lay under one continuous blanket of snow and glittered in the sun. Periodically, the motorcycle column would halt, the motors were turned off, and one of the men put a megaphone to his mouth and announced that at eleven o'clock that morning, the Reich president, General Field Marshall von Hindenburg, had appointed the Führer Adolf Hitler chancellor. To mark the occasion, there would be a live broadcast of tonight's rally on the radio, direct from the Reich Chancellery in Berlin. On all German stations. Whoever believed in Germany's salvation should come to the Station Restaurant tonight.

Of the Brownshirts, Johann knew only Herr Brugger, Schulze Max (who rode behind Herr Brugger with a flagstaff in his hand), and Herr Häckelsmiller, who sat on another passenger seat. From Adolf, Johann knew that Herr Brugger had paid for the uniforms of Schulze Max and little Herr Häckelsmiller, from their caps to their boots.

Again, Johann noticed how Schulze Max's creased and wrinkled face didn't go with his cap.

Of the people who gathered in the spare room late in the afternoon, Johann knew only two: the Sauter sisters. They had a little cottage on the road to Nonnenhorn, right after the house with the tower. When he and Father delivered coal to them, his father always had to come into the living room and drink a cup of maté tea, and then Johann had to take from a plate a soft something of uncertain color that was as good as not sweet at all—maybe a slice of dried apple. Johann said hello to the two Miss Sauters and was pleased they remembered him. Today, the spare room smelled like the Sauters' house. They were all drinking rose hip, peppermint, or chamomile tea. Last week at the kaffeeklatsch, the whole house smelled of coffee. Johann's favorite meeting was the kaffeeklatsch. He was allowed to eat as many donuts and pieces of *Bienenstich* as he liked.

After Elsa had served the beverages, Father stood up and said that when he sent out the invitations to this gathering on the day after Epiphany, he could not have known that the next to last day of January would be such an unsettled one. He had worked out what he had to say long before this January, which was becoming more ominous with each passing day. His desire to speak here today had its basis in all the troubles they had had to endure since 1914. For years he had been keeping a record of what was going on in the world and had put his reactions down on paper. But before he told them what he saw himself compelled to do after all he had experienced, he had another announcement to make, something that had only reached his ears this noon on the telephone: his friend Hartmut Schulz, about whom he had spoken to some of those present today, was dead. Two weeks ago, Hartmut Schulz had taken his own life. Hartmut's father had not deemed it necessary to inform him until today. Herr Schulz senior had been most anxious to let him know that he had succeeded in burying his son in a military cemetery, since his unfortunate deed could thus be acknowledged as a result of the war. Father said he had met Hartmut in a French POW camp in 1918. Everything he wanted to say and suggest today ensued from Hartmut's biography: repatriation 1919, study of Lutheran theology, pastor in a small town in Swabia, doubts about his calling to the ministry, near to despair, finds a woman from the Youth Movement who for a while writes his sermons for him—Hartmut always said those sermons were half Midsummer Night celebration, half Pietism, assertive and vague at the same time. He gives up his post, gets a divorce. Takes a job as tutor in the home of an eccentric millionaire in Arosa. But not for long. They said he had a harmful influence on their children. In the meantime, his path had led him to theosophy. He opens a health food store in Oberstaufen that sells Graham bread, vitamin cream, herbal tea, soybean sprouts, and peanut butter. Invents a magnetizing apparatus no one is willing to invest in, goes into bankruptcy. Kills himself. Just last fall, Hartmut Schulz had ridden his bicycle all through Switzerland, knocking on the doors of Illuminati in Basel, Rosicrucians in Überlingen, cosmosophists, neo-theosophists, magnetopaths, natural healers in Teufen, Urnäsch, and Gais. Sympathy everywhere, but no help anywhere. "Dear friends," said Father, "if you agree, I propose that we name the theosophical community we intend to found today the Hartmut Schulz Circle. Our goal is to escape all suffocating divisions, or as Jakob Böhme says in his *Theosophic Epistles*: It is time to seek oneself. It was a religious transgression to split the self into a body and a soul, and ever since, we have gone astray, we Europeans. Perhaps just in time, natural science has also discovered that the entire evolution of humankind is preserved in twelve chromosomes. The fact that those twelve chromosomes correspond to the twelve houses of the zodiac will come as a surprise only to someone who subjects himself to suffocating divisions. Everything proceeds from Oneness. Jakob Böhme granted only to the Devil a separate, strangulating will, so that the Devil—whose name is Separator—vegetates away, devoid of light, unperfused by the fluid from which the universe developed and continues to exist. Materiality is nothing in and of itself, not a substance but an oscillation that is in harmony or disharmony. We can call that which maintains the oscillation whatever we want. Franz Anton Mesmer calls it Fluid. He used the word *Magnetism* for the attraction and repulsion constantly occurring within us. Magnetism, he says, is an invisible fire, the result of the reciprocity between two poles. Ebb and flow, the terrestrial breath, is such a result. The universe is a result of that reciprocity. The fluid of this reciprocity is *de spiritu quodam subtilissimo*, finer than the rays of light, heat, or sound. Most emphatically at work on the nervous substrate of all life, but also even on so-called lifeless things like iron or glass. We are a part of this movement, subject to it, multiplying and amplifying it. It suffices for one human to be beside or facing another to have an effect on him, to engender in him one's own special and characteristic potential. But the fullness and entirety of the planetary influence on every one of our cells is also always at work. Always take everything into account. Plant trees when the moon is waxing, cut them down when the moon is waning. Swedenborg traces illness back to the sins of mankind. We expose the word *sin* to reciprocity until it is no longer a word but a movement. To think without words, that is our goal. For as Jakob Böhme says, conjecture and opinion only lead to discord. But to think without words, to think as Franz Anton Mesmer tried to learn and teach a hundred and fifty years ago, that we can learn from the East, from the ancient Brahmin of Marapur, leader of the school of Uttara Mimamsa wisdom, who teaches the indivisibility of being and thinking. I recall to your minds the second legend of Rabindranath Tagore. The first legend ended ' . . . each in his own way—each in his own way.' In the second legend, the boy Rabindranath is sitting before his father's house and sees a zebu and a donkey standing side by side. He sees the zebu tenderly licking the donkey's coat. And the boy is overcome by an epiphany. Pervaded by universal feeling, he begins to sing without words. Someone who overhears him says he sang, 'I must love—must love.' As students of the wisdom of Gautama, of the Buddha, the model for the dissolution of form and structure, we know what we no longer say, what we no longer need to say when we know it, yet doubting ourselves, we must say again and again that—"

At that moment, the door from the restaurant was flung open and in strode, in his brown shirt, Herr Brugger with two other Brownshirts behind him, Ludwig Brand and Schulze Max. Ignoring the meeting in progress in the spare room, they began to push open both sides of the folding partition. Even while Father was still speaking, it had gotten so loud in the restaurant that he had to repeat sentences two or three times. Each time he had gestured with one hand toward the source of the babble of voices. Now, he managed a last, "*N'etam mama*. You do not belong to me, you do not belong to me. Uttered to everything: to the world, to our fellow man, to ourselves."

Father sat down. A few people clapped. Herr Minn came over and told Father that they really didn't mean to disrupt his meeting. On the other hand, this was one of the greatest, most joyful days in the last thousand years of German history, and now the day was to be crowned with a speech by Joseph Goebbels, one of the most faithful companions of Adolf Hitler, who from this day forward was to be the chancellor of the German Reich. No one—no person of good will—should be left out on a day like this. "Let's put an end to anything that divides us, cuts us off, any misguided competition. We're all comrades in the *Volk*, men and women together. Down with whatever divides us!"

There were cries of Bravo from both rooms. Everyone crowded around the radio that sat on top of the shelves of glasses behind the bar. You had to be as tall as Elsa or Mother to reach the dials. For a long time, they heard nothing but the sound of marching feet. Then an announcer came on to say that for hours, tens—no, hundreds of thousands had been marching past the Reich Chancellery, that young people had climbed the trees between the chancellery and the

Hotel Kaiserhof and were chanting in chorus, declaring their love and devotion to the Führer and Reich Chancellor Adolf Hitler. And now, Dr. Joseph Goebbels would address the German people from the balcony of the chancellery.

As soon as Dr. Goebbels began to speak, Johann felt shivers running down his back such as he felt only in church when Herr Grübel sang the Benedictus, or when he watched the volunteer firemen train and his father, a squad leader and master hoseman, gave the order, Water on! His father wore a brass helmet shiny as pure gold and topped by a little brass post and a gleaming ball when he gave the command, Water on! When Mina said that in the picture, Johann looked as good as any prince, he immediately thought of his father with the golden helmet and the shiny gold post and shiny gold ball. No other fireman's helmet had a ball, only his father's. It was true that after every practice, Johann had to rub and rub the helmet with Sidol brass polish until it gleamed, but when the water rushed forward in the hose, swelling the flat tube with a swishing sound until it was as firm and smooth as steel, and then shot juddering out of the nozzle that Tone Messmer held fast with both hands and pointed at the onion tower that had been chosen to practice on this time, and when the water then pelted down on the onion tower and church roof, the shivers wouldn't stop running down Johann's back.

From the first, Dr. Joseph Goebbels's voice was cracking. He informed them that there were hundreds of thousands marching by to demonstrate their love and devotion to the beloved Führer. And that the hundreds and hundreds of thousands were carrying torches, burning torches, and that now they were all happy, all the SA men and Hitler Youth, yes, all the people who were comrades in the *Volk*, mothers and fathers carrying their children in their arms and holding them up toward the Führer's window, yes, now everyone was happy and he, Goebbels himself, was immeasurably happy. This was the rebirth of the nation in a frenzy of enthusiasm. And then he cried at the top of his voice that now the Führer and Reich Chancellor was appearing at his window, only a few yards away from where the aged Reich

President, that mythic hero General Field Marshal von Hindenburg, could be seen, and now, now, there was nothing more to hold them back, Germany had awakened at last, one wanted to laugh and cry, and that's why people were singing. He would join the song surging up from hundreds and hundreds of thousands of throats, the Horst Wessel Song, "Aloft the flag, our close-set ranks are marching. . . ."

The people in the restaurant sang along. Herr Brugger, Herr Minn, little Herr Häckelsmiller, Schulze Max, and the other Brownshirts stuck out their right arms. Fräulein Agnes too, of course. And next to her, Frau Fürst. Johann was bowled over that Frau Fürst was singing, and how she sang! Her mouth, stitched shut by pain, now wide open in song. Gradually, non-uniformed people stuck out their right arms, too. Not Father. But over by the bar, his mother did. She didn't stretch out her whole arm, just her forearm. Whenever she stood still somewhere, speaking or listening, his mother would always hold her left forearm across her body, below her chest, and rest her right elbow in her left palm, so that her right hand ended up just below her chin. If she laughed, she would raise her right hand and cover her mouth with it. She didn't want anyone to see her laughing mouth. If someone wanted to imitate his mother, all they had to do was strike this pose: left forearm across the body, right elbow in the left hand, right hand at the chin or covering the mouth to hide laughter. And now, she just kept that pose and took her right hand away from her chin, not to put it in front of her mouth (which wasn't laughing), but to leave it hanging in the air next to her cheek and chin.

Herr Seehahn had of course stood up too and was now stretching his pasty-white right hand quite far out. But since Herr Seehahn could say his text without taking the cigarette out of his mouth, Herr Minn went over to Herr Seehahn and—since he thought Herr Seehahn could then more easily sing along—carefully removed the cigarette from his mouth and laid it in an ashtray, but without stubbing it out. Instead of his medal from the Holy See, Herr Seehahn was wearing his party pin today. But he was sticking to his usual text—Johann could tell from the way he moved his lips. Mother had never put on the party pin Herr

Minn had brought over to the house on Epiphany. She wasn't wearing it today, either.

When the song ended, Father leaned over from behind Johann and whispered into his ear, "Come along now." In one hand Father held his papers and in the other, the little black case. They threaded their way cautiously to the door from the spare room into the central hallway.

Niklaus and Hanse Luis were sitting in the kitchen drinking beer. From the bottle. Mina behind the stove, the Princess at the sink. Hanse Luis jumped up as Johann and Father came in, raised his crooked right hand to the place where his hat brim should have been, and said, "Beg to report, two fillies at work, two bums drinkin' beer." "As you were," said Father in the same tone. He had it on good authority, said Hanse Luis, that he wasn't personally qualified to give the new salute because his paw was so crooked. But since he'd rather go swimming with a millstone than cause any trouble, he'd made himself scarce when the arm-stretching began and came to keep Niklaus company, who hadn't even gotten out of his foot rags from the last war. Some guy had asked him where you could find an ass these days, and Hanse Luis, who used an ass to plow his tiny patch of dirt, had told him: only in Austria.

Father said, "Isn't that the truth."

And Hanse Luis: "An Austrian on Bismarck's throne."

Mina said, "No politics in here!"

And Hanse Luis responded, "*Etz bin i gemuent, hot der Spatz g'seet, wo'n d'Katz Bodestieg nuuftrage hot.*"

And the Princess, furiously, from her sink, "*Jetzt bin ich gemeint, hat der Spatz gesagt, als ihn die Katze die Dachbodentreppe hinauftrug*"— She must mean me, said the sparrow, as the cat carried him up the attic stairs.

But the whole time, Hanse Luis had been listening with one ear to the radio voice drifting in from the hallway. He turned to the Princess and said in the precise accents of Dr. Goebbels, "When some people die, their mouth has to be killed off in a separate operation." At that moment, Herr Brugger came through the open kitchen door.

"Aha," he said, "the wise guys are holding their own caucus." Hanse Luis immediately fell into a coughing fit. Johann had never seen anyone cough like that before. He threw his head forward and back and his eyes were bugging out of his head. Luckily, he was able to put his stogie into the ashtray just in time. He could barely bring out a few words between bouts of coughing. They amounted to: he hadn't wanted to interrupt Goebbels's speech with his whooping cough. "Hanse Luis can find an excuse faster than a mouse finds a hole," said Herr Brugger.

"A good cough means a long life," said Mina from the stove where she was still busy frying bratwurst. She said it in the same tone the priest used when he said Peace on Earth, Goodwill to Men.

Hanse Luis said, "Worthless has a longer life." And he stood up and said, "Gnats in January on the farm, fodder may well come to harm. 'Bye all!" And was gone.

"I prefer *Heil Hitler*," said Herr Brugger, turned around, and continued down the hall to the lavatory.

"Come, Johann," said Father. "Time for bed."

Father was still holding the little case with the magnetizing apparatus in one hand and his papers in the other. Together they mounted the stairs that creaked under every step.

Josef was reading *Robinson Crusoe*. When Johann started to tell him everything that had happened, he didn't want to hear about it. He preferred *Robinson Crusoe*. Then Johann lay down in bed and listened to what wafted up from the restaurant: radio announcers, marching feet, chanting voices, and again and again from what they called throats without number, *Sieg heil!* The guardian angel in the picture holding his hand over the child on the bridge without a railing now looked like he was listening to the noises, too. Apparently, what you hear determines what you see.

PART TWO

The Miracle of Wasserburg

CHAPTER ONE

The Past as Present

CAN ANYTHING BE AS TRANSPARENT as a village that no longer exists? Wallflowers in bloom welling up out of shoemaker Gierer's low-lying garden. A pudgy tailor, sweating and crying in his grass skirt, does a dance on top of the regulars' table to get people to look at him. Herr Gierer drives each wooden nail into the leather sole with a single blow. The man Mother addresses as Battist sits right down at one of the two tables by the windows facing the station. This Battist (the *p* in his name must have been replaced by a second *t*) is their first guest on this Sunday morning. And as long as he's the only customer, he talks to Johann's mother. He talks and Johann's mother listens. As soon as Schmitt the tinsmith comes in (his thirst having held off and allowed him to sleep a little longer since it's Sunday morning), Battist clams up. The third guest on this Sunday is the blondest blond of the whole village: Semper Hagen's Fritz. Evidently his apprenticeship with the master tinsmith is in effect even on Sunday morning. Semper Hagen's Fritz is as good as entirely silent as long as he's sitting next to his master. Today's lesson is clearly about learning to drink. It was Helmer's Hermine who first asked him how he'd chosen tinsmithing as a profession, and he told her he wanted to be able to make himself a tin wreath for his grave so he could hear the rain. When you tell Helmer's Hermine you've already heard that one from Hanse Luis, she says, "And who do you think he heard it from? Me."

The fourth guest at the regular's table: Herr Schlegel. Herr Schlegel has barely sat down when Hagen's Fritz—already a journeyman tinsmith, after all—says in a fresh voice: "Pernambuco?"

But the builder replies quite cheerily: "Seventy-seven and a half hours!"

And Hagen's Fritz, even more cheeky: "Lakehurst to Friedrichshafen?"

And Herr Schlegel: "Fifty-five hours."

"And?" cries Fritz.

"You rascal!" says Herr Schlegel. Which means he's impressed that Fritz wants to know the Zeppelin's flight times down to the last minute.

"Come on, out with it!" cries Fritz.

"Twenty-three minutes," says Herr Schlegel as Luise serves him his glass of lake wine. Taking his sweet time, he picks it up and begins a sip that doesn't end until the glass is empty. He must not have had a single drop of wine all last night.

When Johann is again alone with his mother, she says not to tell anyone what he heard Battist say or they'd all lose their lives: the guest, Mother, and Johann. Mother always says, "lost their life," no matter how someone dies. Johann nods; he probably should have told her that he wasn't even listening and doesn't know what it is he mustn't tell. The whole time he was wondering if he could put on another record before more guests arrived. The record player is right next to the table where Battist was sitting. Father's favorite record, with Johann's favorite song, "Wer nie sein Brot mit Tränen ass," sung by Karl Erb, who started life as a meterman in Ravensburg and was a relative of Grübel's Ludwig. Father is hardly in his grave when Johann is sorry he never got around to singing "Jägerlied," the song Father liked most to hear Johann sing while he accompanied him on piano. "Only four years old, Hartmut, and Schubert's "Jägerlied" down pat!" his father had said the last time his friend Hartmut visited them from Oberstaufen, and he'd sat down at the piano and Johann had to sing the "Jägerlied." At the end, the only thing Johann wanted to sing was "Von Apfelblüten einen Kranz," which his father wasn't that fond of accompanying. In the meantime,

Johann is able to accompany himself, since Lehár writes easier notes than Schubert.

Johann is marching beside Wolfgang, the second Wolfgang in his life, out to the flak battery in Schnetzenhausen. They pass a troop of men, also marching in formation, but instead of uniforms they're wearing dark and light stripes and round caps without bills and Wolfgang says softly, so no one but Johann can hear, "From Dachau." And it occurs to Johann that he has forgotten that man named Battist and also forgotten that he had forgotten him. The only thing Johann heard while not listening on that Sunday morning was "Dachau." When Johann returns home after flak training and comes into the kitchen where his mother is sitting with the great-uncle they call Cousin, his great-uncle is just saying, "Whatever happens, we'll be the ones to pay the price." Mother says, "Shhh." Her face is feigning something. Johann recalls her face after she talked to Battist. He's forgotten that face and forgotten that he'd forgotten it.

So they won't be sent back to the front by one side or taken prisoner by the other, Johann and his buddies Richard and Herbert have kept to the ridgeline for days, walking first north from the Inn Valley, then west. And then once, between Mittenwald and Garmisch, they couldn't avoid crossing a valley and got stopped by two men, wearing that same striped outfit, who threatened them with pistols and forced them to hand over all the weapons they still had on them. Which they do. When they're back in the cover of the forest and starting to climb again, Herbert says, "They were from Dachau." Again Johann recalls what he'd forgotten and that he'd forgotten it.

Father took his drops on little pieces of zwieback. Father hit him only once in his life. Johann had tied a solid rubber ring on the end of a string and was whirling it around. The ring came loose and flew into hundreds of glasses from the previous day's holiday festivities waiting to be washed. It sounded like every single one of them was breaking. Followed immediately by a not-very-painful box on the ear from his father, who was standing next to him. Since the box on the ear came before he had time to fear it, it didn't hurt. When Mother is at her wits'

end with Josef and Johann, she has to herd them into the darkest corner of the cellar, paddle them with a cooking spoon, and say something
she probably picked up in Kümmertsweiler: that she should use one of
them to beat the other to death. When they emerge from the cellar, all
three of them are crying. Every time it happens, Mina right away gives
Josef and Johann a piece of candy she calls a *zickerle*. She always places
the candy on her palm, holds her hand up to Josef or Johann's mouth,
and they take the candy from her palm the way a horse would.

How was one supposed to know how valuable whatever was happening would be for one's memory? It's impossible to simultaneously
live and know anything about that. Which wart was more prominent,
more grand, the one on the left side of Helmer's Hermine's nose or
the one on the upper lip of Customs Official Heym's wife, the deputy
leader of the League of National Socialist Women? The Frau Heym
wart, of course, was the later of the two to shed its glow on the village. And before that could happen, two houses holding three customs
officials' families had to be built on the southeastern edge of the village. From deepest Bavaria and even Franconia, dialects were imported
that one could then encounter every day in town. Frau Hopper flung
open the door to the mail room and said, *"Schnöi a Bockl aafgemm"*—
Schnell ein Päckchen aufgeben. Gotta package to mail in a hurry. The
postmistress knew that to achieve immortality, this sentence had to be
passed on to Helmer's Hermine. Helmer's Hermine passes everyone's
house on her way home from the lower to the upper village, where she
lives behind a wall of arbor vitae. Frau Heym, who was responsible for
bringing the competing wart into the village, also uttered a sentence
that had come to Helmer's Hermine's attention and had thus gained
permanent currency: "Heaven is in Erlangen." That's what the pale-
cheeked, six-foot Franconian native and deputy leader of the League
of National Socialist Women said, so people in the village would know
that Frau Heym feels in exile here. Frau Heym's wart is darker and
flatter than the one that beams like a purple lighthouse from the left
side of Helmer's Hermine's face. Purple is the most distinguished color
in the Church year. Helmer Gierer's Hermine is related neither to the

bank Gierers nor the butcher Gierers, nor the saddler Gierers, nor the baker Gierers, nor to any of the many other Gierers in the villages of the parish, but she is distantly related to all the Gierers in Nonnenhorn, Hege, Hattnau, Bodolz, and Enzisweiler, but obviously, visibly related only to her brother, Helmer's Franz, who was able to play dead in that sappers' post near Soissons, thereby avoiding the POW camps. In the darkness, he removed his boots and foot rags and then, because it seemed like the safest thing to do, he walked barefoot and with a pitchfork on his shoulder that he had taken from a bombed-out farmstead—always looking like he was just coming from or going to his fields—all the way from Soissons to Wasserburg. Father always said that Helmer's Hermine cleaned houses without demeaning herself in the least. Apparently, she ennobled the villas of the summer people by cleaning them. She is a queen. Who wasn't a queen? Was Frau Fürst perhaps not a queen? All of a sudden, she'd become the leader of the League of National Socialist Women and was hanging the Maternity Medal in gold, silver, or bronze around the necks of mothers and working for the Winter Relief Committee. All of a sudden, she was giving speeches that were then reported in the newspapers she delivered. And who wasn't a king? No question but that in this village there were only kings and queens. And that led to conflicts. It always does when kingdoms are squeezed too close together. On her way home from cleaning, Helmer's Hermine reports to Frau Gierer from the bank what there is to report about those conflicts and struggles. Frau Gierer from the bank walks back and forth between the two chestnut trees and listens to what Helmer's Hermine has to report. Anyone who sees these two women walking back and forth on the gravel between the two chestnut trees must realize the importance of what Helmer's Hermine has to report. Johann keeps the gravel as spotless as he inherited it after Grandfather was discovered one morning dead in his bed next to the sleeping Niklaus, who was supposed to be keeping watch over him. Helmer's Hermine walks like no other person in the whole village has ever walked or ever will. Summers and winters those lace-up boots of soft black leather covering her ankles were always carefully tied.

Nothing careless could ever be associated with Helmer's Hermine. At every step, the pointy-toed boots fly energetically outward before the brakes are applied. Dancers walk like that. An energy peculiar to Helmer's Hermine is visible in her step; with each step she actually kicks an invisible ball and then puts down her heel with such force it looks like she's trying to hack a hole in the gravel or the pavement. Of course, she has left the village in no doubt about where these black, pointy-toed boots of fine leather came from. Helmer's Hermine's feet fit perfectly into the shoes of Frau Professor Bestenhofer, over whose floors Hermine bends and stoops in her proud way, which all by itself is enough to keep them shiny. During her reports to Frau Gierer from the bank, Hermine never looks at the woman walking right next to her. But Frau Gierer from the bank gazes uninterruptedly at Hermine, whose speech seems directed upward rather than straight ahead. And Helmer's Hermine speaks only High German. Yes, she does say *hofele-hofele* instead of *sachte-sachte*, but that and a few sayings that would lose all their juice in High German are the only dialect words anyone's heard her utter. Her brother speaks only dialect. Since no one has ever witnessed a conversation between Helmer's Franz and Helmer's Hermine, it's hard to imagine what language they could have spoken with each other. It's easier to imagine that they've never spoken to each other. Or that they had a language not dependent on words. They certainly didn't see each other every day, since Helmer's Hermine was out of the house during the day and Franz was out of the house at night, mostly sleeping in his shepherd's trailer at the edge of the parish woods. He poached in every district. Adolf, echoing his father: "Franz lends a hand when a man is needed."

Thanks to their high walls, even higher gates, and the bushes and trees that hid them even more, the world of the lakeside villas would have been unimaginable without Helmer's Hermine's bulletins. As it was, one learned that Herr Streber had been able to build the extensive house that rose directly from the lakefront wall on the western shore of the peninsula's neck with the profits the First World War had yielded to a manufacturer of gun stocks and rifle barrels, while Herr Geisler owed his lakeside villa to the peaceful and even pious production of silver lace and gold braid and perhaps even ecclesiastical vestments. And if certain people were curious which villa owner was their actual father, they were able to learn that fact from Helmer's Hermine as well. Hermine says that Eschig, the tobacco merchant from Bremen, visits his wife and son so infrequently that he still brings his son Edgar, known as Knupp, teddy bears, even though the boy is already a troop leader in the Jungvolk. And from whom if not from Helmer's Hermine were we able to find out that there was nothing going on between Frau Eschig and Herr Halke, even though the latter—an art photographer from Berlin who had started working as an aerial photographer for Dornier in Friedrichshafen and always wore a leather coat—had found accommodations in her villa. We know from Helmer's Hermine that the wife of the eminent physician Professor Bestenhofer, also from Berlin, is already his second wife and used to be his head nurse. Even without Helmer's Hermine we know that she's always taking off on her much older husband, trotting into the village, and shoplifting whatever will fit into her purse in all the stores, since the Herr Professor is always going around town paying for what his wife has stolen. From Helmer's Hermine one learns that in high society, such shoplifting is defined as an illness, and your better class of people even has a special name for it: *kleptomania*. And the fact that the village's name has been in the twenty-four-volume *Meyers Konversationslexikon* since as long ago as the turn of the century, because Professor Hoppe-Seyler died here, would have gone forever unnoticed if not for Helmer's Hermine. On account of his protoplasm research, she tells us, the professor was so famous that they had to put his place and date of death into the encyclopedia. *Protoplasm.* No sooner did Johann hear this word for the first time than it soared up into his word tree and now sits shining along with *pleurisy, Popocatépetl, Bhagavadgita, Rabindranath Tagore, atmosphere, theosophy, Jugendstil, Swedenborg, Balaam,* and *Bharatanatyam.*

From one of his bedroom windows, Johann would be able to watch the two women off-loading their freight of information between the two chestnut trees. But he doesn't. Whenever he's passed the two gravel-walkers coming from the train station, he's always given them a proper greeting. He would say hello, even though they're women and Johann has learned that in contrast to men, women you neglect to say hello to as good as never complain to Mother. He says hello, but doesn't realize what a chance he's missed to observe the keen, majestic, upright posture one assumes during the lucid narration of nothing but things of the utmost importance.

The fact that even Hermine herself, adept at and even addicted to High German, insists on stressing her own Hermine-name exclusively on the first syllable, is at least as much a part of her essence as the miniature purple lighthouse, known as a wart, to the left of her nose. Now that it's past, one understands why Frau Gierer from the bank can only receive Hermine's reports between the chestnut trees. Herr Schlegel built his building, in which the bank Gierers live and have their business, next to the Station Restaurant after Johann's grandfather himself had designed and built the Station Restaurant to harmonize with the train station in stone, style, and color. Herr Schlegel's building stands on the other side of the restaurant, not in competition, but rather like a sister with long hair, overgrown by wild grapevines and with flowers and a lawn in front. And that's exactly what would not have gone with receiving a report from Hermine. What does go with it is the crunch of gravel at every sentence and every step.

The object of such visitations can begin to suspect that the past only obtrudes to make one suffer at its irretrievability. As long as it was happening before our eyes, we didn't look at it, because from one second to the next we were engrossed in expectations that we now know nothing about. We probably never live, but just wait to begin living soon; afterward, when all is past, we wish we could find out who we were while we were waiting.

Along with falling water, big fish slither down a steep, rounded hillside. Johann must catch at least one of them. As fast as he can, he snatches one and holds on tight. The giant lake trout tries to escape his grasp, wants to be stronger than he is. He can't allow that. He's got to bring one home. He has to kill it. He hits it on the head with a slippery stone. Its face contracts like a small child's about to cry. It's Adolf, isn't it? Soon it won't be. He strikes again and again. It gives a last shudder. Gives up the ghost. Dreamwork complete. He'll bring the trout home.

In the last autumn before Father died, Mother said, "A crow's never flown that close to our window before. Almost hit the pane, but veered off at the last second." When people ask if they can get a hundredweight of coal on credit, it becomes her habit to let them know with a wave of her hand that that hundredweight isn't worth mentioning again.

CHAPTER TWO

La Paloma

When Johann got home from confirmation class, he saw that La Paloma Circus had arrived in town. As Johann started to dash across the terrace into the house, Tell should have been pushing open the swinging door with his nose even before Johann reached the two steps from the terrace up to the front door, which was standing open, and should have been jumping up on Johann until he let him put his front paws on his shoulders and lick his neck. Then the two of them would have continued at a run down the long, wide hallway into the kitchen. Johann would have sat down on the long bench to the right of the door, slid into the corner, and waited for Mina or Mother to bring a crepe and put it down in front of him, straight from the pan. But there was no Tell to be seen, just circus wagons shimmering blue and white and red through the trellised pears that closed off the south end of the terrace.

Johann hadn't come home up the Dorfstrasse, otherwise he would have seen the circus wagons in the courtyard from a long way off. He'd come via the Moosweg, through the meadows outside the village. Adolf had made fun of Johann's haircut. Johann knew—or thought he knew—that Adolf would have liked to have hair as long as Johann's. On his father's orders, Adolf always had to get his cut like Johann's used to be before he started school: most of his head shaved, with only a little tuft left in front. Now Johann was allowed to grow his hair so long it almost covered the back of his neck. Plus a part, like Josef's. Josef rode the train to school in Lindau every day. Josef said anybody with a half-shaved head would be laughed at in Lindau. And since this week Josef was at ski camp and hadn't taken the bottle of hair oil with him to the military prepared- ness ski course, Johann had been able to avail himself of this bottle for the first time. With the aid of the hair oil, he had styled a jaunty wave sweeping up to a frozen peak. He had paraded this coiffure like a crown through the upper village and the lower village, from the station to the lake. At every step he could feel his hair shudder, and so he walked care- fully in order to convey his tonsorial crown to the church unharmed. After confirmation class, Johann had to visit his father's fresh grave, sprin- kle it with holy water, and say three times: Lord, give him eternal peace, may eternal light shine upon him, Lord, let him rest in peace, Amen. The others were already standing outside between the castle and the Crown Hotel. Johann had hurried to catch up. Adolf had shouted, "Careful, don't let your tango-mane slip!" And Guido had added, "Nothin's gonna slip, his hair grease'll keep it in place." Everybody laughed. *Hair grease* was the term Luise used when she bought hair oil for Josef from Häferle the barber, whose wife washed and set Luise's hair. The phrase immediately spread through the entire village. When the regulars ordered their glass of beer from Luise, they added, "But without hair grease, please." And Luise would blush fire-engine red. She came from a mountain farm near Kaltern and had been brought to Wasserburg by Herr Caprano the wine merchant, who traveled to that region to purchase his Kalterer See and St. Magdalener for the village. There was no one Johann liked listening to better than Luise. Hers was the language of the South Tyrol, and he'd just heard Luis Trenker speaking it in the movie *The Call of the Mountain*. From deep in Luise's throat, those same angular sounds emerged more gently. Talking was by no means a matter of course for Luise. Actually, she was silent. Or mute. When she opened her mouth, Johann could tell she was taking a chance. As if she was walking a tightrope in front of an audience. Luise said *woll* instead of *ja*.

But even worse than encountering the words *tango-mane* and *hair grease* was when Adolf concluded the discussion of Johann's haircut with the words, "Now that his father's dead, there's no one to tell him he can't have a tango-mane."

Johann's father had been buried on Epiphany. If anyone had something against long hair and unusual haircuts, it was his mother, not his father. Strictness wasn't in his father's nature. Maybe he was too sick or too weak to be strict. And now, according to Adolf, Johann had taken advantage of his father's death to get himself a tango-mane.

Johann had felt he ought to defend himself. Adolf was beating up on his crown of hair and the others were laughing. They were on Adolf's side. He thought of Wolfgang, Wolfgang Landsmann. Edi (who was to be addressed as Edmund ever since he became troop leader in the Jungvolk)—Edmund the troop leader had thrown Wolfgang's bicycle down a bank into a ditch at their first muster after summer vacation last year. Then he'd taken his position before the troop that was drawn up in front of the new gymnasium and festival hall and said that he was under orders from higher up to dishonorably discharge Wolfgang Landsmann from the Jungvolk. Then he withdrew from his right breast pocket a little book they were all familiar with: the troop's roster. He slid the little yellow pencil out of its loop, moistened the pencil lead with his tongue, opened the roster, and painstakingly crossed something out of the book; everyone knew it was Wolfgang's name. Never since Edmund Fürst had become the Jungvolk troop leader had he spoken such High German during muster. Then he commanded, "Wolfgang Landsmann, step forward!" He stepped forward. "You know the score," said Edi.

"No, I don't," said Wolfgang.

"You're a Jew," said Edi.

"I'm half Jewish," said Wolfgang.

"I've got my orders!" bellowed Edi, as if he'd been insulted.

Wolfgang said, "Yes, sir," and snapped to attention, hands at his trouser seams, heels together, shoulders back, chin thrust out. Then he left, but looked around one last time. He lowered his head, raised his right arm as if in the Hitler salute, and looked back at them once more from under his right arm. His long, dark hair hung down. He'd had that long hair from the first. Apparently, he was allowed to have his hair as long as he wanted. Then he straightened up, went down the bank to where his shiny balloon-tire bike lay, picked it up, pushed it up to the street, and rode away. Only then did Edi bawl out, "Troop tennn-*shun*, Riiight *face*. Song?" Josef called out, "'*Steig ich den Berg hinan*,' three four." And they all started belting out, "Hiking the moun-tain paths, Is what I love. Hiking the moun-tain paths, Is all my joy. You have such lovely lovely eyes, That are so true, And two such rosy lips to kiss, Kiss black and blue." Johann liked that song because on the chorus he could yodel out above all the other voices. Whenever Wolfgang came along on his balloon-tire bike, Adolf had always called out, "Caution, tango-boy on the right!" Wolfgang was the only one who rode a bicycle to muster. He was the only one who had a balloon-tire bike. Wolfgang had only been there half a year at most when he was sent packing like that. In that brief time, he had made a soccer team out of a scrum of kicking boys because in Stuttgart, where he was from, he had played on a team with a coach. Now they only mentioned Wolfgang when they played soccer. They used the words he had introduced: dribble, tackling, goal.

When Adolf said that thing about a tango-mane and everybody laughed, Johann had said that he had to pick up a prescription from the doctor's. Since he had just learned to sort sins into this kind and that kind, he reckoned this lie was a venial one.

Coming home via the Moosweg, he had mounted the terrace from the train station side, seen the circus colors through the leaves and first blossoms of the pear trellis, and now pushed two stems aside. La Paloma Circus was written on all the wagons. The circus people were sitting around a table in the warm April sunshine. One of them was wearing a short blue workman's smock like Herr Schlichte the master electrician. This man kept jumping up, sitting down, jumping up again, talking, and gesticulating; they were all laughing. This gesticulator had a huge thatch of hair, a dense carpet of curls. At first sight you could have mistaken it for a fur cap. When this curly-head jumped to his feet, he was shorter than the others. As soon as he sat down, he was the tallest, not least because of his enormous fleece of hair. That anyone could argue about how to get a few wisps of hair cut by the barber seemed to Johann ridiculous in the face of this hairy fleece. It probably wasn't possible to cut this fleece at all. There was no way the little giant would allow anyone to get near him with a pair of scissors. The color of his skin was as remarkable as his magnificent coiffure. Bluish-red and shiny, that was his skin color. His ears also shone forth bluish-red from beneath his fleece of hair. Enormous ears. One saw only the lower third, which was already bigger than any normal ear. You could imagine how far up under his hair fleece those ears went. Once, he raised his hand and pointed his finger straight up. That suited him to a T! When he spoke about something above him, he pointed his finger straight into the air. Johann felt it in every fiber: this man was the circus. He was the circus despite his electrician's smock. Beneath the projecting roof of the carriage house, several horses were lying and standing on freshly spread straw. Or were they ponies? Someone had moved Tell's doghouse down by the last carriage house door. But no trace of Tell. A powerful black beast with huge, curving horns stood tethered to the Gravenstein (always the first to bloom) by a chain wrapped around its trunk. That was the circus too, that buffalo. Did he like it? asked a girl's voice. He turned around. And knew at once that her name was Anita. Close-set, dark eyes, a rounded forehead, but mostly: short bobbed hair and bangs. Bangs above the rounded forehead. And when she said she was Anita, he wanted to tell her he knew that already. But of course he didn't say so. And he wasn't so sure after all that he had known it right away. He didn't have time to think about that right now. She hadn't said her name was Anita, she said she was Anita, and he approved of that.

He hoped she wouldn't think he was trying to get a free look through the pear trellis. He could see right away that she belonged to the circus. Nobody here in the village would wear a sweater like that, especially not a girl. It was one giant explosion of color from top to bottom: blue and red and some white as well. Johann didn't know how to tell this girl that he didn't need to sneak a free look because he belonged to this house and had always been able to see the evening performances of all the traveling circuses that came to town without having to pay admission.

"That's Vishnu," she said.

"A buffalo," said Johann.

"An Indian water buffalo," she said. From down below came a shrill whistle. "That's my father," she said. "He's waiting for his cigarettes." And she held up the pack of R-6s and ran down the terrace steps to the street and along the fence to the open courtyard gate and over to her father, who was sitting with the others at the table that was covered with a blue tablecloth, waiting to smoke his after-lunch cigarette. Johann had never seen a man wearing a jacket like that one. It only reached down to his hips and was covered with large red-and-black checks. And this wasn't the first traveling circus to set up its rings in their courtyard. Evidently, word got around from one circus to another that the Station Restaurant was the best place to set up in Wasserburg. Three circus wagons to close off the area from the street and the carriage house running along the west side and the large main restaurant building on the north side meant that three sides of the rectangle were secure. And the large apple trees with their low-hanging branches were the guarantee for any circus that couldn't yet afford a tent that no one could see anything from the south side either without paying admission.

It was Johann's dream to be able to whistle like the girl's father. Edmund Fürst, five years older, could do it. Josef, two years older, could, too. Adolf, no older than Johann, could, too. Stick two index and two middle fingers into the mouth, stretch out the corners of the mouth left and right, and you got the shrillest of all possible whistles. People just had to respond to it. Look how it made the girl take off at a run. Yes, Tell came when Johann pursed his lips and whistled, but he would come even faster to a four-finger whistle. When Johann stuck his fingers into his mouth and stretched out the corners, no whistle emerged. It was mostly just a hiss with a slight squeak. His theory was that his fingers were still too skinny, and he kept trying to see if they had gotten thick enough yet, but they were still too thin. Adolf had thicker arms and muscles than he did, too. But when they wrestled with each other, Adolf lost as often as he did. Johann wasn't any weaker. Whether on the mat or finger-wrestling or cock-fighting or diving or high-jumping or shooting air rifles, he didn't even want to be the winner all the time. Sometimes he had to win, sure, but not always. Nothing would have been more unpleasant to Johann than an Adolf who was always the hopeless loser. To be honest, Johann liked it best when Adolf believed that he, Adolf, was better than Johann in everything and Johann could only beat him now and then by accident, so to speak. It was important to Johann to keep Adolf happy. And if victories over Johann could contribute to that end, then Adolf could go ahead and be the winner. What was important was that Johann knew he could beat Adolf. When necessary. Not that it was easy. Nor was it ever a sure thing. But he could do it quite frequently. At least, as often as necessary. At the moment, however, when he thought about how nasty Adolf had been about his tango-mane, he had the feeling he would beat Adolf every time from now on. At wrestling, finger-wrestling, cock-fighting, high-jumping, target-shooting, diving—no matter what, Adolf had to lose. Until he stopped talking like that. Tango-boy, tango-mane—those weren't Adolf's words, they were the words of his father who marched at the head of the SA on holidays, didn't attend church any more, and had said to Adolf—who had repeated it to Johann—that when your name was Adolf, it was your duty to be better at everything than everybody else.

Even before he got to the kitchen, Johann was asking where Tell was. Mother first greeted him, then said she had locked Tell in Johann's room upstairs because he wouldn't stop barking at the black buffalo and the ponies. Johann ran upstairs and released Tell, mixed his dinner for him, and as always, put the bowl out on the landing on the west side of the house, from where the back stairs went down into the courtyard. He stayed with Tell until he had emptied his bowl. Tell wouldn't touch a morsel unless Johann watched him eat. When Tell was done, they went back into the kitchen. Johann slid down the long bench next to the door into the corner and waited for the crepe that Mina brought round the stove and set down in front of Johann. The apple sauce was already on the table. It was there every day, no matter what was for dinner. On Friday there were crepes, and along with them the book that was always waiting for him in the corner. Currently, it was *Winnetou I*, and with Tell's muzzle between his knees, Adolf's mean remarks could vanish into thin air.

Mother said Josef had called: a torn ligament; he'd be home tomorrow or the day after. While climbing up the Nebelhorn, his whole group had been caught when a snow slab broke loose. It could have turned into an avalanche this time of year, late April. Josef must have a guardian angel, thank God for that. Johann should remember that this afternoon in church. Two boys had broken legs. Josef was lucky it was nothing worse than a torn ligament. Johann said, "Oh no, poor Josef," and saw in his mind's eye the dark blue, gold-framed picture as wide as the dresser in which all the shining brightness was concentrated on the angel holding his hand over the head of the child crossing the suspension bridge without a railing. On his back, the angel has a large but folded pair of wings.

Suddenly, Anita was there in the doorway with a woman behind her. The woman leaned forward and knocked on the open door. The woman said that Anita (she pointed to the girl) would like to take part in the First Communion day after tomorrow, the Sunday after Easter. She'd had the necessary instruction in all the towns they had performed in during the last four weeks. But the best thing would be if Anita could participate in communion class today and tomorrow.

Clearly, Mother had told the circus people that Johann was going to take his First Communion on Sunday. Frau Wiener—Mother had called her by that name—asked Johann if he would take Anita with him that afternoon. Now that Anita was going to First Communion with him, he realized that he'd thought she was older. She couldn't be ten or eleven. She must be at least twelve if not thirteen. Maybe in previous years on Low Sunday they had been in the Diaspora, which the priest always talked about in a way that made the Sahara seem an oasis by comparison.

Johann agreed at once to take Anita along today and tomorrow, and of course on Sunday, too. Frau Wiener said she had already made an appointment with Father Dillmann, whose housekeeper, Fräulein Maria, had said she could speak with the Father at four.

The two were gone as suddenly as they had come. Tell had growled when Frau Wiener and Anita appeared at the door. "He doesn't like me because I chased him away from Vishnu," Frau Wiener said. Frau Wiener was not much taller than Anita. But Anita was taller than Johann. Not a lot taller. A little bit taller. But taller all the same. Johann's father had been shorter than Johann's mother. Not much shorter, but shorter all the same. His grandfather, who had died four years ago, had been a giant, but stooped. Father had always held himself erect, especially at the piano. At the piano he even leaned back a little. He played as if someone up above was listening.

Johann went up to the second floor to watch the circus people from the lavatory window. Luckily, Grandfather had built the house with the lavatory on each floor facing south, so Johann could watch what the circus people were doing from three floors. In the meantime, they had assembled a circus ring from a pile of beams and were just scattering sawdust to give it a soft footing. Three rows of benches were already arranged around the ring. Two shorter poles faced each other with a taller central pole between them. All the wires had been strung. From the wires hung white and red light bulbs, as yet unlit. Over the entrance they had erected inside the courtyard gate stood the words LA PALOMA CIRCUS. Between the courtyard gate and the circus entrance was the ticket booth, painted blue and white and red. Two ponies were just pulling a mini-version of an ancient Roman chariot out into the street that ran down into the village. Johann had seen such a chariot in the book *Our Day in the Light of Prophecy*. The caption under the picture of the chariot in the book read "Philip and the Eunuch." The circus chariot was driven by a muscular man whose sun-tanned head was completely bald. Behind him, on a sort of throne, sat the little giant with the fleece of hair, beating a large drum slung from his shoulders. His bluish-red face was shining. Down by the linden tree where all five streets of the village ran together, they came to a stop. The little giant announced today's program. The fellow with the bald head played "La Paloma" on the trumpet. Johann would have loved to run after them. The music attracted him, but he couldn't move. The music held him spellbound, too. They would probably make another stop in front of the Bruggers' house, and then Adolf would already know about the circus when they saw each other at communion class. So Johann wouldn't have to spend much time explaining who this olive-skinned girl with the round forehead was. And what eyelashes she had, too! Johann resolved to take a good look at other girls and women to see if they had lashes like that. And you could see both of this girl's incisors. Her lips didn't close completely. Since the itinerant photographer had taken his picture, Johann knew that his lips didn't always close completely either. He ran to his room and checked to see in the mirror. His right incisor stuck out shamelessly. Johann's upper lip, which was too short to begin with, had to constantly be on guard to keep this pushy individual covered up as much as possible. In Anita's mouth, the same incisor didn't jut out at all but only emerged a tiny bit, as if to protect the incisor next to it. No unsightly pushing ahead, just gently taking a near relative under its wing. Johann liked standing in front of the mirror for a long time. Now it was something else he'd have to confess and do penance for. And resolve never to do again. I have been proud. He had broken seven of the Ten Commandments, the first seven. He hadn't really broken the fifth. He hadn't killed anyone, just beaten them. It was self-defense. But Jesus didn't defend himself. Would the priest recognize him? It was dark in the confessional. But the priest could look through a slit in the curtain and see who was just leaving the pew and needed only two or three steps to be kneeling at the priest's ear in the dark confessional. Johann would have liked it better if the canon had taken confession from the boys. But you never knew ahead of time. I have taken the Lord's name in vain. I have spoken holy names in anger. That's how it started. It helped to get you going. Just don't get stuck. Keep going, plow right on through.

At four thirty, Johann was standing at the entrance to La Paloma Circus, his hair freshly oiled and carefully styled in a single wave. He didn't dare go farther in. He knew which trailer Anita would emerge from, because from the lavatory window he had seen her mother and father, the one with the short, red-and-black checked jacket, disappear into it.

Anita joined him. Now she had on white stockings, and instead of the loud sweater, she was wearing a dark blue knit dress. She looked too much like Sunday. No village boy or girl would come to communion class in such Sunday clothes. He should have told her, but he was too timid. And besides, he'd put on his own new corduroy knickers and his knee socks were practically new. But over his sport shirt he was wearing the sweater he'd gotten for Christmas five years ago and then immediately burned a hole in while blowing out the candles. The place on the left forearm where Mina had darned it was visible. He'd arranged the sleeve so people couldn't see the spot. As soon as he caught sight of Anita coming out the door of her trailer, he knew that he shouldn't have worn this sweater. It was obvious that the bottom edge and the ends of the sleeves had been lengthened.

She came down the three steps and over to him. "Let's go," she said. And because he obviously was unable to move a muscle, she said, "Before we put down roots," and laughed and said, "That's what Papa always says." Johann thought: The last time I heard that was when Schulze Max said it one Christmas Eve.

Now, was he going to take the main street to the church with Anita, more than half a mile with her between all those houses on both sides till they were finally all the way down the hill and in the church out on the peninsula? Not on your life! Just think of all the people they might run into! No, no, no. He would take her by the Moosweg.

If Anita had remained silent, he certainly would not have uttered a word either. But she talked almost nonstop. She wanted them to quiz each other on the questions that would be asked in class and say the *Manual of Confession*. "You start," he said. And she did. But before she did, she said she wasn't confessing, just reciting the manual. And then she recited it, unbelievably fast and not leaving out a single point, not even the one that talks about unchastity, alone or with other people. Alone or with other people, Johann thought. Then she recited all the conditions that had to be fulfilled before contrition is true contrition. Then she recited all the things that mustn't happen between confession and communion if you want to be allowed to take communion.

"OK, now it's your turn," she said. Johann shook his head but didn't look over at her. Instead, he started to walk faster. She said she had to be back by six thirty. The performance began at eight o'clock. So then why did she have to be back by six thirty? To change, put on her makeup, and warm up. She was part of the main act of the evening: the Viennese trapeze artists. It was her family's act. Her father did most of the work, of course, but he needed her and her brother, too. Had Johann seen the pole in the middle of the ring? They performed on that pole, from the bottom all the way up to the top, fifty feet above the ground. He'd be able to see them. Luckily, they could set up the ring here so that people in nearby houses couldn't see their tricks at the top of the pole without paying admission. That was always the biggest problem with their performance. Here, the top was only visible maybe from the street or from the restaurant terrace. "But we'll be sure to pass the hat there," said Anita and laughed.

As they entered the churchyard, Johann said he had to pay a quick visit to his father's grave and she would have to enter on the women's side, anyway. He pointed in that direction, turned right toward the grave, sprinkled it with holy water, and said three times to himself: Lord, give him eternal peace, may eternal light shine upon him, Lord, let him rest in peace, Amen. Then he went in on the men's side. Inside, he saw Anita sitting way up in front. On his side, he walked just as far forward, nodded to her, and she nodded back.

He had left the house so early because he wanted to get to the church with Anita before anyone else was there. It had worked. Johann pictured himself standing at the pulpit the way Father Chrisostomus had stood there during Missionary Week and called out with outstretched arms: Why do the heathen rage? And below him, in the first row, Anita would be sitting. And he would preach just for her.

The other girls and boys gradually trickled in. The priest emerged from the sacristy, and before beginning the class, he went over to Anita and spoke to her, his stiff goatee going up and down without Johann being able to catch a word. Adolf had sat down next to Johann and glanced over at the girls. Then he whispered to Johann, "The girl from the circus." He gestured with his head when he said "the girl." Johann gave a vague nod, as if he weren't as sure about that as Adolf obviously was. How come Adolf knew it already? In a village, you can never tell how it comes that everyone knows everything immediately. The only thing you can be sure of is that everyone does know everything immediately. Adolf's shirt had a much finer check than Johann's. And instead of a sweater, he was wearing quite a long jacket that was held together by a belt of the same fabric.

The priest said that now they were not six but seven girls and eleven lads. In the priest's language, boys were always lads. He said he was pleased to announce that Anita Wiener was well prepared to take her First Holy Communion along with the children from Wasserburg. Johann felt a shiver run down his back. He had to take a hurried, deep breath. His ears were ringing. Was he flying or falling? Quickly, with the nail of his right thumb, he dug a letter into the soft wood of the pew. He cut an *A* into the wood, then a *W*. But he screened what he was doing to keep Adolf from seeing it. Suddenly, he heard Adolf whispering that Johann didn't have to hide it with his hand because he, Adolf, had already seen it. And he pulled Johann's hand away from the pew. Evidently, Adolf was going to urge the other boys to look over here and see what Johann had just done. Johann stared fixedly at the priest, as if he couldn't be distracted right now. And in fact, the priest was just enlarging upon how bad it would be if the communicants, after making their first confession tomorrow afternoon and departing the church in a blessed state of grace, were then to put that state at risk by some sinful negligence or even destroy it entirely by committing a mortal sin, and then take their First Communion on Sunday morning in an unworthy state. That was the most severe, the blackest, most terrible sin there was—to receive the Body of the Lord in a defiled condition. It sounded like anyone who did such a thing could expect to be struck by lightning or have the earth open up and swallow them.

When the priest had ended the class, it occurred to Johann that he still had to say an Our Father and a Hail Mary for Josef's guardian angel, who had let him survive with just a torn ligament. Actually, the worst is ready to happen at any second, and as much as possible you have to prevent it by faith and prayer, supplication and entreaty, so that only the second or even third or fourth worst thing happens.

By the time Johann finished his two heartfelt but hurried prayers, the others had already left the church. He ran.

In two separate groups, the girls and the boys were walking up the Dorfstrasse, the boys some distance behind the girls. The girls had Anita in their midst as if to make sure nothing happened to her. You could see and hear that Anita was the center of attention. Did Anita notice that she was the only one with bobbed hair? All the others had braids. He was the only boy whose hair was not simply pushed back toward the middle of his head. If she hadn't noticed, he couldn't tell her.

Of course, they didn't return by the Moosweg, but up the main street. Johann would have rather shown Anita the third possibility to return to the village from the church: the path along the lake, a walled walkway in front of the villas, protected from the waves by huge stones that had simply been piled there as a breakwater. Anita had already said she thought the pastures in the broad hollow through which the Moosweg ran were beautiful, because from one side to the other cuckoo flowers and buttercups were in bloom. Johann didn't notice all the flowers until Anita said she wanted to pick a bouquet for her mother on the way home. And now she was being led up the main street like a captive queen. He and Anita on the path along the lake, Johann thought. The waves ceaselessly trying to get at them yet always failing—Anita would surely have liked that. Anita could have walked on the wall side and he on the water side. In that case, however, she would be walking on his left and could see his darned sleeve. So he would have had to let her walk on the lake side after all, impossible at this time of year: April, snow melt, all the water from the mountains, the lake overfull and right now, stormy.

After they had passed beneath the big walnut tree that stood right at the edge of the street, they saw their teacher coming down the steps from the barber shop. He had his hair cut even shorter than Adolf's, every hair on his entire round head cropped down to a third of an inch, maybe on account of the silver plate still in his head from the war.

The girls greeted him with, "Heil Hitler, Herr Teacher." The boys, too. Adolf was the only one who shot out his arm when he said it. He even put his left hand down to his fabric belt and stuck his thumb under the belt as if it were the buckle of a leather uniform belt. The teacher said, "Heil Hitler, dear children" twice, and unhurriedly stuck out his right arm. "Well, now," he said, "everybody listen to this. Come on, come on, no shilly-shallying," he said when the girls and boys failed to cluster around him at once. "It's enough to make a person sick the way you greet your teacher. How do you expect to teach your parents to do it? What was that I gave you to write into your National Rebirth note-books about how to greet each other? Firstly . . . Adolf?"

And Adolf piped up, loud and over-enunciated, as if speaking to the hard of hearing, "Firstly, we on Germany's southern border must insist on the German Greeting in place of all older customs and despite any stubborn resistance."

The teacher: "Secondly . . . Anneliese?"

And Anneliese, just as loudly and excessively enunciated: "Secondly, it is a sign of weakness to let one's style of greeting be influenced by the person one is addressing."

"Good, Anneliese!" cried the teacher. And they all knew he was thinking of the last day of school before Easter when he had to give Anneliese a box on the ear because she was erasing an incorrect answer to a math problem in her notebook but denied it when confronted by the teacher. "The worst thing is not that the answer was wrong," the teacher had scolded, "but that you lied about it. A German girl doesn't lie," he'd said and given Anneliese a slap that sent her sprawling so hard against the harmonium that its key got broken. The teacher then gave the girl a kick while she was still on the ground. Then he turned to the blackboard, hammered with both fists against it, and screamed, "She's a liar. She lied, and then she tries to deny that she lied."

When there was a change in the weather, it often happened that the teacher hammered against the board like that. When he thrashed Franz Döbel because he'd taken fifty pfennigs from the Winter Aid collection box to buy glue for his model airplane, the teacher hadn't hammered the board just with his fists, but with his head, too, which made his dentures fall out of his mouth. Franz Döbel, still lying on the floor, picked them up and gave them to the teacher, who put them back in his mouth. Everyone knew: from the war, the silver plate in his head. That's why he was always so quick to fly off the handle.

"Thirdly . . . Johann!" the teacher cried.

And Johann piped up, "Thirdly, whoever insists on answering the German Greeting by doffing his hat or cap or with some mishmash such as 'Good day, Heil Hitler,' whoever keeps answering evasively when we greet him with a raised arm and Heil Hitler—such a person will be stricken from the list of those we greet."

"Any exceptions?" asked the teacher. "Irmgard?"

"An exception," Irmgard spoke up, "is during Carnival. When tomfoolery reigns in outward appearances, the German Greeting is to be avoided."

As he recited his answer, Johann knew that he would not be able to greet the regular customers, whom he was obliged to greet whether he encountered them in the restaurant or on the street, with Heil Hitler. On Memorial Day at the war memorial, the priest had raised his hand in the German Greeting. Even so, Johann would always greet the priest with *Grüss Gott*. There were people such as the teacher or Frau Fürst who you said Heil Hitler to automatically. In every house where she delivered the paper, Frau Fürst called out as she came through the door, "Heil Hitler, everybody." Every time she said that, Johann remembered what the teacher had said: that the German Greeting was "Heil Hitler" and any addition was forbidden. Someone ought to let Frau Fürst know that sometime. After all, in the meantime, she'd become a leader in the League of National Socialist Women. She'd had her daughter Eva's name changed at the municipal registry; she was Edeltraud now. Frau Fürst explained in every house she entered that Eva wouldn't do anymore because Eva was Kyra von Strophandt's deputy. When Kyra von Strophandt, the leader of the League of German Girls, married an SS Obersturmführer from Halle and was inducted into the Community of SS Families, a picture of Edeltraud had appeared in the newspaper

that her mother delivered to every house—Edeltraud standing right
next to the bride. And ever since Edi Fürst became a troop leader, you
really couldn't call him anything but Edmund. As troop leader, track
star, and gymnast, he was in the paper even more often than his sister
Edeltraud. You could tell immediately by the way Frau Fürst tossed
the paper onto your table that her children were in the news again.
Sometimes when Johann was sitting at the table, she even opened the
paper to the Bulletin Board column and among the eleven or twelve
announcements pointed right to where it said, "Troop 36/320," and
especially to the last line: "No excuses accepted." Although Johann
nodded, she pointed to another line in the announcement: "Don't forget to bring overdue payments for Sports Day badges." Johann stood
up and said "*Jawohl!*" with just a bit of exaggeration. And Frau Fürst:
"If only they were all like you, Johann! But there are shirkers, pansies,
and saboteurs, Johann, who make life damn difficult for Edmund."
And with, "Heil Hitler, everybody," she was gone.

After the teacher had strolled off in the direction of the peninsula,
Adolf said they had greeted him like a bunch of magpies and he pre-
dicted there'd be hell to pay. Hell to pay. Johann could hear from the
sound that it was one of Adolf's father's expressions. Today, Adolf looked
like he could be the teacher's son. Because the teacher was wearing the
same kind of jacket, with buttons all the way up to the collar and a belt
of the same material. It made an especially elegant impression that the
buttons were concealed from view. Probably Adolf's mother had seen
the teacher wearing that kind of jacket and had ordered one made as
much like it as possible by Zwerger's Anna or the wife of Gierer the
shoemaker or Fräulein Höhn or even Frau Schmitt, the tinsmith's wife.

Johann had given a start the minute he saw the teacher emerging
from the barbershop. Of course, the teacher knew where the children were coming from, two days before Low Sunday. The teacher
had stopped playing the organ in church three years ago, no longer
entered the church at all, and signed all his notices and placards with
"Heller, Head teacher, NSDAP Member and Propaganda Warden."
On election day two weeks ago, all the schoolchildren had to run up

and down the village reminding everyone they found without a voter's badge to be sure to do their duty and vote. When you voted, you got a badge. In the days before the election, they had to memorize the sentence on the ballot and chant it in chorus along the Dorfstrasse: *Are you in favor of the reunification of Austria with the German Reich, carried out on March 13, 1938, and will you vote for the candidate list of our Führer, Adolf Hitler?* And then they all yelled, "Yes!" twice as loudly. The week after the election, the teacher brought the newspaper to class. They had been practicing percentages. In the Lindau district, 99.2 percent had voted Yes. How many people was that out of a total of 20,422 eligible voters? And in Wasserburg, 659 Yes votes. What percentage of 665 eligible voters was that? Then the teacher said, "Six No votes, we'll bring them around, too." Johann thought, Thank goodness his father wasn't one of the six No votes. Not anymore. Hitler means war. Johann had never repeated this sentence of his father's out loud. He had never told Adolf or Ludwig or Paul or anyone else how Strodel's Traugott had died in the August sun with his guts spilling out and his father and Helmer's Franz unable to stuff them back in. "Where's our host?" Adolf's father, who'd been too young for the war, had demanded whenever he came into the restaurant. "Is our host bedridden again? Or is he just reading?" Adolf's father liked to criticize Johann's father. Adolf's father was in the SA, the Reich Hunter's Association, the National Socialist Automotive Corps, and the Party. Johann's father was a member of the choral society, the veterans association, the alpine club, and the volunteer firemen. Luckily, Mother was in the Party, with a membership number in the first million. As Mother had foreseen, party meetings were held in the Station Restaurant. And the teacher had even given a lecture there one winter, "Our Armaments and Those of Other Countries Compared." The teacher had been a captain in the war. So many people came to hear the teacher they had to open the folding partition. Father was not one of the audience for that lecture. That didn't attract attention, since Father was seldom seen in the restaurant anyway. Only Herr Brugger had noticed. As long as Father was still alive, it had given

Herr Brugger no rest to know that only Mother had joined the Party. Mother had to repeatedly explain her husband's absence. Mainly, she had to repeatedly fend off bankruptcy. Otherwise, what happened first to the Brems, then to the Hartmanns, then to the Capranos, and finally to the Glatthars would have happened to them, too. When all of the Glatthars' belongings were auctioned off after Frau Glatthar died, Johann could see that nothing worse could ever happen to a family than a foreclosure auction. The whole village comes, everyone strolls through your rooms and notes down what they want to bid on: 1 sauerkraut crock, 2 nightstands with white marble tops, 1 grandfather clock, 3 washtubs with accessories, 1 laundry mangle. Johann had never seen anything as terrible as the auction of all the Glatthars' possessions. He didn't have to be asked twice to do anything to help stave off foreclosure. The whole time Frau Glatthar was bedridden, he and his father had gone to visit her. Father always brought her some of his teas. Frau Glatthar had some kidney disease that no one else far and wide had ever had. She said so herself. Johann had never heard anyone speak so softly. It was amazing you could hear her at all. It was the gas pump that had bankrupted them, she said. Anyone could pump gas up into the five-quart glass and then let it flow into his tank without having to come into the store and pay for it.

After his auction, Brem the carpenter, who even with his pistol hadn't been able to keep people from inspecting all the things to be auctioned off, was usually to be found sitting behind the house that no longer belonged to him. He sat at a table with his air rifle and would shoot the wings off the flies that landed on the table. He did it with the air pressure alone. The rifle lay on the table, which was strewn with crumbs of food. Herr Brem waited with his finger on the trigger until one of the flies wandered in front of the muzzle, then he pulled the trigger. Adolf had watched him and said that he wasn't trying to kill the flies, just shoot their wings off.

When Herr Brugger showed up at the restaurant, Johann often recalled what Elsa had told him and his mother when they came back from the savings and loan. Herr Brugger had just left the restaurant, loudly proclaiming: We're gonna pull the plug on that piano player tonight.

Johann had hoped that as soon as the boys and girls reached their houses or the side streets where they lived, they would disappear one after the other. Well, the boys did turn off. And if the girls had also turned off where they should have, Johann would have been alone with Anita. The last ones would have been gone by the time they reached the linden tree. But the girls didn't turn off or disappear into their houses. They led Anita through the courtyard gate and up to the circus entrance and didn't go home till they had promised to come to the performance that evening. Johann had heard it as he passed them. Then he ran into the house and up to his room and threw himself on the bed. He lay on his stomach, and when Tell jumped onto the bed, he pulled him close. Tell licked him, and that was all right with Johann. When he raised his eyes, he saw that beneath the picture of the guardian angel that was as wide as the chest of drawers, someone had put a bouquet of primroses. That was Mina. Mina thought of such things. Mother thought of what would prevent foreclosure.

CHAPTER THREE

Anita, Anita

JOHANN WAS SITTING IN THE CORNER where he always shoved his school bag after school. Today he was looking at the book lying open before him, but he wasn't reading. The grownups counted on him reading. Herr Brugger wouldn't be saying the things he was to Johann's mother right now if he wasn't confident that Johann was reading his *Winnetou*.

"Remember, you're not even thirty-eight yet," Herr Brugger said in a loud voice. "Count your blessings you're rid of that namby-pamby. He would have voted No for sure. Someone should have reported him to the police long ago. And someone would have, if he hadn't been such a pitiful specimen. You voted Yes, I know you did," said Herr Brugger, "but he would have voted No."

"I don't think so," said Mother, much quieter than Herr Brugger. "It would have been all right with him if Austria was back in again," said Mother. "After all, he was in the alpine club."

"And the Führer managed to do all that without a war," said Herr Brugger in a loud voice. "Not a drop of blood spilled. A stroke of genius. And that know-it-all namby-pamby of yours, what did he leave you with? Bills and more bills. And who's going to keep you from going down the drain and maybe losing your whole business? Strength through Joy and the German Workers' Front, that's who. They'll bring you more customers than you've ever had. But Mr. Know-It-All, that idiot, that namby-pamby, that fool . . ."

Johann's mother went "Shh, shh." She must have been trying to remind him that Johann was sitting there.

"Don't worry," said Herr Brugger. "He's reading. Just like his old man. Stick a pin in him and out would come ink instead of blood. I'd whip some sense into my boy if he had his head stuck in a book all the time."

Mother said that Johann would be going to the grammar school in Lindau soon, just like his older brother Josef.

"Waste of money," said Herr Brugger. "They'll both end up with ink in their veins, and we'll have to support them when they can't afford to feed themselves."

Johann was afraid he was going to blush. Often he really would get so absorbed in his reading he didn't hear what they were talking about. But he couldn't help listening. Finally, Herr Brugger left.

Almost immediately the music started drifting up from the courtyard. Johann wished he could run at once to the lavatory window on the first floor. But the Princess (who seldom turned around but still managed to keep an eye on everything) would have known why he left and might have called out after him in a loud voice.

An accordion, a trumpet, and assorted drums. Hit tunes. Sad tunes. Funny tunes. The funny ones were played by the accordion, the sad ones by the trumpet. Suddenly, Anita was there in the doorway. She already had on her makeup, was wearing a gaudy yellow bathrobe, and had some kind of turban on her head, a red one. Johann shushed Tell. Anita said she just wanted to see how many complimentary tickets they needed. "One," said Johann. The others would watch from the windows. Anita put the ticket on the table, wished him lots of fun, and was gone.

Mina said, "What a sweet little thing."

"And a poor little thing, too," said Mother. Mina didn't think so. Mother insisted that a girl who went from village to village in a trailer and had to perform for people every night was a poor thing. She came to Communion, at least. Thank goodness for that.

Johann shut Tell in the bedroom, then stood outside, by the entrance to the courtyard, waiting for Adolf, Ludwig, Paul, Helmut and Helmut, and Guido and Berni. The girls were already standing around laughing at what one of them was saying.

Johann would rather have sat in the third row, but Adolf said, "First come, first served." So far just a few little colored lights were on, which merely made the circus ring that much darker. Only the three musicians were brightly lit. Behind a set of drums and cymbals and triangles sat the Little Giant with his head of curly hair corkscrewing in all directions. Whenever he belabored the drums and cymbals, he rolled his eyes deliriously. Everything he did was exaggerated. He started a drum roll on a little snare drum and let it swell until just before the peak, then ended it with a cymbal crash that he gently extinguished with piously cupped hands. He stretched and twisted his large body as if the music wasn't being made by the instruments but by that body itself. Next to the Little Giant with his head of hair, the other two musicians were almost invisible. The muscleman with the glistening bald head who had driven the Roman chariot played trumpet. He had changed into a shiny silver suit with a hat to match. Golden ringlets peeked out from beneath it. Anita's mother played the accordion. Suddenly, a musical flourish and the lights went up: in the ring stood a gentleman in tails and top hat, the tails deep blue and the hat light blue, with a whip in his hand that he proceeded to crack several times. He bid everyone in the audience welcome, he said, large and small, fat and skinny—but he couldn't continue with clever and dumb, for whoever came to a performance of La Paloma Circus proved thereby they had a good head on their shoulders. The music swelled. People clapped. He promised them an international program that evening: Cuba, India, Italy, Vienna, and the Orient were all represented in La Paloma Circus. But not only Cuba, India, Italy, the Orient, and Vienna. No, even— listen closely now, be amazed, and rejoice—even Mixnitz on Murr. A brief drum solo by the Little Giant made it clear that he himself was from Mixnitz on Murr. People clapped. Then the rhythm turned Cuban, the trumpet struck up "La Paloma," the accordion fell in with a sigh, the drums intimated mystery. "Cuba," cried the ringmaster, cracking his whip and bowing toward two boys dressed in shining white who led the black buffalo into the ring. And immediately, with a solemn beat of her wings, there floated or flew in from one side a white dove: Anita. In she glided, evidently suspended from a wire, and once above the buffalo, she stopped beating her wings and settled into a small golden nest the buffalo carried on its back. Hardly had she landed when she shed the winged costume with a single sweep of her hand and tossed it to the ringmaster, who caught it and bowed deferentially. Now Anita stood in her nest as a Cuban girl, swaying to the music of "La Paloma" and urging herself on to ever more daring twists and turns with a pair of black castanets. Suddenly, the wings were passed back to her, the music subsided into pure languor, and Anita was a dove again, beating her wings quite slowly, as the buffalo bore her from the ring. Everyone clapped. Anita returned with her wings but without the buffalo, and bowed. The ringmaster was applauding as well and cried again and again, "La Paloma in person, Anita Wiener, Anita Wiener from the internationally renowned Wiener family of circus artistes." Then two ponies pulled in a cage. Inside knelt the muscleman, now wearing a sleeveless jersey and tight-fitting breeches and bound and shackled with multiple ropes and chains. Blond ringlets fell to his shoulders. The ringmaster introduced him as Samson, Strongest of the Strong, and asked for volunteers from the audience to inspect the ropes and chains tying Samson down. Adolf, first in line, examined and nodded and said, "They're real, all right." The ringmaster thanked Adolf and said he was the kind of young person we had need of today, a lad who couldn't be hoodwinked.

Samson flexed his muscles, and with each exertion one of his bonds snapped off. A drum roll celebrated the triumphant bursting of each rope or chain. When all his fetters were broken, he seized the chain, tore it in two, bent apart the bars of his cage, and sprang into the ring to thunderous applause. But the ringmaster acted frightened. He ran around in the ring as Samson came after him with powerful, ominous strides. The ringmaster cried, "Delilah, help! Delilah, help!" And in came an oriental woman who began to swivel her hips in front of Samson: Anita. She performed a belly dance, and Samson knelt down in front of her. She pulled out a dagger glittering with jewels, scalped Samson, held up his wig, and threw a slender noose around his neck. Samson was so weak he could hardly lift his arms, and she led him from the ring. Thunderous applause. The ringmaster called after her, "Thank you, Delilah. You rescued us from the terrible Tartar. Thank you, Delilah."

Of course, this scalping scene reminded Johann of Karl May's first Winnetou novel and the farewell banquet for the greenhorn from Germany, when Sam Hawkens removes his hat and his hair comes off with it. An absolutely bare skull appears—scalped by the Pawnees. But the muscleman's skull wasn't as bloody red as the skull of the frontiersman Sam Hawkens, whose every other sentence ended with: Unless I'm very much mistaken. Johann loved Sam Hawkens because he always said, Unless I'm very much mistaken.

Anita wasn't in the next number. Johann watched but didn't really take it in. He only woke up again when the Little Giant and his head of hair reappeared, this time as Dumb August the clown. The ringmaster was his straight man. On top of his mop of hair, the Giant wore a little metal basin with a lip, and he had on a tailcoat stitched together from burlap bags over a shirt hung with tiny bells. When he shook himself, they jingled. He shook himself whenever he didn't agree with what the ringmaster said. The ringmaster said, "My dear Herr August . . ." August shook himself. The ringmaster: "Herr August . . ." August shook himself. "August, you are . . ." August kept still, and nothing jingled. "Aha, so we're on familiar terms with each other," said the ringmaster.

August: "If you like, Herr Director, sir."

Ringmaster: "But then you have to be on familiar terms with me, too."

August: "Your wife is on familiar terms with you, and when I see the way you treat her, I think I'd prefer to be on formal terms."

Ringmaster: "Why? How do I treat my wife?"

August: "Just the other day, after the doctor examined her, he said, 'Herr Director, I don't like the way your wife looks,' and you replied, 'Then we have the same taste in women, Herr Doctor.'"

Ringmaster: "August, I've always said that my wife has a unique inner beauty."

August: "Then maybe you should have her turned inside out."

Ringmaster: "Is that possible?"

August: "Nowadays, anything's possible. Two months ago I was an Austrian from Mixnitz on Murr, and today I'm a German."

Ringmaster: "But that's completely different, August."

August: "Not at all, Herr Director. Your wife has her beauty on the inside, just like we Austrians had our Germanity on the inside, but now it's on the outside. Sunday before last, 99.7 percent of all Austrians said Yes to their inner Germanity."

Ringmaster: "My dear August . . ." August shook himself, setting all his bells ajingle.

Ringmaster, cautiously: "August . . ." When nothing jingled, he continued, "I only hope you, too, voted Yes on April 10th."

August: "Of course, Herr Director, I simply overthrew myself."

Ringmaster: "How's that? Overthrew yourself?"

August: "You know what the expression 'throw up' means. Well, it's just like that. Except that when you throw up it comes out, and when you overthrow it goes in. I told myself right away: now you're going to overthrow yourself, just like 99.7 percent of all Austrians."

Ringmaster: "But August, there was no way you could already know on election Sunday that 99.7 percent of all Austrians would vote Yes."

August shook himself indignantly and said, "None of that argumentative tone, if you please, Herr Director! Of course I knew the Austrians would outdo the Germans in Yes-saying. Next time, I swear it'll be 102 percent."

Ringmaster: "A hundred and two percent? That's impossible."

August: "Not very good at math, eh, Herr Director? A hundred and two per cent is 102 out of 100."

Ringmaster: "You must take me for a bit retarded, August."

August: "But Herr Director, I don't judge a book by its cover." People laughed. The ringmaster gave August a slap in the face, and August pretended to be almost knocked down by it, but he transformed being almost knocked down into searching for something in the sawdust on his hands and knees.

Ringmaster: "Did you lose something, August?"

August: "Nothing much, just my faith in humanity."

Ringmaster: "You've lost your faith in humanity and you call that nothing much?"

August: "I only had a little bit left, anyway."

Ringmaster: "August, what's your job in La Paloma Circus?"

August: "I'm Dumb August, the clown."

Ringmaster: "And what about me?"

August: "You're the ringmaster."

Ringmaster: "And what's the difference between Dumb August and the ringmaster?"

August: "The same as the difference between coconuts and hazelnuts?"

Ringmaster: "And what would that be?"

August: "They're both nuts."

Ringmaster: "I see you can't do it, you're too dumb to figure out the difference between a ringmaster and a Dumb August."

August: "I don't like figs any more than I like Wagner."

Ringmaster: "What in the world do figs have to do with Wagner?"

August: "I don't like either of them, isn't that enough? I bet you like *Der Freischütz*! But I don't, see?"

Ringmaster: "But August, *Der Freischütz* is by Weber, not Wagner."

August: "So, he didn't even write *Der Freischütz*. What about *Die Zauberflöte*? Didn't he write that, either?"

Ringmaster: "That's by Mozart, August."

August: "At least he was an Austrian."

Ringmaster: "So today he'd be a German."

August: "Right, they're all nuts."

Ringmaster: "That's enough politics, August. The weather . . ."

August: " . . . is getting better and better."

Ringmaster: "Finally we agree on something, August. I was walking by the lake today . . ."

August: "The water's rising higher and higher." August raised his hand higher and higher, like giving the Hitler salute.

August: "It's almost up to our necks already."

Ringmaster: "It's like that every spring. The snow's melting."

August: "Well, as an Austrian—"

Ringmaster: "As a former Austrian."

August: "Right. As a former Austrian, I must protest your trying to make the snow melt responsible for the level of Lake Constance getting higher and higher! All you had to do was bend down and dip your hand into that water rising higher and higher to feel at once that it's Austrian tears of joy making Lake Constance rise higher and higher and still higher, our tears of joy at rejoining the Reich. Shake a leg, Herr Director, romance calls, the Führer needs more soldiers."

Ringmaster: "Agreed, August, I'm with you a hundred percent."

August: "A hundred and two, Herr Director. In the meantime we can't accept anything under a hundred and two."

The ringmaster: "Count me in!"

He goes to embrace August, but August pushes him away and cries, "Röhm's turning over in his grave!" Protecting his behind with both hands, August waddles out of the ring. Fanfare, applause.

Johann saw that Herr Brugger and his wife weren't clapping. Herr Brugger's right hand was playing piano on the back of his left hand. His wife waited to see if he would clap.

Then the ringmaster presented four ponies that could count and dance and stand on their hind legs. One pony could even cry when the ringmaster told him a sad story. And another could laugh when the ringmaster told him a pony joke. The ringmaster introduced the Wiener family as the high point of the program. Anita's father came leaping into the ring, flanked by his two cart-wheeling children. Drum roll, furious glissandos on the accordion, the trumpet blew a charge. Anita and her brother followed their father up the white pole in the center of the ring. They shinnied up so fast that everyone clapped in astonishment.

All three were wearing loose costumes of pink silk. Half-way up, brother and sister undid purple belts and fastened them around the pole. The belts allowed them to lean out away from the pole and act as counterweights to their father, whose tricks overhead made the pole bend perilously. But there were other tricks in which they clung to each other and wheeled around it, the father holding on to the pole, the son to the father, Anita to her brother. She flew in a circle, far out from the pole. Their silk pants and tunics fluttered. The audience clapped and clapped. Johann clapped loudest and longest. "All without a net!" cried Adolf. As the three of them climbed back down to the ring at last, the applause swelled to a roar.

They had barely exited, walking backwards and bowing, when the music took an East Indian turn. Anita's mother was bowing an instrument with many strings. Dumb August blew on a flute. The ringmaster cracked his whip and called, "Vishnu, Vishnu, Vishnu, Vishnu," turning in a different direction each time. With the final "Vishnu," he turned toward the blooming apple trees. And out from under them, the water buffalo emerged. "Vishnu," called out the ring-master, now in a different tone of voice. "Vishnu in person, from whose navel the lotus grows and blossoms, the blossom in which Devi sits enthroned, the goddess of all gods, who will now dance Baratanatyam and with all her many arms trick Shiva, the god of Death." The music fluttered up like a flock of tropical birds. Anita, Indian from head to toe, dancing in the white blossom. The black buffalo carried the image in a circle. Anita had more than two arms, and all her arms were moving. But Johann could tell which were the real ones and saw that black hair grew in Anita's armpits. The buffalo circled the ring twice. The music became more and more Indian. The buffalo stopped. Anita stood up, jumped off, and collapsed in the sawdust of the ring in a small heap of all those arms. Only when the buffalo came and stood in front of her did her head emerge. Anita rose and held out both her hands to it. It licked them in fervent devotion. The music swelled to a crescendo. People applauded. Johann had a feeling of bliss. Then the buffalo knelt down on its forelegs, inviting Anita Devi to take a seat between its broad, spreading horns. Which she did. Vishnu stood up and, to triumphal music, bore Anita Devi out into the darkness beyond the Gravenstein tree to which he had been tethered all day long. The audience clapped. Johann clapped as hard as he possibly could. He wanted to infect the others with his enthusiasm. *Bharatanatyam!* A word from his word-tree! He felt that he belonged to the circus now. Adolf clapped considerably less than Johann.

On the other side of the ring sat Herr and Frau Brugger, also in the front row. Herr Brugger hardly clapped at all. With one of his hands he patted the back of the other hand. Oh, Herr Brugger, thought Johann and felt a sort of sympathy for Herr Brugger. He wanted at least to draw Adolf over to his side, away from his father. Over to Johann, to Johann's father. As soon as the ringmaster said "India," Johann thought of his father, especially at the word *Bharatanatyam.* When his father was no longer able to hold a book himself, Johann had read to him. Anselm, the three-year-old, would be put in bed next to his father. Johann always read until both of them—Anselm and Father—fell asleep. Rabindranath Tagore was the poet whose works Johann had to read. The chapters were called "The Counsel of the Heavenly Ones," "The Two Animals," "The Path of the Sun," "The Flower Greeting," "The Tale of a Child's Soul," "The Sacrifice of Song," "The Reconciliation," "The Shining Track." He probably would have found it boring to read. But not to read aloud. *Rabindra, however, sang movingly in an ancient, sacred language from the Upanishads. And what he sang brings a blessing—brings a blessing.* When the buffalo licked Anita's hands, how could he help but think of Rabindra's great epiphany!

One day the lad was sitting on the doorstep of his father's house, looking out. And he saw a zebu and a donkey standing side by side. The zebu, however, was tenderly licking the donkey's coat. Just as the two beasts—so foreign to each other and with completely different natures—sensed their common, eternal oneness beyond everything that divided them, so too the boy suddenly beheld the inner connection of the whole world and all its creatures. And permeated with universal feeling, he experienced the essence of love, of not being able to do anything but love, and he spoke: I must love, must love.

Johann always went upstairs to his father after school, even before he had something to eat, and when he asked him how he was, his father said, "Come, read me the tenth song of the *Bhagavad Gita*." And then whenever Johann read *I am the active element in the realm of powers / The sunlight in the heavenly choir of suns . . .* he had the feeling he was growing as he read. In December, his father's favorite had been the "Night Song." "Come, read me the 'Night Song' from *Zarathustra* again," he would often say in December. In fact, the "Night Song" was Johann's favorite to read aloud. When he read it, he had the feeling he was singing. When he read, *It is night: now all the gushing fountains speak more loudly. And my soul, too, is a gushing fountain*, he had the feeling his voice was singing all by itself. Every time he read his father the "Night Song," his father said Johann's favorite sentence: "You're amazing, Johann." Now, as Vishnu carried the many-armed Devi around the ring, Johann felt that through his father, he was closer to Anita Devi than anyone else in the audience. *I must love, must love.*

When it was over, everyone who had performed paraded around the ring to a blaring march, led by the ringmaster. The ringmaster made a final appeal to the audience to recommend La Paloma Circus to their friends if they had enjoyed it. Then the spotlight over the ring went out and the house lights came up.

Adolf whispered to Johann that they had to get rid of the others first, and he'd be right back. Then he said out loud, "So long, got to rush off," and ran down the village street. The others ran after him. Johann walked the short distance to the terrace, climbed the steps that led up to it, walked across the terrace to the trellised pears, and bent the slender stems apart. The lights over the benches were now off as well, but lights were burning in all the trailers. He knew which trailer Anita was in. But what good did that do him? He might have stood there all night if Adolf hadn't come back. Right away, he asked, "Which trailer does she live in?"

Johann said, "In the one under the Prince Ludwig tree." He had played and fought with Adolf under these same trees at every season of the year, so he knew which apples grew on which trees.

"Then we have to approach from below," said Adolf, and ran down the terrace steps to the street and down the street to the path below the orchard. Johann simply ran after Adolf. Adolf ran far enough along the path so the light from the street couldn't reach them anymore, and then clambered over the high fence. Johann climbed after him, and Adolf and Johann both jumped down into the orchard, landing at almost the same time. Adolf apparently knew exactly where the compost pile was and bypassed it. Then he whispered to Johann, "The Welschisner tree." That was the tree closest to the Prince Ludwig tree. When they reached the tree's thick trunk, Adolf whispered, "Boost."

Johann put his back to the trunk, interlaced his fingers, leaned back against the trunk, and whispered, "Ready." Adolf placed one foot in Johann's hands, climbed onto his shoulders, and pulled himself up into the branches. Then he slid out along the biggest branch that extended toward the trailer. He took no further notice of Johann. Johann stared at the wide, low window of Anita's trailer. It was bright, but a curtain was pulled across it from the inside. He looked up at Adolf, who had now stood up on the branch, steadying himself on thinner branches, and was poking his head up above the foliage. And then he whistled. Not the loud four-finger whistle, but the one with the index finger and thumb of one hand. It wasn't such a sharp whistle. Instead, it slowly fell and got softer and then rose again and got louder. Johann thought it was shocking to draw attention to yourself like that. But Adolf didn't stop making the tone that fell and got soft and rose and got loud. Johann hissed, "Stop that!" But Adolf didn't hear or didn't want to hear. Johann wondered if he should take a fallen branch and poke Adolf to make him stop whistling. Then the door of Anita's trailer opened. Anita stood in the doorway, her bathrobe yellow, her turban red. Adolf stopped then. As soon as the door opened, Johann had jumped behind the thick trunk. Someone inside must have told Anita to close the door. She stepped back, the door closed, and Adolf clambered down and said, "That was her." It sounded like he had accomplished everything he wanted.

They climbed back over the fence onto the path, ran out into the street, called, "So long!" to each other, and took off in opposite directions, Adolf down the street and Johann up the street.

A babble of voices from the inn told him that the regulars' table was more than full. The chairs would be crowded around the table in a big circle. Johann went up to his room, stretched out on the bed, and let himself be licked by Tell, who'd been waiting for him. Why had Adolf run away so fast? So long! and he was gone. Johann just barely had enough time to say So long! himself. They could have talked everything over. That's the way it had always been with them, hadn't it? In the evening, even when it got quite late, they would never part ways so abruptly. Adolf would walk Johann home, but they weren't ready to split up yet. They simply hadn't finished discussing the most important thing, and so Johann would walk back down the village street with Adolf, turn right at the linden tree, and then, fifty yards farther on, left at the entrance to the Bruggers' house, where they stood on the steps talking, and while still talking, they would just naturally set off again, back up the street to the terrace steps. And if at that point Johann's mother or Adolf's from the Bruggers' house hadn't turned up to put an end to the two of them walking back and forth, they would still be far from finished. Perhaps would never be finished. There was always so much that was important. And now nothing but, So long, So long, and gone.

Johann was unable to read or fall asleep. He tiptoed into the lavatory and opened the window. Fortunately, it was large and he could lean out and gaze down on the three trailers where lights were still burning. Since at this time of year they weren't renting out rooms yet and his mother was still busy in the restaurant and Josef was still at the ski hut and his father dead, no one needed to use the lavatory. Johann could lean out the window until the lights had gone out in all three trailers. Then he went back to Tell and finally went to bed himself.

CHAPTER FOUR

The First Time

JOHANN NEVER READ WHILE SPOONING up his breakfast of bread in warm milk. At all other meals, he read. It wasn't like at the Bruggers' or other families where everyone ate together. In Johann's family, everyone ate when they had time. If Johann was alone in the kitchen with the Princess or Mina, he couldn't read, either. Sometimes he did prop a book in front of his plate, but he was always much too distracted by the Princess or Mina to be able to read. Mina preoccupied him even more than the Princess. Every time he looks up, Mina looks at him. She has a small face framed by curly reddish hair, pulled back and tied at the nape of her neck. And her eyes are intensely blue. Mina is certainly the nicest person who ever lived. In the beginning, when he was little, it was she who had gotten Johann dressed and undressed. She even bathed him, in fact. He would stand in the sink while she rubbed the washcloth up and down his body. But before washing him, she always had to shoo away the Princess. "You have to watch out, or she'll stare some part right off of you," she always said. Five years ago at Christmas, she had repaired that awful burn hole in his Norwegian pullover. "That's invisible mending as only Mina can do it," said Mother when she saw it. Which meant that she herself could not have darned that hideous hole in a way that you wouldn't even notice the catastrophe unless you knew it was there. And when Johann had outgrown the sweater, Mina had knitted extensions to the sleeves so it fit him again. Since Johann preferred not to wear a piece of clothing that was important to him in order to protect it, his pullover had stayed so beautiful that Johann still felt like the Silver Knight when he wore it. The only time the pullover didn't pass muster was when he was with Anita.

Sometimes Mina simply came around the big stove, bent down to him, and ran her hand two or three times over Johann's hair, but without doing the slightest damage to his haircut. Quite the contrary: Johann had the feeling that his haircut had been blessed. Since Luise had begun working there, Johann had become aware of the possibility that there was another person with a claim to the title of nicest person that ever lived: Luise from the South Tyrol. Johann knew he would defend Luise against any approach that aimed at more than just ordering a beer. Mina would be leaving soon. There was no one he could tell that, if it wasn't for Luise, Mina's leaving would be unbearable. Mina had given notice for December 31st and had planned to get married in January. Alfred had already leased a farm in Höhenreute and was waiting for her, and Johann had already typed up her letter of reference on the Continental: *She has always performed the tasks assigned to her to our complete satisfaction. Fräulein Mina is leaving us voluntarily.* Johann had the feeling that this reference was a poor reflection of Mina's importance. Mother had taken what she dictated to him from references that had been written for her, years ago.

Then when Mina saw how poorly Father was doing, she decided to stay into the new year. And when Father died on January 3rd, she said, "I can't leave now." Her mother had come from Niedersonthofen to take over all the jobs Johann's mother was, for now, incapable of doing. Mina held little Anselm on her arm as Father's coffin was carried out of the office. She put off her departure until Easter. Yet now it was just before Low Sunday, and she was still standing at the stove. "I'll leave at Pentecost," she said, "or Alfred's going to go to the dogs." Mina spoke the way they do in the upper Allgäu: she said *dong* for *getan* and *long* for *gelassen.*

Today when Johann looked up and saw Mina looking at him, she didn't come around the stove. "Awful news, just awful, awful," she said. In the middle of the night, they'd had to run for the doctor.

August from the circus had been found lying in front of his trailer with his hands and feet tied, and beaten black and blue. Mina said they'd hung a sign around his neck that said "Compliments of the 99.7%." It was uncertain whether August would be able to perform today. If Herr Seehahn and Semper's Fritz hadn't found him, and if Semper's Fritz hadn't rung the doctor out of bed right away, Dumb August would have choked on his own blood.

Johann recalled Wolfgang Landsmann and his balloon-tire bicycle and how Edi Fürst had thrown it into the ditch. Then Wolfgang had raised his right arm and looked under it, back at his comrades. He thought about that muster again and again. Edi, at the time still a troop leader in the Jungvolk, pulls out his roster, moistens his pencil tip, and crosses out Wolfgang Landsmann. A song two, three, four, *Steig ich den Berg hinan, das macht mir Freude.* Josef had once told Johann that Edi was probably the only troop leader in the entire squadron who came to every muster in jackboots. Edi Fürst was a bit on the short side. Yet even though he really wasn't tall, he beat them all at high jump, to say nothing of horizontal bar. The face he made when he landed on the mat after performing a giant flyaway and quickly snapped to attention was exactly the same face that he made when he stood before his troop in high boots. When he stood before the troop with that face, everyone could see there was nothing more important than the muster taking place at that moment. Nothing in the whole world. Nobody found anything to grin about then.

Johann would have liked to skip Mass. In the street, he stopped and looked over toward the trailers, where nothing was stirring. The buffalo stood motionless beneath the Gravenstein tree. The ponies lay on the straw under the projecting roof of the carriage house. The trailer doors were shut. Johann walked into the village as slowly as humanly possible. But nothing happened that would have caused him to stop, much less turn around. Since today he'd forgone his hair grease—and that also meant forgoing any kind of coiffure, even one that looked like a crown—he could start running as soon as he passed the linden tree, where all the streets converged.

As he knelt down in the pew next to Adolf, Adolf whispered to him, "They gave it to August last night." Right after this piece of news came a gesture that meant that what he said was for Johann's ears only. Nobody else must hear it. When Mina told him what happened last night, Johann had thought at once of Herr Brugger. When Herr Brugger entered the restaurant with the ivory toothpick in his mouth, Johann always felt like something was going to happen. Mind you, when Herr Brugger led cows and calves or pigs out of his trailer and into their stalls, he was a different person. He sang a quiet *ho-ho-ho-hoh* to the animals and guided them with caressing hands. And the animals followed him without resistance. But when he emerged from his house in his hunting togs with a rifle over his shoulder and Treff at his side, then the sun flashed from his gun barrel even when it wasn't sunny. Johann and Adolf would stop playing, greet the hunter, and watch while he got into his Mercedes and turned on the ignition. The truck that Father had acquired a year before his death had to be cranked, and if he didn't do it right, the crank jumped back and smacked Father if he hadn't pulled his hands away fast enough, hit him so hard that he cried out in pain and had to rub his hands together for a while before he could try cranking the truck again. But Herr Brugger just got into his car, pressed a button, and the motor started up with a harsh gurgle. On special days, Herr Brugger marched through the village at the head of his column of SA. Since an accident a few New Years back, when his car had gone into a skid on glare ice, slid into the Oeschbach, and turned over, he had a bad hip. To tell the truth, he limped. But when he marched along at the head of the SA, he compensated for his limp by a jerking and twitching you weren't supposed to notice. Adolf said that if anybody told his father he should use a cane, his father got hopping mad. Johann avoided Herr Brugger whenever he could. But if Herr Brugger caught sight of him before Johann was able to disappear around the corner of the house, he went right straight to Johann's mother and complained that Johann had made himself scarce so he wouldn't have to greet him, Herr Brugger. Johann had never before heard the expression "made himself scarce," but he understood right away what it meant. And then Mother gave Johann a dressing-down in front of Herr Brugger. She really read him the riot act. Wasn't he ashamed to be sneaking around a corner just to avoid saying hello to Herr Brugger? She was at her wits' end with him. Your own children let you down. Herr Brugger let Mother finish her whiny, despairing scolding, then he removed the toothpick from the corner of his mouth and said to Johann, "You listen up now, laddie boy." Fortunately, Mother didn't use the words of the person who had lodged a complaint when she scolded him. She never said Make yourself scarce, thank goodness. Johann could only feel comfortable at Adolf's house when he knew Herr Brugger was on the road selling livestock, hunting, or commanding the SA or the National Socialist Automotive Corps. Of all the mothers of his schoolmates, Frau Brugger was the friendliest. You couldn't go to the Bruggers' without her giving you something. Of course, Johann knew that it wasn't Herr Brugger who had beaten up August from the circus. But he knew very well that Herr Brugger knew who had. Something made him whisper to Adolf, "Who did it?" Adolf rebuked him sharply with a condescending glance while repeatedly tapping his index finger against his temple. Which meant: Are you crazy? That's top, top secret! Anyone who asks a question like that is already a little bit like the one they had to beat up at night. So stop asking such stupid questions!

When Mass was over, the first thing Johann had to do was go to the grave again, sprinkle it with holy water, and murmur: Lord, give him eternal peace, may eternal light shine upon him, Lord, let him rest in peace, Amen. Out by the cemetery gates stood his teacher, surrounded by all the others. The teacher led the way to school. Apparently he had already told the others why they had to hurry off to school, despite its being Easter vacation. They sat down at their desks just like on a regular school day. The teacher said it was his duty to warn the boys and young ladies (the teacher never called them lads, but always boys, and the girls young ladies) of the dangers that threatened the German people from all sides and would continue to threaten them as long as there were complacent elements who gave aid and comfort to the enemies of the

German people. He talked about Dumb August, first without naming him and then, without actually saying the words, about their First Communion. Johann had to admit to himself that he had underestimated Dumb August. He hadn't realized how dangerous he was. But still, he was sorry they'd beaten up the Little Giant with his head of curls. All they would've had to do was tell that curly-head he mustn't make jokes that could be used by the enemies of the German people. The teacher called First Communion an old custom that would sooner or later be replaced by even older customs. Before we were Christian, we had a different religion. Now, he just wanted to remind them that a German boy and a German young lady had no need of confession to be pure. School would begin again on Monday, and then he would tell the children more about how they could stay clean by doing their duty. Then they could dispense with rattling off their prayers on bended knee. In the meantime, when they got home, the first communicants should read what it said in the parish magazine about Widukind. Then they would know how little the truth was worth to the church. The heathen Duke Widukind makes a pact with the devil because he intends to murder Karl, the Christian kaiser. Sneaks into the kaiser's camp— on Christmas Day, of course. Kaiser Karl is kneeling unarmed at the altar, devoutly praying to the Christian God. According to the parish magazine, the wild Saxon duke suddenly goes strangely soft. Walks up to the kaiser, confesses his evil plan, and at once the baby Jesus rises from the white Host in the priest's hand like a miraculous rose on a cold winter night. Widukind gets himself baptized, and the devil forsakes Germany for good. The first communicants should please enlighten their parents and tell them what he, their teacher, had told them about Widukind and Karl, so that their parents would know what to think of the parish magazine.

As they went home, not a single boy or girl said anything about what the teacher had told them, though they usually made fun of everything he said. For a while they walked up the street as if the teacher was still there among them. Adolf wore a face that made him look like he was the teacher. Or the teacher's son. He was wearing that jacket again, the one with buttons up to the collar and a belt of the same material. It was impossible to simply talk to Adolf. Not until they encountered Crooked Hat did they start running and hooting as usual. Whenever this man had been shopping in the village, he walked his bicycle back home. He always wore a stiff hat on his head, and it was always askew. A tiny brim ran around the hat like a gutter. No one knew where he lived. When they called after him, "Crooked Hat!" he turned and lifted his hand to ward them off. He had little gold-rimmed glasses and an old-fashioned face. When Johann was by himself and encountered Crooked Hat, of course he didn't call him names. Johann would look him in the eye and say *Grüss Gott*. Crooked Hat always looked like he had to be careful not to fall with each step he took. And then, what a funny-looking rucksack he had. You couldn't buy a rucksack like that anywhere, so baggy and light-colored—almost white. Crooked Hat must have made it himself. That rucksack was never full, not even when Crooked Hat was on his way home. The whitish thing always just hung there limply against his back. His purchases were in the basket clipped to his bike rack. As soon as the girls sang out, "Heads up, here comes Crooked Hat!" the boys took each other by the hand and formed a chain across the road. Crooked Hat pushed his bike through the girls, came toward the chain of boys, and stopped right in front of Adolf and Johann, who were in the middle of the chain. No one said a word. His front wheel was almost under Adolf's and Johann's hands. Johann could feel the pressure of Adolf's hand. He returned it, which meant: You can count on me. I'm not giving in. He won't get past me. Crooked Hat kept looking straight ahead, even after he'd come to a stop. Johann thought that Crooked Hat stood there like an animal. Like an animal that doesn't know what to do next. Then he raised his face, and you could see his eyes, enormously magnified behind his thick lenses. Then he opened his mouth, and they heard him say, not loudly, but quietly, "Thank you very much." And he took his bicycle, carried it into the field, and, once in the field, around the end of the chain of boys. He set it down carefully on the road and set off again, still walking it. Adolf said, "We should've reset the chain along the edge of the road so

Crooked Hat couldn't get back up onto it." Everyone agreed. Nobody wanted to take responsibility for the mistake they had all made.

Johann recalled a black cat with yellow eyes that had once strayed into the lower carriage house. Johann had closed the door. He wanted to pet the cat, but she got away from him. So he had to chase her. He caught her and suddenly threw her into the air, so high into the air that she hit one of the wooden ceiling beams. And he chased her again, caught her again, threw her against the ceiling again. Each time he threw the cat against one of the beams, she yowled. And each time, it was more difficult to get his hands on her again. She scratched and bit. Johann's hands were bleeding, and yellow mucus was dripping from the cat's eyes. When the cat fled onto a beam where Johann couldn't reach her anymore, he gave it up, opened the door, waited outside for a while, and then lost interest in the cat and went to join the other boys in the village. But he had no desire to tell Adolf or Ludwig or Paul or Guido or Berni or Helmut One or Helmut Two what had just happened. He hadn't seen the cat give its dying shudder. That was an Adolf-word for the last twitch, and not just of cats. Adolf claimed that women did it, too, when a man was lying on top of them. Johann didn't forget that the day he had chased the cat had been a Friday.

Adolf announced that the Bruggers were going to drive Anita to church tomorrow. Adolf was saying something that his father had told him. You could tell from the way it sounded. Johann thought about how Herr Brugger was often the first guest at the regulars' table on Sunday morning and—until Schlegel the builder, Schmitt the tinsmith, and his apprentice Semper's Fritz arrived—the only one. Herr Brugger would then tell Johann's mother and Johann, who had been to early Mass, that he didn't need the Church. The forest was his church, where he was closest to his Lord. He always said: my Lord. Mother always said: our Lord.

Adolf said that Anita's parents could walk with Johann if they wanted to go to church, since Johann's mother would have to be at the stove all day. His father had already reserved a table for the celebration.

A table for eight: Adolf's father, his mother, his godparents, Anita and her parents, and Adolf.

Johann had planned to take Adolf along. Maybe they could help the circus people haul hay, or curry and water the ponies. But when he heard that Anita was to ride in the Bruggers' car on Sunday, which was tomorrow, he had to come up with a white lie. His brother was coming home with a torn ligament, he said, and he had to pick him up from the train and carry his skis and rucksack. And then he ran home, fetched Tell, and took him to the carriage house. There stood the green Ford truck in which Father, toward the end, had gone on his salesman's rounds because he didn't want to be a restaurateur. Fruit, shortenings, wood, and coal. But neither Niklaus nor Johann's father could manage to lift a hundredweight sack from the scale onto the bed of the truck. Father was too sick, Niklaus too old. Josef could manage it in the meantime. Johann could almost do it. Johann, in the meantime, was able to carry the hundredweight sacks from the handcart—which they were again using to transport coal to customers since Father's death—into people's basements or to the basement window and empty them just as well as Josef. On level ground or downhill, no problem. Only when the way was up several or many steps was he not quite able to do it yet. Niklaus could fill the sacks by himself, since they had acquired a tipping scale and stiff coco fiber sacks. When Josef and Johann got home from school and had eaten something, they loaded the sacks onto the handcart, which could hold a good ten hundredweights of briquettes or twelve hundredweights of hard coal. Since they had just purchased twenty-five new coco fiber sacks, Niklaus could always fill twenty-five hundredweights in the morning while Josef and Johann were at school. Then, while they made the deliveries, he could fill another ten or twelve hundredweights. And so between noon and evening they could deliver between eighty and a hundred hundredweights to their customers. Since Father had died and his truck stood idle among the piles of coal in the carriage house, they used Herr Waibel's horses and wagon to supply their larger customers directly from the coal cars, as they had in the past.

Johann got into the Ford with Tell. The car was going to be picked up soon. Xaver Noll from Hengnau had already paid for it and was going to modify it for his own purposes. Xaver Noll was a farmer who they said could run circles around any engineer.

Johann had already gotten hit by the crank when it jumped back; since then, he hadn't dared to try cranking it again.

Actually, Johann was sitting in the Ford, waiting for Anita to come and sit beside him. But since he had shut the carriage house door from inside, how could she know he was sitting there? And even if she had known, it would hardly occur to her to sit in a coal truck. Nevertheless, Johann sat and waited for the door to open and Anita to come and squeeze between the pile of coal and the truck and get in beside him. The carriage house door did open, but it was Niklaus. He started to fill sacks with coal. How was Johann going to get out of here without Niklaus seeing him? Although Niklaus didn't hear so well anymore, you could never tell with someone who was hard of hearing what they heard and what they didn't. The coal that Niklaus shoveled onto the tipping scale, weighed, and slid into the sack below made a pretty loud noise. He could take advantage of that to slip out behind Niklaus. If Niklaus discovered Johann there, he would have to tell him what he was doing sitting in the truck on a Saturday morning. Johann couldn't think of a white lie. Just sitting behind the wheel? Practicing switching gears! That was it. Johann started to practice coordinating the clutch with the gearshift. It felt good the way the gears got along with each other up there in the transmission, far away from Johann, just because with a foot and a hand he was operating a clutch and a gearshift lever. And when he did it right, he could feel how smoothly the gears meshed in the transmission.

Suddenly, Tell jumped up and started barking. Johann got out of the truck at once and squeezed out between the coal and the side of the vehicle, shooing Tell ahead of him. Niklaus was not surprised at all to see Johann emerging from the depths of the carriage house. Niklaus recited the list of people they needed to make deliveries to that afternoon: Frau Haensel, Fräulein Hoppe-Seyler, Herr von Lützow, and Frau von Molkenbuer. All summer people, small accounts, people you could only deliver three or four hundredweights to at a time because they had no space for more. True, Fräulein Hoppe-Seyler got seven hundredweights. That wasn't so bad. But Frau Haensel only got three. You had to carry them up to the second floor and through the whole apartment onto a covered balcony and empty them into a bin. She always laid a path of newspapers through her apartment so not a speck of dust could fall on her carpet. Herr von Lützow had a little bin next to his stove that held only a single hundredweight. Also on the second floor. At least Frau von Molkenbuer had room for eight hundredweights in her attic. Plus you didn't have to carry the sacks all the way up there. Her apartment was in a renovated barn, and under the gable there was still a winch for raising bales of hay. With it, you could pull up one sack after another. On the other hand, her house was way out in Nonnenhorn. But today was Saturday, Johann's Nonnenhorn day. Every Saturday at the canon's house, he could exchange the Karl May novel he had just finished for a new one. The canon in Wasserburg had only boring books with titles like *When I Was Still a Backwoods Farmer Boy*, all bound in the same boring paper bindings. The books in school had titles like *Barrage against Germany*, *The Command of Conscience*, and *Army behind Barbed Wire*. For Johann, the war books were even more boring than the stories of backwoods farmers.

So now he knew he would have to change his clothes. They would put three hundredweights for Frau Haensel into five sacks and the hundredweight for Herr von Lützow into two sacks. There were too many stairs. If Josef found out, he would make fun of them. But Johann didn't want to be forced to turn back when he was halfway up the stairs. He knew it wouldn't be long before he would be able to carry any hundredweight sack into any attic. Josef couldn't do it till he was thirteen, either. And when Johann was thirteen, he'd be able to do it, too. At Fräulein Hoppe-Seyler's house, you could push the handcart between the huge trees right up to the cellar window and dump the sacks in. But only if you did it *hofele-hofele*.

So, the first load to Frau Haensel and Fräulein Hoppe-Seyler, and the second to Herr von Lützow and Frau von Molkenbuer, whose first name was Ereolina. Johann knew that from typing up the bills. Josef refused to do bookkeeping. And so all the paperwork, from discharging the waybills after the coal cars had been shoveled empty to billing the customers, fell to Johann. He always admired the way Josef would declare that bookkeeping was out of the question for him! Josef was an artist. And bookkeeping was out of the question for an artist. Until last winter, Father had taken care of all of the paperwork. His handwriting was admired even by people like Herr Brugger. But then, as Father became more and more worn out and you couldn't expect Josef to do the bookkeeping, it was natural that Johann had taken over the purchase ledger, the billing, and the correspondence with the tax office and with the banks. Of course, Mother took care of placing the orders and paying the bills. That had always been her job. But it was Johann who wrote everything down. It had always been fun to sit at Father's desk, try out the rubber stamp, pound away on the Continental, or even dip one of Father's expensive fountain pens into the inkwell and then imitate Father's extravagant handwriting on the back of some envelope. He had always been attracted even by the inkwell, which was inserted into a little glass cube and closed with a domed lid of silver leaves. To say nothing of the fact that the telephone stood on the desk. Their number was 663. Which meant, Johann thought, that they had the six hundred and sixty-third telephone in the Lindau exchange. Only Johann was allowed to turn the wheels on the rubber stamp that changed the day and the month. The weaker his father became, the more exclusive was the control Johann gained over the highboy. Mother and Joseph were not interested in this unfathomable piece of furniture with more secret compartments than it had drawers. Since Father's death, Johann had been discovering more and more of them. Inside were father's report cards from the Royal Bavarian Middle School in Lindau and little notebooks filled with his beautiful penmanship. But what they said was not so interesting to Johann. It reminded him of the things his father had been talking about in the spare room that night when the folding partition from the main room was shoved aside so that everyone could hear what was happening in Berlin. Johann and his mother shared responsibility for the safe. How he loved it when the heavy steel door sank closed with that sighing sound. The safe looked like it belonged in a knight's castle. The two critical keyholes were concealed behind armorial shields that you slid aside.

Johann returned, dressed in his work clothes, and he and Niklaus heaved the ten sacks onto the bed of the handcart. Then they placed a wooden frame with exactly the same dimensions as the bed of the cart around the sacks to keep them from sliding off when they went downhill or around a curve. Since the level path across the courtyard and onto the street was blocked by the circus ring, they had to push the cart around behind the house and up the steep untarred entrance ramp that was full of ruts from the recent rain. The two of them couldn't manage it alone. Johann fetched his mother, Mina, the Princess, and Luise. All together, they were able to do it. And then: around the side of the house and hell-for-leather down the Dorfstrasse, so that Niklaus struggled to keep up. Johann didn't brake or wait for Niklaus until he knew that Anita would no longer be able to see him if she came out of her trailer. Already, while loading, he kept glancing over to the trailers. He just didn't want Anita to see him this way, in his old coalman's jacket with pants and boots to match. With the customers or anywhere in the village, he wasn't the least bit embarrassed to be seen in his coalman's clothes. Quite the contrary: the more coal dust on him, the more fun the work was. It was a pleasure to look in the mirror and see that everything in his face was black except his eyes and his teeth. But he didn't want Anita to see him that way. At five o'clock, they were supposed to be in church for their first confession. At four thirty, he would be standing at her trailer, freshly washed and waiting for her to come down the three wooden steps. If she came out at all. Perhaps the beating of Dumb August had changed everything in some utterly unimaginable way. Perhaps there would be no more circus. Perhaps when he came back from the first delivery, or from the second, they would have vanished completely.

Frau Haensel was a pianist from Munich. Her shiny clothes looked as if they were made of material that wasn't dyed but possessed some natural luminescence. And she always wore long pearl necklaces. Slung two or three times around her neck, they still hung down to her black patent leather belt. There was a concert grand in her living room. Frau Haensel was always quite pale, almost yellowish, and had dark spots on her face, hands, and arms. She wore several rings on her fingers and bracelets on both wrists. Johann knew from Josef that you had to show her how cautiously you walked along her newspaper trail so that not a speck of dust could trickle out of a sack. It was easy for Johann to carry the two hundredweights in three sacks, shuffling out to the balcony in slow motion for Frau Haensel's benefit. There he slowly emptied the sacks into the bin, turning and pulling them up carefully to let the coal slide out slowly. Frau Haensel praised him and tipped him fifty pfennigs. Downstairs, he passed the coin on to Niklaus, because he felt he was the boss and accepting a tip was beneath him.

The second load went to Nonnenhorn. For this trip, *Winnetou I* was carefully wrapped up and stowed among the sacks. Nonnenhorn meant up the steep ramp again, then straight out of the village toward Schäggs, from there downhill at a trot, taking advantage of the momentum that lasted almost to the doctor's house. By that point they were also almost at Herr von Lützow's.

Viktor Baron von Lützow lived on the second floor of the house at Hagenau's chicken farm and was one of Johann's favorite customers. When the singing society practiced on Thursday evenings and Johann lay in bed reading, he often heard the powerful song with the refrain, *That was Lützow's wild swashbuckling charge, that was Lützow's wild swashbuckling charge.* Then he thought of his baron, who more than any other customer praised you for bringing him his coal and emptying it carefully into the bin next to his tiny stove. The baron even patted you on the head. The baron was never without a scarf, one end hanging down in front and one behind, and always wore suits of coarse, speckled material with trousers that ended just below the knee and were cinched there with buckles. In the street, he always wore a billed cap of the same material as his suits. You never saw him other than all alone. Every time Johann greeted Herr von Lützow in the village, loudly and cheerily, he always said to himself, He's going to buy bouillon cubes and teabags. And maybe some biscuits. That was really all he ever bought. From Ludwig, Johann had heard that Herr von Lützow used to live in the colonies.

In Nonnenhorn, Niklaus had to wait by the empty cart while Johann trotted into town to exchange *Winnetou I* and then trotted back. Canon Krumbacher packed up *Winnetou II* in the same paper *Winnetou I* had been returned in. He asked Johann if he'd gotten all his sins assembled for first confession this afternoon. Johann tried to laugh and said, "There's not that many of them." Another lie. He was actually almost buried under a heavy mountain of sin. When he thought about how to put his sins in order so that he could mention each one in the right place during his first confession, he thought he must have done nothing but sin his whole life long. It was still unclear to him how he was going to get rid of this mountain of sins in a single confession. He mustn't stay in the confession box any longer than the others. Above all, what was contained in the priest's response to Johann's confession mustn't be any different from his response to the others. If only Canon Hebel would be taking the boys' confessions. Dr. Rottenkolber was well known as a stickler for detail. He had follow-up questions and wanted everything explained in more detail. That's why, since he had become their priest, many grown-ups from the village went to confession in Lindau, and some even as far away as Lochau or Bregenz.

The canon wished Johann a painless first confession and a blessed First Communion. He said it was a truly unique day when one was permitted to partake of the Body of our Lord for the first time. The canon's mother pressed some eucalyptus drops on Johann. The canon said, "Looks like this is your lucky day!" Johann really liked the Nonnenhorn canon. In everything he said, Johann had the feeling that he didn't really mean it that way. He spoke through his nose. It sounded like he was talking into a drinking glass. He talked only because one had to say something, after all. Whether the canon was talking about eucalyptus drops or the Body of our Lord, he would have preferred not to say anything. But since that wasn't possible, he had to say something. When he spoke, he always closed his eyes and didn't open them until he'd said the sentence he had to say. And when he spoke, his mouth looked like he was nauseated by something he'd eaten. For Luise, speaking was a risk, because she had grown up in a language that she had to handle with care, word by word, in order to use it in Wasserburg. But for Canon Krumbacher, speaking was an embarrassment because he would have preferred to remain silent. Even when the canon came to Wasserburg to preach, in every sentence of his sermon Johann could feel the pain it caused him to have to say so many sentences so loudly to so many people. Even in the pulpit, the canon closed his eyes at every sentence, and his lips curled as if he was nauseated. On the soccer pitch, the canon was a different person. After Wolfgang Landsmann was gone, he had taken over as their coach. And he also played with them. If he didn't see an opportunity soon enough, voices would shout from all sides, "Shoot, Canon! Shoot!"

Ever since Missionary Week, Johann had felt sorry for all the local preachers. Father Chrysostomus, the Franciscan from Messkirch— now that was a preacher! Chrysostomus's very first sermon had convinced Johann that he wanted to be a priest. For the entire week, he hadn't missed a single evening sermon. Their teacher had made it impossible for them to hear the morning sermons. But he couldn't keep them from going to the evening sermons. Johann had heard Father Chrysostomus three times. Fathers Gangolf and Barnabas also preached better than the local priests, but nobody could equal Chrysostomus for preaching. "When you hear his voice, do not harden your hearts!" That's how he began. When he spread his arms in his white habit, he looked like a huge bird. He must have been at least six foot six and had a wingspan of more than that. And a face straight off an altarpiece. And a voice that made the church seem for the first time not too large, but two small. The church was more than filled by his voice. Father Chrysostomus preached about boots and sandals. What would get you farther, what did the Earth prefer—boots or sandals? And he talked about the Kingdom of Heaven that the apostles had walked in their sandals. Later, when Josef passed the giant priest in the street, he'd been disappointed to see that he was wearing boots, not sandals.

Why Do the Heathen Rage? That had been his third sermon. Johann got tears in his eyes and could only stare up at that angel. If he wasn't an angel, then who was? Why do the heathen rage? That question, called out repeatedly, propelled the sermon forward. And everyone had sensed who was meant by the heathen. Why do the heathen rage? And why are their ideas worthless? He posed one ringing question after another. He was only repeating what the mouth of the psalmist had been crying out for three thousand years. And with the psalmist, he answered today as the psalmist reported the heathen answering so many years ago: "We are free! We need no God. We have no need for this alliance!" And the psalmist replied: "Eternal God can only laugh at that. But then God gets angry at that pack of fools. He's going to show the scoundrels what it means to deny Him."

Never before had it been so loud and then so quiet in the church.

But did Johann still want to be a priest? On the one hand, what more could he wish than to stand in the pulpit and preach to Anita? On the other hand, he was more attracted to singing than preaching. He could still hear his father saying: Four years old, and Schubert's "Jägerlied" down pat! You're amazing, Johann! Johann could tell that his father liked his singing as much as Josef's piano playing. And since Father played piano four hands more and more often with Josef, Johann was also asked to sing something his father could accompany. If Johann had known that his father was going to die soon, he wouldn't have refused to sing anything but "Von Apfelblüten einen Kranz." Since Father's death, he sang nothing but Lehár, "Von Apfelblüten einen Kranz" or "Dein ist mein ganzes Herz." Those were melodies he could lose himself in.

As Johann was thanking them for the eucalyptus drops, the canon remarked that Johann had come not just from Wasserburg to Nonnenhorn, but had walked all the way across Nonnenhorn, too. He'd give Johann a ride back to the handcart. "But be careful!" called his little old mother as the canon started up his DKW 500. Johann climbed onto the passenger seat, clutched his *Winnetou* in one hand, and held on tight with the other, and the two of them roared away down the long straight street. Johann knew that their roar could be heard all over Nonnenhorn. Riding in the car was nice, too, and the great-uncle they called Cousin sometimes drove really fast. But basically, it was just the car that was moving. On a motorcycle, you were moving yourself. Johann would always drive a motorcycle, just like the canon.

Through town, across the tracks, and out to Niklaus, who was sitting on the empty coco fiber sacks, and if Johann hadn't come, he would probably be sitting there to this day. What Niklaus did wasn't waiting. Whether sitting or standing, he did it as if nothing would ever change. Johann jumped off, and the canon roared off with as much style as he'd shown on the way there. Johann wanted to call after him: Canon, shoot! Johann gave his eucalyptus drops to Niklaus. He didn't like eucalyptus drops. Niklaus, who accepted everything that was given to him except socks, said, "God bless you."

At home, Josef was sitting at the long kitchen table, but on the stove side of the table, with his right leg resting on a chair and with a bandage instead of a shoe on his foot. Johann immediately envied Josef's tan. A tan like that was worth a torn ligament. Josef had just gotten home. His skis and rucksack were still at the station. Josef had limped over on crutches. Mother said Helmer's Hermine had just asked if Johann would still have time to take a hundredweight of briquettes to Zwerger's Anna today. Johann hated orders like that. Even if Josef hadn't had a torn ligament, it was always Johann who had to make these small deliveries. Usually it took a wrestling match to get him to do it. He wouldn't agree until he was pinned flat on his back with Josef kneeling on his upper arms. Today there was no match and no argument; Johann cursed and went to do it. When he heard himself cursing, he thought of this afternoon and his first confession: I have taken the Lord's name in vain, I have spoken the Lord's name in anger. Then he rode the cart down the Dorfstrasse at the speed they called hell-for-leather, swung the hundredweight sack into Fräulein Zwerger's coal bin (the usually freshly shaved fräulein lived on the ground floor),

plodded home, rinsed himself off with cold water from the hose in the
laundry room, lathered himself up, rinsed off once more, and while
he rinsed he sang in the highest register of "Von Apfelblüten einen
Kranz." Then he ran up to his room with only a towel around his waist.
Tell had, of course, been listening the whole time and complained that
Johann hadn't come back sooner. Johann checked the mirror to see if
there was still a bit of coal dust around his eyes. He thought he looked
more interesting with dark circles under his eyes. But it hadn't been
dusty enough today. No circles. Too bad.

After depositing the payments he'd collected in the safe, Johann
went into the kitchen. Mina insisted that for once they all eat together
today. "Not like cows out to pasture, every man for himself," she said
in her Allgäu accent. But then Mother had to get up and go out to the
dining room after all to greet Herr Hartstern the architect and Captain
Knorr and his wife. Mina scolded Luise for announcing every time
she put in an order who was having brisket of beef, who was having
schnitzel, and who was having a pair of bratwurst with mixed green
salad. Mina liked to scold Luise. Stubborn as a mule, she was. Couldn't
just do as she was told, had to think over if she should or even if she
would. She apparently had to prove that you couldn't just order her
around. She'd only do things she thought were right and proper and
necessary. Johann liked the way Luise would demur and then nod: Okay,
she'd do it. But only because she understood that it had to be done, and
by her. Johann thought it must be a typical South Tyrolean trait.

Josef told them about what had happened. He was the third one to
start down the mountain. The two ahead of him had broken their legs
when the snow suddenly gave way. But since it wasn't a big slope and
there was an opposing slope that followed it immediately, the snow mass
didn't develop into an avalanche. The only problem was how the nine
others would get the three injured boys back to the hut. Mother told
Luise to take a beer to Herr Deuerling over at the station. In the meantime, the stationmaster had brought Josef's rucksack and skis over to the
restaurant. Luise thought about it for a moment and then said, "Agreed."

"Aggrieved!" said the Princess.

"She'd rather have said no," said Mina when Luise had left the room. "Such an obstinate thing she is!"

Josef asked about the circus. Johann described it with muted enthusiasm. Josef had a girlfriend already, but everyone knew he was a lady-killer. That meant Josef could steal Anita from him without a second thought. So Johann only told him about what had happened to Dumb August. "Who did it?" asked Josef.

"Don't even ask," said Johann, attempting to convey some of the admonitory mood in which Adolf had reacted to the same question. But Josef said they absolutely had to get to the bottom of it. It was cowardly for a gang to ambush one guy in the dark, especially if he was smaller. Edi Fürst should look into it, Josef said.

Mother said, "Don't always get mixed up in things that aren't your business."

"I could say the same to you," said Josef. Mother had little Anselm on her hip, and he kicked his leg against Josef's foot. Josef cried out in pain. But then everyone thought it was good that the little tyke had seen that his mother needed defending against Josef's sass.

"Have you heard the latest from Helmer's Hermine?" asked Mina. "When Semper's Fritz got back to Herr Seehahn with the doctor, Herr Seehahn had Dumb August's head in his lap and was just saying to him, 'If you come with me, your Eminence, I'm placing you under arrest. If you take the back door, you've given me the slip.'"

Johann closed Tell in his room, went into the lavatory, and gazed down on the circus grounds.

The circus people were sitting at their table, talking and smoking. Herr Wiener in his short red-and-black checked jacket and Anita in her yellow robe and red turban. They were all looking at the Little Giant. He wasn't jumping up and sitting down, jumping up and sitting down today. He was sitting and not moving. His florid face was half covered in bandages, and one hand was wrapped in gauze. The way he was sitting on that bench today, no one would think to say that Dumb August *was* the circus. Dumb August had given aid and comfort to the enemies of the German people, their teacher had said. The teacher hadn't attended the performance. When he said that, it made Johann think of Versailles. The previous year they had performed *The Death of Schlageter* in the gymnasium, and Johann had played the part of the Red Death of Versailles. He had to wear a fire engine–red costume knitted by Huth's Jossi and say nasty lines about Germany, and then Frommknecht's Hermann, who got to play Schlageter, tied him to a stake and burned him with flames of silver paper. Germany awake! the others had cried in unison. Death to the specter of Versailles! The Germans would have to toil another hundred years, the others chanted, a hundred years of slavery for the shameful Treaty of Versailles. But the Führer had ripped up that shameful treaty. That's why the enemies of the German people didn't like him. And the Little Giant had given aid and comfort to those enemies. Unfortunately.

Johann put on a jacket Josef had outgrown. It was still a little too big for him. But he had to wear it now. It was from Mother's uncle, the one they called Cousin. Whenever Josef and Johann went to Allgäu to visit him, he picked them up from the train station in Wangen in his Ford and drove straight to Bredl's store to buy them clothes. This unmarried uncle whom all their relatives called Cousin was stout and had the handsome brown face of an Indian. He would seat himself in an armchair in the store, and Josef and Johann had to try everything on and walk back and forth in front of him and look at themselves in the big mirrors, and then choose. He always wanted them to choose between one suit with plus-fours or another, one gabardine coat or another. Then they drove like fury out to his house next to the cheese factory, which displayed the name Alpine Bee in big letters. In the evening, he would take his freshly-suited boys to one of the taverns in the neighborhood and stand everyone drinks while Josef and Johann had to sing for them. Johann sang melody and Josef harmony. Johann thought he had the more beautiful voice, but Josef was more musical. After all, Johann just had to sing the melody, while Josef improvised a second voice that went with it. Josef never sang the same harmony twice. There was always lots of applause in the tavern. Cousin Anselm didn't applaud, but on the way home in his Ford he praised the two singers. Sometimes they had to sing at his house, just for him. He had a piano on which Josef would accompany the two voices. The piano always sounded like it had fallen fast asleep since the last time Josef had woken it up. There was always a dark red velvet cloth with gold embroidery covering the keyboard.

In the morning they would drive to church in Cousin Anselm's car, and that was the whole visit. But he had already told them he would come the following year for Josef and Johann's confirmation. They were going to be confirmed together, because the bishop of Augsburg only got to Wasserburg every other year. Cousin Anselm had announced that he would buy each confirmand a gold wristwatch for the occasion. Their godfather and godmother were coming to their First Communion. The latter, the baker's wife from Kressbronn, had never been seen without a smile on her face, and their godfather, Mother's oldest brother who ran the family farm, was the biggest, strongest man in the world. Above his eyes, one thick, bushy, continuous eyebrow with no gap in the middle. Johann was going to walk through the village with this giant godfather and his smiling godmother. Anita's parents would probably choose to walk behind him and his godparents. Johann couldn't imagine his godmother and godfather conversing with Herr and Frau Wiener. Whenever his godfather came down from Kümmertsweiler and sat at the regulars' table, he would swing his head around exaggeratedly to look at the person who was speaking, and then the same with the next speaker. You could tell by watching him that what people talked about here on the lake didn't count for much up in Kümmertsweiler. He almost looked amused as he listened. He never said a word himself.

Johann experimented in front of the mirror with how many and which jacket buttons he should leave open.

Suddenly, he took the jacket off again. He took another jacket that Josef called a sport coat out of the closet. Josef had outgrown this jacket, too. Johann knew at once: this was the one. A very light-colored sport coat. The palest imaginable blue-gray with just a hint of purple. But with a pattern of nearly imperceptible reddish lines that formed a few large checks in the almost purple blue-gray. Johann had been waiting a long time to inherit this sport coat. It was still just a little too big for him, but he couldn't wait any longer. He tried it on in front of the mirror and couldn't get enough of his reflection. He grinned at himself a few times. He would confess that today. I have been vain. And not just confess it, but repent it, too, or else the priest could say *ego te absolvo* a hundred times, but without complete repentance there would be no forgiveness of his sins. That was his great fear. What if he couldn't manage to repent them completely? And without the intention of never again doing what one had done, there was no complete repentance. They said you had to pray for the strength to repent completely. The strength to say: Never again. On his own, he didn't have the strength for it. Some more hair oil for his hair? He thought he needed a bit more to give his hair a more reliably jaunty shape. Not as much as the other day, but at least a little more. Then he could confess his vanity right away. But what about repentance? Could he repent his vanity while still wearing a haircut like a crown?

At four thirty, he was standing at the foot of the three steps that led to Anita's trailer. The door opened, and Anita appeared, in light blue today, white stockings, and on top, a soft, light blue bow in her hair. As soon as she came down the three steps, he turned and walked before her, hoping she would follow. He felt hot. But he definitely could not puff as he usually did. He thought that his voice was getting better by the week. His voice, he thought, was the best thing he had. When he sang, he could lose himself in his voice. It was as if he weren't the person singing anymore. It was just his voice, which he found as beautiful as the voice of Karl Erb or Ludwig's father. Ludwig's father sang as beautifully as Karl Erb. When Ludwig had said that they—the Grübels—were related to Karl Erb, Johann had sensed that he should spend more time with Ludwig and less with Adolf. Ludwig said Karl Erb had told his father: Cousin Anton, if you'd had the training, you'd be my main competition today.

Even before they reached the Moosweg, they could see the two nuns forging ahead. They were basically always on their way from the hospital in Hege to the church. Because of the high grass, only their upper halves were visible, the huge, angular, white superstructures of their wimples floating above their darker habits. As if two black ships with white sails were running before the wind that rippled through the grass. The green of the meadow foamed with the purplish-white and yellow of cuckoo flowers and buttercups. Sing something, thought Johann. Best would be "Von Apfelblüten einen Kranz" or "Dein ist mein ganzes Herz," or something from the Agnus Dei last Sunday. Or "Wer hat dich du schöner Wald." If only she doesn't start talking. He can't say anything. He wouldn't be able to get a single word out.

She asked if he had seen Axel Munz. Had he seen what those scoundrels had done to him last night?

Johann was glad she had started talking about that. It was easier for him to answer that question than if she'd asked him something about confession. "Yes," he said. "It was a cowardly thing to do, all against one and in the dark, too, those cowards."

"And the way they ambushed him," said Anita. "They were actually lying in wait for him." She said that after the performance, Axel Munz had had a beer in the restaurant, and no one dared say a word to him. But when he was walking back to his trailer, alone, they jumped him, those scoundrels.

"Those cowards," Johann added.

Suddenly, she laughed and said, "I hope I don't forget any of my sins." Oh no, thought Johann. He remembered the hair in Anita's armpits. Was armpit hair something you had to confess? He thought it probably was. She said she was going to be driven to church in an automobile tomorrow.

"In a Mercedes," he said, and was immediately annoyed at himself for making propaganda for Adolf's car. She said she would have liked just as much to walk to church with Johann.

"You and I make a good pair, don't we?" she said and looked over at him and laughed. Johann could feel himself getting red.

"Anita, Anita," he said.

"Yes?" she said. All he'd meant to say was Anita, nothing more. And accidentally, he said her name twice. He knew that as often as he said Anita, he would always say Anita, Anita. He could have said Anita a hundred times in succession. Of course, he wasn't about to do that, but twice was all right, wasn't it?

"What about your parents?" he asked in order to say something.

"They don't have time to go to church," she said.

"My mother doesn't either," he said.

"That's right," she said. "The two of us could have done it by ourselves anyway." Since he didn't reply, she said, "Isn't that right?" Was she making fun of him? "That's a stylish jacket," she said.

He said, "Anita, Anita."

"Now let's wish each other a good confession," she said when they reached the cemetery.

"I hope so," said Johann, and had no idea what he was trying to say.

She walked to the door that led to the women's side while he went toward the side facing the lake. But before the gravestones blocked their view of each other, she looked over at him once more, raised both hands, made little fists, pumped them even higher, and smiled. Johann couldn't smile. He hurt all over from happiness. Birds were singing in the bushes and trees along the cemetery wall. They had never sung so loud before. It echoed as if he was already indoors. His steps crunched the gravel of the cemetery path so loudly it scratched his ears. He didn't stop at his father's grave. In the distance across the lake, Mount Säntis was closer than ever. As if Mount Säntis stood before a wall of gold. "Mount Säntis is a mother hen," his father had said once, "two million years old."

Once Johann was kneeling in the pew, it was time to start examining his conscience. But first he cast a quick glance across the aisle. Anita was already on her knees. So go ahead, examine your conscience. He called up the individual items. His numbered sins announced themselves. Then he summoned up complete repentance by the usual formula. It appeared. That is, it filled him up. He was almost surprised. Is it really complete repentance? he asked himself. Is your Never Again genuine? Do you think that's possible? You just have to resolve to do it, and that's sufficient, to beg for the grace that helps you not do it again. Just beg for grace. With grace, everything will be all right. But then it was already his turn. With numb feet, he walked the three steps from the pew to the confessional, heard the priest's breath, started breathing himself again, rattled off his confession, and there was no problem at all. But the priest's response was too loud. Everybody out there must have heard what he said. Yet earlier, when the priest had spoken to Adolf, Paul, Ludwig, Guido, Berni, Helmut, and Helmut, Johann hadn't been able to make out what he was saying. You couldn't understand him until he started in with the Latin, but what he said in Latin was the same for everyone.

Even after saying the penance he had been given, Johann stayed in the pew; not till he saw that Anita was getting up and leaving did he go outside himself. Not immediately after her, of course, but soon. Outside, most of the others were standing around between the castle and the Crown, boys and girls in separate groups, even more separated than usual. And they remained so as they set off toward the village. Guido asked if the others had gotten as much penance as he did and laughed. He was surely the only one who could ask that and laugh at the same time. But at least they could talk about it now. Of course, not so loudly that the girls walking up ahead could hear what they were talking about. It was reassuring to learn that everybody had been assigned three Our Fathers and three Hail Marys. It was a bit disappointing, too, or so Johann thought. Everyone doing the same penance! But he didn't say that. After all, they'd committed most of their sins together. Everybody had contributed a couple pfennigs so Edi could buy sauerkraut in Brodbeck's store. Frau Brodbeck had to leave the shop to get the sauerkraut out of the barrel, and Edi was able to pilfer four bars of chocolate before she came back. They flung the sauerkraut against the wall of Zürns' new house and divvied up and immediately ate the chocolate by the lake. And was it a sin to steal boxes of cheese from Müller's cheese shop when they turned out to be just shop-window dummies? They had run straight through the village and down to the bay, and only when they were deep into the reeds had they opened the boxes: no camembert, just wooden discs. Now Paul asked if the others had confessed to that. He hadn't. They were just fakes. None of them had confessed to that failed mission. And when the girls in front of them started giggling, the boys took it as a pretext to catch up with them. Adolf asked what they were giggling about. Trudl Schnell gave Leni a nudge so she would tell the boys. Day before yesterday, a rural constable had gone to Lattermann, the man who made hay-drying racks and props for fruit tree branches in Hege, saying that another complaint had been lodged against him for trespassing in a private woodlot, but before Herr Lattermann could answer, Frau Lattermann stepped in and told the officer she was surprised the police were looking into that since they'd already confessed it all in church.

Adolf asked—and Johann admired his courage—what penance the girls had gotten. Had they, like the boys, all been given the same penance? The girls looked at each other and decided they weren't going to tell. Ludwig said they probably didn't get any penance at all, their sins were so tiny. But Leni corrected him sharply by rattling off a saying. And in rattling it off, she demonstrated how well known it was and how unshakable the truth it expressed: "*Biechta und it biassa, isch wia Lade und it schiesse.*"

"Bingo," said Paul, and everybody laughed.

Adolf translated for Anita: "*Beichten und nicht büssen, ist wie Laden und nicht schiessen.*"—Confession without penance is like loading without shooting. Fortunately, Anita said she didn't need a translation to understand it. Today, not the single boy or girl accompanied them beyond the linden tree. That meant that Johann had about sixty-five yards alone with Anita. And it was clear that not a single boy or girl would come to the performance today, either. For one thing, the teacher had as much as forbidden it, and for another, it probably wasn't proper to go to the circus in a state of sanctified forgiveness, anyway. Since he thought it would flatter her, he said he would watch the performance again today, but from the window. He did not say, however, that it was the lavatory window. She had no idea that as he walked along next to her, he was constantly saying something other than what he meant. This talking one way and thinking another was like a hum inside of him. It felt grown up.

He asked if he could show her something after the performance. Yes, he could. Okay, he'd wait for her over at the station. "Good luck."

"Thanks," she called and ran off to her people.

He dashed up to his room, threw together the things he needed, then ran out of the village with Tell, past the fir-tree hedge, and then instead of going down past Schäggs', they went across the tracks and uphill onto the Lausbichel. To his right and left, apple and cherry trees were all in bloom. Just before he reached the top of the hill, he turned off into the high grass. Tell sprang ahead of him, as if he knew where Johann was headed. Johann put the things he had brought with him onto the grass at the base of a cherry tree and returned to the path.

He heard the sounds of Josef playing piano in the spare room. Josef had started playing even before Johann went to confession. Josef had to make up for his two pianoless weeks on the Nebelhorn. Johann was not as excited as Josef when it was time for Jutz the organist to come. Herr Jutz always came by bicycle from Kressbronn, leaned his bike against one of the two chestnut trees, locked it, and unclipped his pant legs, setting the material free to ripple at every step around the legs of the nonchalantly approaching organist and painter. A circle of black hair around a shiny brown glabrousness, Gypsy eyes, and a sharply angled nose: that was Jutz the artiste. To tell the truth, Herr Jutz was only interested in Josef, and Johann could tell.

When the circus music began, Josef stopped playing and hobbled down to the courtyard. Johann ran upstairs. Tell had to stay in his room. Johann went to the lavatory, opened both halves of the window, and leaned out. The same program as the day before, except that the Little Giant wasn't making any beautiful gestures.

There were only pitiful remnants of his drumming and bell-ringing. When he played Dumb August, people laughed because they thought that all the sticking plasters and bandages were part of the act. Today, he didn't shake himself to set the little bells ajingle in answer to the ringmaster. Today, the jingling was constant. But not loud. Maybe he couldn't shake himself anymore, but he could still tremble.

The ringmaster said in a loud voice, "August, August, what a sight you are!"

And August answered contritely, "I look like a man who's gotten to know his wife from a new angle."

"When did you first get to know your wife?" the ringmaster wanted to know.

"Six weeks after the wedding," said August.

The ringmaster: "But she's never thrashed you like this before."

August: "And I've never contradicted her like this before. Just imagine, she claims that four minus one is three."

The ringmaster: "She's right."

August: "Interesting that you agree with her. An example: four sparrows are sitting on a wire. I shoot one of them. How many are left?"

The ringmaster: "Three."

August: "Zero. The others flew away."

The ringmaster: "Since your wife has already banged you up so badly, I'm going to make an exception and not slap your face today."

August: "That's the difference between you and a scoundrel."

The ringmaster: "How so?"

August: "You give me a slap from in front. A scoundrel jumps me from behind." The ringmaster raised his hand but didn't slap. People laughed. Johann saw Josef laughing, too.

Johann was only waiting for Anita's entrances, especially when she appeared as the goddess Devi riding on Vishnu and deceiving Shiva the God of Death with her many arms. Johann was waiting to look at Anita's armpits. Viewed from the second floor, Anita's armpit hair was no longer hair.

When the applause finally died down, he ran down and waited for Anita at the train station. He couldn't sit still on a bench. He couldn't stay standing in one place. He was sure Anita wouldn't show up. But he intended to walk up and down in front of the station, go halfway around the station, and return to the front. He was going to walk back and forth here all night long until it was finally time to go to church.

But she did come. "Anita, Anita," he said. She was wearing a jacket and her hands were in the jacket pockets. She said it had turned cool, but Johann knew nothing about that. "Come on," he said and set off, more running than walking out of the village in the direction of the grade crossing. She kept up with him, even when they went uphill. The moon was so bright that the trees in bloom along the path leading upward were almost blindingly white. The path was white with fallen cherry blossoms. On a moonlit night in April, Johann was humming rapidly "Von Apfelblüten einen Kranz"—A Wreath of Apple Blossoms. Anita had no reaction. If only he could sing now! "Dein ist mein ganzes Herz"—I'm Yours with All My Heart. That was it, and he hummed with all his heart: I'm yours with all my heart, Without you I am all undone. Just as the flower fades, If it be not kissed by the morning sun . . . Josef disliked Lehár just as much as Father had. Johann loved to lose himself in Lehár, his favorite. Now if only Anita had hummed along. Lehár with her, now that would be something. But she didn't join in. Johann said, "There it is!" He made his voice sound as rough as he could, somehow angry or threatening or coarse. In any event, he meant to scare Anita. Stupid girl, he thought, scaring himself. Suddenly, he didn't know how to proceed. Could he . . . Did he want to . . . What? Stupid girl, he wanted to say. He wanted to grab Anita and throw her against something. Like the cat in the carriage house.

"Come here," he said, took hold of her, picked her up in his arms, and carried her through the grass to the tree he had chosen. He said they weren't supposed to trample down the farmers' tall grass, so it was better if only he walked through the grass and she let him carry her.

"If you can do it," she said.

"No problem," he said. And in fact, in his arms she wasn't very heavy. But even if she had been, it wouldn't have mattered to him. "You don't weigh anything at all," he said and carried her through the high grass. Just like three years ago, when his godmother had carried his little newborn brother to the priest who was waiting at the baptismal font to baptize the tiny child, Anselm. He thought of the beer deliveryman, too, who carried in his arms blocks of ice as big as railroad ties into the cellar. He wore red, slit-open automobile tires on his arms.

Under his cherry tree, Johann set Anita back down on the ground. "What now?" she asked.

"Your Bharatanatyam dance was great," he said.

"How do you know about Bharatanatyam?" she asked.

"From my father," said Johann, as if it was nothing special.

He took out his flashlight, the one he used to read under the blanket in bed when he just couldn't stop, and shined it on the bivouac he had set up at the base of the big cherry tree. On a blue hand towel lay the cigarette pack with the transfers. There was a sponge in its canister and a tin of Leo Fucidin ointment, which he handed to her. "Anita, Anita," he said, "it's for you." She laughed. "Not so loud," he said. He thought the quieter they talked to each other, the more beautiful it would be. He picked up the cigarette pack and the sponge canister, Anita sat down, looked up at him, and he kneeled down in front of her and opened the cigarette pack. "Transfers," he said. "Your knee," he said. Luckily, she was wearing knee socks. So he only had to push her skirt back a little bit and then moisten a spot on the inner side of her right thigh with the sponge. Anita shivered. Then he positioned the transfer and ran the moist sponge over it. He pulled away the film and immediately placed the second transfer on her other inner thigh. Skirt up, skin moistened, transfer placed, sponged over, film lifted off and put in his pocket—done. Johann was so assiduous that Anita had no chance to say or ask anything. He felt that at that moment he was just as assertive as Adolf. He was afraid, however, that Anita would jump up and run away. Had he ever been so afraid in all his life? Once the two images had dried, he shined his flashlight on them and said, "A whale spouting water and Popocatépetl erupting."

"What's it called?" asked Anita.

"Popocatépetl," said Johann.

"Is there really such a place?" asked Anita.

"What do you think?" said Johann. "My father said he wanted to climb Popocatépetl before he died."

"And did he?" asked Anita.

"He didn't make it." And when Anita was silent, Johann said, "A thirteen-thousand-footer."

Anita said, "It's a funny name."

"It means Smoking Mountain," said Johann. "It's near Puebla." And then, as if it was self-evident, "In Mexico." And he jumped to his feet, pulled Anita up, took her in his arms, and carried her back through the high grass to the path lying white with blossoms in the moonlight.

He needed to leave so abruptly because he had nothing more to say about Popocatépetl. The transfer could be any old volcano. He didn't know himself why he had suddenly said it was Popocatépetl. What he had really wanted to do was show Anita how the Eskimos greeted each other. But he didn't get to that. Slowly, they walked downhill. Johann had a solemn feeling and hoped that Anita felt the same way. He couldn't say a thing. Apparently, Anita couldn't say anything, either. They walked down the hill at the same measured pace without touching each other.

Anita stopped, and so did Johann. For a second they stood facing each other. Anita said quietly, "Good night." Just as quietly, he said, "Good night, Anita, Anita." Then she walked and he ran. Upstairs, he was greeted by Tell as if the dog had experienced everything along with him.

Johann lay in bed and was glad Josef wasn't there yet. He pulled the blanket over his head and knew that he was about to commit a sin. He thought of Adolf. When they groped each other in the reeds or the bushes, Adolf called the thing they touched their manhood. And it was obvious that he got that word from his father. Everything that Adolf got from his father lent what he said an unmistakable assertiveness and confidence it otherwise lacked. When Adolf talked about his or Johann's manhood and meant by that nothing more than that particular part of their anatomy, Johann had always been surprised that Adolf didn't find the word funny. He put his hand on the part of his anatomy he had no word for. Everything has a name, he thought, except for you. And since the part now responded to him, and the bigger it got, the warmer and more alive it felt, he thought how strange that it had no name! No name for the thing he now had in his hand and slid open and closed, open and closed and open again. The boys who were three or four or five years older—Edi, Heini, and Willi and Fritz—called it a dick and said balls (one heard about it without having to be there when they said it). Words like punches, thought Johann. Johann could not take in those words without a kind of trembling or shaking. Unimaginable that he would ever use such crude words. Johann felt that he needed to protect his member from words like that. There probably was no word for this part of his body, because it was not supposed to be touched or thought about. This part was not supposed to exist at all. And yet it did exist so . . . so much. And now he was completely overwhelmed by the feeling that he only existed thanks to this part. Whether it had a name or not. He would protect this part from any disparagement by a crude name.

He couldn't get enough of this feeling, a feeling he awakened by handling himself, and so he increased it by handling himself more vigorously while reciting some syllables to himself that made no sense, but had a rhythm, a Herr Seehahn rhythm. Yes, he felt like Herr Seehahn, spitting out syllables and sentence fragments. Anita-Anita occurred most often among the expectorated syllables. The thing he had touched for the first time in the shed behind the dairy with Irmgard was called her plummy. Plum—it wasn't just something crude but also something delicate. Between the women's beach and the men's beach, there was a new beach to which both men and women could go. It was called Plumkiln Beach. In a meadow beside the lake, someone had wanted to construct an imitation of the grotto in Lourdes and had already brought in a Madonna from Lourdes. They had imported from Switzerland all the stones they needed for the grotto, but then Rome had not approved the project. So what remained was just a swimming beach. Plumkiln Beach. If the word *dick* struck Johann as completely crude, the word *plummy* seemed to him both crude and delicate.

Narrow, sublime, both soft and firm. It was inconceivable that he would ever say it out loud to anyone. But now, alone, he could say it. When he said "plummy," he felt that the plummy letters said what he imagined to be between Anita's legs. Plummy. And himself. His member. That he had to call You, because he had no name for it. Only: You, you are who you are. He felt how his member responded to his syllables: I am who I am. And Johann: You are who you are. And again: I am who I am. You are who you are. I am who I am. Johann felt it shooting up from within, up and out of him. And felt himself falling. Because he had never been so high up, he fell lower than ever before. In what abyss was he lying, in what darkness and cold? Divided from himself. And yet it was he who lay there. Undone.

Now he'd committed a sin. A mortal sin. He could not be the person who had done that. He was the person who wanted to separate himself from the person who had done that. Forever. He was the person who had had that done to him. The person who could not get away from the person who had done it. Who had done it to him. And since he could not get away from the person who had done it, he knew he had never had to suffer like this. Not when they buried his father, not when they buried his grandfather. What should he think now? That it would subside.

When Josef tiptoed in, Johann pretended to be asleep. But how could he sleep when he had just destroyed the blessed state of grace? When he was contemplating committing the greatest, weightiest, most terrible of all sins: taking communion in a state of unchastity. Nothing could be worse. It was almost good for him that he felt more miserable than ever before in his life. It serves you right, he thought. You're going to feel this miserable as long as you live. Why wasn't he lying in the grave beside Elsa and Valentin? But they were buried in two different places, Elsa in Einöd bei Homburg on the Saar, and Valentin in Mindelheim. Johann wanted to lie in Einöd. Spooning. Elsa had once explained it to Herr Deuerling when, for a change, Herr Deuerling was not sitting on her lap on top of the coal bin behind the stove, but she on his. When you are lying next to each other like two spoons,

Elsa had explained, they called that spooning in *Ainaid by Homborsh*. Herr Deuerling said, "Get goin', get along with ya!"

Johann recalled that just as Elsa was explaining the spooning position, he happened to be reading the sentence in *Winnetou*, " . . . for there is nothing I abhor as much as, for example, a mouth full of bad air."

And when Schmied, the dockworker who made fast the steamers when they landed, came to say they had found them back there in the bay, Elsa and Valentin, along with their capsized boat, Johann had been sitting on the dock with a fishing pole in his hand, waiting for his cork to start dancing and then be pulled under by a perch that had taken his bait and thought it could shake itself loose by a wild dive. "From all that rolling and rocking," the dockworker had said. "And then, both of 'em non-swimmers, a-course," the dockworker had said. And then he said extra loud, since a couple of strangers waiting for the boat were listening, "All men must die, said the Yid, maybe even me." It often happened that Johann remembered most what he understood least.

Johann had pulled his line out of the water at once and discovered that the worm he had wrapped around the three-pronged hook was no good anymore. So he reached into the tin can filled with dirt and took hold of a fresh worm. And began tugging the worm—which was growing harder and resisting—steadily but carefully (he didn't want to tear it in two) out of the can. He skewered it on the triple hook until it was a squirming tangle, then he threw his hook back in. But he couldn't wait until one of the perch hanging around in the water finally got interested in his worm. He pulled his hook back out, tore the worm apart while dislodging it from the points, and threw the torn pieces into the water, making a present of them to the loitering perch. Holding his fishing pole, he ran over to the bay. But he got there too late. Elsa and Valentin had already been placed into a black automobile. He wanted to show Anita his swimming certificate. *Fifteen minutes in still water,* it said.

Anita should watch him some time, the way he skewered a worm onto the triple hook at the end of his line, pushing it down over the barbs until it stopped wriggling. He couldn't get enough of imagining it down to the smallest detail. He wanted now to think about nothing except the twitching and squirming of the worm on the triple hook. Do nothing but crouch down and imagine it. Nothing else.

CHAPTER FIVE

Low Sunday

WHEN THE BLINDS CLATTERING in the wind woke Johann up on Sunday morning, it felt good to be under his blanket. When it wasn't just the blinds on the two west windows that clattered but also the ones on the north windows, facing the station, it meant a storm was coming. And this morning, nothing was more important to him than a storm that would delay everything. If only the whole world would collapse. Johann stretched under the blanket, curled up again, and his hands wandered to the thing for which he had no name. Should he call it, provisionally, dick? Name?—Provisionally Dick. Then the mere thought of it would be a deadly sin, his blessed state of grace banished forever, i.e., he was headed straight to hell. You are who you are. I am who I am. You are who you are. I am who I am. IAWIA. That could be hidden, tucked in among KDF, NSV, NSKK, and WHW. He sensed that his member would accept the name IAWIA. The more he said IAWIA, the closer IAWIA and his member became. There ought to be a baptism. But please, not today!

Johann jumped out of bed and ran to the lavatory to look down at the circus. They needed it to be warm with no wind! So all wishes: About face! Please, no big storm! The black buffalo Vishnu waited patiently under the Gravenstein tree while the wind covered him with a snowdrift of white petals. The ponies lay under the carriage house eaves and stared at nothing with great concentration. Tell had come running after him and put his front paws on the windowsill so he could look down, too. No one was stirring in the trailers. Tomorrow the circus would move on to Langenargen. Johann put his right arm around Tell and pulled him close until he could feel Tell's nose at his neck. Tell knew he was supposed to lick him now, and he did.

As Johann donned the glad rags known as his First Communion suit, he began to feel the solemnity of the occasion. Long before Easter, the great-uncle they called Cousin had taken him to Bredl's store in Wangen to pick out this dark blue suit, along with a shirt, knee socks, and cap. The shoes were from Schorer's, his very first low shoes ever. White knee socks. White shirt with a collar so wide the points covered his suit lapels and reached almost to his shoulders. The cap spoiled everything. But you couldn't be a communicant without a cap. He took the communion candle, decorated with green and gold tendrils and a red Sacred Heart, out of its fancy box and practiced the best way to hold it in front of the mirror. Not too much piety, but not too little, either. And in his other hand, he held the Schott prayer book and hymnal, bound in leather with gilt edging. Cousin Anselm had asked him to carry it for his First Communion. Not a bad impression overall. Low shoes, knee socks, short pants that weren't too long and actually didn't even come down to his knees, a well-fitting jacket, the wide white collar, the elegant candle, the positively sparkling prayer book—but then that stupid cap topping it all off. Which mustn't be crooked, not even a little, nor sit too far back on his head. So, jammed down on his forehead nice and straight. Voilà.

Downstairs, Mina and Luise applauded. "What a sweet boy," Mina cooed.

After her usual hesitation, Luise said, "*Woll.*"

Josef, already at the table with his bandaged foot on a chair, said, "Agnus Dei in person."

The Princess smacked her lips and said, "Yummy."

Mother, who hadn't said anything yet, gave her a severe look and said, "Behave yourself, Adelheid!" And to Johann, "Time to go." As always, she carried three-year-old Anselm on her hip, and he repeated everything his mother said. It had become a habit, because every time he repeated his mother's words, the grown-ups would laugh. Johann's godfather and godmother were sitting at the table beneath the clock, all ready and waiting for him. The folding partition was open, and Luise had set all the tables for the post-communion banquet, with a vase of daffodils on each one.

"Here comes our communicant!" cried his godmother with a big smile on her face.

Mother said, "If only his papa could see him now," and started to cry. Little Anselm didn't repeat that. She went out of the room and returned at once, now holding the three-year-old by the hand. It almost looked as if the three-year-old had gone to fetch her and was now leading her back into the room.

His godfather said the important thing was that the living were doing well. It sounded like a reprimand. In the meantime, Josef had hobbled on his crutch over to the piano in the spare room and started to play.

"He's really good," his godmother said.

Johann's godfather said nothing, but looked over at piano-playing Josef as if to say: You don't have to play so fast for me, you show-off!

As they were leaving, Mother said (as she always did when someone was heading for the church) they shouldn't forget to visit the grave, too. She was tormented by the thought that because of the business, sometimes an entire month went by before she could visit the grave. She was sure her dead husband was registering her repeated failure with disappointment. And she was not at all sure he would accept her duties in the business as an excuse. Perhaps he was only aware that she didn't visit his grave every week, and in his dead state did not know why she hadn't come. But his grave must absolutely not be without a visitor on Sundays and holidays, because people might talk. To say nothing of lacking flowers. And what would people say if barely three months after his death no one visited the grave anymore! That was her constant refrain to Josef and Johann. And when Frau Hotz or Frau Ehrle, who tended the neighboring graves, told Mother that her sons had just dashed by after High Mass, sprinkled holy water on the grave, and taken off again, then mother was so distressed she could hardly speak. Her conclusion: now she knew what would happen to her when she was under the ground. No one would come to her grave and pray for her. When she talked like that, little Anselm would lay his head on her shoulder.

Johann walked proudly down the Dorfstrasse between his huge godfather and his smiling godmother. His godfather from Kümmertsweiler and his godmother from Kressbronn were not unknown in the village. People greeted them right and left. It had taken his godfather almost an hour to get from the farm in Kümmertsweiler to Wasserburg. He'd considered harnessing up the chestnut and coming in his little racing cart, but then thought better of it. A day of rest in the middle of spring planting would do the chestnut good, and besides, the streets in Wasserburg were almost all tarred, and the chestnut didn't like that. Johann's godmother had come by train. As they walked down the length of the village among growing crowds of people, she could not simply remain silent, of course. It would look like they'd had an argument.

"Spring's in an awful hurry this year," she said.

His godfather nodded.

"I can't recall a year," she said, "when things blossomed so early."

His godfather nodded. Then he finally opened his mouth and said, "Never known there to be so many hares as this year." Johann got the feeling that his godfather wanted to say there was something special about the year of his First Communion. But as if he realized that it would sound too positive coming from him, he added, "Wouldn't be bad if we got some rain."

No trace of Anita. How on earth would Herr Brugger ever get his Mercedes to the church through these crowds? Herr Brugger had probably already picked Anita up, and she was now sitting at their house on the big leather sofa with the fluted brass buttons that always gleamed like gold. Not a trace of Anita's parents, either.

Unfortunately, the wind was gradually blowing the clouds away. The day didn't look so threatening after all. Johann's godfather had to hold on to his hat and Johann to his communicant's cap. Even before they reached the church, the pealing of the four bells washed over them and just at that moment, the clouds parted and the sun streamed down. People going into church nudged each other and pointed.

In the churchyard they went their separate ways. When everything was over, they would meet at Father's grave.

Candlesticks had been set up to hold their candles. Adolf was already there. So Anita must be, too. In fact, Johann was the last to arrive. But it wasn't even nine o'clock yet.

As soon as he knelt down, he couldn't think what to do next. He wasn't able to make a quick confession before early Mass because if he had, it would have drawn everyone's attention to his wicked life. So he was going to his First Communion with a mortal sin on his conscience. Everyone knows that breaking the sixth commandment is a mortal sin. Not one of your little secondary, venial sins that Heaven punishes with earthly penalties—sins you could even get rid of without involving a priest at all by just repenting and praying—but a mortal sin which, if he, say, were to die right now, would be followed by immediate and eternal damnation. In fact, sinning against the sixth commandment was the biggest sin of all. The only thing worse than this biggest of all mortal sins was if, stained with this sin, you took communion anyway, which was exactly what he was doing. Was going to do, unless a bolt of lightning, an earthquake, or the earth opening up and swallowing him prevented the sacrilege. He was unconscious. He was not the person going through all these practiced motions and saying all these memorized words. He didn't want to be that person, that most dreadful of boys who went to the altar rail in a state of mortal sin. He kept stealing glances at Anita. She knelt with a straight back, her head held high and adorned with a white wreath. She was the tallest, or at least the straightest, in the girl's pew. To see Anita was something beyond all damnation. On the other hand, she was the source of all damnation. But he still had to keep stealing glances at her.

The priest droned on as always. "Before we begin to ponder these words from Holy Scripture, let us pray: Our Father, which art . . ."

Whenever the priest in the pulpit got going on a prayer like that and everybody started praying along, you couldn't hear him anymore. You only saw his beard bobbing up and down. He started to pray with his head bowed and then raised it, which meant that he could see anyone who wasn't praying.

Johann didn't take in a single word of the priest's sermon. But later during the Mass, he heard Herr Grübel's voice soaring above the others in the choir. And he was kneeling next to Ludwig Grübel, whose father's voice was the equal of Karl Erb's. Johann didn't just hear the voice, he saw it. It was the Light of Lights. He felt pierced through and through, as though he himself was singing, singing against mortal sin. Against all punishment. He sang.

When the consecration had been completed and the communion bell rung, Johann followed the other communicants and bowed his head along with the rest. As he knelt and saw the priest's white hand emerge from the golden chalice holding the white host, and as that hand with the host approached his open mouth and laid it on his proffered tongue, he thought: Don't let it dissolve. Don't swallow. If you can somehow take it out of your mouth, you haven't committed a crime. But then, what was he to do with the host? It was the Body of Christ, so deep-sixing it or throwing it away was just as criminal as letting it melt in your mouth in a state of mortal sin.

And then he was back in the pew, kneeling. The host melted in his mouth. Dissolved in him. And he was still alive. He thanked the Lord for that. Thanked him with a prayer that really should have been prayed earlier: Oh Lord, I am not worthy that Thou shouldst come to me, But speak the words of comfort, My spirit healed shall be. He was probably the only one who was unworthy. But then why this prayer? Don't try to split hairs, you.

And then, with lighted candles, the solemn recession of the boys and girls who had just received the Body of the Lord for the first time. Johann had kept a sharp eye out to see Anita stick her head forward to receive the host. And then the way she went back to her pew! Not went, floated. La Paloma.

When the procession reached the entrance to the cemetery, it began to break up, and Johann saw Herr Brugger approaching from the direction of the Crown. Adolf ran over to the girls to fetch Anita, and then they went to meet Herr Brugger. Of course, Anita was going to ride back in his Mercedes. Johann had to go back to the cemetery, to the grave, pray three Our Fathers and three Hail Marys, and each time think: Lord, give him eternal peace, may eternal light shine upon him, Lord, let him rest in peace, Amen. Turning to his Grandfather's grave: And same to you. There was no point in praying fast, since he could not stop praying before his godmother did. His huge godfather stood looking not at the grave, but at nothing. But with great concentration.

And on the way home, Johann thought about what excuse he could invent so as not to have to eat in the restaurant with his godparents. He didn't want to have to watch Anita sitting at Adolf's table and laughing. She was sure to be laughing, because Herr Brugger always told stories that made people laugh. Tell occurred to him; so he said to himself, but loud enough so the others could hear, that it was high time he looked after Tell. His godfather patted him on the shoulder in approval. At home, Johann ran straight upstairs, said, "What would I do without you?" to Tell, who was jumping up on him, led him out through the back door, over the grade crossing, and up the path to the Lausbichel. They turned off to his little bivouac under the cherry tree, and he sat down on the blue-checked hand towel he had left there last night. Tell stretched out beside him. The wind had blown down even more cherry blossom petals. It was like sitting on a bed. When he heard the clocks strike twelve, Johann knew that everybody who was coming to the banquet at the Station Restaurant was now seated, and he could go back.

He went into the kitchen with Tell and slid into his corner seat, but without a book today. Mother was sampling Frau Lutzenberger's gravy. On special occasions like this, Frau Lutzenberger always helped out, and Mother always praised what she did so much that Frau Lutzenberger blushed. And Mina had to sample the gravy after Mother and praise it just as much. And the object of so much praise smiled as though she didn't take what they said as seriously as it was meant.

It was no news to Johann that everything made and done in the village was better than anywhere else in the world. When he stood behind the bar in the dining room eavesdropping on the conversation at the regulars' table, he heard in great detail about all the things that were better in Wasserburg than anywhere else in the world. Schäfler the wainwright made the best wagon wheels, Frei the blacksmith the best fittings, Groh the locksmith the best locks, Werner the baker the best rolls, and Gierer the butcher the best bratwurst. "And all that in a community," as Schäfler the wainwright had once proclaimed, "where if one farmer falls down, he lands in another one's field." And Brem the carpenter once declared, also at the regulars' table, that he might not be the best carpenter in the world, but he would see to it that his son would be— guaranteed. And it made Johann really happy to be living in precisely the village where everything was better than anywhere else in the world. For instance, when you heard what kind of cabinets people had to settle for from cabinetmakers in other towns, compared to the cabinets created by their cabinetmaker Rechtsteiner, you just had to thank your lucky stars you were permitted to live here. So it was only right and proper that Frau Lutzenberger's gravy was the best gravy that ever was.

Johann accompanied his godmother to the station, where she caught the train to Kressbronn. His godfather had said *Behüt dich Gott* and set off in the direction of the grade crossing. Over the Lausbichel, down to Mittelsee, up the Winterberg, not quite as far down to Hengnau, uphill from Hengnau, then down the Atzenbohl, then a really steep climb and he was back home in Kümmertsweiler, seven red roofs afloat among the treetops, back home with Johann's other grandfather, who was much shorter but also much broader than his tall slender wife, the grandmother who always made sure that when Johann was sitting at her table in the midst of his hungry, long-armed uncles, he got his share of the fried potatoes that were served straight from the pan, back home with the chestnut and the bull and the seven cows whose names Johann knew by heart because he'd filled all their troughs with feed and also seen to it that they all got their share.

At three o'clock, there was a prayer service. Johann was waiting by the trailer with blue curtains at two thirty. Anita appeared at the door, three steps above him. He had never seen her from close up in this dress before. Gleaming white like the wreath on her head. And white gloves. And a little purse with a white cord, just like the one his mother was holding in her wedding picture. Frau Wiener also came to the trailer door but didn't look the least bit festive. So he knew Anita's parents had not been in church or sat at the Bruggers' table. Only Anita. Johann was happy when Anita came down the three steps and stood beside him in the grass. She probably thought his cap looked stupid. He looked like Schmied the dockworker. Not that he had anything against Schmied the dockworker. But he didn't want to look like him.

"Is the Moosweg all right with you?" asked Johann.

Anita said she didn't know which that was. Johann explained it was the path they'd taken yesterday, and she said that was fine with her. Johann stopped holding his breath. He had been afraid that the Bruggers were going to chauffeur her in their Mercedes to the afternoon prayer service, too. Although even that morning there had been something funny about it: Herr Brugger chauffeurs his wife, Anita, Adolf, and Adolf's godfather to church and then withdraws into the Crown Restaurant, referred to by many in town as St. Alternate's.

Had Anita washed the whale and the volcano off her inner thighs? That question preoccupied him more than any other.

And as if she could read his thoughts, she said, "The pictures are still stuck on. They tug at my skin when I move my legs."

When she said that and laughed, he was unable to look at her. He walked a little faster. He was afraid he would blush.

"They really do pull."

"Tomorrow it's off to Langenargen," he said.

She asked what Langenargen was like. Were there people there, too, who would ambush you at night, tie you up, and then beat you?

Johann said the men who had done that were not from Wasserburg.

"How do you know?" she asked.

He shrugged his shoulders and made a face as though he couldn't say any more about it.

"My father wants Axel to go to the police," Anita said, "but Axel says it was the police who did it."

"Damn cowards," said Johann.

"Poor Axel," she said. "There isn't a nicer person in the world, and he's the one they beat up."

"That's how it always is," said Johann.

"What do you mean?" she asked.

"That the nicest people get beat up," said Johann. He could tell that now Anita was looking at him admiringly. It made him feel good.

And this wind, fortunately blowing up a storm again. The sky full of racing clouds so low they seemed to boil right up out of Nonnenhorn. The reeds that ringed the entire bay responded to every gust, bending down and springing back up and bending down again. The meadows billowed as though they wished they were water. Did Anita notice that one and the same wind blew against her forehead and his? It made him want to break into song again. But you almost never can do what you want to do. Not even say how great it is to be walking into this storm wind! The poplars! He could say that, couldn't he? Look at those poplars, the way they're bending! All fourteen or fifteen poplars on the path around the reeds and the bay, just look at how they're bending all together. Anita, Anita, just look at them! That's what he would have said if he could have said anything. Then he would have run ahead of her, so that she would follow him all the way down to the reeds and through the reeds to the place where the boat drifted ashore last summer, the one that capsized and drowned Elsa and Valentin at night when they rowed out onto the lake and tipped over from all their groping and grabbing and rocking. Both of them non-swimmers, of course.

"Do you know how to swim?" asked Johann.

"What do you think?" she laughed. The wind blew the bangs from her round forehead. He was also convinced that hers was the roundest forehead in the world. And almost as brown as Josef when he came back from skiing. And how blue her eyes were, and her mouth always open a little.

He wished the storm wind would blow the cap off his head and far out into the meadow's yellow and purple billows. He could run after his cap, Anita behind him, and they could at least fall down together and then see what happened after that.

He asked Anita if she'd read *Winnetou*. She didn't know what *Winnetou* was, and he couldn't explain it to her. Then he said, "Do you want to go home by the path along the lake afterwards?" It would be beautiful in this stormy weather. "If you're not afraid," he said.

"Afraid?" she said. "Afraid of what?"

And suddenly he couldn't think why she should be afraid. Anita, afraid? Anita, who flew around the tall pole and rode on Vishnu, Anita Devi, Anita Anita. Suddenly, it was clear to him that this wind bore her name. If anyone was afraid, it was him.

When the graveyard gravel crunched under their steps, he began to walk so fast she couldn't keep up. He couldn't walk beside her among the graves.

In church, the seat beside Adolf was still free. How could he let Adolf know that Anita—over with the girls now, the most visible of all—had a whale and a volcano on her thighs? A baleen whale (What, you've never heard of one?) and Popocatépetl (And you don't know what that is either?). And if Adolf answered: You can kiss my ass, you and your Popocattywhatever! then he would punch him right in the face, punch him like he'd never been punched before. And then they would fight and Johann would win this time, that was for sure. He couldn't do it in the church pew, however. He'd have to postpone his inner-thigh report. Now he was itching for a fight with Adolf. For at least a year, Johann had been noticeably taller than Adolf. Adolf might be stronger, stockier, but was still an inch or so shorter. All Johann had to do was grab him in a flash, grab Adolf's neck with his right arm, throw a headlock on him. Then force him to his knees, then onto the ground, then onto his back. Johann would kneel on his upper arms the way Josef always kneeled on Johann's upper arms when he had him on his back. But then Johann wouldn't stand up and release him like Josef did. He would bend down to Adolf, put both hands behind his head, and raise him up gently, saying: See? Boast like ten naked niggers and you get pounded into the ground! Come on, get up, you old cannon fodder. And he'd even help him to his feet and maybe add something that Adolf had been saying lately, something he must have gotten from Herr Brugger: You old swindler, you.

During the service, Johann whispered to Adolf and Paul that they were going home by the path along the lake. He said it the way Adolf always said things. And in fact, to his right and his left there were nods of agreement.

Johann sang along with the hymns that were part of the prayer service, sang as though he was all by himself, with just the organ accompanying him. At least, all he could hear was himself and the organ. He kept looking over at Anita. Couldn't she hear him? She must be able to. He was singing for her. But she didn't look over. Johann had never ever sung like this before. "Star of the Sea I Greet Thee," and *Holy, holy is the Lord upon his throne, Holy, holy, holy is the Lord alone. He from the beginning, Father, Lord, and friend, Whose reign endures forever, Kingdom without end.* Truly, he'd never sung like this in his life. No one ever had sung like this. Stained with the worst mortal sin, he had partaken of the Body of the Lord. It didn't get any worse than that. But he would sing. Schubert. *Holy, holy is the Lord upon his throne.*

At the grave, he recited his prayer—Lordgivehimeternalpeace—faster than he'd ever done before. He had to keep them from going home up the main street. Adolf greeted him with a mocking yodel. Johann didn't join in their laughter. "Let's go home by the path along the lake," said Johann. Adolf said that was fine with him, since he had on sturdy footwear. Johann thought of the word *manhood*. Sturdy footwear, that was Herr Brugger talking for sure: *sturdy footwear, consequences, role model, bad example, bootlicker, fop, womenfolk, litmus test.*

They walked between the Crown and the teacher's house and down to the lake. Guido called to the girls to come, too. "Along the lake!" shouted Adolf. The girls conferred. They didn't all come, but most of them did. The path along the lake was not continually under water, but each wave was topping the breakwater and flooding parts of the path before streaming back. You had to run forward while the wave was receding and before the next one came. Johann thought they should run forward, wait, and run forward again along with the girls. He wanted to show Adolf that not he, Adolf, but he, Johann, was there to protect Anita from the waves breaking onto the path. But Adolf blocked the way and said, "You have to answer a question first before you're allowed to use the path. If Lake Constance sinks by half an inch, how many cubic feet of water does it lose?" Not a single boy or girl could answer. Adolf: "One hundred sixty million cubic feet. If you didn't know the answer, you have to pay. A toll."

Manhood, consequences, sturdy footwear, toll, thought Johann.

Adolf explained that a toll was a fee. Fees used to be called tolls.

He was barring the way with his thick communion candle. He really did have the thickest one of all. He said, "Boys pay a pfennig, girls pay with a kiss." He said, "If you can't pay, you have to go home by the usual route or you have to beat me. Then you can go past."

Now he was holding his candle like a sword. Paul pointed and yelled, "Look, there's the customs boat!" Adolf turned around to look and in that second, Paul, Guido, Berni, and Ludwig shot past behind his back. Helmut One, who always had change in his pocket, paid a pfennig for himself and Helmut Two. The girls blew kisses to Adolf, and he let them pass.

Johann could tell that Adolf had staged this whole toll business just for Anita's sake. "You and me are staying together," he said quietly to Anita. Except for Anita and Johann, everyone had now gotten past Adolf. Already they were running, waiting between waves, and running again. The boys began each run by yelling to give themselves courage. The girls uttered high shrieks.

Johann walked toward Adolf, lowering his candle so that it was also like a sword. As they began to duel, Anita took advantage of their candle fight to slip past Adolf. She ran after the others, but before reaching them she stopped and looked back. Johann was aware that she had stopped, although he needed to concentrate on Adolf.

They would each try to knock the candle out of the other's hand. The closer he got to Adolf, the more Johann lowered his candle. That way, Adolf couldn't just strike at Johann's candle. They got so close that the candles they were both holding quite low touched and rubbed against each other. Who would be first to cock back his arm and strike? Johann had advanced so steadily toward Adolf that Adolf had taken a step back. Should he crowd him to the edge of the promenade so he would fall in the water? A wave they couldn't pay attention to washed over their shoes. Johann sensed that he would not be able to withstand Adolf's stare much longer. He wanted to say: Come on, let's make peace. But he couldn't. He sensed that he couldn't glare at Adolf the way Adolf was glaring at him. And then Adolf was already doing what Johann had only thought of. Cocking his arm and instantly striking with his candle. Johann's candle broke, and he was so startled that he dropped his Schott. A wave washed the beautiful book against the wall. Johann grabbed it before it could be pulled back into the lake.

Adolf snickered, said, "One to nothing," and ran to join the others. He soon caught up with Anita, walked beside her on her right, on the lake side, and yelled, Stop! when a wave came and, Go! when the wave receded and left the path free. Then he ran forward to the next starting line, holding Anita by the hand. Johann followed slowly with his broken candle and sodden Schott. Up ahead, where the path left the lake and continued past Hoppe-Seylers' park to the Dorfstrasse, they all gathered. Main topic of conversation: Adolf's victory. Everyone felt sorry that Johann's candle was broken and his Schott soaked. Ludwig put his arm around Johann's shoulder.

Adolf said, "He started it."

Johann thought: Started what?

Ludwig told him to cut the wick of the candle at the spot where it was broken. Then Johann would already have a candle that had burned down to where the others would be after the last May devotions. Johann said he would. He wouldn't relight his candle until the others' candles had burned down to the same length. But what about his Schott? It was ruined. Johann knew he would never get another leather-bound

Schott with gilt edges. Now he would just have one in boards with red edging, like Franz Döbel's. And it didn't seem to bother Franz in the least. Franz was three years older and had missed his First Communion when it was his class's turn because of his flying. He lived out on Bichel Pond and built gliders that really flew. He wanted to be a pilot when he grew up. Flying was the only thing that interested him. He knew every type of plane in the world and had even been inside a Zeppelin. He had a Schott in boards with red edges and that didn't seem to matter to him at all.

From the linden tree on, Johann was alone with Anita. She was silent. He was silent. She might have said that it wasn't so bad to have a broken candle and a sodden hymnal. But his Schott was supposed to last him a lifetime. You were supposed to be able to pray the stations of the church year that are assigned to each Sunday for fifty or sixty years with that book. But his father hadn't had a Schott either, just a small prayer book that was printed in shorthand. He surely must have been the only person who had a Gabelsberg prayer book that was so tiny and still had everything in it. Should he tell Anita: As soon as I've learned shorthand in Lindau, I can use my father's shorthand prayer book anyway? He couldn't say that.

As the restaurant came into view, they could see that the circus people were taking things down and packing up.

"Yes," said Anita, "we're leaving today. In weather like this, it's better to be in the trailer and on the road."

And in fact, it was just starting to rain.

Johann said, "Yes, of course."

He had to get used to it, arm himself. Arm himself against the moment the orchard would be without Vishnu and the circus ring and the circus wagons. The circus was leaving because it was raining, because Dumb August had been beaten black and blue, because it could have been the police. Arm himself.

"Johann," Anita called him back when he had already turned to go. He stopped, and she came and held her candle out to him. "Let's trade," she said. Wherever they were going, she wouldn't be attending May devotionals, since they usually started so late it would make her miss her performance. So she didn't need the candle. And as a memento, Johann's broken candle would serve just as well. And then he'd have one that wasn't broken. "Come on," she said. He gave her his candle and took hers.

As he lay on the bed in his room with Tell (when Tell lay next to Johann, he stretched himself out as long as a person), he asked himself if it was good for Anita to have a broken candle as a memento of him.

CHAPTER SIX

Follow Her

As JOHANN CARRIED HIS brother's bicycle down the back stairs shortly before six o'clock on Monday morning, he had no pangs of conscience. Josef wouldn't be able to use his bicycle for the next two days anyway.

The yard looked desolate: the grass under the trees trampled flat, remnants of straw and sawdust everywhere, puddles from the rain that had also brought down more apple blossoms during the night. And no more La Paloma Circus. Late yesterday afternoon, Xaver Noll had come on his homemade miracle tractor and pulled all the circus wagons out of the courtyard. Typical that he did it, even though it was Sunday. He called himself godless. He marched in the parades in his black SS uniform. At the regulars' table, they said he was the world's smartest farmer. Besides being able to build for himself all the machines he needed, he heated his house with the gas from the liquid manure in his barn. Where else in the world would you find such a thing?

Johann had watched the departing wagons from the lavatory window. Of course, the circus people had come to the door before they left to pay the rent for the space. But Mother had waved them off: No, no, she wouldn't take any money from them after what had happened. Frau Wiener tried to hug Mother, but Mother was able to fend her off because she was almost two heads taller than Frau Wiener. Anita shook everyone's hand, Johann's last.

"Well," she said, "until next time." She was wearing her wild sweater again with the red, white, and blue nap. Anita, Anita, he thought to himself. She even turned back and said, "Don't forget all about me." Johann nodded. "You either," she added to little Anselm, who was watching it all from his mother's hip as usual. Johann thought Anita should have said her sentence about not forgetting only to him, and not to little Anselm, too.

Later, the ringmaster and director of the circus came up to the restaurant, too, and thanked them even more profusely than Frau Wiener had that there was no rent to pay. "Dear lady," he said, "I can only tell you that your generosity will never be forgotten! You will be in our prayers. Au revoir, dear lady." Johann saw that his mother had the same expression on her face she wore when she had pains near her gallbladder.

Luckily, his mother had not called out as he crept along the upstairs hall whose every floorboard creaked. When he reached the stairs, he slid down the banister to avoid any further noise. If you snuck past Mother's door at an unusual time of day, you could expect her to call out: Johann, is that you? She could tell Josef from Johann by the way each snuck past. And even when she slept, she was apparently able to hear everything going on in the hall.

Before he went to bed he'd unbolted the back door, and now he didn't latch the door behind him but left it slightly ajar. He wasn't going to run any risks. He felt like what Franz Döbel had told him pilots feel when the plane leaves the ground. He had hidden a chocolate bar under a loose roofing tile on Peter Schmied's bakehouse last night. It was from his godmother's bakery, and she had given it to him as a First Communion present. As he unwrapped this fabulous bar of Waldbaur chocolate, his first thought was to share it with Anita. Where and when he would do so was unclear. He could have kept the chocolate out of Josef's clutches by hiding it in his secret compartment in the highboy, but that would have meant opening the office door this morning and Mother might have heard the latch click. So last night he had quickly slipped the chocolate under this loose tile. The bakehouse was a tiny building on the edge of the orchard in front of Peter Schmied's house and barnyard, a little house just for baking bread, and so low to the ground that it was easy for Johann to reach the roof tiles. He often hid things he didn't want Josef to find under those loose tiles. Because Josef immediately gobbled up whatever treat they were given and would eat Johann's portion, too, if Johann didn't hide it. For Johann, sharing it was as much of a pleasure as eating it.

He wrapped the chocolate bar in a blue scarf he had brought along, clipped the little package to his luggage rack, and set off. Set off, as if he had somewhere to be by eight o'clock. He rode down the Moosweg to the bay, then turned onto the poplar avenue that led to Nonnenhorn. The poplars and the reeds were not moving at all today, not a cloud in the sky. It couldn't be better weather for what he had planned. As he rode along between the reeds and the fishermen's huts, it occurred to him that in or near Langenargen, there must also be a net-drying rack and huts where the fisherman repaired and stored their nets. Although he had some money with him, since he had access to the safe, he didn't want to spend the night at an inn.

He was still riding as if he had to be somewhere by eight, and he began to perspire. He pretended he was Old Shatterhand's strawberry roan, sweating big flakes of foam.

He had never ridden his bicycle beyond Nonnenhorn before. But didn't Jutz the organist ride his bike from Kressbronn every Monday to give Josef and Johann piano lessons? And so slowly, both coming and going, you would think he was trying to demonstrate how slow he could ride without falling over. Kressbronn couldn't be all that far away, if such a slow rider came from there every Monday to give piano lessons. Johann's lesson was this afternoon. He began pedaling even harder. Let's get out of here. Don't think about that. Five marks per hour. If you didn't cancel your lesson ahead of time, you had to pay for it, even though you missed it. He could picture Mother's face contracting, and her mouth getting tight as she handed Jutz the organist his ten marks even though he'd only given one hour of instruction. But perhaps she would be so worried that Johann was missing that the money wouldn't matter. And a boxcar of straw was supposed to arrive today, too. Starting at noon, the farmers would be driving their empty wagons onto the truck scale. The scale had to be cranked up, the empty wagon weighed, and its tare printed out on the scale receipt. Then each farmer would drive out to the tracks, get his load of straw, and return to be weighed again. The gross weight was also printed out, but the weighing fee was charged only on the net weight. When his mother had no time and Josef could not tear himself away from the piano, Johann would stand at the weighing booth under the chestnut tree all afternoon, raising the heavy scale bed with the big crank. The scale bed would swing free of the ground, Johann would slide the small weight along the beam until it stopped swinging, too, then he would print out the receipt, crank the bed back down, and call out: Next, please! They didn't earn much weighing wagonloads of straw, beets, and windfalls, but Mother was loath to give up the weighing business. The Linden Tree had a truck scale, too, one that was roofed over. If you didn't think too clearly—and who did think clearly, anyway?—you would probably think you'd have to pay Johann and his mother extra for the weight of the snow and rain. Which was ridiculous. Whatever precipitation there was, was included in both the gross weight and the tare. So the net weight was the same in either case. But some farmers made comments while being weighed in snowy or rainy weather, comments Johann found humiliating. Why didn't they go ask Herr Witzigmann about it? He organized all the loading and unloading for the savings and loan and totaled up all the carbon copies of the scale receipts every evening. What came out as the total net weight was more or less exactly what the boxcar had contained.

Pedal harder. Go, go, go. Langenargen, Langenargen. He didn't want to think about anything else now. On his left, between the path and the lake, came the villas where the summer people lived. The newest ones belonged to Ribbentrop and Streicher, big houses with tall hedges and fences. They bought their coal somewhere else. Helmer's Hermine had declined to work in either Ribbentrop's or Streicher's villa. She had been asked to, of course. But both lay within the Nonnenhorn town limits. And Helmer's Hermine said she never cleaned in Nonnenhorn. Semper's Fritz had laid all the pipes in Streicher's villa, and he told the regulars that the house had an underground escape tunnel. And when everyone asked where to, Fritz had pulled down one eyelid with his index finger and said, "To the boathouse. He's got 140 horsepower in there. If things get too hot, it's off to Switzerland." The smallest house Johann rode past belonged to Martha and Elisa Sauter. Did the Fräuleins Sauter know Father had died?

If they read the newspaper, they did. Johann had read the newspaper article about his father's funeral, which took place at two o'clock on Epiphany. Frau Fürst had not tossed the newspaper onto the table in her usual energetic manner, but laid it down carefully, sat down on the bench under the boiler next to Johann, opened the paper, and pointed to the headline: A Sad Day. And she sat next to Johann until he had finished the whole article. The newspaper said it had snowed day and night for three days and hadn't stopped until the middle of the day, shortly before the funeral. The newspaper said that the village was buried in more than twenty inches of snow. It said they had to plow the streets free. Then people had waded through the snow behind the hearse driven by Herr Waibel and pulled by his two horses. Johann had never seen so many people on the Dorfstrasse. In front of every house, people dressed in black were waiting to join the procession. Maybe one could see the people clad in black so clearly because everything was covered with white. The newspaper reported who had spoken at the funeral on behalf of Father's schoolmates, his fellow POWs, the Kyffhäuser Bund, the volunteer firemen, the choral society, his comrades from the Prince Karl of Bavaria Infantry Regiment, his comrades from the former Royal Bavarian 20th Infantry Regiment, the restaurateurs' association, and the Benevolent Association for the Survivors of the Fallen. Later, in the overcrowded church, it was the priest who spoke the longest. Johann didn't register a word of what he said but only how his goatee had bobbed up and down. Except once, when the priest spoke directly to him, Josef, and Anselm. He told the three forsaken lads of the dear departed— departed before his time—that they should always revere the memory of their brave father. Of course, the newspaper didn't mention the bit about the forsaken lads. Nor that the church was overcrowded. But it did say who the speakers were. The newspaper said that Father was forty-seven when he died and listed all the places he had fought. There was nothing about the fairly large bird that wouldn't be shooed away. Nor did it say that Senior Postal Inspector Zürn, speaking on behalf of the Kyffhäuser Bund, was the only person wearing two armbands: the armband of the Kyffhäuser Bund and the armband with the swastika. Hurrah-Zürn, his father had called him. He, too, addressed the three lads who would have the privilege of growing up in happier times than their father, summoned all too soon to the great muster in the sky.

In Nonnenhorn, Johann was just passing the farm where Frau Molkenbuer lived: Ereolina. That had been one of Father's words too. *Popocatépetl* . . . or was it *Potocapétepl?* He repeated both words to himself until he couldn't tell them apart anymore. And felt ashamed. To revere the memory of his father and then so soon forget his words! He could see the word tree. *Popocatépetl* or *Pototapécetl*—the word swung in its lower branches, he just had to concentrate on it—*Popocatépetl*, of course it was *Popocatépetl*, what else? *Pleurisy, Rabindranath Tagore, theosophy, Balaam, Jugendstil, Bhagavadgita, Swedenborg, atmosphere, protoplasm.* And then the upper branches came back to him, Father's favorite words: *trepidation, bijoux, curiosity, exuberance, whitecaps, freckles, weeping willow, reincarnation, kingdom of heaven, chattels, memorial.*

Before he was even as far as the center of Nonnenhorn, he heard a sound he knew and feared, the thin whistling that means your tire has picked up a nail. He stopped immediately and saw he had a flat. Because he'd gotten distracted! That damn word tree! He howled, but quietly, just to himself. He'd learned how to howl quietly from Tell, into whose ear he'd whispered phony words of consolation this morning. Josef was always a sound sleeper, but if Tell had insisted on his morning routine, it would have woken Josef up. And that had to be avoided at all costs, because Johann could not have explained anything to him.

Johann laid his bike down on the grass. Good thing he had a repair kit with him. It must be there, if Josef had put in everything that ought to be in a saddlebag. But Johann had never repaired a flat before. Whenever he got one on Josef's bicycle, he just walked the bike over to Franz Hotz's in Hege. Franz worked for the railroad, but in the evenings he repaired anything that could go wrong on a bicycle. And as long as Hotze Franz did the repairing, Johann preferred scratching the ears of Franz's nanny goats to watching him work, so he hadn't learned how to do it himself. Should he walk the bike back to Hege? Impossible. So he had to repair the flat himself. If the nail wasn't still sticking in the tire, he would need a pan of water to find the tiny hole. You had to pump the tube back up again and then run it through the water and watch for rising bubbles to reveal the hole. Should he go to a house and ask for a pan of water? Again, this feeling of needing to arm himself. He had to arm himself.

"So, *büble*, what seems to be our problem?" said a voice behind him. He turned around. Oh jeez, it was Crooked Hat. Johann couldn't get out a single word. Did it have to be Crooked Hat, the nickname they always shouted to needle him? Johann could only point to his bike lying in the grass.

"You got a flat," said Crooked Hat. Johann nodded. Crooked Hat leaned his own bike against the nearest tree. Then, as if someone had assigned him the task, he took the repair kit out of Johann's saddlebag, stood the bike on its head, rotated the rear tire, and then brought it to an abrupt stop. "Lucky for us," he said, pulling the nail out of the tire and the tube, a real cobbler's nail with a square head. He unscrewed the valve cap, pushed the valve out of the rim, and could then pull the tube out of the tire at the spot where the hole was. He abraded the area with the emery paper, spread adhesive on it, chose the size patch he needed from the repair kit, positioned it over the puncture, and then pressed down with both thumbs for quite a long time. While he pressed he gave Johann a cheerful smile. Then he pushed the tube back into the tire, reseated the valve, and pumped it up. "So, *büble*, all set to go." Where was Johann headed?

"Langenargen," said Johann. He had meant not to tell anyone where he was going. Now he had betrayed himself.

"Then you'd better get going," said Crooked Hat, "before you put down roots." Anita had told him that her father always said that. Crooked Hat returned to his bicycle and then looked back.

Johann said, "Thank you very much." Fortunately, Crooked Hat heard him.

"You're welcome," he said. "Maybe you can scratch my back sometime in return." Then he mounted his bicycle and rode off, the large, light-colored rucksack hanging limply from his shoulders as always.

When Johann went to stand his bike right side up, he saw a piece of paper lying next to the saddle. Written on it in the cursive handwriting he knew was Father's, a single word: *Beatrijs*. It was harder for him to throw something away than to hang onto it, so he stuck the paper in his pocket. As he pedaled through Nonnenhorn, *Beatrijs* found a place in his word tree. *Beatrijs* now swung between *Swedenborg* and *Balaam*. Johann's word tree was the opposite of a Christmas tree. It was more motion than tree: a tree made of motion, always moving and always a tree. An apple tree in motion.

For a while, Johann looked down at the road he was riding on to avoid the next nail. But then he forgot to. Simply kept on riding. On through Nonnenhorn. When he passed the wine shop where Edmund Fürst was an apprentice, he wished he could stop by. Every morning, Edmund took the 6:00 a.m. train here. When he comes home in the evening, it's either a muster or he embroiders. He spent one entire evening meeting explaining about the embroidery. When he finished the explanation, he said, "So, now you all can laugh." His father had started doing it when he was out of work, and Edmund had taken it over from him. There's a company in Offenburg that sends postcards with pictures of Rothenburg or Dinkelsbühl. Edmund embroiders copies of them, and the company pays him for them.

One hundred eight thousand, six hundred twenty-four embroideries for Nuremberg. His mother gets one pfennig per newspaper per day. After having his lunch in Memmingen, his father is about to get into Herr Mehltreter's car. Hans Schmied is already behind the wheel. Herr Fürst raises his foot to step in and falls down dead. It is Frau Fürst's doing that all their names have to begin with E. Her name is Ernestine. Eva is now Edeltraud. When she announced the new name in all her houses, Frau Fürst explained it was according to Section 11.

Keep going. To Thunau, Goren, Langenargen. As he came up to the bridge over the Argen, Johann dismounted. The bridge was suspended on thick steel cables from four massive stone piers that looked like they belonged to some palace or castle. They would go well with the door of the safe in the office back home. As he pushed his bike across this bridge, he had a solemn feeling. He couldn't imagine a river bigger than the Argen. Or more transparent. You could see every rock and every little stone. Most of all, he couldn't imagine any river livelier than this one. How the water hurried forward and broke into silvery ripples against the rocks and rushed forward again, as if wanting to reach the lake as quickly as possible. This was not the first time he'd seen the Argen. He had been on its banks more than once. Two years ago this fall, with relatives farther upstream in Apflau. They had gone to fetch a big barrel of apple cider. While their father was in the house, Johann and Josef had taken turns cranking the handle of the fruit press. Johann just had to try out every crank he encountered. Josef had gotten his hand caught in the gears, and while he screamed, Johann had to turn the crank backwards, and at first he turned it the wrong direction, but then back. Josef's hand looks crushed and bloody. Afterwards, they say it was a miracle none of his tendons had been injured. Josef has the ambition to be something that will involve piano playing. Mother said his guardian angel had never intervened so clearly before. His hand between the gears, and no injury to his tendons! Or only to the one on his little finger, and even then just barely. Ever since, Josef was unable to move his little finger over next to his ring finger. It didn't affect his piano playing at all. But when he gave the German Greeting, you could see the little finger standing off from the others a bit. The first time the squadron leader Edmund saw Josef giving the salute like that, he said, "Well, there goes your chance to be in the Adolf Hitler Lifeguard Regiment."

Johann didn't get back on his bicycle at the other end of the bridge. He didn't know where he was going.

When he passed a boy his own age, he asked as casually as he could where the circus was in Langenargen.

"On the Hirschenwies," said the boy.

"Oh," said Johann, "on the Hirschenwies." The other boy could tell from his face that Johann didn't know where that was.

"Straight down from the train station toward Klosterstrasse, then into Klosterstrasse and along the wall." Johann's expression said that now everything was really clear to him.

"Merci," he said, and, "So long." And he pushed his bicycle forward, hoping that at least he was going toward the train station. You always come to the train station in a town. Or does he just think that because he lives across from a train station? Langenargen was obviously a much bigger town than Wasserburg. Here every street had its own name. Suddenly he heard the trumpet playing "La Paloma." He mounted his bike at once and rode toward the music. Then he heard the voice of the muscleman and in answer, the voice of Dumb August. And then he saw the two of them with their Roman chariot and the two ponies. They were announcing this evening's performance of La Paloma Circus on the Hirschenwies. "Marvels never seen before, neither here nor anywhere else. Come tonight, folks. Come, look, and be amazed. Money-back guarantee if we fail to amaze you."

"With compound interest," August added.

Johann had the impression that August and the muscleman were drunk. They were constantly laughing about what they themselves had just said. Suddenly, he felt sorry for both of them.

Johann had only to follow them to reach the Hirschenwies. It was much bigger than their back courtyard. The six wagons were arranged so that from outside, you could only see the feet of the circus people walking back and forth. So he would go in. Hello, Anita . . . He had practiced the speech a hundred times while riding here. But that didn't mean that when he stood facing Anita he would be able to get out even a single word. Adolf had simply jumped into the circus ring, strode over to the cage, reached between the bars, felt the ropes and chains, and said: They're real all right. The drum and the accordion had played a fanfare for him; the ringmaster praised him. And rightly so. It was really fabulous the way Adolf jumped into the ring without the least hesitation. Fabulous, Adolf. Johann now regretted that he had not asked Adolf to ride with him. If Adolf had been with him, it would have been no problem to walk around the wagons and go in: Well, so here we are. Hello everyone. But it was unthinkable to visit Anita with Adolf. Johann would rather not do it at all.

He went back to his bike and rode down to the lake. He sat on the retaining wall and looked at the water. Today it was absolutely still, that water. Should he go to a restaurant and eat something? The restaurants in Langenargen had already set tables outside. Back home, they would probably set the tables on the terrace, too. Although Herr Kalteissen the bailiff had not been in the restaurant for a long time to mark the piano, the gramophone, the highboy, and the safe for repossession, Mother still sent Johann into the village to ride slowly past Café Schnitzler and the Linden Tree and count how many guests were sitting outside. Should he simply ride home now and carry the bike up the back stairs? On New Year's Day, the dark bird had perched on the transom above the back door, and when they shooed it away, it kept coming back until January third, when Father died. Then the bird had disappeared. Herr Waibel's two horses that had pulled the hearse wearing their black caparisons were the only things audible on the long ride from the house to the cemetery. What would Mother do when she discovered he was missing? Couldn't be found anywhere? Yes, Josef's bicycle would also be gone. But what would she think? He couldn't imagine how his mother would explain his disappearance to herself. He had to go home. But he had to see Anita, too. At least to bring her the chocolate bar. Then he could ride back.

He rode back along the lake in the direction of Wasserburg, back to the mouth of the Argen. The landscape became more and more wild. There were a few fishermen's huts there, everything more shaded by trees than in the bay at home. He tried the door to one of the huts. It was open. Inside it smelled of tar and fish. This hut might do. Back into town. Back to the Hirschenwies. And this time he just rode straight there and then around the farthest circus wagon. The ring was set up. The pole for the Wiener family had been raised along with the two shorter poles. Anita and her parents were sitting at a table. Anita saw him before her parents did. He would not have gone closer if, being able to see him, she had not seen him. If she had not seen him now, he would have gone home at once. But she did see him, jumped up, and cried, "Johann!" Her father invited him to sit down. No, said Anita, she hadn't seen anything of Langenargen yet and wanted to take a stroll through town with Johann. *Stroll* was a word he had, until now, only heard Adolf say. Once Adolf had said that he wasn't about to stroll through life when he could march. Johann had never heard this word from the House of Brugger before, because it didn't occur in the books he read.

He was going to leave his bike against the nearest tree, but Anita said, "Let's take the bike along." As soon as he was beside her, pushing the bike, he realized it was a good idea. That way, both hands had something to do and he knew why he was walking next to Anita—in order to push the bike. They went toward the lake and then along the shore the same way he had ridden earlier. He played the local authority, suggested they walk as far as the mouth of the Argen. Last night, she hadn't even noticed they were driving across a river and had no idea it was a suspension bridge. He said they could walk along the Argen until they reached the bridge. It was one of the most beautiful bridges in the world, if not the most beautiful. Said it as if familiar with all bridges and especially all suspension bridges.

"How is Axel Munz?" he asked.

He wasn't hurting anymore, but he was quite gloomy. He wanted to quit. Get away from the circus, away from everything. When you asked him where he wanted to go, he said: Where there's different police.

When they got to the mouth of the Argen, Johann said, "There," and pointed to a bench. He acted as if that had been his goal all along. Emerging from under the bench were the mighty roots of the tree that arched above it. And there was a view of the lake. Johann sat down on the front edge of the bench. Anita leaned back against the armrest and put her feet up on the bench. She rested her chin on her knees and hugged her legs with her arms. Johann got out the chocolate bar and gave it to Anita.

"For you," he said.

"Thank you," she said, took the bar, tore open the paper, and held the chocolate out to him so he could break off a piece for himself. Then she broke off her own piece. And they kept at it until the whole bar was gone. Every time Anita held the bar out to him to break off another piece, he looked at her. He broke off only the tiniest of pieces so he could look at Anita more often. How round her forehead was. And the same with her bangs. And she had eyelashes like no one else in the world. He realized that when she hadn't been there in person, he had imagined her much too vaguely. In front of them, two swans flew across the water with necks extended. Their huge wings made a sighing noise.

"The air is crying because the swans are beating it with their wings," said Anita. Johann longed to ask her to say something else like that. But you can't ask something like that. You know exactly what you can and can't say. And what one longs to say is what it's least possible to say. Sentences that he could not articulate occurred to him. In the books of poetry Father had left behind, which he almost preferred to Karl May, there were sentences he would also have liked to say. To Anita. But they were unsayable. It would have been obvious that someone else had written them for a different girl. Make up some of your own. Open your mouth, count on something coming out that would be possible at this moment: Anita on this bench, under this tree, not twenty yards from the lake, and on the far shore above the lake was the Säntis, that white-powdered mother hen of stone, as Father called it, sitting there and letting the sun roll right off its back. He couldn't say that, either.

The poem he read more often than all the others in his father's books began: How beautiful, Mother Nature, The splendors you invent To scatter across the meadows. He must have repeated that to himself a hundred times. And now he couldn't. What if Anita laughed? Would he seize her and throw her in the water? He snorted.

"What are you thinking about?" asked Anita.

"Me? Nothing," said Johann.

"Same here," said Anita.

Too bad, thought Johann. Then he said, "My father told me that Eskimos greet each other by rubbing the tips of their noses together."

Anita laughed. Then she said, "Shall we try it?" He shrugged. "Come on," she said, and was already kneeling on the bench. He knelt facing her, she moved her face closer, he also moved his a little toward hers, but less than she moved hers toward his. Then they rubbed the tips of their noses together, each nose circling the other and rubbing against it. "Nice," said Anita.

"Yes," said Johann. "The Eskimos are a great people. There are no curse words in their language."

"How do you know that?" she asked.

"My father told me," he said, jumped up, ran down to the shore, and tested the water. It was cold melt water from the mountains. He took off his shoes and socks anyway, waded in up to his knees, and called back, "Come on."

She came down, took off her shoes and socks, and waded into the water, too. She shivered, and that was all the signal Johann needed. He went over and hoisted her up. Careful now, don't slip on a rock. Anita uttered little squeals. She put her arms around his neck. When he'd carried her through the grass, she hadn't done that. He carried her farther into the water.

Quietly, Anita said, "Not so deep, Johann."

He made a face as if he didn't want to comply. Back on shore, he put her down carefully, then ran to fetch the scarf he had packed the chocolate in. He used it to dry her feet and legs. Up to the decals of the whale and the volcano.

"Neat," he said.

"What?" she said.

"That the whale and the volcano are still there."

"Did you think they wouldn't be? You still have my candle, don't you?"

"Of course I do. Did you think I didn't?"

Johann dared not stroke the whale and volcano. To stroke those two pictures at this moment, or even be allowed to touch them with his bare hand, without the scarf or the drying—that would be the most beautiful thing in the world that could possibly happen. All forbidden. He dashed off to the tree and the bench, sat down, shoved his hands under his thighs, and stared at Anita coming up slowly over the rocks. She sat down next to him, and shoved her hands under her thighs just as he had. But instead of staring out at the lake as he was doing, she looked at him. He couldn't understand how she could look at him like that, now. Turn her smiling face toward him! Now! He felt like the world had yet to be born. And it was up to him how it turned out. My God! And then she was smiling as if nothing was at stake.

"Anita, Anita," he said. He drew his right hand from beneath his thigh and placed it on the bench between himself and Anita. When Anita didn't notice, didn't notice immediately and answer by drawing her own hand out and placing it next to her, he felt he would boil over. He had to jump up and run over to his bicycle. He stopped beside the bike. He stood still without turning back to look at Anita. He would stand like that until . . . until . . . until everything was over. A thunderous noise broke in; an airplane roared over the lake, pulling three huge words: PERSIL—ATA—HENKEL. And soon became a mere rumble in the distance. When you couldn't hear it anymore, you could still see it.

"Man!" said Anita.

Johann said, "Right."

He pushed the bicycle, and she walked beside him. Anita suddenly took hold of his left hand, which he didn't need to push the bike, and swung it in time to their strides. And whistled "La Paloma." Goodness, how she could whistle. Should he drop the bike and clap? Anita was swinging his left hand so vigorously with her right that they should have been able to take off and fly away, but he had the wrong reaction and tensed his hand and arm. By the time he noticed, it was too late. Anita laughed. He was glad when they finally reached the Hirschenwies and Anita said, "Here we are." He could only nod. At that moment, he would have agreed to his own execution.

Anita said, "Safe trip home."

At least he was able to shake his head no. He managed to say that he would come to the performance that night and then say goodbye. Where was he going to spend the night? With relatives. In Apflau. It was right nearby.

"Wait a second," she said, disappeared behind the wagons, and returned with a red ticket. COMPLIMENTARY ADMISSION, it said. "Well, Johann," she said, "see you soon."

He said, "Yes, see you soon." She waved. He walked his bike toward the lake, returning the same way he had just come with Anita. Then he sat on the bench where he had sat with Anita. And although he didn't open his mouth, two lines took shape in his head:

> Oh, that early in the day
> I should be so lonely.

He didn't try to stop those two lines repeating themselves over and over inside him. He even allowed them to rise to his lips. Quietly, but nevertheless still audibly, he said over and over and every time with a feeling of acquiescence,

> Oh, that early in the day
> I should be so lonely.

CHAPTER SEVEN

The Miracle of Wasserburg

WHEN JOHANN TOOK A SEAT on a bench in the third row and saw that, in Langenargen, they had room for five rows of benches around the circus ring and all five were filling up with people—in fact, there were even more people who had to stand to watch the performance— he felt ashamed of their courtyard back home and of Wasserburg in general. Langenargen was really a different story entirely. That was already obvious at the bridge suspended from four piers that could have been the towers of a castle. You could already hear the hum of the town to be reached by crossing a bridge such as this before you even got there. And how the Argen foamed over the rocks! He had greeted the water of the Argen as an old friend, because when he and Josef visited the great-uncle they called Cousin during school vacations, the first thing they did was to run down to the Argen (which also flowed past there), dive headlong into the dark green stream from the outcroppings of bright rocks, and swim straight across. Whoever was driven farthest downstream by the current was the loser. That was always Johann, of course—so far.

People in Langenargen laughed louder and clapped more than people in Wasserburg. Compared to the people in Langenargen, the people in Wasserburg now seemed to him cowering, suspicious, and almost furtive, as if they weren't there to have a good time but to decide whether everything was being done as they thought they had a right to expect. Or was it because he couldn't forget the way Herr

Brugger had scratched the back of his left hand with his right instead of clapping? Or because Axel Munz had been mistreated? There was no question that people in Langenargen were better dressed. Or did he only think that because he knew everyone in Wasserburg, so their clothes didn't seem so fine? People were laughing so hard at the ringmaster and Dumb August that they couldn't stop making jokes. This time the ringmaster kept confusing "I" and "me." When August said something right, he got a slap that knocked him over every time. Then August would peer up at the ringmaster and say, "What if it turns out I'm right after all?" And every time the ringmaster would shout, "Me never confuse 'I' and 'me.' Come with I and me will teach you to speak German." The lesson, larded with slaps, didn't end until Dumb August couldn't say anything right, either.

Johann realized the only thing he was interested in was Anita's performances—the way she floated in as a dove; the way she whirled around the pole with her father and brother, her pink costume lit from below and fluttering against the night sky; the way she was carried around by Vishnu as the goddess Devi! Again, he gazed at her armpits and knew he would never ever see anything as beautiful as Anita Devi's armpits, the hair in Anita Devi's armpits. Fortunately, everything was decided now. He would follow her and gaze into her armpits every night when she made her entrance as the Hindu goddess. He was happy when suddenly it became so clear to him why he had been born and what he was to do. He would tell Anita about it right away. And if he couldn't get it out, well, she would see him sitting in the audience night after night and see that he was always the one clapping longest and loudest.

When everyone had left, the lights were turned off, and the ring lay bathed in moonlight, Anita came out of her trailer. She was wearing the yellow robe and the red turban. Then Johann knew that he could not tell her now. Now he could only say something about the performance.

He said, "Great."

She said, "Thanks."

He said, "It was so great."

She said, "It was better today than in Wasserburg. Maybe Axel Munz will stay after all, because he sees how much people like him." Then she hummed the melody the circus band had played today as the lights were gradually dimmed: "Sag beim Abschied leise Servus." Johann realized he couldn't stand there forever facing Anita like that. He had already shaken her hand and said—he couldn't remember what.

"So," he said.

"So," she said.

Again he moved his head as he did when rubbing noses, but without expecting her to come closer with her nose. Instead, he turned around, went over to his bicycle, and then turned back to her. Anita stood there and even raised her hand and waved. Then she called out, "Tell Adolf hi from me. He should've come to see me again, too!" Turned, and walked toward her trailer.

Johann didn't get on his bike. He pushed it toward the lake, then along the shore in the direction of the mouth of the Argen. Because the lake multiplied the moonlight, it was much brighter here than in town. He found the fisherman's hut again. So much moonlight was pouring through the open door from the sky and the lake that he could see the nets he was going to spend the night on. Johann took a heavy rubber apron that was hanging from a nail and used it to make a sort of cave in the mountain of nets. Then he lay down and howled quietly, like Tell. Whenever Tell knew he was innocent, although everyone was scolding him, he howled quietly like that. It sounded like he was only howling to himself. But of course he knew that they heard him and would respond sometime. Johann knew that nobody heard his howling and that no one would respond. Still, he couldn't help howling. He didn't want to think anything now, he just wanted to howl.

When he opened the door, it was already light outside. His saddle was wet with dew. He dried it with the scarf he'd used to dry off Anita. He had dried her up as far as the whale and the volcano. He started riding toward town. Toward the Hirschenwies. No sign of life. As hard as he looked, nothing was stirring. The ponies lay on the straw, the buffalo stood beneath a tree. Luckily, no one was awake yet.

The worst thing that could happen would be to see Anita again. Tell Adolf hi from me. He should've come to see me again, too. Oh, that early in the day, I should be so lonely. That sentence popped up again and wouldn't go away. Johann had to sing it. And so he rode out of Langenargen, and as he pedaled across the castle-like suspension bridge, he sang out loud, but fairly quietly: Oh, that early in the day, I should be so lonely. He sang it the way Karl Erb, the meterman from Ravensburg, sang *Wer nie sein Brot mit Tränen ass*. As the big onion-domed tower of the Wasserburg church loomed above the trees, he switched to the Mass. He rode along the upper path called the Langgasse. For half a mile, it was bordered left and right by a dense wall of blossoms, flowering trees standing in the fields like bouquets. If he were to write a composition in school about riding between these walls of bloom, he would write: There are three kinds of white. The greenish white of pear blossoms, the pinkish white of apple blossoms, and the pure white of cherry blossoms. Unconsciously he slipped back into his old "Von Apfelblüten einen Kranz." The coloratura felt good. The more confidently he sang, the lighter he felt. He had the feeling it was lifting him from his saddle, or with his saddle and bike into the air. Basically, he was riding in the air above all the blossoming trees. Down there on his right: the lake, the bay, the long peninsula presided over by the church.

What would he say when he got home? Mother had probably not been to bed all night. For sure she had telephoned Stadler, the rural constable, and had him call around asking after Johann. By now, Rural Constable Stadler was surely sitting at the regulars' table, and from the inside breast pocket of the coat he never took off (when he sat down, he didn't even undo the coat corners he had clipped up for bicycle riding, because despite a companionable nature, he was always in a hurry to get somewhere else) he was taking out his notebook and writing down the case: Unexplained disappearance of the second oldest son of the widow, etc.

Johann rode as fast as he could. If the rural constable had not yet arrived, Mother would be standing outside on the terrace or on the side facing the station. She would be pacing up and down between the two chestnut trees, both hands balled up in the pockets of her apron.

And to every passerby she calls out: Have you by any chance seen Johann? He's been missing since yesterday morning. Maybe even since the evening of day before yesterday, with Josef's bicycle. Without leaving a note behind. It's not like him at all. Something must have happened to him, but what? Perhaps she could not even imagine he was still alive. If Johann was still alive, he surely would have sent her some sign. The guardian angel! What else could she do but implore Johann's angel to protect him and see to it that Johann returned halfway unharmed—a thing, however, she really no longer thought possible.

He stayed on the road that ran into the village from the west and led directly to the linden tree, where he turned and started uphill in order to approach from below, turn into the courtyard, walk the bicycle around the house, carry it up the back stairs, and leave it in the passageway. As if nothing had happened. Then he would go into the kitchen, let the storm break over his head, and not defend himself. Pull a long face and maybe cry. Before he could even turn into the courtyard, Tell raced down from the terrace. Johann had to lean the bike against the gate post and brace himself for the assault. And how he did bark! And howl! And leap at him! Until finally, with his paws on Johann's shoulders, he calmed down and licked Johann's neck.

Obviously alerted by the barking, Niklaus came out of the carriage house where he was filling sacks and asked what was wrong with the dog. Johann said he had no idea.

"First he doesn't eat anything for two days," said Niklaus, "then he goes crazy."

"Didn't he eat anything?" asked Johann.

"As if you didn't know. You were complaining yourself that he didn't touch a bite."

Johann looked at Niklaus. Maybe Niklaus was getting a little soft in the head after all. When Johann saw that Niklaus hadn't left a single speck of sawdust or blade of straw from La Paloma Circus, he praised him. Niklaus had also mowed the trampled grass and carried away the cuttings. That could not have been an easy job. Niklaus said he couldn't have done it without Johann.

Or anyway, not so quickly. Johann patted Niklaus on the shoulder, pushed the bike to the rear stairs, and carried it up and into the house. As he entered, he saw his school bag on the landing. He picked up the bag and took it into the kitchen as if he were coming from school. He gave the bag a shove so it slid into the corner and then slid down the bench himself. He felt Tell's head between his knees and thought that now the trouble would start.

Mina was alone in the kitchen. She asked if school had let out early today.

Johann said, "Yes." Tell pushed his nose against Johann's knee and thigh, repeatedly. And in between, he barked.

"He's hungry," said Johann.

"About time," said Mina. "I'd let him beg a little more if I were you. Yesterday he turned down everything like we were trying to poison him, and now he acts like he's complaining."

Johann dashed off to get Tell's bowl, filled it, filled his water bowl too, and put both on the landing by the back door, then watched Tell eagerly devour his food and quench his thirst with noisy slurps.

Mina watched out the kitchen window. "Can you believe it? Yesterday he wouldn't touch a bite and now he can't get enough."

"Didn't he eat anything yesterday?" asked Johann.

"What's the matter," said Mina, "are you losing your memory? Yesterday he acted like you were some stranger. I guess the beasts have their moods just like us, right?" Johann nodded, then came back into the kitchen with Tell. Tell laid his head on Johann's feet.

Johann opened his school bag and took out the notebooks he needed: math and composition and geography and history. He opened his composition notebook and read the essay he hadn't written, "How Much Homeland Do We Need?" It was dated yesterday and written in Johann's handwriting.

Things started to dance in front of Johann's eyes. He clapped the notebook shut and stuffed it into his school bag like something he had to hide. Mina said his mother was waiting for him. I'll bet she is, thought Johann.

"I'm sure she wants to tell you herself," said Mina. And the words were barely out of her mouth when Mother was standing there in the doorway. Oh jeez, thought Johann. Mother sat down across from him.

"I'm glad you're home early," she said. She told him how happy it made her that now he had gained the confidence not just of the farmers, but of Herr Witzigmann too. Since he must have been gaping at her like a half-wit, she went on: Yes, that morning Herr Witzigmann had come by with the paper on which he added up the weights. Thirty-two separate weighings and the sum of the thirty-two net weights was the same—down to the pound—as the net weight of the straw that had been unloaded from the boxcar yesterday and distributed to thirty-two farmers. And last night, some farmers at the regulars' table who had picked up straw and had it weighed by Johann had praised him to the skies, saying how friendly he was and how precisely and quickly he worked. They had downright congratulated her on her son. It really did her good to hear it, because she was always afraid one of her children would do something other people wouldn't understand. She had already had enough of that with Papa. If things had gone on like that, she would have been at her wits' end. That's why she was so relieved today. My God, you can't live against people when you have to live from them, can you? And when Herr Witzigmann said things like that about Johann, then it meant something. Johann could picture him. At Father's funeral, he had spoken on behalf of the choral society. Since he had praised Father's voice and musicality, Johann had been able to listen to what he said. "Now that his warm and soulful voice has fallen silent, we are the poorer for it." That's what he said, the strict Herr Witzigmann, whom one always anxiously awaits because he always comes with the list on which he compares the weighed loads with the total net weight. A certain difference in weight is to be expected, as long as it's not too big. And especially if it isn't to the disadvantage of the savings and loan! For instance, when the waybill says that a boxcar with 135 hundredweights has been delivered, and the loads that Johann and Mother weigh come to only 129 or 131 hundredweights! So when you weigh, you always have to weigh a little bit in favor of the savings and loan. But the farmer you're weighing is, of course, standing right next to you and watching to see that the two pointers on the scale are right next to each other when the weighing is done. And now, this great triumph. Herr Witzigmann said he was glad to see that Johann was growing up to be a boy one could count on.

When Josef limped into the kitchen, he said his bicycle was back again. He just wished he knew who had taken it.

Mother said, "Well, thank goodness for that."

When Josef saw Tell lying under the table, he said, "Is he back to normal again?"

Mina answered right away, "At least he's eating again."

Mother said, "Thank the Lord."

Josef said that yesterday, he really thought they would have to shoot Tell.

"Are you crazy?" said Johann.

"Don't pretend you didn't think he had rabies, too. He'd never barked at you like that. I could see you were afraid of your own dog. And he wouldn't take a bit of food. Maybe he had just a touch of it and now he's gotten over it."

Johann stroked Tell's head. Tell laid his head between Johann's knees. Johann jumped up and went to the office. From one of the lower drawers of the highboy, he took out a purchase ledger for the restaurant and hotel trade in which each new month started on a new verso, even if the previous month had only filled up half the two-page spread. At the end of every month, there was a lot of blank space below Mother's unsteady handwriting. On the two-page spread for January, he drew a line from the left to the right margin and wrote, more in his father's handwriting than his mother's:

> Oh, that early in the day
> I should be so lonely.

Then he hid the book in the lowest drawer. Now, if lines like that popped into his head again, he would know where to put them.

When Johann returned to the kitchen to eat with the others, Josef said, "Herr Jutz said if you always played the way you did yesterday, maybe he could make a pianist out of you after all. He'd never heard you play with such a fine touch before."

Johann said, "Oh, sure."

"I'm just telling you what he said," Josef replied. Then he said he had talked to Edi Fürst last night. The attack on Dumb August hadn't been Edi's doing. Dumb August was a rum customer, all right, but it was people from outside who had beaten him up. He guessed they were SS militia.

"Hush now," said Mother.

"Axel Munz is a great artist," said Johann.

"You think anyone who can make a funny face is a great artist," said Josef. But that didn't mean you had to beat them up, and Edi Fürst agreed.

"That's enough now," said Mother. "There's lots of other things to talk about." And she started to cry. Everyone was silent. Little Anselm, who was sitting on her lap, raised his eyebrows and looked reproachfully from one person to the next. It's all your fault that she's crying. That's how he looked at his brothers. Mother said it was all she could take that Father had nothing but trouble with the new people and they had almost lost everything. Wasn't that enough? Couldn't they be quiet now? Hadn't the family been in enough trouble already?

Luise came in and ordered two specials for the customs officials. "Just be quiet now," said Mother and went into the dining room, little Anselm on her hip, to wish the two customs officials bon appétit.

Johann and Tell ran upstairs. Johann took his school bag with him. He pulled out his composition notebook and read: "Man is a pitiful thing without a homeland, actually just a dry leaf in the wind. He can't defend himself. Anything can happen to him. He's fair game. One can never have enough homeland. There is always too little homeland, never too much. But everyone should know they are not alone in needing a homeland. Other people do, too. The worst crime, comparable to murder, is to rob others of their homeland or drive them from it.

As Winnetou's noble father Inchu Chuna says: The white man steals the red man's land, kills off the buffalo that provide the red man food and clothing, destroys the mustang herds, and ruins the prairies with railroad tracks, thus destroying the red man's homeland and, consequently, the red man himself. The white race acts superior. As long as it destroys other races, it is inferior, worse than any other race. And besides that, it is Christian in name only."

In the notebook, there was also a half-page of text and music. One sharp, four-four time. Text: Georg Schmitt. Music: Ernst Heller. That was their teacher. And Georg Schmitt was Schmitt the tinsmith. Johann read and hummed:

> *How oft on a flowering hillside*
> *or at rest by a freshet's flow*
> *have I gazed upon northern beauty*
> *or felt the southland's glow.*
> *But nothing has stilled my longing,*
> *not mountains or meadows or streams,*
> *till you, dear German homeland,*
> *fulfilled all my fondest dreams.*

He would be able to play it more precisely later on the piano, but now he was too excited. Was he excited? Muddled is what he was. Lying on his bed, he could look directly at the picture of the guardian angel that hung at an angle from the wall. Tell lay next to him, and he hugged him tight. Beneath the picture of the angel, primroses—a bit faded—and a burning candle. He jumped up, went over to the picture, and for the first time looked closely at the guardian angel. But the angel was concentrating entirely on the child beneath his protective hand, crossing the abyss on the bridge without a railing. Johann knocked on the glass. The guardian angel did not react. Tell sat next to Johann and looked up at the guardian angel, too.

"Come," said Johann, and he and Tell went downstairs and outside. First in the direction of the linden tree. Between the houses: trees in bloom, bushes in bloom, and the sun shining on everything. He had a solemn feeling. He turned off, went straight on until the Schorers', then turned left and continued downhill toward the firehouse. Of course, he said hello to Herr and Frau Schorer. They wanted no fruit trees or bushes in front of their house, only roses, small bush roses they spent all their time tending. Herr and Frau Schorer always said hello to Tell, too. When Johann got to the Hagens', he saw Helmut on his knees in the grass. Lichtensteiger's Helmut was pulling up grass from the meadow in front his uncle's house and barnyard—grass for his rabbits. On the other side of the street, Frommknecht's Hermann was trying to crank the motor of his modified Brennabor. When he saw Tell, he called over, "Hello, namesake!"

Johann said to Tell, "Yes, boy, look over there. That's what the real Tell looks like."

When he was finally allowed to have a dog, Johann knew he had to call him Tell. Frommknecht's Hermann had just played Wilhelm Tell in the gymnasium. Josef played the son from whose head the apple gets shot. The heavy green curtain had barely risen when Josef sang,

> The lake is laughing, inviting us in,
> The boy is asleep on the shore's green rim . . .

How Johann wished he could have been Josef.

"Hi, Helmut," said Johann, and began to pull up grass blades, too. Beneath the wooden stairs on the outside of the house leading up to the second floor where the Lichtensteigers lived, Helmut kept a whole wall full of rabbit hutches. Johann sent Tell home. It was his favorite trick. Tell's face got very sad whenever he was sent home. Johann had to repeat his command, had to say, Go home! three times before Tell slowly turned and set off for home at a morose trot.

Frau Schorer was digging in her rose bed while Herr Schorer applied his clippers to the tops of the bushes like Häfele the barber his scissors and comb to your hair. Frau Schorer straightened up and called to Tell sympathetically in her high, penetrating voice, "He has to obey, poor thing!"

"Go home," Johann said again. Tell obeyed.

Helmut's rabbits would get restless if Tell was nearby with Johann. And there was nothing Johann liked better than to fill the twenty feed troughs with fresh dandelions and then take some of the big rabbits out of their hutches, one after the other. How soft and heavy they were, lying in his arms! He liked the white ones best. They had had white rabbits, too, before he'd started school. Unexpectedly, Father had brought home some angoras. They had to be combed every day, and Father collected the wool picked up by the combs and took it to Lindau-Reutin. It was supposed to bring in some money. It didn't. After half a year, they took the white rabbits with the red eyes back to where they had gotten them. They didn't even try to start that business with the silver foxes once they had taken a look at the silver fox farm in the Allgäu. When Father and Johann got back from Ellhofen and reported that raising silver foxes was not going to work out, Mother had uttered a fairly loud: Thank God. The last attempt had been with silk worms. A room on the top floor was cleared out, the worms were fed, but then they died instead of producing cocoons from which the silk was supposed to be made.

Helmut thought Johann's clash with the teacher had been really great.

"What do you mean?" asked Johann. "What was so great about it?" he persisted. Helmut said that when Johann read his composition out loud about how much homeland people needed, the longer he read, the more the teacher shook his head. But then when he started to give Johann a lecture about homeland and race, he didn't have much to say. And the teacher's last sentence was really really great.

"Which last sentence was that?" asked Johann. Helmut said the teacher had said: You're wrong, of course, but you're a very good speaker.

"Oh, you mean that," said Johann.

"And you can forget the thing with Adolf," said Helmut. Adolf just had a grudge against Johann because Johann had defended his composition in such a really great way and Adolf hadn't even gotten a chance to read his.

"You think so?" said Johann.

"Yeah, I'm telling you," said Helmut. Adolf always wrote exactly what the teacher wanted to hear. And then the teacher goes and chooses Johann, has him read his out loud, and there was such a long discussion that Adolf didn't get to read his. And you better believe that peeved Adolf.

When all the troughs were full and the only sound coming from all the hutches was munching—the quiet crunch of dandelion greens between the teeth of the rabbits—Johann said that he'd just remembered something he had to do at home.

"So long, Helmut."

"Hang on a second," said Helmut. He just needed to show Johann the postcard that had come from Madeira today. Did Johann think he should bring it to school tomorrow? Johann deciphered what Helmut's father had written: Madeira, a heaven on earth. Each day more beautiful than the last on his KDF vacation. Still, he was really sorry to have missed Helmut's First Communion. Heartfelt greetings from your father.

"Whadd'ya think?" asked Helmut.

"Absolutely, bring it along," said Johann. Then another, So long, Helmut, and So long, Johann, and Johann took off.

"Somebody's in a hurry," said Frau Schorer as Johann dashed by, and Herr Schorer also held his hobby gardener's clippers motionless for a moment.

Luise was washing glasses and Johann, still panting heavily, asked if she was running low on tobacco products. Luise thought about it and then said, "*Woll,*" and counted up how many packs of Salems, R6s, Niles, and Khedives and how many stogies and Virginias she needed. Then he went over to the office, where Mother was sitting at Father's desk but not writing anything. When she sat at the desk like that, she was adding up accounts receivable and debts and then subtracting the former from the latter.

He said he needed her to sign a blank check to buy tobacco products. He got it and ran out. After a quick apology to Tell and a promise to return soon, he ran back down into the village, this time all the way to the linden tree, where all the streets converged. He turned off at the Linden Tree, their competition, and at the firehouse entered the big courtyard behind the Bruggers' house. Frau Rauh lived on the Bruggers' second floor and sold tobacco products wholesale, and if you were going to her place, you had to use the back steps. Herr Brugger's hunting dog, Treff, was sitting right in front of the door. German short-haired pointer. He greeted Johann. Treff probably remembered that Johann had stood next to him a week ago when Herr Brugger delivered his lecture, Adolf to the left of Treff, Johann to the right of Treff, and Treff standing between them. Herr Brugger had whistled them over from where they were playing, each hopping on one foot with their arms crossed and trying to see who could knock the other over by bashing into him. You lost if the foot you were holding up touched the ground first. The battle—or game—was ten to nine in favor of Adolf when they heard Herr Brugger's whistle. Herr Brugger had a long, drawn-out whistle that ended abruptly with a short, deeper note specially for Adolf. When they were in position to the left and right of Treff, Herr Brugger stood before them with his legs apart and said that Treff had been disobedient and must now be taught a lesson that would stick. That's why the boys were there to witness it.

And then he started in: "My dear Treff, you are a beautiful beast, a proud representative of your race, lithe and quick. Your fur is shiny, your eye sparkles, and your passion for the hunt leaves nothing to be desired. But more is also expected of such a highly talented dog. If you ever run off into the underbrush again or stray into someone else's hunting ground, you'll get a bullet in the head. A good hunting dog is always true to his master, or else there would be an end to any proper hunting. If you can't learn to control yourself, you'll get a bullet or never be allowed into the woods again. You can stay at home, lie around, and be lazy, and the next time you disobey, you'll be sold to a farmer who will chain you up. You won't get much to eat, your fur will lose its shine, your eye become dull and your voice hoarse. Soon you will be just one more mouth to feed, you'll be given away to a cottager who has nothing, and you'll end up in his stewpot. Fate? You have often performed splendidly, Treff. I'm proud of you. But your temperament is both your strength and your weakness. Either you and I are bound together forever, day and night, or it's the bullet for you or a miserable life on a chain and ending in a stewpot. It's up to you, Treff. I'm counting on you, Treff. Understood?" And Treff had gone over to Herr Brugger, stretched out his front legs, touched the tips of Herr Brugger's shoes with his nose, all the while emitting soulful sounds until he felt Herr Brugger's hand. The hand scratched his neck. His tone got deeper and he sat down, this time next to Herr Brugger. Herr Brugger said, "We understand each other, Treff. I'm glad." Treff had briefly rubbed his face against Herr Brugger's calf. "Good dog," Herr Brugger had said, and to Adolf and Johann: "Remember this, you two. It applies to all of us."

Johann climbed the stairs. As always, Frau Rauh opened her door at the first ring. Although the packages of tobacco products were stacked to the ceiling in her living room, it smelled of perfume. Frau Rauh was a lady. One time, Cousin Anselm had taken Josef and Johann to a shop in Wangen that carried nothing but perfume. He had bought himself some cologne and the salesman had sprayed Josef and Johann. Both of them had been terrifically fragrant.

Downstairs, Adolf was standing beside Treff. He said that whenever Johann mounted the stairs, he could hear right away that it was him. Nobody climbed stairs as slowly as Johann. Johann was glad Adolf had come out. Johann would not have dared ring at the Bruggers' glass door. But he didn't know how he could have gone home if Adolf had not been waiting for him now. Johann put down the bag full of tobacco products by the wall of the house. Then he faced Adolf, raised both hands, and spread his fingers. Adolf understood at once. He laced his spread fingers between Johann's spread fingers and the contest began. Each tried to bend the other's hands so far back that he was forced down and ended up kneeling before the winner. It was the kind of contest in which Adolf had almost always proved to be stronger on account of his thicker, more powerful forearms. Adolf was an enthusiastic splitter of wood. With big axes, he split firewood into bright piles. Beneath the overhang over the door to the lower carriage house, Johann also split the wood they needed. The lower carriage house was then stacked to the ceiling with the wood Johann had split. But Adolf split wood not just for the Bruggers, but also for other people who were not—or were no longer—able to do it themselves. Adolf's mother sent him out to needy, elderly people and admonished him not to accept anything for the work. Johann thought about that as he felt how difficult it was to bend back Adolf's hands even a quarter inch from the perpendicular. And Treff was also jumping up on Johann and barking. He was on Adolf's side, of course. But then gradually, Johann managed to bend Adolf's hands back a little. By standing on tiptoe and using his full weight and pressure from above, Johann now really should have been able to bend Adolf's hands completely back and force him to his knees. But Adolf simply wouldn't give in. Although his hands were bent back at an angle, he resisted any further pressure. And suddenly, the counter-pressure came. Adolf regained the perpendicular. They were back where they had started. And Treff barked and barked. In Adolf's face, Johann saw a sort of certainty or calm or confidence. Johann realized that Adolf thought he was stronger, and Johann remembered the greeting: Tell Adolf hi from me. He should've come to see me again, too. Johann felt the power gathering within him for the next, final assault. If Adolf was going to attack, Johann would see it in his eyes before he felt the pressure in his hands. He had learned that from Old Shatterhand in his fight with Metan-akva, the Kiowa they called Lightning Knife. A sudden dilation of the pupils would herald the decision to attack. But then came a jolt and pressure without Adolf's eyes showing anything beforehand. Johann was forced down until he was on his knees before Adolf. Treff finally stopped barking. Johann stood up.

"Serves you right," said Adolf, and grinned. And suddenly Johann didn't really mind that he'd lost to Adolf. Of course, he would have liked to force Adolf to his knees. If anyone, then Adolf. But if anyone was going to force Johann to his knees, then it should be Adolf. And here in the Bruggers' yard, where Herr Brugger might turn up any minute, Adolf just had to win. Johann would have been embarrassed to beat Adolf before the eyes of his father. And since Adolf had grinned at him like that, it was easier to talk to him. Adolf walked Johann home, just like always.

Adolf said that he hadn't liked Johann yesterday and this morning. Johann stooped down and picked up a big nail.

"What are all these nails lying around here?" he asked.

"Just rusty ones," said Adolf. He wouldn't bother bending over to pick up one like that. Johann dropped the nail.

The teacher hadn't been happy with Johann, either, said Adolf.

Johann said, "Let's just drop it." They walked on without saying anything until they reached the steps to the terrace. Usually Johann would now have gone back down the hill with Adolf and Adolf come back up the hill with him and on and on, back and forth, until either Adolf's mother or Johann's mother intervened. But Johann couldn't go back with Adolf today. Adolf was waiting for him to, he could see that. It gave him a good feeling. He hoped Adolf would think it wasn't right for Johann to simply not come back with him. He hoped Adolf would be annoyed and get mad. Adolf said he didn't think Johann's composition was very good. For the first time, Johann sounded like a show-off to him.

All Johann could say was, "Let's just drop it."

"So," said Adolf.

"So," said Johann.

Adolf turned and walked away. He didn't just walk: he marched. That was abundantly clear. He swung his arms and his back was exaggeratedly straight. Suddenly, he took off running.

Johann turned, went into the house, and delivered the tobacco products to Luise.

When he saw Johann coming back, Tell had left his place in front of the doghouse and, since Johann did not order him away again, he went with Johann up to his room. They both lay down on the bed. Johann looked over at the guardian angel, who reminded him of Anita. She'd worn wings, too, when she was a dove. When he closed his eyes, he saw Crooked Hat riding away with his droopy, light-colored rucksack. Now he was happy to think about Crooked Hat. Hadn't he had wings, too? But most of all, he liked to think about La Paloma. The goddess, the dove, the goddess. He got up again, went into the next room where his parents had slept until his father had to be moved to the room on the other side of the hall. From the bookcase he took out the book from which Father had last had him read the passage with the word *correspondence*. It was the last word about which Father had said: You just have to look at it. It had been in this book, written by someone named Emanuel Swedenborg. Johann wanted to find the pages he had read to his father between Christmas and New Year's. He found the page where it said that one calls everything in the natural world that arises from the spiritual world a correspondence. And the doctrine of correspondence was a doctrine of the angels. He read that a few times. Each time it was easier to read. Like when you practiced some difficult passage on the piano until it wasn't difficult anymore. The doctrine of correspondence was a doctrine of the angels. *Correspondence*. It belonged in the tree next to *trepidation*, *bijoux*, *curiosity*, *exuberance*, *whitecaps*, *freckles*, *weeping willow*, *reincarnation*, *kingdom of heaven*, *chattels*, *memorial*, *Beatrijs*, *correspondence*. To his surprise, *Beatrijs* no longer floated among the names, but between *memorial* and *correspondence*. So you can look at it, Father would have said.

There was one sentence he looked at again and again: Accordingly, all bodily processes in feature, speech, and gesture are correspondences.

Maybe someday he could allow an entire sentence to fly into the word tree, so he could look at it at any time.

The burning candle was reflected in the glass of the picture of the angel. The reflection of the burning candle left only the angel's wings and head visible. He got up and blew out the candle. Tell stayed on the bed. Johann lay back down even closer to Tell than before, petted him as he had never petted him before, got the Bible out of the bookcase, and read to Tell what Father had read to him last winter when they had talked about angels. *Balaam's donkey*. That's you, Tell. You're the only one who noticed that it wasn't me but an angel. Like Balaam's donkey that saw the Angel blocking the path, tried to squeeze past him, and then because the angel wouldn't allow it, went down on his knees and was beaten three times by Balaam until the Lord opened Balaam's eyes so he could see the Angel of the Lord standing in the path.

He would never, ever deliver Anita's greeting. It was painful to separate from Adolf. Unless he distanced himself from Adolf, he could not neglect to do what Anita had asked. Anita and Adolf belonged together. He was alone. Since no one was there, he did some howling, but only a little bit. When Tell started to howl with him, he was able to stop. He recited to Tell the two lines he was going to make into a poem someday:

> Oh, that early in the day
> I should be so lonely.

He would wrap himself in this language as soon as he couldn't stand it here anymore. *Trepidation, bijoux, curiosity, exuberance, whitecaps, freckles, weeping willow, reincarnation, kingdom of heaven, chattels, memorial, Beatrijs, correspondence.* He compared his father's words with the words that Adolf had from his father: *manhood, footwear, consequences, role model, bad example, bootlicker, fop, womenfolk, litmus test.* He didn't envy Adolf the word *manhood*, but only the ease with which he said it, as if it was a make of car. He could not use his provisional *dick-*word, even when he was speaking only to himself. He had heard the kind of people who said *dick* and how they said it. It wasn't the way he wanted to talk about the most precious part of himself. He couldn't even say *ass*. Mother always said *anus*. It was the only High German word in her language. Whenever she said it, she looked uneasy. Johann would certainly never say that word. All these proffered words pained him.

"You are who you are," he said. And his member responded: I am who I am.

And Johann said, quietly, "IAWIA, can you hear me?"

Josef said, too, that he preferred to play the piano for himself alone. Johann would find words for himself alone.

CHAPTER EIGHT

Taking Leave

JOHANN FEARED THE MOMENT when his eyes would meet the teacher's. In the village, the teacher was both referred to with reverence on hundreds of occasions and feared for his fits. People said they came from his silver plate. In any case, Johann wet his much-too-long hair and combed it as smooth and flat on his head as he possibly could. Whenever the teacher mentioned tango boys or love-locks, Johann felt he meant him.

He was glad when he ran into Göser's Trudl and Lichtensteiger's Helmut. When Trudl started talking about yesterday and the day before, he didn't know where to look. She thought it was swell the way he'd stood up for her. He could only shake his head and say, "Aw, come on, Trudl!" But she insisted.

"It's really true," she said, while Helmut One nodded vigorous agreement. "It really is. That lunatic would have beaten me to death if you hadn't stood up and said: Herr Teacher, may I please be excused? And the look he gave you—I was really afraid for you. When he turned toward you, I got right up off the floor and put the key back into the harmonium. It had fallen out when I crashed against it. Then I snuck back to my seat because I could see it was your turn now. You caught him off guard. We all know he's a good-natured person, but when he gets one of his fits, anything is possible. I thought I was done for. And then you pipe up: Herr Teacher, may I please be excused? And even though you interrupted him at his touchiest moment—when he's giving someone a thrashing—he didn't just smack you one. You know as well as me he only gives excuses during recess, and then you go and ask him in the middle of a fit. Oh jeez, I thought, poor Johann. Did you see the way he looked at you? But you—you meet his stare, stare back cool as a cucumber, but friendly-like. He walks toward you, slowly, but instead of pasting you one that would have sent you flying into the harmonium, if not worse, he walks right past you, goes to the door, opens it, gives a little bow, and says: At your service, Herr Johann, you may be excused. And you walk past him—I think you even said: Thank you, Herr Head Teacher—and all of a sudden he was our nice Herr Heller again, our beloved teacher!"

Since there was nothing Johann could say, he started talking about something else. He would rather not have said anything at all. He had to pull himself together now, get ready so he wouldn't just run away at the first glance from the teacher. Everybody in the schoolroom was talking about yesterday—about Johann.

Adolf whispered, "Now you can show off again like ten naked niggers, can't you?"

The teacher came in, went to the front of the room, called out, "Heil Hitler," and received the pupils' "Heil Hitler, Herr Teacher" in return. The teacher looked only at Johann. And how he looked at him, milder than ever before.

After school, Ludwig said to Johann, "You would've thought he was trying to cozy up to you."

Adolf said, "Sure, since Johann's playing the show-off now. Tango hairdo, love-locks, artist's mane—a regular dandy."

However, today was also Johann's next-to-last morning in this school. From Monday on, he would be attending the secondary school in Lindau. Two of them, he and Berni, were going to be secondary school pupils starting next Monday.

When the bells started tolling eleven o'clock, the teacher interrupted his lesson as always and struck a pose so everyone could see how much he suffered from the clanging of the church bells, booming loudly over from the church next door. He held his ears. His face: one huge grimace of pain. After the bells had finally come to rest, he said, "Adolf, go open the door for the poet." Adolf, his favorite pupil, was used to such assignments. He was at the door at once, opened it, and in staggered—and almost fell—Schmitt the tinsmith. Johann probably knew the master tinsmith Schmitt better than anyone else here. Almost every day, he was the first at the regulars' table. The master tinsmith had never shown up later than nine. They started drawing his beer as soon as he entered the dining room. When Johann watched the tinsmith drain his glass without once setting it down, he sometimes had the impression he wasn't drinking for his own sake but rather to water his magnificent mustache. Today, Johann could tell as soon as he saw him that the tinsmith had watered more than just his mustache. Johann had never seen him so unsteady on his feet—or, yes he had, once before, when the tinsmith had forgotten who he was. Mother had had to call up Frau Schmitt and ask if her husband was at home. Only when the master tinsmith heard from his own wife that he wasn't at home did he concede it was possible that the person who was not at home was himself.

Adolf grabbed the hand of the staggering man and led him to the teacher at the front of the room; he offered him the chair behind the teacher's desk. Once the master tinsmith was seated, the teacher said they all should greet the poet with the German Greeting. He himself at once raised his right arm and stretched his hand out so flat and straight that the fingers actually curved upwards a bit. Everyone followed his example and cried out, "Heil Hitler, Herr Schmitt." The tinsmith stood up, clicked his heels together, laid his hands along the seams of his trousers like a soldier, lowered his chin a tiny bit, cried, "Yes, Sir," and then slumped back onto the chair. He realized he had forgotten something, jumped up again, stretched out his right hand, cried, "Heil Hitler," and—almost while still uttering this acknowledgement—collapsed back onto the chair.

The teacher called, "Irmgard, Leni!" Both jumped up and took a wreath out of a basket that stood next to the harmonium—a rather small wreath, actually much too small for four hands. But it had apparently been agreed upon or ordered to be that way. Together they had to

take the little wreath out of the basket, carry it with their four hands
to the master tinsmith, place it on his head, and maybe even press it
down on his head to make sure it didn't slip off first thing. The tinsmith
looked startled but left his hands where they were, resting on his knees.
As soon as the wreath was on his head, he made an effort to straighten
up as much as he could.

The teacher said that with this laurel wreath, the Wasserburg School
was honoring the outstanding poetic achievement of the regional poet
Georg Schmitt. The fact was that he was more than just a regional poet.
His verses were intended to be sung all over Germany, as proved by the
song for which he, the teacher, had written a melody so that everyone
could sing it. He gave them the pitch with his tuning fork, said, "Three,
four!" and led all four classes, who had risen from their seats, in singing:

> *How oft on a flowering hillside*
> *or at rest by a freshet's flow*
> *have I gazed upon northern beauty*
> *or felt the southland's glow.*
> *But nothing has stilled my longing,*
> *not mountains or meadows or streams,*
> *till you, dear German homeland,*
> *fulfilled all my fondest dreams.*

"You will now sing this song while you escort the poet through the
village as his honor guard." Again he called out, "Adolf!" Adolf fetched
the master tinsmith, led him out, and saw to it that he made it down the
broad sandstone steps into the schoolyard without falling. Then they all
lined up, the tinsmith at the head between Adolf and Guido, and behind
them the four classes. The teacher called, "Forward, march," raised his
hand in the German Greeting, and the column set off. Frommknecht's
Hermann, who was in charge of everything having to do with music, led
the singing, and the song resounded. It was repeated until they arrived
at the Schmitts' little house. Frau Schmitt, the only seamstress in the
village whom everyone referred to as a tailor, had prepared a basket full

of soft pretzels. The pretzels were sliced open and spread with butter. She removed the laurel wreath from her husband's head and then passed the pretzels around to the boys and girls and praised them all for their singing. Johann was well prepared to sing along, because he had learned the melody the day before. Everything above a high C was his specialty. He competed with Ludwig, who also had a voice that reached the high notes without effort. . . . *noooothing has stiiiilled my loooonging.* It went up to a high F sharp. Johann had the feeling that the others were only singing to allow him and Ludwig to rise to the high notes. Too bad Adolf didn't think much of singing. Music's okay, he would say. Music at the proper time and place. He sounded like Herr Brugger.

Afterwards, when everyone had dispersed, Adolf stayed beside Johann and continued on with him past his own house; once past the linden tree, they were finally all by themselves and Adolf said, "I could have killed you yesterday and the day before."

Johann thought: I'd like to see you try. But all he said was, "Sometimes I could kill you, too."

"Yesterday and the day before were the first time for me," said Adolf.

"The day before was the first time for me," said Johann.

"Then we're even," said Adolf. When they reached the steps to the terrace, they turned around. And it was back down the hill to the Bruggers', and back up, and back down, and back . . . They no longer took Main Street down to the linden tree and from there around the Linden Tree Restaurant to the Bruggers'. Now they took the back way that ran along beneath and between blooming trees almost the whole distance, and wasn't tarred.

Thank goodness Adolf had said that about wanting to kill him. Since Adolf said it, Johann could look him in the eye again. Now they could talk to each other again. As they walked back and forth, neither said anything that the other didn't already know. But nothing was said the same way it had been said before. This day was the day that had never been before. They talked as they were able to talk only on this day. They were something like kings. They felt that way because they were walking back and forth between their houses, and everything that occurred to them was at their command. Johann was waiting for Adolf to begin talking about Anita. He would say: She sent you her best. Actually, she was waiting for you. She only wants you, not me.

As more and more sentences went back and forth between him and Adolf, as they both sensed that this talking to each other would never come to an end, as Frau Schorer—when they went past her for the third time—called out, "My, don't you two have weighty things to discuss!", as Johann sensed that it made no difference at all what they talked about, he also felt that he could forego Anita. He would convey her greeting, degrade himself to a mere messenger who had no chance with her. You're the only one who has a chance, Adolf, he would say. She started talking about you, sent you her best. But to be the first to mention Anita—that he couldn't do. He could look at Adolf when Adolf was talking. Despite his terrible haircut, Adolf had a beautiful head. You could see so clearly the way his neck joined his head, because there was no hair to cover even a quarter-inch. It wasn't a long neck. Adolf was a ram. A clean-shaven ram.

And suddenly, Anita's name was uttered. Adolf said Anita was kind of a lame goose. She's anything but, thought Johann. Adolf probably saw a completely different Anita. Maybe he meant the way she acted when she wasn't in the ring, wasn't flying around the pole, wasn't riding on Vishnu. A lame goose, clearly one of Herr Brugger's expressions. Never had Ludwig or Guido or Paul or Helmut One or Helmut Two said about a girl that she was a lame goose. Johann was happy that Adolf had said something so completely inappropriate about Anita. He admired Adolf for not sinking to the ground in pure adoration. Instead, he was able to say something that, though untrue, still had some pride and independence to it. How strong, how lofty Adolf must be to be able to call Anita a lame goose. For Johann, it was a reason not to deliver her greeting after all. The fact would remain his secret. It felt good to have a secret like that. Not to mention, how was he going to prove to Adolf that he had been in Langenargen? For Adolf, he had been here. Adolf would think it was just showing off if Johann said that he had been in Langenargen and done thus and so. And yet Adolf was the only person who would have understood what had happened to Johann, because he had experienced something similar himself. And he had told only Johann about it, no one else. Because Franz Döbele lived far out at the edge of the village, the Bruggers let him eat lunch at their house in the winter. Once, Franz had spotted a tree trunk sawed into boards in the Bruggers' yard. The boards were separated from each other by blocks of wood so they could dry out. But the way they had been stacked up, you could still see exactly what the tree trunk had looked like. Adolf said Döbele Franz had almost shed tears when he saw those boards. If he could have some boards like that, the airplane he was planning to build would be as good as finished. Adolf immediately gets the handcart out of the shed—his father was on the road in the Allgäu—and because Franz's enthusiasm is infectious, he says, "You can have two of them."

And Döbele Franz says, "The two in the middle." They load them on the handcart and pull them out to Wasserburg Hill, where the Döbeles and other families who don't have much live together in a way that people in the village can't even imagine. As they are unloading the boards, Adolf hears the whistle—his father's whistle. The long-drawn-out whistle that drops abruptly to a short, deeper pitch, the whistle Herr Brugger uses to call Adolf from wherever he is. But not when Adolf is at least a mile outside the village! Nevertheless, he does hear the whistle and runs back home, pulling the empty handcart behind him. Right away he spots his father's car. So his father is back sooner than expected. Adolf himself can't understand why he did it. Döbele Franz bewitched him. Stealing—just about the worst thing you could do. A scoundrel. He's going to be punished worse than ever. He sees his mother in the open doorway, and his father appears next to her. "Good thing you're here," he calls to him. "I just bought seven head of cattle in Simmerberg and resold them to a man in Konstanz. They have to be put onto a boat in Lindau. Getting seven cows to go peacefully up the gangway—nobody's as good at that as my Adolf." And he's already heading for the car. Adolf follows, and the car is parked right next to the boards, of course. And what does Adolf see? The two middle boards, the ones he carried off with Döbele Franz, are no longer missing. Adolf said he had felt so light he could have risen into the air the next moment. Döbele Franz, he thought, would have called it taking off.

Johann felt awful. Adolf had told him everything. But he was keeping everything from Adolf.

They had reached the Bruggers' again and were standing behind the house.

Suddenly, Adolf said if he were Johann he wouldn't go to school in Lindau.

"Man, why don't you stay here?" said Adolf. Johann would have to admit, wouldn't he, that Herr Heller was the best teacher far and wide, a once-in-a-lifetime role model. "Remember those productions of *Wilhelm Tell* and *The Death of Schlageter*? Nobody else can teach you as much as Herr Heller." Johann could not disagree.

Josef was taking French and would soon start learning Latin. Father had said whoever couldn't speak French was unfortunate. Neither Ludwig nor Guido nor Paul, neither Helmut One nor Helmut Two expected him to stay in Wasserburg. But Adolf did. And Johann was happy that Adolf expected it and even demanded it. Fortunately, Adolf could not accept the fact that Johann was going to school in Lindau.

"Whadd'ya say?" said Adolf, and gave Johann two or three punches in the chest. Johann didn't defend himself. They weren't really punches, just touches, invitations. Johann was supposed to admit that Adolf knew better than Johann what was right for Johann. Adolf started in again about going to school in Lindau. Now came the words his father used against educated people: *ink in your veins, starveling, loafer, drudge, shirker, pansy*. Adolf could not know that Johann had already heard Adolf's father use these words against Johann's father, and also against Johann and Josef.

"Well?" said Adolf.

Johann said, "Well, see you tomorrow, Adolf." And turned and walked toward the linden tree so slowly that Adolf could easily have called him back.

"Oh, Johann," he heard Adolf say. But it sounded as if Adolf was saying it more to himself then calling to Johann.

Johann felt miserable as he walked toward the linden tree. He could not turn around to look. If Adolf called to him again he would turn around. And stay. With Adolf. Forever.

In order to make the turn at the linden that would hide him from Adolf's view, he said all the words to himself that Adolf got from his father: *manhood, footwear, consequences, role model, bad example, bootlicker, fop, womenfolk, litmus test.* Johann had always admired the way Adolf lifted his chin when he used these words in a sentence. The words that moved Johann's tree, he sensed, could not be said aloud: *trepidation, bijoux, curiosity, exuberance, whitecaps, freckles, weeping willow, reincarnation, kingdom of heaven, chattels, memorial, Beatrijs, correspondence.*

Johann had just turned into his street at the linden, where all streets converged, when he saw two men coming toward him whom he had never seen together before: Herr Schlegel and Hanse Luis. Herr Schlegel was more dragging his walking stick than wielding it. One could not imagine him ever again drawing out the sword by its elegant handle and declaring: A personal gift from Frederick the Great after the Battle of Leuthen! The large, ponderous man now walked as if he had become too heavy for himself. Perhaps he would not have been walking at all if Hanse Luis had not taken him by the hand and pulled him along. Herr Schlegel let himself be pulled.

Johann said his *Grüss Gott* and Hanse Luis asked in a loud voice, "Where is Manila?"

"In the Philippines," Johann replied.

"Pernambuco?" asked Hanse Luis.

"Seventy-seven and one half hours," said Johann.

"Lakehurst to Friedrichshafen?" cried Hanse Luis.

"Fifty-five hours," cried Johann.

"And twenty-three minutes," added Herr Schlegel weakly.

"My respects," said Hanse Luis, and without letting Herr Schlegel's right hand go, he made a graceful bow to the huge old man.

Herr Schlegel mumbled, "Up against the red wall and shoot him!" Hanse Luis let go of Herr Schlegel's hand, placed his left forearm between his chest and his stomach, rested his right elbow in his left hand, quickly covered his mouth with his right hand, and then turned his hand and froze it in the German Greeting. Johann laughed to show Hanse Luis he understood that his mother was being imitated.

Hanse Luis could imitate anyone. No one need be offended when Hanse Luis did his impression of them. Hanse Luis always imitated what was most characteristic of you. You could see how much enjoyment he got from doing impressions so well that everyone could tell immediately whom he meant. At the regulars' table a few weeks ago, he had imitated Herr Harpf. Herr Harpf was the new local group leader. Herr Minn didn't want to be local group leader anymore. He had resigned of his own accord. His son had been insulted, and in the Station Restaurant, too. Head Teacher Heller was giving a talk entitled "Yuletide, a German Holiday" and had made fun of the Virgin Birth. When Mother told Josef and Johann what had happened, she said she thought the Lord God could not allow a thing like that to be said. Somehow she feared for the safety of the house in which such a thing had been uttered. She thought that because she had listened without protest and without defending our dear Lord God from such disgraceful slander, the restaurant would collapse immediately and bury them all. She was hardly able to breathe, much less say anything. But no one else, not a single man or woman, had said anything, either. A few even smiled—she left it to Josef and Johann to imagine who they had been. Those were the lost souls, beyond help. And then young Minn raised his hand. He stands up, dressed in the uniform of the Navy SA, to which he belongs, and protests against the way the head teacher was talking here about a Christian article of faith. He, Max Minn, was a Lutheran. It wasn't his article of faith. But he felt himself insulted by the words of his fellow party member, Head Teacher Heller. Now, young Minn has the habit of covering everything over with *sh-sh*, and even more so when he's upset. Mother said it was almost all hissing sounds, but you could understand it anyway. The people who had been smiling before jumped up. Either Max Minn apologized to the head teacher, or they would throw him out on the spot. He did not apologize. And so, even though he would surely have left on his own, they threw him out. Five or six or seven of them grabbed for him. There wasn't enough of him for all the hands that were grabbing. His glasses got knocked off and trampled. The next day, Herr Minn Senior resigned and turned in his membership book. One other person turned in his membership book, too: little Herr Häckelsmiller. Since little Herr Häckelsmiller never went to church, but his wife went more than once a day, people assumed his resignation from the party—and after all, he had been a member since 1924—to be the work of his wife. The assumption was that her prayers had finally been answered, and she had prayed her husband right out of the Godless Party.

Fräulein Agnes, the Lutheran sacristan (the Lutherans had been able to build their own church in the meantime, because everyone was making money again)—Fräulein Agnes, whose membership number was not a year younger than that of little Herr Häckelsmiller, was supposed to have refused to fetch her neighbor Häckelsmiller his milk every evening because he had left the party.

Since then, the customs official Herr Harpf had become the local group leader. He spoke Franconian-Bavarian dialect in a bright, tinny voice, and in his capacity as local group leader moved like a figure from a mechanical clock. Hanse Luis couldn't resist imitating him. In the Station Restaurant recently, he was doing his impression of the local group leader and everyone was laughing. They didn't notice that Herr Harpf himself had entered the room and had seen and heard everything. Fortunately, he had to laugh himself. If he was ever sick, he said, Hanse Luis could stand in for him.

Johann watched Herr Schlegel and Hanse Luis until they disappeared from view between the nursery and the butcher shop. They were probably going to have a drink with Boger's Paul the cooper, since the restaurants weren't allowed to serve Herr Schlegel alcohol anymore.

Public Notice: Prohibition from Consumption of Alcoholic Beverages for Herr Schlegel. Frau Fürst had not simply laid their newspaper on the table. She'd opened it herself and asked that Luise be brought in to hear what she would read from the page she had opened. Taverns and restaurants were officially prohibited from waiting on the builder David Schlegel because of alcoholism. Whoever served him alcohol would lose their concession. Frau Fürst looked from one to the other to assure herself that they had all taken in the announcement. Then she said in a more friendly, conciliatory tone, "Heil Hitler, everybody!" and left. That means no more David parties, thought Johann. On his name day, Herr Schlegel always invited all the Davids in the parish to drink lake wine with him. Last year there were eleven Davids. Over and done with.

Tell jumped up when he saw Johann coming. Johann ordered him to stay by his doghouse beneath the carriage house overhang until Johann came to him. Carriage house—he would probably always think of Adolf when that word came up, because Adolf had tried to prove to Johann that the thing Johann called a carriage house was a barn. Adolf had said that a larger lean-to was a shed. An even larger one was a barn. The upper, smaller carriage house was a shed. The bigger one, a barn. Nobody in the whole village said carriage house when they meant shed or barn.

Johann had accepted the fact that what they had was not a highboy even though he still called their secretary a highboy. But in the case of their two carriage houses, he wouldn't give in. He did, however, avoid using the word carriage house in Adolf's presence. Adolf clearly could not accept Johann's calling both a shed and a barn a carriage house.

Johann and Tell passed Niklaus, who was busy filling sacks, and went up to the house. From the spare room, Josef with his never-ending Bach pieces. "They keep going in circles," the Princess once said, "but they're good to wash dishes to." Upstairs, he lay down on his bed with Tell. Outside, a train was signaling its departure. Footsteps crunched in the gravel and then rang hollowly on the planks of the scale, but then Josef began a crescendo that drowned out everything else. The sun slanted in through the window, sharply dividing the room into planes of light and shadow. The leisurely ticking of the warning bell as the crossing barriers were lowered penetrated through Josef's piano playing after all. Johann whispered his two lines into Tell's ear:

> Oh, that early in the day
> I should be so lonely.

Tell shook himself. Of course, Johann had to turn to him, take him by the neck in both hands, and give him a good shake. Because that was what Tell considered bliss: to be shaken by Johann.

PART THREE

Harvest

but the present. After all, it too is as good as nonexistent. And the future is a grammatical fiction.

Instead of the past, should we call it the character of having been? Would that make it more present? The past does not like me trying to capture it. The more directly I approach it, the more clearly I encounter, instead of the past, the motive that at the present moment enjoins me to seek out the past. More often than not, it is a lack of justification that directs us into what is past. We are looking for reasons that could justify the way we are. Some people have learned to repudiate their past. They generate a past they deem more favorable. They do it for the sake of the present. One learns all too precisely what sort of past one ought to have had if one wants to come off well in the currently prevailing present. More than once, I have watched people positively slipping out of their past so they can present a more favorable past to the present. The past as a role. There are not many things in our conscious and behavioral economy that have such a pronounced role-playing character as the past. Is it wishful thinking that people with unstandardized pasts should be able to live together as the different individuals they are by virtue of—among other things—their pasts? In reality, our dealings with the past become more stringently standardized with each passing decade. The more standardized these dealings, the more what is displayed as the past is really a product of the present. It is conceivable that the past will be made to disappear entirely and will serve only to express how we feel now—or rather, how we're supposed to feel: the past as a wardrobe department from which one can choose a costume as needed. A past completely available, approved, well-lit and laundered, and totally suitable for the present. Ethically and politically revised. Modeled for us by our most immaculate, our best and brightest. Whatever our past may have been, we have freed ourselves from anything in it that was not the way we would like it to be now. Perhaps one could say we have emancipated ourselves. Then the past exists within us as something we have overcome. Something we have mastered. We must come off looking good. But not so mendacious that we would notice it ourselves.

CHAPTER ONE

The Past as Present

MAGDA IS GOING TO CUT a piece from Johann's lower lip wit
scissors. He wasn't able to stop her from getting hold of the s
can already see that he won't be able to keep Magda from c
his lower lip. They're in a train. It's fairly dark. The train sto
manages to get his luggage thrown out, two suitcases. Johann
he's escaped. It's the Wasserburg station. One of the suitca
even belong to him. That's an embarrassment. On account
He has used some sort of trick to escape her. He shouldn't
that, he thinks.

The past is contained in the present and cannot be separa
way you can extract one substance contained in another su
means of some clever process, and then you would have it as
past doesn't exist as such. It exists only as something contai
the present, a decisive or suppressed factor—and in the latter
sive, although suppressed. The idea that the past is slumberir
can awaken it, for example, with the help of a lucky turn o
the relevant smell or some other long-forgotten signal—by
intellectual or sensual data—is a delusion you can surrender
as long as you don't notice that what you thought was the rec
is really a present mood or whim for which the past has merel
the material, but not the spirit. Those who most long to rec
past are in the most danger of thinking that what they have
is what they were seeking. We are unable to admit that there

To wish for the past, a presence over which we are not the master, with no conquests to be made after the fact. The goal of our wishful thinking: a disinterested interest in the past, and that it would meet us halfway of its own accord.

CHAPTER TWO

Harvest

THIS FALL, HE WASN'T BAREFOOT on the ladder. He had a sack hung over his shoulder that held many more apples than the little bag he used to use. As Johann let apple after apple slide into the sack, it got so heavy he wouldn't have been able to stand barefoot on the rungs. He had never been so seldom barefoot as this year, and his feet weren't toughened. In the spring, the laced boots of his home guard flak battery; in the summer, the jackboots of the Reich Labor Service. And soon—hopefully soon—would follow the hiking boots of the mountain troopers. If you volunteered, you got to choose. Johann had chosen the tank corps like Josef, had been rejected because he wore glasses, and had then chosen the mountain troops.

The gentle snap of the breaking stem as he picked each apple from its branch. Still in his ears: the percussive chopping of the twin-cannon flak. He preferred the hard *hack-hack* of the two-centimeter canons, however, to the booming of the eighty-eights. In Chieming, where he finished his sharpshooter training, he had filched one of the long, slim, two-centimeter projectiles. They lay in your hand, so cool and smooth and lovely. For two weeks, a plane pulled a tattered square of target across the sky, and they had shot at it from morning to night without ever scoring a hit. In April, Friedrichshafen gets bombed to ruins in a single night, and that same night they practice shooting tracers into the black skies above the Chiemsee. Johann wanted to hit something. When he aimed, he was an aimer and nothing but an aimer. The target

positively sucked him in. It was unthinkable that he would not hit it
dead-on. His Jungvolk target practice log was sacred. He kept it in his
secret compartment. He had long since inherited Josef's air rifle. Even
before Josef joined up, he had lost interest in shooting at the targets
thumbtacked to the door of the carriage house. In the meantime, the
door was riddled with holes from which the small lead pellets, deformed
on impact, peeked out. In Fürstenfeldbruck, Johann the Reich Labor
Service man had shot thirty-three of a possible thirty-six points, prone
and without support. Thirty-four would have earned him a Sunday
leave. Mother waited day and night for at least one of them—Josef
or him—to come home. In July, right after the awards ceremony in
Stralsund, Johann had caught a train to Berlin and stayed only long
enough to transfer to the first train heading south. The others from his
team were going to continue on later. They wanted to get out and gape
at the smoking ruins of Berlin.

When Johann stepped down onto the platform in Wasserburg after
a twenty-six-hour journey, Herr Deuerling said, "Get goin', get along
with ya! What took you so long?" Josef had just left on the noon train.

Johann hadn't known that Josef would also have leave and come
home. He had only hoped he would. Josef was done with training
and already a non-com, but not yet tested under fire. Before that:
home leave.

Johann had hoped Josef would arrive before August, when Johann
had to enter the Reich Labor Service in Fürstenfeldbruck.

Coming directly from Stralsund, it would have been great to meet up
with Josef and tell him how they had fared in Stralsund—in Dänholm,
actually, but Josef knew that already, since he had himself competed in
the Marine Hitlerjugend national championships two years ago. This
year, they were only fourth in the crew race, by half a boat's length. But
first in technical rowing and in semaphoring, too: Reich champions,
thanks to Johann. The next best, a Berliner, had read his ten words in
1'40" with twelve errors, Johann in 1'30" with no errors. He could
have done it in 1'20" or 1'10", except that the signalmen provided by
the navy took much too long to start the next word after Johann had

shouted out the word they were signaling before they had even finished it. Johann could guess any ten-letter word in the German language after only the first three letters—or four at the most. If they signaled H I N . . . Johann shouted HINDENBURG. If they signaled S T E U . . . and STEUERMANN had already been sent, Johann shouted STEUER-BORD. If they signaled R E G E . . . Johann shouted REGENBOGEN. If they signaled T A N . . . Johann shouted TANNENBAUM. If they signaled F L A G . . . Johann shouted FLAGGLEINE. If they signaled S I G N . . . Johann shouted SIGNALGAST. If they signaled A N K . . . Johann shouted ANKERKETTE. If they signaled K O E N . . . Johann shouted KÖNIGSBERG. If they signaled L E U . . . Johann shouted LEUCHT-TURM. But by the time the signalman received the next word from the timer standing beside him and started signaling it, another second had been lost. At least. But he was Reich champion in semaphoring nevertheless. Wolfgang—the second Wolfgang in the village—was the best runner with 12'0". In total points, they were eighth out of thirty-nine teams. And if Josef had still been on the team, they would have been second like two years ago. Everybody said so, and he would have delivered it to Josef hot off the presses if Josef had been home. With Josef as starboard stroke, they would have been the first cutter across the finish line this time. They would have beaten the pants off the Berliners and Hamburgers and Heidenheimers good and proper. They couldn't win a race without Josef to set the stroke and accelerate to the limit. All ten of them in Stralsund said so, and so did the cox.

It's stupid when things go wrong like this. He breaks his neck to get home, and Josef has left already. It hadn't been a pleasant journey. July heat. Crowded compartments and corridors. Nothing but soldiers. Disgruntled soldiers: bawling, bellowing, bitter, silent. Wearing dirty, disheveled uniforms. Johann the only civilian. He had taken off his Marine Hitlerjugend uniform in the men's room of the Stralsund station and stuffed it into his rucksack. He thought the Marine Hitlerjugend uniform was overdone, almost dandyish. It was only wearable near or actually on the water. The round cap was especially hideous: a circular lid with no visor and a bit of material

stretched above a wide, stiff rim. Join the navy? Never! He was never
going to wear a cap without a visor. It was incomprehensible to him
how anyone could volunteer for the navy, despite the uniform. He
was embarrassed every time he had to walk to muster through the
village in such a getup, and he never put the cap on until he was
down by the lake.

Between Stralsund and Berlin the train had suddenly begun to sway.
Johann knew at once what was happening. He was surprised no one
sprang to their feet except him. He couldn't stay put on his jump seat
in the corridor. If the train was going to tip over, he didn't want to get
caught in the corridor again. If the train fell onto the corridor side, the
car wall would be torn open and crushed against the compartments.
He couldn't say anything to these drunken, smoking, bawling, or dozing soldiers. He had to find a conductor or an emergency brake. When
the train began to accelerate into the next straightaway, the last car,
which was swaying the most, would jump the rails and tip over, pulling
down the next-to-last car, which would pull down the next car, until
the train that was already dragging the last car through the ballast with
its side ripped open could be brought to a stop. That's exactly what had
happened last March 4th between Dornbirn and Bregenz, a Sunday
evening when Johann and Gerhard were on their way home from skiing. When Johann saw out the window that they were leaning toward
the ballast and heard the terrifying grinding and shattering, he had just
enough time to take off his glasses but not to stick them in his pocket.
There was a last shudder and bang, and then silence, except for something still trickling down. Gerhard and Johann had been standing in the
corridor, and the wall of a compartment had slammed down between
them. Johann struggled up through the compartment door, clambered
out the window, and then back down through the next window and
into the ripped-open corridor and found Gerhard, head-first up, to his
belt in gravel and filth. Johann recognized him only by his ski pants.
He started digging and clawed away the gravel until he came to the rav-
aged face and smashed head. Despite the four-year difference in their
ages, Gerhard was the best friend Johann had ever had. Not a whiff of

competition. Each wanted only to please the other. In the woods, they whistled in harmony. And they made fun of each other at every opportunity but never took anything seriously. Except perhaps what could be expressed by their eyes. Johann had ridden home on an emergency replacement train. Gerhard's parents had already been notified by Herr Deuerling. Johann's mother couldn't utter a sound but only moved her lips. Seven dead, all in the last car. Everyone else injured, except for Johann. The first thing Mother was able to get out: Your guardian angel. And now he was in a train that was about to tip over, just like in Haselstauden in the Vorarlberg! Johann looked for a conductor he could tell to warn the engineer: Slow down, or you'll throw us off the track. But he couldn't find a conductor, only soldiers he couldn't talk to. They were talking about the front, about their wounds, about nurses they had banged first this way, then that way. And how they'd blasted away with the new MG 42 until the Russians had taken to their heels with their socks smoking. Johann thought of the smoking Berlin. When they emptied a bottle, they threw it out the window, far out—not carelessly, but intentionally, as if it was a hand grenade. They did what was forbidden on purpose. After every bottle they threw out, they shouted the slogan that was meant to get people to be frugal and economize with everything: "Fight waste!"

"Leuna," said the soldiers, as the train rolled for half an hour past a wilderness of pipes and rods. It was where they made gasoline from coal. Once they achieved autarky, the war was as good as won! One of the soldiers bellowed, "Tonight or never." Another joined in, "Autarky, autarky." Since the first four-year plan, everybody knew what *autarky* meant and that it was the most crucial thing for Germany. Johann thought of Herr Breuninger, the art teacher in Lindau. In sixth grade, he had them illustrate the word *autarky* as a struggle for raw materials, and for each new sixth-grade class, he would recite the couplet he had penned himself but pretended he was making up on the spot: Don't throw potato peels away, They may prove useful one fine day. Johann would have liked to tell that to the soldiers who were singing the praises of autarky. But maybe they hadn't even noticed him.

Which was all right with him, since his short-pant civvies must look ridiculous among these uniforms. And yet these dark green corduroy shorts were his favorites. They made him feel historical. The soldiers were telling one dirty joke after another, and then one of them finally did point to Johann and say, "You're settin' a bad example for this little guy." His tone of voice reminded Johann of Elsa with her sagging lower lip, spooning with Herr Deuerling, and the expression she used to report some outrage: I thought I was gonna eat my own feet. Elsa from *Ainaid by Homborsh*, capsized in the moonlight, the non-swimmer, with the non-swimmer Valentin from Mindelheim. Amazing that even at that news, the Princess's response was: Shake a leg, romance calls, the Führer needs more soldiers.

Johann slid each apple carefully into the mouth of the sack and didn't let go until it touched the apples already collected in the bottom. Far overhead in the unending blue of the October sky, the little glinting sliver needles of the bombers flying in from Italy nosed forward almost soundlessly. In the evening, they would learn from the radio whether it had been the turn of Stuttgart or Ulm, Augsburg or Munich. The only bombs that got dropped around here were on the return flight, the few they hadn't released over the cities—seven between Lochau and Bregenz not long ago.

When the sack got full and heavy, and the cord started cutting into his shoulder, Johann backed down the ladder rung by rung. He lifted the cord over his head and passed the sack to the waiting Niklaus, who insisted that only he, holding his arm out as a brake, was able to let the apples roll slowly and gently enough from the sack into the crate that they didn't get bruised. Before Johann hung the empty sack across his shoulder again, he gazed at the place beside the trunk of the Gravenstein tree where last year Tell had sat and watched Johann deliver the sacks to Niklaus. Tell's favorite spot. The letter from nine-year-old Anselm had arrived in Fürstenfeldbruck the first week in September: "Johann, we had to have Tell shot. Herr Brugger had to do it."

From the very first day in Fürstenfeldbruck, Johann had always waited until he was lying in bed to read his mail. When they were shown their quarters, he had insisted on taking the top bunk. He said he got nightmares if anyone slept above him. When he read Anselm's letter, he turned to the wall and howled. Anselm wrote that after Johann had been drafted into the labor service, Tell had refused to take food from anyone else. He had run away twice, had to be caught, and had snapped at anyone who approached him. Finally Herr Brugger, the hunter and livestock dealer, got a muzzle on him. Then Herr Brugger led him into the courtyard and Anselm had to show Herr Brugger Tell's favorite spot. They tied Tell to the Gravenstein trunk and Anselm had to maneuver the handcart into position in the grass two yards from Tell, stand in the cart bed, and call: Tell, look up here! Tell looked up and in that second, Herr Brugger pulled the trigger. Tell hadn't suffered at all.

Johann couldn't eat anything for two days in Fürstenfeldbruck. He had to report in sick. You can't line up for mess hall and then not eat anything. And besides, it had become his duty to recite a saying for the day. When everyone had gotten their chow and they were all standing at their places in the mess hall, someone had to recite a saying for the day. Sometimes it was one person, sometimes another. One day, no one volunteered. "Outside!" bellowed the sergeant. "Around the hall at a run until someone has a saying!" After the third time around—and it was a rainy day—Johann had had enough and volunteered. Everyone went back inside and stood before their cold suppers while Johann intoned in his clear voice the rhyme he had just concocted:

> The sun is bright, the world is wide,
> We're comrades marching side by side.
> Within our hearts, the sun it shines
> Despite the darkness of the times.

Fortunately, no one had laughed when Johann had the sun shining on this rainy day. From that day on, they all relied on Johann. Every evening before going to sleep he rhymed a saying for the next day:

Our foes have weapons that can kill,
But none to match our steely will.

After reading Little Anselm's letter, he knew he couldn't eat a thing, not ever again. So he would give one of his buddies the saying for tomorrow and sayings for all the days to come. He couldn't just holler out

With joy we wield the pick and spade,
Proud to be Germany's youngest brigade.

and then not eat anything. That wouldn't do. Not only would he never eat again, he would never see or hear anything, either. Never feel anything. In every letter he wrote home, he'd reminded Anselm to please, please read his letter to Tell, too, send Tell his greetings and let Tell sniff the letter. He would spit on the upper left corner of every letter, draw a circle around the spot, and write next to it, "Let Tell sniff here!"

After Tell had refused food from anyone else during Johann's visit to Langenargen, Johann should have known that he could never leave Tell alone. But then he had to go and volunteer so he could get away before anyone else and be drafted into the labor service before anyone else. It couldn't be too soon for him! *He* had killed Tell, not Herr Brugger! Two weeks later, Mother wrote that Herr Brugger had been picked up, arrested, called a parasite on the *Volk* for doing something against the wartime economic rules—trafficking in livestock for a lot of money. Poor Adolf, thought Johann, and wrote asking Mother to send him Adolf's address.

Every time Johann came down the ladder and gave Niklaus the sack, he saw Tell's spot next to the Gravenstein trunk. He had sat in the grass against that trunk with Tell, had read and translated *Childe Harold's Pilgrimage* and read it aloud in English and German to Tell. And he had read him odes by Klopstock. It would never have occurred to Johann to read prose to Tell. Poems, yes: they flowed, swung, danced, and sung, and Tell had a feel for that. You could see it when you read to him.

Of course, you also had to let him feel the rhythm through your hand on his neck. Little Anselm was going to bury Tell under the Gravenstein tree, but Herr Brugger said he wasn't allowed to. Dogs suspected of having rabies had to go to the rendering plant. And he tossed Tell into a tin tub and took him away with the help of Dusan, who lived with ten other Serbs and Poles in Galle Schmied's barn.

Johann spent two more days without eating and then got a letter from Josef, written in Ostrowiece, a town he said was south of Warsaw. He wrote that Little Anselm had sent him a sweet letter. Main contents: They had to have Tell shot. In the evening of the day he got the letter, Josef and a Polish musician he was quartered with—an excellent jazz trumpeter who played regularly on Radio Warsaw—had played the funeral march from Chopin's Sonata in B flat minor, Josef on accordion. After hearing Anita's mother play the accordion in the circus, Josef had knocked on the door of the Wieners' trailer the following morning and asked if he could try playing it. Right off, he played "La Paloma." Then he pestered Mother until he got an accordion of his own, and after a few months, he could play practically anything on it.

When Johann arrived too late from Stralsund, even though he basically ran directly from the awards ceremony to the train station and rode straight through without stopping anywhere, Mother said that during his home leave, Josef had done almost nothing but play piano.

"Scales," said Johann.

Mother nodded. Already during Holy Week, when Josef had come home on four days' leave, they had the impression he had come only to practice scales, especially the ones in contrary motion with four or five flats that were beyond Johann's skills. Josef just rippled them off like nothing, even though the tendon of the little finger on his right hand was injured. When they practiced giving the salute in the barracks yard, the little finger always caused some trouble at first. Every slave driver of a drill sergeant had to see for himself if he couldn't force Josef's finger into the prescribed position, and then had to admit that as soon as he let it go, it jumped right back off-sides. One of them had said that with a finger like that, Josef would never have gotten into the reserve officer training course in peacetime.

From Palm Sunday to Good Friday, Josef suddenly wasn't the nineteen-year-old brother of a seventeen-year-old anymore. Not the brother you had to argue with about every little thing, the brother who was always snatching something from you or forcing a job on you he didn't want to do himself. Suddenly, Josef was confiding in him. Wanted to know everything from and about Johann right away. Except for Magda, for whom and to whom Johann wrote poems, he hadn't admitted to a soul that writing poetry was his favorite thing to do. Now he could tell Josef. And Josef hadn't laughed but had said seriously—not too seriously, but without the least hint of mockery— "Will you let me have a look at one some time?" Johann had been unable to answer. He probably turned red as a fire engine.

Johann had walked Josef to the train to return to Böblingen. Johann didn't like the cap that went with Josef's black uniform. A gleaming, totally rigid visor—and black, to boot—beneath a top that was too stiff, too round, and too formal, despite being greenish. The cap of a mountain trooper that he would be wearing was more dashing, and above all, softer and more comfortable. But since Josef had a narrower head, his stiff, puffed-up cap was easier to accept. But a stiff, rounded cap like that on Johann's round skull? Impossible! Sometimes when Johann looked in the mirror, he thought people might take him and his round head for hydrocephalic. Although for years he had been shoveling coal out of boxcars, shouldering sacks, and carrying them into cellars and attics, nothing strong-looking had developed on him except his arms and shoulders. When he and Dusan shoveled three hundred and twenty hundredweights of briquettes from a boxcar into Waibel's wagon between seven in the morning and three thirty in the afternoon, and then the four o'clock freight dropped off a boxcar with three hundred and seventy hundredweights of hard coal and they had emptied that, too, by eleven thirty at night, and during that whole long day they'd only had two or three hours of help from Magda's brother, Wolfgang, Johann totted up what they'd accomplished in his letter to

Josef the following day, because he knew Josef would be impressed. Before: Johann the weakling. After: Johann who empties two boxcars between seven in the morning and eleven thirty at night. Johann had the feeling there was nothing he couldn't do. And much faster than anyone would expect. He wanted to surprise them all, and Mother the most. Actually, only her. He wanted everyone to shout Bravo! But not for his own sake. For his sake, only for her sake.

Sometimes there was so much going on inside him, Johann just couldn't hold out on the ladder. He rushed down, tossed the half-full sack to Niklaus, and wanted to run off to his notebooks, his poems. But then he climbed back up the ladder after all. He had to finish. For her sake.

His favorite apples to pick were the shiny, red, plumply oval Prince Ludwigs, each one more beautiful than the last. You could tell by looking how delicious this variety was. He didn't need someone to set the ladder for him anymore. When he came home from the labor service and encountered the Princess for the first time in the passageway—she now washed dishes for the man who was leasing the restaurant—she'd looked him over, up and down, with her one good eye, and he looked her over with both of his. She had a magnificent new coiffure, dense and curly like Dumb August's used to be.

Then she said, "O pain, be gone."

And Johann said, "How goes it for Princess Adelheid?"

Still taking stock of him, instead of answering, she said, "The expert is astonished, the layman rubs his eyes." And then: If she didn't act soon Johann would be too old for her. And she laughed. She never laughed in a genuine way, but always went *Ha-ha-ha-ha*. Never more than four *ha*s. Then: "Well, you great big man, shake a leg, romance calls, the Führer needs more soldiers."

Johann had replied in her tone of voice, "O pain, be gone."

As he set his foot on the stairs, she had said, "In your dreams, my friend." The only thing still missing was: Schiller dead, and this character still walks the earth. Then she would have run through all her sayings. But he felt he would rather have stayed with her than gone upstairs. Maybe there were sayings he had forgotten. What did it matter what someone said, anyway? The way the Princess fired off her sayings! The way she stood there! On tiptoe at the end and waving her arms as if treading water. Her uneven eyes no longer bothered him. The mass of curls compensated for everything, they and her over-large mouth. Had he forgotten that the Princess had such a huge mouth? And since the beginning of the war, they had taken to calling her The Stuka. Everybody except Mother called her by the name of the dive bomber. O pain, be gone. But really, there were women everywhere you looked. The town was crawling with women, women dressed the way women here had never dressed before. All big city women, bombed-out refugees. Maybe they had sewn these clothes themselves, trying to look like Hilde Krahl, Hansi Knoteck, Ilse Werner, Brigitte Horney, or Marika Rökk. Fantastic collars and bodices, hemlines and cuffs. And every one with two to four children in tow.

Beneath the trees that Johann had to have picked by All Saints' Day, because otherwise Mother would be embarrassed to face her fellow churchgoers, Frau Woschischek's children waited for drops. Bombed out in the Ruhr region, living in the annex that used to be a stall— the horse stall that Mother had rented to Herr Mehltreter for the production of floor wax. Now bombed-out people had priority over floor wax. Frau Woschischek and her three children were housed in the right half of the ground-floor annex. The left half was still a pigpen where a mother sow was nursing nineteen piglets at the moment. There had been twenty-four to begin with, but she had already smothered five of them. Johann and Niklaus took turns standing watch all night and moving the piglets, but if you nodded off, another would get caught under its enormous mother. They hoped to get twelve or fifteen of the strongest through the ordeal. Once her children were asleep, Frau Woschischek received visitors next door and accepted money for it. Master craftsmen, journeymen, apprentices, vacationers, farmers, hired hands, and even schoolboys sneaked to her door after dark. The barred windows, wider than they were tall, were hung with red curtains. But the wall between stall and stall was thin, and when Johann stood watch by the mother sow at night, despite the radio that was constantly on, he could still overhear sounds and scraps of conversation that kept him awake. He felt like an explorer on an unknown continent. When Herr Woschischek came home from the Russian front on two weeks' leave, Frau Woschischek, by her own account, was the happiest woman in the world. Herr Woschischek was no taller than the really short Frau Woschischek, and his glasses were so thick you couldn't imagine him being able to see through them at all. And in Russia, no less. Lucile knew only a few words of German, but with gestures she could characterize or imitate everyone who came into the kitchen. Whenever Frau Woschischek passed through, Lucile would make the fingers of her small, white left hand into a tube and bore into it with her right index finger. Lucile's hair was even redder than Mina's—Mina who had long since become Alfred's wife. Alfred had enlisted early on, and Mina ran their farm in Höhenreute. Lucile's skin was also much paler than Mina's. It was essentially white, Lucile's skin, Snow White white. And from Paris. Twenty-three and divorced. Everyone who mentioned Lucile said the same things: Paris, twenty-three, divorced. Ever since Lucile had been running the kitchen, the Princess had a new saying: Paris is shit, London is bigger. She now used this sentence to express her disapproval of anything: Paris is shit, London is bigger. Lucile was probably the only person who never understood the saying, although it was aimed at her. Lucile now cooked for the man to whom Mother had leased the restaurant for as long as Johann was in Fürstenfeldbruck as a labor service man and composer of daily sayings. The lessee had had two hotels in Friedrichshafen destroyed by bombs in a single night in April. Now that he was back from the labor service, Johann occupied Rooms 8 and 9 along with his mother. Room 8 had been made into two rooms by the addition of a wooden partition. Lucile slept in the smaller of the two. In the other there was now a small stove, a sofa, and a table, and the delicately carved cherry chest of drawers from Grandfather. Johann slept on the sofa. Mother and Anselm slept in Room 9. Now Johann was no longer able to go to the kitchen and pretend to be reading on his bench in order to listen to how the men pestered Lucile. But at night, when it wasn't his turn in the pig pen, he lay next to the partition and listened to all of Lucile's noises. He heard her turning over in bed. And he heard her when she hummed or sang "Komm zurück" to herself. He liked to imagine that she knew he was listening, that she only hummed and sang because he was listening. He hummed "O sole mio." He'd already been a hit with his tenor solo of "O sole mio." But Lucile didn't react, not even to an "O sole mio" that literally melted from its own passion. So close to Lucile and yet separated by the partition, he couldn't fall asleep. He had to fiddle with his still nameless—and thus still known as—IAWIA until he found relief. When he did, he imagined he was crossing a finish line like the sprinters in the newsreels, hurling their entire being into the last tenth of a second as if trying to beat even themselves. Across the line, across the line, across the line.

On the other hand, he was already going with Magda, the sister of Wolfgang number two. Also from the Ruhr, but from a completely different family. Being from the Ruhr district obviously had no special significance. Frau Woschischek and all her children looked as if they didn't even know enough to wash themselves every day, so when they did get washed for a change, one was astonished. My respects, Herr Schlegel the builder would have exclaimed had he still been alive.

But Magda and Wolfgang were the most beautiful apparitions imaginable. When they came to the train together each morning, Johann couldn't decide which one he liked looking at more. He wrote poems, however, only for Magda. Not a day went by that he didn't write her a poem, but he gave her only every tenth poem at most. He had a clear sense that it would be to his disadvantage to hand over everything he had written every day. Sometimes, sitting on the edge of his bed and thinking of Magda, he simply could not stop before he'd written five or even six poems into the oilcloth-bound notebook spread on his knees. He felt many things when he was with Magda, things he had to respond to, things he needed to celebrate in order to feel them entirely. His tone was always dictated by whichever poet he happened to be reading at the moment. He read nothing but poetry now. The stuff in the newspaper: unreadable. Novels: unreadable. Only poems. Now he selected only the poetry books from the books Father had left. During home guard flak training, during labor service training, he read nothing but poetry and wrote more poems than he read. For each poem he read, there were two if not three he wrote. Even as he broke the stems of Prince Ludwig apples beneath the thin, ethereal hum of silver bombers in the sky, there was no stopping the poem in him. Faster than was good for that special, delicate, red-bellied variety, he would sometimes clamber down the ladder, swing the sack off his shoulder to Niklaus so that the old man complained that he wasn't taking proper care of the apples. Then he raced up the back stairs into the house and up to the second floor, grabbed the latest notebook and his fountain pen out of the drawer of Grandfather's chest (which was so beautiful it made everything else in the partitioned room look ugly), and wrote down his newest poem so not a word was lost and every word was in its proper place. But he wrote more slowly than he had run, his hand moving in exalted solemnity. Poems were solemn affairs, one's own included. Then there it stood, in black and white, in letters not quite so rounded and arched as his father's, but more like Father's looping curves than like Mother's splintery and rather crushed individual letters. Mother's handwriting had become nothing but individual letters; each one looked crumbled, like a Gothic ruin. Mother could not have forged a signature now as she once had. When he finished writing down a poem (they all ended with a solemn flourish), Johann always returned to the orchard much slower than he had left it and climbed back up the ladder. As he started to bag the red, oval apples again, the poem he had just written formed on his lips. Very quietly, of course, but repeated several times, like a litany.

> These are no earthly pains
> Burning through my veins.
> Your body pressing into mine,
> We leave the spirit far behind.
> Destroying, blessing flows the fire,
> An ultimatum to desire,

Cauterizing every sadness
And freeing us to boundless madness.

Schiller and Magda felt equally close to him as he wrote, Schiller
maybe even closer than Magda.

Unless the world bears your sign,
ennobled by your worthiness,
And beauty apes your every line,
Then life itself is meaningless
And I will live no longer.

Of course he had written poetry before, but one fine morning there
was Magda, coming along the line of fir trees from the direction of
the Schäggs' house. As soon as he saw her, he knew she was the one
he would write for. When all the others were crowding onto the train
they took to school, she still stood there as if she didn't even want to
go. She was solemn, serious. Had he ever been able to call someone
fine before? Or even *noble*? Her hair seemed to shape itself on its own
into an oval that framed her face, but softly, not severely. And at the
back of her neck the oval came together in a pigtail that was no ordinary pigtail but a Mozart pigtail. And from her dark brown velvet dress
gleamed gold embroidery. She emanated a gravity that required one to
convey one's thoughts to her only in poems. That's how Johann felt.
At last! At last he had an addressee. The hope of being understood was
exciting. He had not had a girlfriend since he started going to school
in Lindau. He couldn't imagine getting to know any girls in Lindau.
Besides, he wasn't a leader in the Jungvolk or the Hitlerjugend. They
had it easier. Last summer he had just dropped his hook into the
water off the steamship landing when the daughter of the family who
owned the Crown and the daughter of the doctor came down to the
dock. They both went to school in Lindau, too. When he saw them
approaching, Johann pulled his line back out of the water and quickly
tore the worm off the hook. At that moment, the two girls passed

close behind him without stopping. They didn't say, "Hello, Johann," to him, either, as would have been natural since they went back and forth to school in the same train every day. They were completely fixated on the steamer that had just arrived and was tying up at the dock. Now Johann could see that the girls were meeting two Jungvolk leaders from Lindau. They were standing on deck, wearing earthen-colored capes over their dark uniforms, and each raised an arm in greeting. It looked good, the way the two boys in uniform raised their hands above their caps. The hands paused in the air. The two girls waved excitedly. Then the uniformed boys were on the dock, hands were shaken, and they headed toward shore. Johann had tossed his line back in the water without a worm just in time and pretended to be concentrating on his cork, which was bobbing wildly as if God only knows how big a fish was nibbling at his bait. Johann knew, of course, that it was only the waves and eddies from the boat that had landed and was now pushing off again that made the cork dance around, but he needed a distraction. He didn't look at them until they had gone past, but he heard them pass behind him. The boys from Lindau were wearing the flared pants they called breeches and the jackboots that went with them, and they thundered across the planks of the dock with the two girls hovering beside them. Johann became aware of the fact that he was barefoot. But it was the middle of summer, wasn't it? A beautiful day, and no muster in the village that he knew of. The two Jungvolk leaders from Lindau—he recognized them; they were two classes ahead of him in school, Uhlmann and Dummler were their names—had come over by boat in their uniforms and boots and capes just to visit these two girls. As they were passing behind Johann, one of the girls said, "A boy with glasses gets no lasses." He hadn't just imagined it, he'd heard her. And he knew which of the two had said the sentence that could only have been meant for him, the boy with glasses. He pulled out his line for good and walked home on the Moosweg, hanging his head as though looking for something he had lost, because here he had the least chance of running into anyone. When he got home, he wrote on a new page of his oilcloth notebook the necessary poem.

You groan for light in crabbed times,
And empty dreams in blaring colors,
Unforgiven victims, o my rhymes,
Of dark designs by hateful others.

But when Frau Woschischek appeared at the stall door to call her children, or when Frau Helling wobbled by in her high heels, there was a pause in his poetizing. Frau Helling lived in the basement of the house next door, where Frau Fürst and her children used to live. Frau Helling was from Berlin. Her husband was a war photographer, but only of the war in the air. He often landed in Friedrichshafen and was able to visit his wife. A bald-headed man with a permanent smirk, Herr Helling smoked as much as he drank, and even so, smoked and drank much less than his wife, the most made-up woman Wasserburg had ever seen. Either he was in the restaurant, or she was. If he was there, it meant she had a visitor, just like Frau Woschischek. But Frau Helling had been a dancer. She wasn't short and big-hipped like Frau Woschischek. She had no truck with children. On the other hand, the most made-up woman in the world also walked on the highest high heels in the world. Everyone thought it was a daily miracle she could walk at all in shoes like that.

Although Herr and Frau Helling never came into the restaurant together, both of them, independent of each other, stood at the exact same spot at front of the bar. Neither one ever sat down. They stood, and for as long as they stood, they drank—beer and schnapps. And in neither case could one have told by the clothes they wore whether it was a Sunday or a weekday. In general, it was a distinguishing characteristic of the evacuees and out-of-towners that the better-situated among them wore their Sunday best even on weekdays, while the poorer wore their work clothes even on Sundays. Of course, the regulars talked about what it was like with Frau Helling, but never when Herr Helling was present. While Herr Helling drank his beer and schnapps, all he talked about was his wife. He expressed his admiration, sang her praises, and described what a wonderful artiste she had been in Berlin before falling victim—on account of the war—to alcohol. Despite all he had heard, Johann could not have said for certain if Frau Helling had more contempt for the men who came to visit her, or vice versa. The men at the regulars' table praised Frau Helling just as much as they despised her. Without praising her, they couldn't have despised her, and without despising her, they couldn't have praised her. Frau Helling was able to despise her clientele without feeling any need to praise them. She named no names, but from her over-painted lips there issued nothing but scorn. And the regulars' table laughed about it. Semper's Fritz shouted, "She sure gives it to us." For some reason unknown to Johann, Frau Helling and her clientele had the need to outdo each other in contempt, which made for the accumulation of an extraordinary contempt-potential. But that accumulation was nothing compared to the contempt that filled Herr Helling when he spoke about his wife's clients—without naming names, of course—and his wife. He took no offense. He expressed next to nothing. But he despised. You could see it. His mouth was one straight, lipless line that twitched a little when Herr Helling was despising. That sufficed.

Johann heard everything, registered everything, but didn't know why or what for. He sensed, however, that it had something to do with research. It had nothing to do with poetry. Only Magda had to do with poetry, just as poetry had only to do with Magda.

Every Sunday after church, he ran home as soon as he thought he had stood at the grave long enough to be noticed by the people at the neighboring graves. He ran into the partitioned Room 8 to fetch from the drawer the poems he had composed during the preceding week and had made fair copies of on Saturday night, in order to take them to Magda.

If a boy went with a girl, people in the village said he was flirting her. When the Princess, who apparently only washed dishes but actually kept track of everything, asked Johann once in the passageway if he was still flirting that girl out there— "You know the one I mean, over toward Nonnenhorn"—he had twirled his finger at his temple in a gesture cruder than he was and made the most horrid face he could. The Princess called after him, "I'm just saying, every broom finds its handle. Ha-ha-ha-ha." When the topic was girls and women, there were some words Johann simply could not stand. If somebody said he was going with Magda, he made no comment. He would not put it that way. But he wouldn't allow it to be called *flirting*. He didn't know what to call it himself. That's why he wrote poems. And delivered them. Magda gave no indication of whether she read his poems or not, whether she liked them or not. Johann was rather happy about her reticence. In moments when he was not writing poems, he could imagine that for someone who didn't think poetry was the most important thing in the world, it could be embarrassing to be addressed like this:

> Whip up action in the tangled
> bodies of your transient team.
> Drive them on with urgent cry
> Toward your peaks ablaze with evening.

It was just conceivable to him that there was nothing Magda could say about his poems. What he could not conceive of was not to bring his poems to her, to say nothing of not writing any more.

By the time Johann had fetched his poems from home, Magda— who of course had also been in church and had been observed by Johann—was always sitting at the piano. Under the pretext of saying hello to her mother, he first assured himself that she was busy in the kitchen. Then he entered the living room as silently as possible and laid the week's poems on the pile of music on the piano, stood behind Magda, and touched her hair, first with his hands and then with his mouth. He moved on to her neck. With his hands. And only once: under her collar with one of his hands, which slid forward and down her neck in the direction of her breast. Magda stopped playing at once. That startled Johann, he snatched back his hand, and Magda resumed her playing. Her mother called from the kitchen asking if Johann wanted to stay for dinner. No, thank you. On the stairs, he met Wolfgang Two coming up. Wolfgang had started going with the daughter from the Crown. She wasn't from here, either, and was even a Lutheran.

"Hey, brother-in-law," said Wolfgang, and went back downstairs with Johann, sat down on the bench that encircled a thick tree trunk, and patted the bench beside him. Johann sat down, too. Then they talked. Wolfgang set the tone. He was going to study medicine, and he already liked to express himself diagnostically. What Johann was feeling and why he felt what he felt—Wolfgang could explain it all exactly, preferably using Latin expressions. For a while they would sit on the bench, then they would head into the village until they reached Johann's house, then turn around and walk back out to Wolfgang's house and then back in again, just like he used to do with Adolf. Since Wolfgang was going to school in Lindau, too, he had replaced Adolf. They were about to turn around for the third or fourth time when Wolfgang's mother called down from the balcony that his dinner was getting completely cold. If she hadn't, they would have walked back and forth forever

When Wolfgang found out that Johann had to unload and deliver coal at the end of every school day, he started to help out, and with an enthusiasm that made working with coal into a sport. Since boxcars were in short supply now, they had to unload them in half a day. It used to be that you had to pay demurrage only on time over twenty-four hours. Now it was after eight hours, and the penalty was three times as much. So he had to skip school. What they were doing was called *important for the war effort*. Since Josef had enlisted and Johann had turned fifteen, he had a driver's license and was allowed to drive the new Tempo three-wheeler. With Wolfgang standing behind him on the cargo bed and maintaining their balance by leaning left or right, they could take the curves fast, despite the Tempo's instability—even if only to scare people, or at least amaze them. Wolfgang was a born athlete with black hair like the first Wolfgang, but curly, not straight. After unloading coal, they hosed each other off in the laundry room. Johann avoided looking at what Adolf would call Wolfgang's manhood. Johann forced himself not to look. He would never have been able drop little innocent, unobtrusive hints to wangle it so that he and Wolfgang both ended up in the train station privy, a little annex whose doorless entrance was screened from the eyes of passersby by a huge wall of arbor vitae. He had been able to maneuver Adolf in there without him realizing right away what Johann was up to. Then, as they stood facing the glistening black, tarred wall of the urinal that smelled more of tar than of urine, Johann had tried to seduce Adolf into something more than urinating—peeing—together. And sometimes he succeeded. But Johann had the feeling that Adolf despised him when he wanted to fiddle with Adolf's manhood. But whenever Johann managed to steer Adolf behind the arbor vitae hedge and in front of the tarred wall, he never did as much as he'd planned on doing. Johann was drawn to the gigantic bulge of the arbor vitae in front of the doorless entrance. Alone or with others, he called it the confessional. The arbor vitae foliage was so dense that neither the trunks nor the branches were visible. When you reached your arm into the hedge, you felt fragrant, soft greenness. Wasn't that its hair? But it was neither possible nor desirable to get Wolfgang behind the hedge. Wolfgang was a year older. He shaved. He was Magda's brother. And just in general. Girls were preferable now. Johann got that without really understanding it. Of all the boys and girls, only the girls were left, even though up to now, he had gotten less from them than from the boys. Once he had written four lines that he would never show to Magda:

> I wonder what you're thinking of,
> what gives your soul its shape.
> What image, when you think of love,
> are you—the vine, or grape?

What Berni said about Frau Woschischek didn't turn him on, or what he had seen of Frau Helling, either. All he felt was an investigative interest. But the Princess—yes, the Princess was another matter. The Princess was a storm, a force of nature. The Stuka was a good name for her. And yet, a poem for the Princess? He couldn't picture it. What about Lucile? She had never given a second thought to who was on the other side, rustling the bedclothes, noisily turning over, soulfully humming, singing, whistling. There was no audible response from her side to which one could respond in turn. Even her look could not be translated into the German of a seventeen-year-old. Really green eyes beneath really red hair and a skin that was nothing but white. Whatever happened, Lucile puckered her lips and raised her eyebrows. Even when the soldiers billeted in the gymnasium drank too much on New Year's Eve and stormed the kitchen wanting to meet the French cook who made the best antipasto and the best deviled eggs, Lucile scrambled onto the stovetop (gone cold by that time), puckered her lips, and fended off the soldiers with a wooden spoon until she had them kneeling on the kitchen floor and singing "Komm zurück" while she used the spoon as a baton. Perhaps women were simply unattainable. It was not at all certain that women were in the least interested in what most interested Johann. Sure, if you paid for it, see Frau Woschischek, Frau Helling, or the bordello women the soldiers home on leave talked about at the regulars' table. Those women could pick up a five-mark coin from the table with their lower set of lips. Or in Paris they could, anyway.

He couldn't talk to Magda about anything like that. Magda sat at the piano or knelt in the church pew or walked beside Johann up the Moosweg, and nothing was as certain as that she was not thinking about what—if he didn't watch out—he was thinking about all the time. Unchastity, it was called in the confessional, and it always spoiled his complete contrition and thus absolution and thus communion. He had gotten used to opening his mouth to receive the Host without being in a blessed state of grace. For which he would have to pay the bill later in the eternity toward which one actually lived one's life. Mother had made it crystal clear how stupid it was to let deadly sins in this short life here on earth spoil your chance for eternal life. Above all, they wouldn't see each other on the other side. He wouldn't be there. His mother would be waiting in vain for him in heaven. And then she would know the truth about him. Of all the people in the world, she was the last one he could have told what he was thinking about all the time. For a while, he had hoped to draw Adolf into the

mood of unchastity that preoccupied him day and night. Last year in
November, he had made one last attempt to share the most important
thing with Adolf, and it had ended in farce. The army physical had
brought all his schoolmates together again. For Johann, the day of the
physical was a day of unprecedented anxiety. Getting undressed and
being naked with Adolf, Ludwig, Helmut One and Helmut Two, with
Berni, Guido, and Paul! Johann knew his IAWIA would not stay still
when he caught sight of the others' significant appendages. He couldn't
even think about their members without his starting to swell, rise, and
stick out idiotically. And the more forbidden it was, the faster his member rose. And then, to walk into the next room and up to the different
tables—medical commission, army doctor, medic, clerk, and so on.
Johann had got across the finish line twice that morning to make himself more relaxed. And once there, he had looked at the ceiling more
than at the others and forced himself to conjure up scenes that would
distract him, like he and Lichtensteiger's Helmut getting caught on an
ice floe late last January and drifting off into the fog; they lost track
of where the shore was, and if the breeze hadn't picked up and blown
away the fog, they probably would have frozen to death on the floe,
which was maybe four yards square. With such scenes and a kind of
intense internal detachment, he managed to keep his member from
rising. But then they went out drinking. Once examined and declared
fit for active duty, you were allowed to drink as much as you wanted.
Fit for active duty—that was cause for celebration. He had managed
to take a giggling Adolf, so drunk he was almost incapable of walking
or talking, home with him. Since Josef had been conscripted, Johann
slept alone in Room 9. But Adolf had been so smashed he couldn't even
get himself undressed. He had collapsed onto Josef's bed and immediately started snoring. Then he threw up and Johann had to clean up
him and the bed. It wasn't a great night, his last night with Adolf. Fit
for active duty, he thought, as he mopped up Adolf's puke with a wet
towel and crept along the dark hall to the bathroom carrying the puke
he had gathered, fearing every moment that the creaking floorboard no
creeping could avoid would wake up his mother and she would call out:

Johann, what are you doing? Nothing, he would answer. She would find out soon enough that Adolf had puked all over the bed. Adolf had volunteered for flak duty. Johann hadn't dared to ask him why. Only cowards and shirkers volunteered as anti-aircraft gunners. If you volunteered for the flak, it was like admitting you didn't want to be sent to the front, that others could go to the front instead. If Johann hadn't wanted to be sent to the front, the last thing he would do would be to admit it by volunteering for flak duty. The others get sent out to the front, and you sit on your behind in some fortification and fire into the air! How could Adolf do such a thing? And not say a word about it. He obviously didn't care what Johann thought.

The following morning, a telephone call from Geiselharz crowded out every other thought. The great-uncle they called Cousin had been arrested. From that point on, Mother could only refer to him as poor, poor Anselm. The nine-year-old who still was most often to be found holding her hand knew that it wasn't him she meant when she said poor Anselm. The cousin they all owed so much to—arrested, in jail in Rottenburg. The last thing Johann had gotten from the great-uncle they called Cousin was a shiny, light-colored, close-fitting double-breasted suit, so bright and well-fitting that—besides Johann— only Johannes Heesters could wear such a suit when he sang to a woman in one of his films. On Johann's sixteenth birthday—Josef was already in the tank corps—Johann was allowed to choose a suit at Bredl's in Wangen. He modeled every suit he tried on for Cousin Anselm, who sat and watched with his knees wide apart. Although no one said why the Geiselharz Anselm had been arrested, it gradually was revealed to Johann that the cousin was supposed to have touched or pressured or abused the workers in his Alpine Bee cheese factory. When people mentioned the cousin now, they called him by a section of a statute. They said he was a hundred-seventy-fiver. When men said it, they did so contemptuously. Women seemed to pity him. "What a disaster," said Mother. "Poor, poor Anselm." If Mother had married Otmar Räuchle, the worker her uncle had picked out for her, he would have left her the Alpine Bee together with the shiny black piano;

red upholstered chairs; a glass-fronted bookcase that contained a multivolume history of Switzerland, *Meyers Konversationslexikon* in twenty-four half-leather gilt-edged volumes, and several shelves of novels; and a grandfather clock, which against all expectation would again and again rouse itself from what seemed like slumber and manage to strike the hour. Mother had kept house for her uncle for a few years. Otmar Räuchle, Cousin Anselm's youngest worker, would smuggle flowers into her room as soon as they started blooming. He picked them at 5:30 a.m. on his way from Amtzell, where he lived, to Geiselharz. Every time he had to make a detour on account of those flowers, since he couldn't approach the cheese factory from the road in front with a bouquet in his hand. The other workers and the farmers, already busy delivering their milk by cart, would have laughed at him. So every day, he made a big circle around the town and arrived at Cousin Anselm's house from the meadow behind it, and then somehow got into the house and up to Augusta's room unseen. Every time, the vase Mother always moved from the night stand to the table was back on her night stand and bursting with freshly picked flowers. Otmar never said anything, but he always stuck one flower in his button hole. If a cuckoo flower smiled from the button hole of his cheese maker's smock, it meant that Augusta would find a bright bouquet of cuckoo flowers on her night stand.

She had nothing against Otmar, but she was receiving letters from Wasserburg and answering every one. She always gave herself time, how-ever. Nothing would have pleased her more than to answer each letter at once, but she demanded of herself that at least a week should go by between the day a letter arrived and the day it was answered. That was more proper, she thought. At least once a day, she would look at the lat-est letter. Before re-reading it, she looked at it, like a picture. The violet ink. The fancy letters, written with a nib that was very fine but could also become quite heavy and broad. Dear Augusta! He was the only person who didn't shorten her name—the first person since the priest, who also called her Augusta. The first time the Wasserburg letter-writer had come to Kümmertsweiler to buy apples, Augusta's mother had invited him to stay for tea. Typical Mother's mother. Mother's father would never have simply invited someone to stay for tea. But Mother's mother was born a Messmer, and they had been livestock dealers as long as anyone could remember; compared to Unsicherer's farm, the Messmer property in Hemigkofen was an estate. Anna Messmer was the first woman to bring a horse with her when she married an Unsicherer. Her predecessor, Augusta's grandmother, came from Bruggach but didn't seem to have a very permanent address. Her trousseau must have consisted mainly of her raven-black hair, eyes shaped like plum pits, and skin that was not that white. Her name, Emritz, suggested she wasn't from around there. It was astonishing that, despite this grandmother, as a child Augusta was said to have had an uncontrollable fear of Gypsies. If Johann bent down every night before going to sleep and looked to see if a Gypsy or some other sinister being was under his bed, he had learned it from his mother, adopted and retained it even though Josef always laughed at him as long as they shared a room. Who did he think was going to come up to the second floor and get under his bed? Here in Wasserburg! Josef was obviously less fearful than Johann and Mother. Mother probably had not inherited her fear that terrible things could happen any moment from her mother, that coddled and well-provided Messmer daughter from Hemigkofen, but from her father, who may have gotten it from his mother, the black-haired Theres Emritz with the unusually shaped eyes. That meant that all through her childhood and youth, Augusta would have bent down to look under the bed—perhaps, in the end, to discover some dangerous relative of hers. They say the well-endowed livestock dealer's daughter who came up to Kümmertsweiler from Hemigkofen with that magnificent chestnut had to battle it out with her black-haired mother-in-law, whose oldest son, Thaddäus, the Messmer girl had stolen from her by marrying him. Fritz, the horse she brought with her, at first couldn't stand it in Unsicherer's stall and misbehaved so much that the cows next to his stall basically stopped giving milk. In the morning his mane and tail were always half tangled. The veterinarian and the priest did what they could, and his nocturnal fits became less frequent, but he still got one now and then. It was a battle. They said that only once the black-haired, plum-pit-eyed mother-in-law was dead—which she was, after only three years—did his restless fits stop entirely. And his mane and tail stayed untangled from then on. But from then on, too, Fritz the chestnut could not step over water, not even a puddle. Either he couldn't stand seeing his reflection, or water in general terrified him. In the rain, you could hardly get him to walk calmly. In a thunderstorm, he sought refuge among the cattle in the pasture. Thaddäus decided to sell him. A dealer from Rorschach seized the opportunity and took Fritz with him, intending to get him up the gangway and on board the train ferry in Lindau, which transported freight to Switzerland. But the chestnut noticed that the gangway ran over water, got excited, reared up and jumped the railing, plunged into the water, and drowned. He'd been paid for. People said he'd always shied from water because he had a premonition of how he would end. Messmer's daughter ran into her bedroom when she heard the news. The following day she gave the priest in Gattnau money to read three Masses for her mother-in-law. Then gradually, the born Messmer became the mistress of her own house, and her Thaddäus, who was shorter than she was, let her have her way. With what he made from selling Fritz, he was able to buy a very well-behaved brown that could find its own way home to Kümmertsweiler whenever Thaddäus delivered wine or hops in Tettnang, drank one glass too many, and nodded off on the box. The oak winepress was already housed at the Unsicherer farm, and now the village snow plow was also entrusted to them. And then, Thaddäus became a member of the borough council and served for thirty-five years. He washed himself every morning outside at the pump, putting the back of his neck under the stream of cold water first, which kept him from getting a toothache all his life. His wife, the Messmer daughter, liked to tell that story. She didn't talk much, but more than her husband, Thaddäus. He worked like it was what he was put on the earth to do and went into the Eckes forest every morning, with or without a gun. The fruit dealer's son from Wasserburg had gotten himself invited to tea and then for a while, he pedaled over three ridges and across two streams every Saturday, always leaned his bicycle against the garden fence on the side where the hollyhocks were blooming, took the clips off his pant legs, and asked for Augusta. He never shortened her name, and that fact alone must have pleased her mother, the born Messmer, who put some stock in appearances. But then suddenly, he stopped coming. When Augusta came home on Saturday afternoons, the first thing she did was go down to Gattnau and tell the priest—who said her full name, just like the fruit dealer's son from Wasserburg—what she considered to have been her sins. Then she walked, or rather ran, back up to Kümmertsweiler, always hoping the bicycle would be leaning against the fence on the side with the hollyhocks, the only bicycle under whose saddle there was a yellow tin tag attached to the frame that said EFFENDI in red letters. From pure joy that the owner of the bicycle was there, she always forgot to ask what that meant. But when the hollyhock side of the garden fence remained without the bicycle of the fruit dealer and restaurateur on seven Saturdays within the space of three months, she had said through the dark grille of the confessional that she had decided to enter a convent. As she left the confessional, she will have had the feeling that the priest was watching her through the gap in the curtains. She must have felt more important than ever before. I want to enter a convent, she had said. As she knelt down to confess, she had certainly not intended to say that. But suddenly, in the midst of detailing her meager sins, it occurred to her: If I go home and the bicycle is not leaning against the fence by the hollyhocks, I'm going to enter a convent. She didn't want to enter a convent. But she also didn't want to keep running around in the world senselessly if that bicycle was not going to be leaning against the fence when she got home. She was twenty-two. Had been keeping house for seven years. Had learned to cook in Liebenau and in The Bear in Tettnang. And her father's brother, Uncle Anselm, wanted to marry her to Otmar Räuchle, his favorite cheese maker from Amtzell. In the pubs where her uncle always stood a round for everyone, if someone asked him why he had never gotten married himself, he would scratch the back of his right hand with his left, give a generous smile—his broad face really seemed to cradle the smile—and then say, "I'm much too impatient for that."

She couldn't run home from Geiselharz every Saturday. It was too far. But then, on this Saturday, suddenly, quite suddenly, she asked her uncle if she could go home on the weekend. He drove her to Wangen in his Ford. She took the train to Oberreitnau and then walked through Unterreitnau and Bechtersweiler and past Rickatshofen to Kümmertsweiler. Then down to Gattnau to confess and told the priest: I want to enter a convent. She thought: If he doesn't come today, I'll go to a convent. It was clear to her that it was a sin to think such a thing. And it was a much graver sin to tell the priest you wanted to enter a convent when you didn't want to at all. But she would enter a convent if she went home afterwards and the bicycle with the EFFENDI tag was not leaning against the fence under the hollyhocks. She would hurl herself out of this life and into the deepest convent, the Poor Clares in Siessen. Tomorrow morning, before Communion, she would need to confess again. Of course. Whether the bicycle is there against the fence afterwards or not, you can't blackmail God. If he doesn't come today, I'll enter a convent—that's blackmail. The priest had said, "What a beautiful decision, Augusta." It was the first time he'd said her name during confession. Most of the time you never know if the man taking your confession has any idea who you are. Hopefully, he doesn't recognize you by your sins. And it's dark behind the curtains in the confessional. She should thank God, the priest said, that He had inspired this wish in her. Not to everyone does God open up such a short, direct path to Himself. Augusta should try to prove herself worthy of this wish that God had inspired. She must care for and nourish this wish like a seed, a seed of the tree of eternal life. And so she didn't dare admit that she wasn't yet completely sure she would enter a convent. In school, she had been the priest's favorite. He had her sit on his lap to warm up the area around his gall bladder. And at the same time, he had her read aloud to the whole class from the catechism. Since the priest's cook suffered from palsy and would often get sudden attacks of tremors, Augusta would be called on to fetch medicine for the cook from Dr. Moser in Bechtersweiler and deliver it to the rectory, since Kümmertsweiler was closer to Bechtersweiler than Gattnau was.

The doctor said that when she was done with school, she could come and work for him, help his wife with the housekeeping. That's what Augusta did, but stayed there only a year, cleaning, cooking, looking after the horse, splitting wood. The doctor's wife, herself the daughter of a doctor, was too fine a lady to be expected to do any work. The doctor at least saw to it that at the end of the year, Augusta got a job in Liebenau so she could learn to cook.

From Gattnau to Kümmertsweiler is uphill almost all the way. But after confession, she ran. She slowed down only when she reached the place where the hill begins to level off before dropping into the next valley. Here a footpath branches off past the dump, and she took it. She pressed a hand against the stitch in her side, and when it wouldn't stop, she bent down, picked up the nearest stone, spat on its underside, and put it back down. That was supposed to help. She had to prepare herself for the sight of the empty place against the fence. Why should he come on this particular Saturday, after all? It's true that the apples were just being picked, but there was no way for the Wasserburger to know that Augusta would come home from Geiselharz on this very day. He wouldn't have any inkling. She had come home on seven Saturdays in the last three months and he wasn't there. If the EFFENDI bicycle was not parked beneath the hollyhocks, she would walk back down to Oberreitnau that same evening, call up Uncle Anselm from there, and ask him to pick her up in Wangen. If not, then she'd walk from Wangen to Geiselharz. But her uncle loved to drive. If the bicycle wasn't there—and it wouldn't be—then the best thing would be to take her bag right away and keep on going to Oberreitnau while it was still light. Between Bechtersweiler and Rickatshofen, you have to go through woods twice. It's dangerous even in the daylight, but as soon as it gets dark, it becomes impassable. If you try, Zürnewible will lift up your hat, pronounce a curse, and put your hat back down on top of it. And worse than Zürnewible were the two fiery horses. Augusta would die of fright if they came jumping at her. Anyone who's ever encountered them has their hair turn snow white.

If Uncle Anselm had to pick her up in Wangen on Saturday, he'd know that something hadn't gone the way it was supposed to. And he'd start in about Otmar from Amtzell again. Every time he handed her a letter from the Wasserburger, he said, "Otmar writes a pretty nice hand, too." If the mailman gave her the letter himself, he said that if what was in there was a beautiful as the handwriting, then she was to be congratulated. Augusta had nothing against Otmar from Amtzell, but she was not going to marry him. She just couldn't. Either the Wasserburger or the convent. Forgetting him could only be done in a convent. And she had to forget him or cease to be. She was already asking God to forgive her for her sin. She hadn't meant it to sound like blackmail, which is the way He might have taken it. She knew Uncle Anselm would try to talk her out of the convent. Why not take Otmar instead? he would say, and list Otmar's strong points: tall, smart, kind. And he's not a bad looker, either, is he? It was painful to refuse her uncle anything. Since she'd left home, no one had done as much for her as her Uncle Anselm. The first time she'd been sent down to the cellar in Liebenau to fill the wine jug—she'd only been there two weeks—she was in such a hurry to get back upstairs with the wine that she forgot to turn off the tap. The barrel had run dry, all that expensive Bolzano—wasted. The boss had screamed, "I don't ever want to see you again!" She cried all night. Before collapsing in her attic bed, she called her uncle from a public phone booth and told him about the disaster. He came the next morning, paid for the wine, and she was permitted to stay. She waved good-bye to her uncle—or at least to the cloud of dust completely obscuring his car—until there was nothing left to see. If Augusta went to church twice on a Sunday, her uncle remarked, "Once would do."

Augusta knew what Uncle Anselm would say when she told him she wanted to enter a convent: that the same thing would happen to her as happened to that nun who stabbed the child she bore and then threw it into the Nonnenbach, and every time you cross the Crooked Bridge over Nun's Creek, the baby always cries out to you to this very

day. Uncle Anselm had also been born in Kümmertsweiler and grew
up there with his three brothers, Thaddäus, Kaspar, and David. When
they finished working in the fields that bordered the Nonnenbach, they
washed themselves in the stream's meanders and coves and listened for
the nun's murdered child to start crying.

As she neared the houses, perhaps she said to herself: You're still
going too fast. What would the neighbors think and say when they
saw Unsicherer's eldest, now in service in Geiselharz, running up from
Gattnau on a Saturday afternoon! So few houses make up
Kümmertsweiler that everyone is basically your neighbor. Everyone
lives under the eyes of everyone else. She passed Becke's, turned off
before Günthör's, and then rounded Unsicherer's—the front door,
which faced south, was only used when there was a wedding or a
funeral—and already saw the manure pile, the barn annex, and the
garden, and by the fence, beneath the white hollyhocks with violet
edges, she saw the Wasserburger's bicycle with the EFFENDI tag.

The wedding was held a year later. Augusta became a restaurateur in
Wasserburg. When she told her father later that she had come within
an inch of entering a convent, he said, "I'd have preferred the Good
Lord to any other son-in-law."

The gentle, always helpful cousin named Uncle Anselm didn't hold
it against her that she didn't choose his Otmar. And now he was in
jail, a hundred-seventy-fiver, a queer, or whatever all those words were.
When Cousin Great-Uncle had Johann pick out the light-colored,
close-fitting, double-breasted suit at Bredl's in Wangen, as soon as
Johann got home he went to Lindau in the suit and had his picture taken
at Eckerlein's photo studio, standing next to an elegant armchair with
his left hand resting on the chair back in such a way that his left sleeve
pulled back to reveal his wrist and the gold watch. Cousin Great-Uncle
had been godfather to both Josef and Johann and gave each of them
a gold wristwatch. Too bad the picture couldn't reproduce the flash
of gold from the watch. Unfortunately, Johann hadn't dared to have
himself photographed wearing the light beige poplin coat as well. It
was another present from Cousin Great-Uncle. The salesman at Bredl's

in Wangen had said it had raglan sleeves. Whenever Johann looked at himself in the mirror wearing the coat, he repeated that word: raglan. He felt like a flower in a vase in that coat. He couldn't get enough of looking at himself. Wasn't he a thing that could fly? All he had to do was spread his arms and they would become wings, the air an element just waiting to support him to any height, into any distance. His life would be a single rising up. He knew it when he stood before the oval mirror in his raglan coat. Of course, he was afraid of rising up and flying high. The higher the climb, the steeper the fall, that was clear. He'd been inoculated with that feeling. And yet he wanted to rise. To rise and nothing else. To prove to his mother that falling was not his lot. On the other hand, the man from whom he had everything beautiful had been in jail since November. The man with bronze skin and short, dense, silvery hair. A loser, demographically speaking, Herr Brugger had called him. Johann would have liked to defend his great-uncle, but he didn't dare to. That made him feel like he was in agreement with Herr Brugger and Herr Deuerling and all the others who talked like that. But that wasn't what he wanted at all. He wanted to contradict them, but he didn't know how. After six weeks in jail, poor Uncle Anselm had lost thirty-two pounds, Mother said. He was just skin and bones. Johann resisted imagining his great-uncle like that. Although poor Anselm was certainly not allowed to wear his beautiful suits there, Johann could only picture him in a suit. His suits enclosed him like liquid become cloth. The liquid impression was reinforced by the fact that the suits had no pattern and no distinct color. Actually, they were always a light purple, but so light that it was more a hint of purple than the color. And now those suits were aglow in the medieval corridors of the Rottenburg prison. Johann imagined the great-uncle they called Cousin bribing the guards with truckloads of butter and cheese so they would let him wear his suits. Johann wanted to save his uncle from prison clothing. If they absolutely had to arrest people, why did they need to humiliate them as well?

Uniforms sometimes seemed humiliating, too. It was an embarrassment to show yourself in public until you were at least a lieutenant.

That's why he asked Josef in every letter he wrote: When will you be a lieutenant? He pictured Josef as a first lieutenant, himself as a second lieutenant, and Mother between the two of them. Then the village would have to admit it had underestimated this family. The village was the embodiment of mankind, precisely represented by Frau Gierer from the bank, Helmer's Hermine, Herr Gierer the saddler, and all the other Gierers, Grübels, Zürns, Stadlers, and Schnells. The whole time Johann was picking apples, they were all constantly passing back and forth in the street and calling up to him in the tree: glad to see him home again, how had it been in the labor service, he was used to hard work, wasn't he, and how long had he been back already and what did they hear from Josef, hopefully he's fine, one's happy just to still be alive, hopefully better times will come, OK Johann, keep it up boy, you've got some nice apples there, you can be glad if they taste as good as they look, OK then, God bless.

But when Semper's Fritz came by and shouted up that children really do eventually turn into human beings, Johann called back, "And soldiers into privates first class."

Fritz shouted back, "Schnapps is good for cholera AND promotion." It was well known that Fritz had been quickly promoted to private first class because he supplied his unit in Eichstätt with schnapps. Fritz insisted that Johann come down at once and join him at the regulars' table. He had to hear about a slap in the face that happened less than half an hour ago. "Come on, Johann, or you'll never see me again." Johann handed Niklaus his half-full sack. Fritz led him out to the street, and before they turned onto the terrace he rounded up Dulle, too, who'd had no intention of going to the restaurant but saw right away that Semper's Fritz was not in the mood to take no for an answer. Semper's Fritz needed an audience. Off they went to the regulars' table, already full of the people Johann always saw there at this time of day. Luise was told to bring lake wine. When Fritz noticed that Johann was just sipping his, he interrupted his narrative and said, "Drink, drink, *Brüderlein*, drink!" He ordered a round of lake wine for everybody at the table: Herr Schmitt the tinsmith—Fritz's teacher in everything—Schäfler the wainwright, Späth the master

mason, Frei the blacksmith, Leo Frommknecht, and Schulze Max. Herr
Seehahn sat at his own table, spitting words. It was the first time Johann
had sat at the regulars' table since they had leased the business. Fritz was
immediately the one everybody else had to listen to. He passed around
his hand-rolled cigarettes. "One rolled by hand is worth two Senussis
in the bush," he announced. Since Fritz wasn't going to take no for an
answer, Johann didn't turn him down, but he smoked as cautiously as
he drank. Once again, he observed how the regulars talked and how
they listened. They all turned their chairs so they could look directly at
Semper's Fritz's prominent mouth with its lips askew. Luise knew to have
a full glass of lake wine ready to replace the one he was just emptying.

"OK, OK, comrades of all ages, listen up to what an enlisted former
apprentice tinsmith wearing the honorable uniform of his nation had
to swallow from a monkey who didn't even finish his commercial
apprenticeship, he was so eager to be in the military, you know who I'm
talking about, I won't say the name—I dunno, my God, our lieutenant
and Iron Cross first class wearer, you know, with his assault gun and
tank corps duds, former HJ squadron leader and embroidery artist who
always tried to ignore this apprentice—later journeyman—tinsmith so
he wouldn't have to say hello. He used to look the other way when the
guy in the tinsmith's outfit ran past. So OK, and now, less than thirty
minutes ago, the former journeyman tinsmith and current private first
class on active duty meets up with the Iron Cross first class–wearing
lieutenant and embroidery artist. Of course, the tinsmith lowers
his eyes and turns to look at butcher Gierer's shop window because
he's caught sight of a pyramid of canned goods and wants to know
what's being offered by a pyramid of cans in the fifth year of this terrible
war the other side started. But the Iron Cross first class lieutenant starts
screaming at the totally undecorated pfc: Back to Hartmann's nursery
this instant and then about face and march right back here and salute
Herr Lieutenant or I'm gonna get reported, and delinquent company is
the very least I can expect for refusal to obey an order! But the former
journeyman tinsmith and current private first class seems to be hard of
hearing, just stands there hemming and hawing like a mule in the rain.

But the lieutenant, son of the newspaper lady, yells at the motionless former tinsmith, 'And along with reporting you, we're gonna finally clear up that shady business at your physical.' That was too much for the private first class on active duty. All of a sudden, that awful mistake made by a not very bright journeyman tinsmith is being called a shady business. You all know what happened. You're just as sorry as I am that the young man I once was marched past the tables of the medical commission, took a piece of paper from each table, corps of engineers and fit for active duty and God knows what all they needed if the Fatherland was going to know what could be expected of you. And the tinsmithing lad I was back then goes out into the hall and, confused as he is, he misses the door where all that paper was supposed to be turned in so that the folks in Kempten could call him to the colors at the appointed time. This dummy, unaccustomed to and confused by the state of nakedness required for the physical, misses out on two years. For two years—and I say this with deep regret—I was not able to do my duty by the Fatherland. What could I have been by now instead of just a private first class! Which, by the way, is what the Führer was, too. But Semper's Fritz could have been more if the physical hadn't led to him making a mistake and taking those papers home with him instead of turning them over to the folks from Kempten. And that's what the Iron Cross first class lieutenant calls a shady business. Wants to dig it up again, i.e., ship me off to a delinquent company, which I'm not exactly longing for. It'd be the end of me for sure. So there's nothing for me to do but to go back to Hartmann's nursery and about face and parade march back past the Iron Cross fist class lieutenant posted by butcher Gierer's window with a salute that was a joy to behold. But then I circled around behind the Bruggers' and came up the back way and then back onto the street. No way I can drink enough to puke as much as I'd like to. Don't get me wrong—it's because I'm horrified. That such a thing can happen to anybody! Let me just say here and now: no one should have to take that. Especially not from our precious Edi Fürst, whom we learned early on to call Edmund. No mistake, comrades, I scare myself. I deeply regret it if I've been the cause of misunderstandings of any kind. I rise and salute our Führer, whom I honor, admire, and love, because I know he can't know about everything that's done in his name by random people. Heil Hitler. Don't salute, Luise, just bring more wine. Man, can't she see how thirsty I am?"

After that, there was no more talk about the incident. Except for Semper's Fritz adding sotto voce, "The Herr Lieutenant used to poach my chicks, too, and leave me the dregs."

Semper's Fritz was the only one still around who could entice Johann down from the ladder. When Herr Taubenberger came up the street, however, Johann jumped off the ladder on his own, tossed the sack to Niklaus whether it was full or not, and dashed into the street to ask the mailman, "Anything from Josef?" There had to be a letter once a week. If Herr Taubenberger had a letter from Josef in the huge letter bag that dwarfed him, he pulled it out before you even got to him and waved it in the air to show that it made him just as happy as the addressee. When he had to answer the question Anything from Josef? with a No, he did it wordlessly, just shook his head and showed that he had to force himself to keep going in order to pursue his cruel profession, a profession that compelled him to tell people that again today there was no letter from the man they feared for day and night because they hadn't had a letter in such a long time. When a letter came, it wasn't opened until all three of them were together. Nine-year-old Anselm insisted on being the one to read Josef's letters aloud, no matter whether they began Dear Anselm or My dear Mama or Dear Ones. Even before the salutation, Anselm always read what was in the upper right corner: Eastern front, September 19, 1944; Eastern front, September 27, 1944; Eastern front, October 6, 1944; Eastern front, October 15, 1944; Eastern front, October 20, 1944. And so they learned that Josef was doing quite well so far, except he hadn't seen any real action yet; farther forward they'd thrown the Russians back twenty miles and he and his tank were stuck in the repair shop, but life here was more fun than in barracks at any rate; sadly his assistant gunner had shot himself yesterday, it was a mystery to them all since he'd had the good luck to be assigned as gunner in a Panther right out of training; everything in Poland had been outrageously expensive, a pound of pears cost ten reichsmarks for example; here in Hungary people brought fruit right up to the train for them; they'd finally reached the Rumanian border, crossed the ridge of the Carpathians that evening, and on September 29th he'd finally, finally, seen some action at last, not too much going on, they were waiting to provide cover for the infantry and the Russkies were firing artillery, antitank guns, and grenade launchers all day long, but to no effect except Josef and his crew couldn't get out of their tank; Josef had soon gotten used to being under fire and was even able to read a book— by Hesse; in the evening they made a foray with a few other tanks, saw two Russian tanks at thirteen hundred yards, a Stalin and a T34, an assault gun fired at the T34 but missed, Josef fired and the Russky was on fire with the first shot, Josef was ecstatic, what luck on his first day, even though the T34 had already been crippled and couldn't move, it was his first hit; right after that they took a hit on their glacis plate, a real good jolt, knocked the can for a loop, if it'd hit a little higher it might have crippled them, but except for some minor damage they were just shaken up; another letter from us yesterday, a nice feeling to know somebody back home was thinking of them way out there, he used to think it would be better not to have anyone, how easy, how carefree it would then be to go to war, but now he thought it would be awful not to have someone to shed a tear for him, without the folks back home there'd be no point to this fight; if possible please have the Lindau paper sent to his new address; suddenly they were being sent forward again, with a few tanks they beat back a Russian battalion, in the night his can took a direct hit and had to withdraw from the battle so he had time to write again; lots of chickens and pigs running around there, they made porridge and coffee with real beans; the Russkies had apparently broken through near Grosswardein and they were on the move through Hungary again; hopefully everything was going well at home, they got almost no news at all; there was so much talk about the new miracle weapons, hopefully they would arrive soon; the local people everywhere greeted them with open arms, the Russky occupation here was terrible: people shot, women raped, the people in Grosswardein brought them

wine and bread and cheese and bacon; he'd been awarded his first dec-
oration, the Panzer assault badge in silver, he would send the certificate
home; how were things back home, he hoped to get a letter soon; in
the fighting around Grosswardein he had put nine anti-tank guns and
two tanks out of action; during the last assault an officer from another
company had climbed into his tank and was going to recommend Josef
for the Iron Cross, which would be super, of course; the Russkies broke
through with eighty tanks yesterday and Josef hadn't been able to take
part because his main gun wasn't firing accurately; he wondered if they
had any news from his friends back home, where was Hermann Trautwein, where was Edi Fürst, where were Saki and Jim, could they please
send addresses if possible; he had hardly been afraid at all so far, of
course when the shells landed close to their tank it did make them pull
their heads in; the commander of their army had gotten the Iron Cross
with diamonds; he was glad Mother had leased the restaurant; the next
time he came home it was sure to be nice, if only the war would be over
soon; the worst thing would be Russians in their beautiful homeland,
they could believe whatever the propaganda said about how the Russians treat civilians, he'd seen it for himself and if that's the way they
treated the Hungarians it'd be much worse for us; at the moment it was
just their own artillery shooting over their heads but you never knew
what the Russians had up their sleeve even though they had suffered
terrible casualties the last few days; by the time Johann got to the front
the war was sure to be over; they were really hoping to get the new
weapons soon; Mother wasn't to worry about him but she should please
pray for him; his division—in fact, his regiment, tank regiment 23—
had been mentioned in the Wehrmacht report; the situation was dicey,
they were surrounded yesterday but today there was supposed to be an
opening, they weren't about to let themselves get captured; day before
yesterday he'd run into the son of Hornstein from Nonnenhorn; today
for lunch they'd made themselves some pancakes, think of that, they
were almost as good as the ones back home; in Grosswardein he'd eaten
so much chocolate he almost exploded; they must get more news about
the war than he did at the front; finally there was mail from home, the

letter with the pictures from his leave made him so happy; he was fine as always, at the moment he was in Debrecen where there was a lot going on, the Russians were constantly on the offensive and always with superior numbers, Josef's division had been a thorn in their side for a long time and the Russians were always trying to bottle them up and had managed to do so, but not for very long; yesterday a cameraman filmed Josef looking for lice in his shirt, he didn't notice him until it was too late, hopefully it wouldn't get into the newsreels; with all my love, your Josef.

In the evenings, they wrote to him. Either Mother wrote, or Little Anselm wrote, or Johann. Little Anselm wrote that Josef should bring him home a piece of shrapnel. Mother wrote: If only the war was over. Johann wrote: I hope I get called up soon.

"Whadda'ya say, young man?" called Frau Woschischek to Johann. When she called up into the tree like that, Johann knew even before looking down that she would be standing there with her legs apart, fists on her hips, and lower lip sticking out. And the most suggestive expression Johann had ever encountered. Frau Helling always looked down her nose at you, as if you were offending her even before you opened your mouth. Johann had to come down anyway to empty the sack and reposition the ladder. He had picked the Prince Ludwig tree clean. Now came—always the last—the Welschisner tree. This variety ripened the slowest. Johann made it abundantly clear by the way he climbed down that he was doing so because his sack was over-full and not because Frau Woschischek had called to him. He handed the sack over so Niklaus could empty them into the crates unbruised.

Frau Woschischek said, "May I?"

"Be my guest," Johann replied obligingly.

"Turn about's fair play," she said, picked out a perfect Prince Ludwig, and took an enormous bite. While she chewed, she explained what she meant: this time Eva was eating the apple and not Adam.

Johann said, "Come on," to Niklaus. Niklaus only had to help him reposition the ladder when he needed someone to brace against the ends of the stringers. It felt good to have Frau Woschischek watching as he laid down the big ladder and then set it up again. But he was also glad to be standing on the ladder again, breaking off one green Welschisner after another and sliding them into the capacious sack.

In addition to what Johann had already observed himself, Berni had told him things about Frau Woschischek that fired his imagination. Berni said Frau Woschischek walked back and forth in front of you in nothing but underwear and high heels, staring at you the whole time. With burning eyes, was how Berni put it. She pressed her index finger to her lips to indicate that everything had to be done quietly on account of the children sleeping behind the curtain. Her under-wear was black. Whether Johann believed it or not, Frau Woschischek's underwear was black. And how fast were you back outside again? In the blink of an eye, that's how fast. In the blink of an eye she saw to it that you squirted, and that was that. That's how it was everywhere. Cost you five marks, damned expensive. But pretty cheap, on the other hand.

If Frau Woschischek and all her brats had been lodged in Berni's house, Johann would have paid her a visit, too. Maybe. But maybe not. But maybe so. But maybe not after all. It must mean something that when he thought about Frau Woschischek—and he thought about her more than he liked—not a single line of poetry occurred to him. He couldn't think of Magda at all without words starting to stir inside him, form lines, and gather into the strophes of a poem. That time in Holy Week when Josef had said he would like to have a look at one sometime had become for Johann the best moment of all between him and Josef. It was a Monday, early afternoon; it had snowed again. He'd had to weigh two wagonloads of straw. He swept and tared the scale, and the farmers drove on and off; Johann, the seasoned scale operator, expertly cranking the scale bed up and then letting it ratchet back down. The farmers hardly glanced at their scale receipts anyway, since Josef, home on leave, was standing there beside him. And since Josef had said he would like to have a look at one sometime, Johann wrote to his brother, who was meanwhile back in barracks in Böblingen, that he, Johann, was going to enter the regional literary competition in the drama category. He didn't dare enter anything in the poetry category. Except for Magda, not a soul had seen his poems. He couldn't imagine showing those poems to anyone they weren't addressed to. And they were addressed to Magda. To her, or to all mankind. He would have shown them to all mankind, but not to just any human being. But he would to Josef. Probably he would. The fact that Josef would have liked to read one—no, not read, would like to see one—made him feel closer to Josef. He could have caressed him. Some day he would let Josef see a poem. But not yet. Except for Magda, there was no one he could permit to see his poems. For now: the drama category. A five-act play in a single week. A week in May, however. In Fürstenfeldbruck with the labor service, the notice arrived: first prize for *The City in Distress*. Over to Augsburg on a Sunday morning, to the biggest hall he had ever seen in his life. A certificate in Gothic script and a book on General Dietl's conquest of Narvik. A war book, not his kind of reading material. He didn't tell Mother about it. Not yet, he thought. His play was set in the fifteenth century. In his next letter, he had to describe for Josef the ceremony in the big hall in Augsburg. He wanted Josef to hear how much he envied the winner in the poetry category. He had to stare and stare and stare at him. The poetry winner put in an appearance, stood on the stage, and accepted his certificate and his book as if he weren't really present. A prominent, rounded forehead, enviably long hair, and in civvies— just imagine, the poetry category, the only civilian in the entire hall, and Johann of course wearing his dreadful labor service getup, jackboots from the Thirty Years War, but him, the poetry winner, in a flecked gray knickerbocker suit as aristocratic as Baron von Lüt- zow's and a dark green bow tie, probably silk, dark green, sensational, but his expression was the most outrageous thing: pure detachment. Dreamer, Johann had thought, and wrote that to his brother. Actually, it was the way he himself would like to be. Afterwards, no one could claim to have been noticed by the winner in the poetry category. He probably lived among his words. Where Johann would have liked to live, too. Just the fact alone of Frau Woschischek's eternal chatter from the ground below was enough to rule that out. She talked like an open spigot. Maybe she didn't even care if anyone listened to her. But Johann felt constrained to look down every once in a while. Niklaus wasn't listening to her, that was for sure. He looked straight ahead. Frau Woschischek was complaining about an army jackass who was permanently two sheets to the wind, a noncom billeted with the soldiers in the gymnasium. This midget pestered her day and night. She said it in a way that sounded like Johann should help her. Johann called down to her that he would come tonight and throw him out. That's what he planned to do. He was familiar with the stocky midget with the crooked nose. Two nights ago he had been down in the restaurant raising a ruckus. Johann had gone downstairs, and, for the second time since they had leased the business, sat down like a customer at the regulars' table. He ordered a glass of apple juice from Luise and asked her to ignore Semper's Fritz, who was sitting at the table in his private's uniform and shouted to Luise, "A half-liter for Johann on Semper's Fritz!" Semper's Fritz spent the better part of his leave at the regulars' table. The little noncom with the crooked nose was parading back and forth, stopping at every table where someone was sitting and shouting that since he was in for it in the next big push, off to Russia, that is—because of that, he could have any woman, no use playing hard to get, he'd lay 'em before they could let out a peep. His orders were already on the way, he'd be in the next dust-up, off to Russia, that is, and not coming back, so now, before he got whacked for good out there, he was allowed to have any woman, otherwise to hell with a hero's death. . . . The only person who reacted to this noisy disturbance with more than an amused or anxious glance was Herr Seehahn. He stood up from the table against the wall where he always sat by himself, raised his right hand in the German Greeting, and sat down again. But Johann could read from the lips of the word-spewing Seehahn mouth that the Seehahn text had continued uninterrupted: False serpent, stupid sonofabitch, miserable prick . . . Suddenly the Princess appeared, addressed the noncom as "little man," and said if he didn't start behaving himself that instant, she would personally toss him out on his ear, even though he wasn't really worth soiling her hands over, and if he tried to get fresh with her she wanted him to know, since he was over thirty, that anyone over twenty was out of the running for her, was that clear?—if not, he wouldn't be the first one she'd thrashed good and proper. And the shouter just put his head on her shoulder and started crying like a baby. In a peremptory voice, the Princess told two soldiers also billeted in the gymnasium to take care of their superior officer, please. They led the drunk out while the Princess accepted the applause of the patrons: Bravo, Stuka, bravo! And with Bravo Stuka resounding on all sides, she took her bows like an actress and disappeared back into the kitchen.

As Johann handed Niklaus the next sack, he said, more in the direction of Frau Woschischek than really to her, that he would stand guard that night. Frau Woschischek gave a little cheer—it sounded like Hip, hip, hooray—and took off. Johann wasn't quite comfortable watching her receding backside tossing left and right. Maybe there would be another full air raid alarm tonight. They had an alarm almost every evening now. Then all bets would be off. They would all sit next to and across from one another in the cellar and listen to the mechanical drone of the bomber squadrons until the all-clear was sounded. By then, hopefully, it would be too late. Too bad. And thank God. But too bad, too. Really too bad. Perhaps the bomber squadrons would take another route tonight. In the blink of an eye, Berni had said and laughed. Guffawed is what he'd done, a throaty sound. What a deep, rough voice he had all of a sudden. And then he'd added that as soon as Frau Woschischek took hold of your dick, you came—mail delivered, meeting adjourned, next please, who hasn't had a turn, who wants another go?

Berni had told him about it the night they walked home together from the movies in Lindau. Johann felt that it was the darkness and the walking side-by-side that enabled Berni to be so crudely blunt. Sitting across from each other in the train, in daylight, not even Berni, who was certainly more of a daredevil than Johann, would have been capable of saying that. He had said *dick* more than once. As they were passing the Schwandholz woods, Johann had an urge to tell Berni what had happened to him on the edge of those woods the night before Pentecost

Sunday. He would have liked to tell Berni about the results of that
night. He had lain there with Luise's sister all night long, on a raincoat
he inherited from Josef, on the moss at the edge of Schwandholz woods.
Next to Rosi, against her, on top of her, behind her and in front of her.
But nothing came of it, despite all his pressing and pushing. Rosi had
been in town for only a few days to visit her sister. On Whit-Monday
she was returning to the South Tyrol. It had turned into an inscrutable
and completely silent struggle. Rosi had resisted but not in a way that
made Johann feel he had to stop. He had gotten farther with her than he
ever had with Irmgard or Gretel. And he was also not sure if it was his
fault that he couldn't get into Rosi anywhere. They rolled around on the
ground, kept at it without speaking, groped each other, searching, panting. In his mind's eye Johann had pictured the illustration he'd looked
up and studied in his great uncle's gilt-edged encyclopedia: the female
genitalia, reproduced and labeled in a vivid steel engraving. Vagina. He
still preferred the word *plummy*. He failed to translate the engraving into
reality. Finally, he broke the silence after all, hoping to create a mood
that would soften Rosi's mute resistance a little. But of course, he was
unable to say what he was thinking. Beating around the bush was no
help. When it was finally light, he had covered Rosi's mouth once more
with his and pressed against it so hard it seemed he would never stop.
Perhaps only to escape suffocation, she had worked her way out from
under him. OK, OK, OK, forget it then, and he jumped up, slowly
folded up the raincoat, and they walked side-by-side back to the village,
slowly and in complete silence again. Johann had thought: I hope we
don't run into shoemaker Gierer's Hedwig or Frau Schorer or anyone
else on their way to early Mass. Again the birds sang louder than ever
before, sang down at Rosi and Johann from all the trees. Not singing,
shouting. At the corner of the courtyard, he touched her neck one last
time, then went in the back door and up the stairs. He couldn't worry,
too, about how Rosi was going to sneak back into bed with her sister.
Luise lived in the house of shoemaker Gierer, where three beds had
become available beneath the sloping roof: Julius, Ludwig, and Adolf
were in all in Russia, and Ludwig already killed in action.

Of course, he failed to reach his room before Mother called out, "Johann, what is it?" Her tone made it abundantly clear that she had lain awake all night waiting for Johann.

He called back, "Nothing," and made that Nothing as hard and mean as he possibly could. He had pains in the area for which he had no name. Sharp pains. He knelt on his bed, bent over, lay down, curled up. Nothing helped. This was what came of his all-night mishandling in the Schwandholz woods. This was his Pentecost. As the pain gradually subsided, he caressed himself. Oh you, he thought. And he almost heard, literally felt, the answer: IAWIA. And thought: He is who he is. And since his Pentecost had now arrived, he understood it as a first name: He is who he is, HIWHI.

Johann couldn't immediately grin with the others when the flak instructor in Chieming illustrated the ballistics lesson with the pinklepipe; to hit a certain point on the urinal wall, you couldn't aim your pinklepipe right at it. You had to hold it higher.

Tonight, Frau Woschischek. Tonight he would offer Frau Woschischek IAWIA. And what if she laughed at him? He could say it was the Arabic word for dick. Or the Lithuanian word. The Lithuanian word was better.

When he was back on the ladder and reaching for the green Welschisner apples, he saw through the branches a yellowish-brown—almost more yellow than brown—at any rate, very light brown uniform coming up the Dorfstrasse. Only the local group leader wore a shiny, light brown uniform like that. And that was no longer Herr Minn, the boat builder with the white goatee—hadn't been for quite a while. It was Herr Harpf, the customs official whose tinny voice and marionette-like movements Hanse Luis could imitate so well.

When he heard the speeches Herr Harpf had to give in the course of the year, Johann would recall that at the conclusion of Herr Minn's speeches, he had always said: May God protect our people's chancellor. Herr Harpf always closed with the exhortation to give three *Sieg heils* for the Führer and Reich chancellor Adolf Hitler.

Since the war had begun, whenever Herr Harpf walked through the village on a weekday in that radiant uniform you could spot a mile away, everyone knew that in the family whose house he was heading for, someone had been killed in action. It was his duty to visit the houses and say that a husband or a son or a brother had fallen. When he saw that uniform, Johann froze. The local group leader could still turn off toward Peter Schmied's and shoemaker Schorer's, or farther on, where the Rehms, Heitingers, and Schäggs lived. Or he could turn off on the other side to the Hagens', or up the hill farther to shoemaker Gierer's. Or just pass by, keep going toward the train station. But Johann saw that the local group leader was turning onto the terrace. Johann slid down the stringers without bothering with the rungs, threw off the apple sack, ran out into the street after the local group leader, trying to get into the house ahead of him. Herr Harpf would have to go through the passageway, then up the stairs to the second floor and knock on the door. Johann caught up with the local group leader as he was setting his foot onto the top step. Mother was just then in the hallway, under the open door to Room 14, also partitioned—a family of five had been quartered there. The wife was standing beside her eight-year-old, Mother next to Anselm. They all heard the local group leader's boots on the creaking stairs and turned toward him. Mother sees him and screams. Anselm screams, too. Mother runs along the hallway into the partitioned Room 8. Johann stays behind the local group leader. The scream, a single tone, doesn't stop. Nothing more from Anselm. Johann has no feeling of his own. He feels only what Mother is feeling. The local group leader goes into the half of the room that is a makeshift kitchen. Mother has left the door open. Mother stands looking at the approaching local group leader and no sound comes from her mouth. Johann has the feeling that her eyes see nothing. Usually, her eyes are like plum pits. Now her whole face is nothing but staring eyes and a mouth neither closed nor open. She knows nothing anymore. Johann squeezes past the local group leader and stands beside his mother, but not on the side where Little Anselm is standing. He needs to let Mother know he is there. Mother, his little brother, and he must constitute a single being. Against this raging storm. The local group leader looks as if he's going to come to attention and raise his hand in the German Greeting. Instead, he removes his stiff cap, transfers it to his left hand, straightens up, and says something about field of honor, soldier's duty, oath of allegiance, something about greater Germany, and then he suddenly puts out his hand to Mother and says, more quietly, "My condolences." Since Mother doesn't take his hand, he withdraws it, says suddenly and even more quietly, "My deepest condolences." Clicks his heels together, puts on his cap, then executes a rather gentle about-face, turns back once more at the door, bows stiffly, and leaves.

Then the three of them are alone. Johann closes the curtain and turns on the light. Mother says, "No." So he turns it off again. Mother starts to scream again, but not so piercingly anymore. Still loud, but not piercing. No longer a scream, but drawn-out wailing tones that rise higher and higher in pitch. And end in a whimper. Johann holds her right hand, Anselm her left. They sit there into the night. They hear or do not hear the air-raid sirens. They continue to sit there after the all-clear. Until Mother says that Anselm and Johann should go to bed now, and Anselm and Johann are finally able to move again.

CHAPTER THREE

Excursion

THE ENVELOPE. THE CALL-UP NOTICE. Herr Taubenberger needed Johann's signature as proof that he had delivered the letter to him in person. Enlisted. At last. To report to the mountain troop barracks in Garmisch on December 5th. But how was he going to show Mother the call-up? Skiing, mountain marches, mule trains on snow-covered trails, long evenings in huts above the tree line, lots of singing, the most beautiful of all uniforms . . . Mother started right in about the Schnells. Two weeks ago, the news that Schnelle Johann had been killed in action. The funeral is arranged and on the day before, his fiancée gets word from his comrades that Schnelle Johann is wounded and in sick bay in Silesia. So the wreaths are returned to the cellar. Two days later: the younger brother, Josef, killed in action. The wreaths are brought back out. The day after that: word that Johann is dead, too. Yesterday: Paul, their youngest, missing in action. Mother keeps repeating, over and over, what happened to the Schnells. Paul, missing in action. And where is Ludwig? Where are Guido, Berni, Helmut One, and Helmut Two? The only thing they know for sure is that Brugger's Adolf is safe. Not with the flak, but—even safer—in a Luftwaffe radio training brigade in France, with the brigade staff for administration of communications equipment, an interesting assignment, but Adolf was not permitted to say anything more about it, as Frau Brugger told Mother when they chatted in the cemetery. Frau Brugger was glad that since her husband got locked up, he'd permitted her to start going to church again.

Mother's suffering turned Johann into a spectator. He was unable to imagine Josef being dead. He had no sense of it. He saw Josef in his mind's eye, in a hundred different situations, alive. He lacked the ability to conceive of death.

Time to be enlisted, what else! But how to escape from his mother? By the time he's done with training, the war will be over. The miracle weapons are about to be deployed. In Fürstenfeldbruck, they've dug trenches for the electric cables along the runway for turbine fighters, rocket fighters, supersonic fighters, Messerschmitt 115s, which have already performed take-offs and landings. A thunder so loud you can't say or hear anything for a while afterward. The first time, Josef thought: Judgment Day. They said these planes were invulnerable. And he'd be in Garmisch: mountain marches with a rucksack only half as heavy as a sack of coal, and no front and no war in sight. He reasoned with Mother.

In the barracks, he followed the signs, ended up in an attic filled with bunk beds, and again took possession of an upper bunk as he had in Fürstenfeldbruck, one against the wall; beneath him, a Jochen from Hannover who cranked up a gramophone on the very first night and put on one of the two records he had brought along from his unimaginable big city, which he then continued to play every evening—one night the first record, and the next night the second one—and every time the foxtrot started up, he was mobbed by listeners:

> Every single man
> any time he can
> plays his little gramophone
> and never needs to be alone.

Or:

> Friend Sigismund can't help it
> that he's handsome.
> Friend Sigismund can't help that

he gets kissed.
You think someone who's handsome
should pay ransom?
Just be happy our friend Sigismund exists.

Everybody showed with their hands and feet how the foxtrot carried them away. Johann, lying directly above the machine, didn't jiggle along, but he sang along. From one evening to the next, more and more of them joined in until you couldn't hear the record anymore.

Johann turned his face to the wall and with his flashlight read the poems he had brought along, poems by Stefan George. Since Wolfgang—Wolfgang Two, that is—had been going out with the daughter from the Crown, he often passed the chaise longue on which SS squad leader Gottfried Hübschle was recuperating from a bullet through his arm and another lodged in his thigh. Wolfgang, who didn't miss much, noticed that the squad leader was reading poems and told him right off that his friend Johann didn't just read poems, but wrote them as well. Johann had to come and meet Gottfried and ended up sitting entire afternoons in a chair beside the chaise. He got up to leave when the squad leader's parents came down on a visit from Hergensweiler, but the squad leader wouldn't let him go, didn't want to hear as much from his father and mother as they did from him—cared nothing about their little farm in Hergensweiler but said he was going to get an estate in the Ukraine when the war was over, unless he decided to remain an officer. Perhaps, in fact, he might return to the Ordensburg in Sonthofen, where he'd spent the happiest, brightest days of his life—bright, fiery days that shone all the brighter the further they receded.

Gottfried Hübschle spoke High German even with his parents. Johann found that astonishing, since neither parent ever uttered a word of High German. They didn't even try. The father didn't say much in any case, but nodded eagerly whenever his son spoke. The squad leader's mother, who clutched her handbag the entire time she was there, exactly like Johann's mother clutched her little white purse in her wedding picture, namely, as if fearing someone would snatch it from her—the squad leader's mother was unfazed by her son's High German. It was almost painful to think of this small, thin, sharp-nosed, worn-out woman trying to speak High German. She looked much older than her husband; you might have thought that he was his son's brother rather than his father and that she was the mother of both of them. Gottfried's parents were glad their son was wounded and thus out of the worst of it. After the parents had left, the son felt called upon to explain his parents to Johann. He talked about them as if they were a species of animal. Lovingly, and full of pity as well. They were beyond help. Bent and broken for good, creatures of hardship and fear. Fear of God above, fear of the powers below. Two thousand years in thrall to religion, feudalism, taxes—thralldom in general. But that was all over and done with now. Man had picked himself up, German Man first of all, but others were already starting to follow his example and now the New Man would be created. Man without fear. Only he was beautiful. And only the beautiful man was worthy of love, worthy of life.

Gottfried Hübschle did not look at Johann as he said these things. They had no need for special emphasis, because they were obviously, unquestionably right, just, and true. He was repeating them only for Johann's benefit. For his part, it wouldn't have been necessary to say them a second time. But for Johann's sake. Since he cared about Johann. They had more in common than could be expressed right now. "We'll talk again after the war," he said, "if we're still around."

There were sometimes words in what the squad leader recited so monotonously that sounded like they came from Zarathustra sentences, but Johann sensed that they were anything but Zarathustra sentences. They were more like sentences from church. Johann was glad when the squad leader opened his book of poems again and read from it. He read the poems in a voice that almost seemed not to belong to him. It was as if he costumed his voice to make it worthy of reciting these expansive and radiant poems. One afternoon he said he would like to leave the book with Johann, now that he had to return to the East. The bullet wounds in his arm and thigh had healed. And every Russian tank he cracked open out there would be one less tank rolling across the border of the Reich. His comrades needed him. Nowhere was he more needed than there. He just had to decide if he should get the number on the underside of his left forearm, which had been tattered by the bullet, re-tattooed or not. Should he take it as a warning from his so-called destiny not to cultivate his SS identity so much anymore? What did Johann think? Gottfried Hübschle was holding Johann's right hand in both his hands as he said that. And the way he gazed into Johann's eyes told Johann that with his question, the squad leader wanted to express how important it was to him to discuss life questions with him. Johann said, "Don't re-tattoo it." Every time there was talk about this SS tattoo on the underside of Gottfried's left forearm, Johann felt a kind of pity for someone who had been branded like that. It was already bad enough to be in the SS, a troop of godless men who were said to do anything they were ordered to do. Obedient submission to the point of self-effacement—that was the SS for Johann. He was sure Gottfried Hübschle was not that kind of uniformed machine. But there were rumors that in the East, the SS took no prisoners. Johann thought it was propaganda, because it couldn't possibly be true, could it, that they would shoot someone who had surrendered. He wanted to ask Gottfried Hübschle about that. But he was too embarrassed to ask such a thing. It was base even to think it might be possible. But then why did he feel sorry for anyone from the village who let himself be recruited by the SS? Just because people said they did everything they were ordered to do. Although the new constable regularly came into the restaurant, he never even hinted that Josef or Johann should volunteer for the SS. It wasn't feasible, given Mother's opinion of their godlessness.

Gottfried Hübschle, who wore the Iron Cross first class and a silver wound badge, suddenly stood up, pulled Johann to him, and said, "Good boy." Then he gave Johann the book and said Hergensweiler was not on the other side of the moon, so he'd see him after the war. He straightened up—he was six three, at least—saluted smartly, and left. For the first time, Johann had poems written in his century. *The Year of the Soul*. A midnight blue book stamped with golden letters.

And what letters they were. Inside, too, the pages sang with these letters of primeval elegance. Johann could gaze at the poems on those venerable pages, pages that seemed almost Egyptian, without needing to read them right away. And Gottfried had told him that the poet had died only a few years ago. What astonishing news. He would not have dared think that such poems could be made in his own century. Poetry—that was Klopstock, Goethe, Schiller, Hölderlin—and that was all. Maybe a few from the Göttingen Grove League, still eighteenth century in any case. But now, poems like these, so recent. Poems that had no less an effect on Johann than those by Klopstock or Hölderlin. And the squad leader had said that shortly before his death, this poet— the very thought was utterly overwhelming—had been in Wasserburg. Johann was already alive when Stefan George was supposedly in the village—no, probably not in the village. He would have been down by the lake, in the Crown. But if by any chance he took a train, he would have passed their restaurant. Johann received this information as a special favor bestowed on him. He loved to imagine himself as a three- or four-year-old sitting on the terrace steps, and this poet walking past in the company of a friend. The squad leader had shown Johann a picture of the poet, who looked just like his poems: primeval, elegant. Since then, Johann had to respond to everything in this poet's tone. Even if he didn't have enough for a whole poem, he wrote down individual couplets that could later be worked up into poems:

> My heart—was it not as full as yours?
> And was not God as great in all my nights?

> I hate the coward's railing on the bridge,
> and seek in much the more I cannot have.

As Johann came down the stairs with his rucksack and bag to catch the train to Garmisch, the girl was just coming out of the kitchen. He'd already passed her a few times in the house or outside on the terrace and nodded to her. And she had nodded back! She played the piano with as much perseverance and expression as Josef. She obviously had the same inner confidence that ensured that the tones always established order, no matter how quickly or slowly they were played. You could recognize the rhythm at once. Like when you glanced into a church and immediately absorbed its spatial principle. When Johann returned from the labor service, he'd been told to go downstairs and introduce himself to the family who were leasing the restaurant. He didn't like having to do things like that. But he went through the motions and saw and heard next to nothing. Afterwards, he ran upstairs as if he were being pursued. Whenever the sound of the piano drifted up from the first floor, Mother would sit down and start crying. When she calmed down a little, she would say: Lena. That was the daughter's name. Every time Mother heard the piano she would say: Lena. She had to say it out loud so she didn't surrender herself to the idea that it was Josef playing. In the meantime, they had received a report from the company commander confirming his death. Even if the circumstances were not clearly described, they were clearer than what the local group leader had been able to tell them; but although the letter informed them that it happened in Nyiregyhaza and that Josef had died with his crew and was buried in the Miskolc military cemetery, row 1, grave no. 7, Mother would not or could not believe it. The company commander had gotten a letter wrong in Josef's name. Obviously he had never seen the name in writing. Mother clung to that wrong letter. She demanded that Johann write again to the Unit APO No. 40-345-E and ask for more details. Johann wrote, and they were still waiting for an answer. God only knew where that unit had gotten to in the meantime. At least Josef's service record book had been mailed to them by the army records section in Lindau before Johann's departure. And fifty-one marks had been mailed from the unit with the handwritten note on the check stub "FLB, 9/1–10/21." Johann checked the math: 51 days = 51 marks front-line bonus. But Mother wanted more facts. Until she got them, she still had to say "Lena" out loud every time the lessee's daughter played the piano. Obviously it was the same with Mother as with Johann: she couldn't imagine Josef dead. Nevertheless, she suffered as if Josef were dead. Johann did not suffer. He wanted to get to the front.

She had come out of the kitchen, probably on her way to the piano in the spare room, since it was still early in the day and no patrons were there yet. But as she saw Johann coming down the stairs and his rucksack and bag revealed that he was leaving—and where one left for at that time was well known—this Lena had taken a step back, so that as Johann passed her she was again standing in the wooden frame of the kitchen door, and this time she didn't just give him a friendly nod but also said, "Good luck."

So he, too, didn't just nod, but said, "Thanks." And then he just wanted to get out of there. As if the train was already signaling its departure.

Upstairs he had shaken Mother's hand. Arriving or departing, they never did more than shake hands. They didn't need more than putting their hands together to express how they felt. Mother knew as well as Johann that, for example, a farewell at the crossing gate would be completely out of the question. Maybe Little Anselm could have gone to the station with him and waved good-bye, but he was in school.

Whenever Johann lay on his upper bunk making poems, he had the feeling that this Lena was watching him. Partly because of the frame of the kitchen door, this Lena had become an image. Bangs like Anita's. Adolf had called them pangs. Adolf was in France now, an administrator of communications equipment, an interesting assignment. This Lena didn't have a bob to go with her bangs. Instead, she had a volcano of hair. Right behind the bangs, a volcanic wave of black hair erupted, hesitated over the middle of her bangs-draped forehead, and then flowed right and left down to her shoulders, flowed not straight, but in waves that hardly touched the shoulders before turning back, turning inward and then upward again; which led to the flood of hair being widest at the bottom. It splashed onto her shoulders and splattered sideways and inward and finally upward again. Plus two completely round and utterly dark eyes with two black but not very prominent eyebrows above them. When this Lena arose in his imagination, framed by the kitchen door, Johann couldn't stop thinking about her. He had preserved that instant. When he wrote, he lived on the idea that someone was watching him. Not from close up, and certainly not over his shoulder. But at a distance from which his feelings as he wrote could be shared by the observer. Johann wanted to be observed. Wanted attention. Since his night on the nets in Langenargen, he was addicted to attention. He had never been as alone as in that night on the nets. Anita had not paid attention to him. She had seen in him only a messenger who would convey her greetings to Adolf. He was haunted by the fact that he had not conveyed the greetings to Adolf; it also made him feel good, annoyed him, and humiliated him. He still approved of his deception. He'd deceived them both, Anita and Adolf. It still did him good. Then the daughter of the family leasing the Crown and the doctor's daughter had paid no attention to him when they met their Jungvolk leaders from Lindau at the dock. Magda had paid attention. No enough, but some. When he said good-bye to her, she said that if he was going to get letters from that Lena who lived at his house, then he would never get another letter from her. Where'd she get that idea? How was he going to get a letter from the girl with eyes that looked like they were there not to see but to be seen, a girl with hair you could bury yourself in! Magda said she should be ashamed to call herself Lena. Lena was part of her own name. From then on, she was going to call herself Magdalena. That was what they called her before she came to Wasserburg. This Lena needed to be shown that the name was already taken.

Johann was amazed at the vehemence with which Magda talked about this Lena whom he hardly knew, whom he didn't know at all. Most of the time she was away at boarding school on the Untersee. And at home she was mostly at the piano. Sure, at the last moment she had been there, had said Good luck; he'd answered Thanks. And they'd looked at each other only for the time it took to say Thanks.

Now he was scribbling in his notebook as if singing the lines:

Still blooming against gray-green rock,
the miracle of red roses.

He sang no further. Or not the way he wanted. He twisted and turned, wanted to feel, to sense himself. He was both arrow and bow.

He would shoot himself high into the air. That was all that interested him, only that. He recited verses to himself that he had read. And when they ran out, he recited his own. If there was one he wanted to remember, he wrote it down:

> At twilight hour when shadows blue
> like sheep were herded down the lane
> I rose up weary from my rest
> and asked if life had been in vain.

They were fitted for uniforms, sworn in, and trained. They were drilled by a drill sergeant, and at night they whispered from bed to bed that when they got into the field, he would be the first they would bump off. He called it a test of courage: from the top of the steep wall of earth that separated the individual shooting ranges, they had to let themselves fall backward, which was unpleasant even though the steep walls were covered with snow. If one of them just wasn't able to let himself fall backward, it seemed to gladden the heart of this sergeant. He would pull that person out of the line and make him do push-ups, sprints, knee bends, and crawl on his belly carrying his rifle until he couldn't go on. And the whole time he kept telling them that once they were out *there*, they would thank him for this training.

Johann had expected the swearing in to be more difficult than it was. The prescribed oath tripped off his tongue like the words of contrition at the beginning of confession, just another formula. Repeat and recite and promise what had nothing to do with you. He had nothing against these texts, but they had nothing to do with him. Just as the songs they sang when they marched had nothing to do with him. They were only there to be sung, and besides, the ones he liked best were the ones that had yodeling parts. He competed in yodeling with a fellow from Lenggries. His name was Sepp, and he reminded him of Josef. This Sepp yodeled better, Johann realized during their very first march. His voice slid much more easily, more smoothly and brightly into falsetto than Johann's did. Johann wanted to ask him how he did it, but he was too shy. But in shooting, Johann had no competition. You lined up the notch and bead sights with the target, rested your finger on the trigger, breathed out, and squeezed off a round. Johann didn't see how anyone could miss.

In January, high altitude training in the Kreuzeck range, the night before spent in a hotel a mile above sea level. Johann brought only one book with him: *Thus Spake Zarathustra.* As they slogged through the snow for six or seven or eight hours straight beneath a bright moon or a blazing sun, Zarathustra's lofty sentences began to sound in Johann's head. In Father's last winter, Johann had read to him from this book when he could no longer hold it himself, and reading Zarathustra sentences aloud had been like singing. He grew, he sang, he grew.

Johann led a mule. And each man carried his own fifty-five pound pack. The mules carried the machine guns and the ammunition. Occasionally someone toppled over and had to be treated by a medic. Johann had the feeling that nothing in the world could tire him— Zarathustra energy.

Rock ledges, snow cornices, blue shadows, sparkling mounds of snow—Zarathustra milieu.

He seemed haughty to himself and enjoyed feeling haughty. He was aglow with loneliness. When they had maneuvers on skis, he loved it, loved it most when the exercises were pointless, but on skis. Fresh snow, mountains, and forests. The peace that lay on the sunny rock walls and the peace on the walls in shadow. Sun peace and shade peace. Loneliness. All the shooting on maneuvers could not disturb the quiet of the wintry world. The shots only increased the quiet. When they practiced advancing downhill on skis, and during the pauses Johann lay in the snow among scattered fir trees, he almost forgot what he was doing here because he wanted to listen to the firs, how silent they were with their covering of snow. The firs lifted their snow out of the shadows and into the sun. Between the widely spaced firs, the light lay on the snow, sunning itself. The snow reveled in its color. The firs, in groups. They could not be arranged more perfectly. Positively ceremonious.

In the evenings, a low-hanging sky. The clouds tore open their bellies on a thousand fir trees and expired in silver. Johann could feel lonely in the midst of a maneuver. Beside him in the snow, above him in the light stood Zarathustra. Johann felt himself taken up. He was convinced of his discipleship. As a lover. When Zarathustra said *brother*, Johann felt he was talking to him. Instead of the ordinary language of the service, he would have preferred to speak a completely different language all day long. And then he said to his master, who stood before him, above him, in the blinding light of heavenly clarity: I was born for this day and want to end with it. And didn't know why he said it. To make his impressions palpable, he needed to respond to them. What he saw, heard, and sensed he answered, and only then did what he saw, heard, and sensed exist. When he had sentry duty and took up his post outside, he took in the wintry mountain scene and felt called upon to respond. The snow builds pretty walls of silence all around, he would say. The flakes called flakes are falling. What are the flakes but the syllables of a poem. Then he said: I watch the snow falling like an action. And only then does it snow.

This falling and floating and swirling and driving of the flakes was replete with a tendency he could only match with long sentences that continually drew back from completion, circling more than progressing, but then, finally unable to deny their direction, they at last settled down in invisibility. Snowfall, a history. Not a poem anymore. Zarathustra's seemingly inexhaustible store of gestures and sounds: a kind of substrate of encouragement. Encouragement to survive the fall from the language of prescription into the language of freedom.

Two hours standing watch, four hours of rest, thus a night of sentry duty trickled away. In the morning, when it was past, he had the feeling of having been in a theater, but as an actor.

When they trained during a snowfall and he was skiing into insubstantiality with nothing visible but his skis, with his elbow resting on the knee over his uphill ski, gliding along into boundlessness, aware only of what the ground beneath the skis was telling his knees, then he would think: no one should be here. But that he was there was all right.

The worst case, for which what they were practicing here was supposed to be useful, was unimaginable. Nothing that happened between the Alpspitze and the Zugspitze could ever serve a useful purpose. As it was, he felt that where he was, was not really where he was.

But he had to keep Mother alive, too. Give her some signs of life. And remind her that the dues for the coal dealers' association must be paid soon. Then, on a Monday morning toward the end of February, the company commander, a school teacher in civilian life, read the names of the applicants who had been selected to receive reserve officer training in Mittenwald-Luttensee. Johann's name was not among them. He went straight to that mild-mannered man who commanded the company. Yes, he said, he was very sorry. He wished he could have started Johann on the road to becoming an officer, but the corporal Josef had been assigned to for training in the Kreuzeck mountains had given Johann such a bad report that he couldn't justify recommending him. He was really sorry, said the Swabian teacher-officer, because his written essays—the one about Bismarck and the other about leading columns of mules through the high mountains—had turned out to be far above average. Johann clicked his heels together, did an about-face, and left. He ran to the dormitory, lay down in his bed, gasped, and struggled not to cry. The company commander had said that if one wants to command, one must learn to obey. Said it in a way that suggested that since Johann had not fulfilled this basic precept of military life, he would understand that crushing his ambition to be an officer had been only fair. Johann had never failed at anything . . . yes, he had, in Langenargen. Now he lay in his bunk as he had on the nets in Langenargen. Rejected. A failure. All over. He was not able to regret the incident that had been the cause of it all. He would have done the same thing again. His group, ten recruits, clustered around an MG 42. One after another, they lay down in the snow beside the machine gun and recited how it worked. A warm, windy day at the end of January. With miraculously expansive visibility. Suddenly, the corporal asked Johann if he was cold.

"No, sir, Corporal."

Then why was he jiggling his foot?

Johann had no explanation.

The corporal asked if he perhaps found training with the MG 42 boring and was that what he was trying to express by jiggling his foot?

Not that Johann was aware of.

The corporal: Because Johann had also been staring off into space. The only thing missing was that he would start whistling. But he, the corporal, would do his best to make things not so boring for the group's number one smart aleck. And he made Johann sprint, lie down on his belly, crawl on the ground, do push-ups, etc. Ordered him back. Then out of the blue: "Snow's really black today, isn't it?"

Johann said he thought it was white.

The corporal was already worked up, and he got even more infuriated. Johann could see his silver wound badge, but there was no backing down now. The more insistently the corporal ordered Johann to admit the snow was black, the less Johann was capable of saying it was black. Now, on his bunk, his hopes crushed, he found that the snow on that warm, windy day in January had been just as black as it was white. But he had not been able to admit it. How would he explain that in the village? No one would ask him. The news that Johann hadn't made officer was enough for them.

Transferred to an infantry company in Oberammergau, a troop with a lot of wounded men, mostly privates first class and lance corporals. As for him, although he got no private first class stripe on his sleeve, he did get the small rifleman's star, the smallest promotion of all. He lay on the upper bunk of a double-decker and thought about Gottfried Hübschle. And felt ashamed. He'd stumbled on the very first step, stumbled and fallen.

Up to now, Johann had always managed to claim an upper bunk in every barracks, and one on the outside wall as well. He would not have liked to sleep in the middle of the bunkroom. Not in Oberammergau, either, where they had commandeered the hall of the Passion Play theater and filled it with beds. The outer wall reminded him of Gottfried Hübschle. On the hospital ship from Libau to Stettin, he and the man beneath him in the bunk bed had been pushed against the steel wall of the hull, at least two meters below water level. There'd been three submarine alarms. Gottfried Hübschle had told the medic that he and the other bed-ridden casualties who had been shoved against the wall would not be able to get up and out on deck if they were torpedoed. The medic agreed and said it was more important that the ones who were still mobile had their beds further forward, since they'd be able to help themselves if they took a hit. So Gottfried Hübschle just lay there and listened to the water gurgling quietly along the hull. In Oberammergau, the spring winds whistled around the Passion Play theater. Johann had flunked and ever since, found himself unable to read *Zarathustra*. The lance corporal on the bunk below his was eager to show Johann his tattoos: a large eagle across his hairless chest, holding a naked woman in its talons; on one arm a snake woman, on the other the head of a young girl. His last posting had been with the army in Courland, in eastern Latvia. The only way to get a leave was to denounce a buddy who had expressed doubts about Germany's ultimate victory. "What all a body won't do," said the lance corporal, "when the noose is around your neck." That was apparently how he got out of East Prussia just before the Germans were cut off. He said it while he and Johann were filling two hundred sandbags for air raid shelters, said it more to himself than to Johann. In civilian life he'd been a mailman. In Güstrow, in Mecklenburg. His special talent was dog imitations. Johann was supposed to guess which breed. Johann asked him please not to do a German shepherd. In the evenings after lights out, the lance corporal would lie on the lower bunk and quietly run through his repertoire of barks. It didn't bother Johann as much as the stink of the feet he never washed, rising up ineluctably from below.

One time, the lance corporal got up again and said, "Can you hear me, Johann?"

"Yes," said Johann.

Then the lance corporal said very quietly that he couldn't stop imitating dogs because as an SA man he had taken part in the persecution of the Jews, and now he couldn't stop wondering if he would have to atone for it. If he could sing, he would sing to distract himself, but he had no ear for music.

What had he done? asked Johann.

"Set fire to their houses," he said, "and beat 'em."

"Beat them," said Johann. He wanted to ask: Why did you beat them? But he couldn't.

"Yeah, beat 'em," he said, and whimpered.

Johann turned to the wall. The lance corporal lay down again but continued to whimper. Beat them, thought Johann, why did he beat them? And then his stinky feet. Of all the stinks Johann had so far been exposed to in his various barracks, the stink of sweaty feet was the most repulsive.

Then, from one day to the next, instead of being sent to some front with this company, he got orders to go to Wörgl for noncom training, equipped for an infantry march: 3 sets underwear; 2 pairs socks; 1 tent pole; 2 tent pegs; 1 complete uniform, twill; 1 complete rifleman's dress uniform; 2 blankets, wool; 1 tent fly; 1 cooking pot; 1 gas mask; 1 steel helmet; 1 bread bag with canteen; 6 cartridge pouches plus rifle and sidearm.

During the ride into the Inn valley, the first sounds of war. Then every day the twin-fuselage strafers roared down the valley, bombing and shooting up everything in sight. The major who directed the training in Wörgl was obviously tortured by the fact that he had to put up with those twin-fuselage Lightnings thundering by, and there was nothing he could do about it but take cover and stay put until they thundered off again. The major, who was plastered with medals—what most caught your eye was the Iron Cross in gold on the right half of his chest—ordered the troops under his command to fire their rifles at the low-flying planes. Especially the men with scopes on their rifles should shoot at the Lightnings. Somebody said that the planes were so well armored that rifle bullets would bounce right off them, but no one dared tell that to the major. He arrived at every muster on horseback. He sat on his white steed and announced that the final victory was at hand. The advanced V1s and V2s were almost ready to be deployed, and the U-boat war was entering a new . . . Johann stared at the spring sky and thought: Blue casque above the valley of the Inn.

When the major mentioned the Führer, Johann paid attention. With the Führer a month ago: what calm, what strength, and how intently he listened, and suddenly quite impulsive, worked all night long into the wee hours, then had the answer, so brilliant in its simplicity that none of his associates had come up with it.

When they went out into the field for training, the white horse would have been too tempting a target for the Lightning gunners. They deployed without the major and scratched their heads about the fact that such an experienced major could have said he expected to get a positive report soon from the riflemen with scopes. Aim three to five plane lengths ahead of them, he'd told them. But that meant there would be nothing but thin air in the crosshairs of the scope or in your notch and bead sights. Someone had heard tell that the major had been a Nazi propaganda officer on the Russian front. Johann did not fire a single shot when they took cover from a Lightning attack at the edge of a forest. It was March and then April; he lay on the edge of the woods looking down at the foaming Inn. The French were advancing from Innsbruck, the Americans from Rosenheim. If the French were already in Innsbruck, that meant they were in Wasserburg, too. So the war was over. Four other guys whose home towns were also occupied were of the same opinion. Since the major rode a hobbyhorse through the barracks when he got drunk every evening, claiming that the Inn valley was the lifeline of the Alpine fortress and the Alpine fortress was the guarantor of final victory, Johann and the other four decided to put some distance between themselves and the speaker. Their rucksacks were filled with canned hunter's sausage. They had been permitted to empty out a storehouse that would soon be captured by the Americans. As soon as darkness fell, they set off uphill, northward. And were amazed when they came to the path leading that way: hundreds or thousands were following it, sleeping in haystacks and going on at dawn. And at a fast clip. Simply following the guys ahead of them. Now always under cover of woods. At some point, the ground stopped rising and began to fall. At some point they ran out of woods. Farther down there would be more tree cover. Suddenly, around a bend, watchdogs and motorcycles blocked their path. Military police, their chests covered with tin, at once started bellowing at them, "Get a move on, march!" Three hundred yards down the hill was a collection point where you were supposed to check in. A fighting unit was being put together to defend the Alpine fortress. When the watchdogs could no longer see them and the collection point was not yet in sight, the five of them walked, as if unintentionally, a bit to the side of the path, and as soon as there were some bushes and trees, they faded into the forest. Everyone else kept going toward the collection point. Wurmser, from Mittenwald, had engineered this maneuver. As soon as the forest absorbed them, they turned back uphill. But when they reached the top, they didn't continue down into Austrian territory but kept to the ridgeline, heading west. They kept sinking up to their bellies in rotting spring snowdrifts. Unexpectedly, a hut in a clearing. They were greeted by a stout little man with a pistol trained on them. Staff commissariat officer. Once assured of their peaceful intentions, he invited them in. The entire hut was full of supplies. They could help themselves. He was living there with two female assistants whose combined ages were less than his.

"We ought to take them for ourselves," said Wurmser.

Richard, who planned to be a priest, said, "Shh."

Ferdl from a family of hoteliers in Garmisch said he wouldn't touch them with a manure fork.

Since their rucksacks were still practically full, they just stuffed packs of cigarettes in wherever they could. So long then, Herr Commissariat Officer.

Toward evening, they descended until they came to a farm. They slept in the hay, exchanged their uniform coats for old farmers' jackets, ate bread dunked in milk out of double-handled bowls, learned that the Reich had surrendered and all soldiers were to report immediately to POW collection points. Anyone caught in possession of a weapon would be regarded as a *Werwolf,* i.e., get shot. They still had their pistols, but they were relieved of them before they had even reached Garmisch. Wurmser had already left them because he lived on a farm near Mittenwald. When he was a hundred yards down the hill, he'd treated them to a farewell yodel. Johann didn't yodel back. He would have given anything to be able to yodel like Wurmser. That last yodel hung in the air like a gleaming, hundred-yard-long whipcord. And not even half an hour later, they were confronted by two men in striped prison garb who relieved them of their watches, pistols, and cigarettes. Johann was glad that Wurmser had already taken his leave, because he was jumpy and obstinate and proud—unpredictable in general. He might have put up resistance. And these two were already armed with pistols. Apparently, they couldn't get enough of them. Johann thought of his father's lovely 8 mm. He was going to return from his war without a pistol. No problem.

Herbert, the apprentice saddler from Mindelheim, said, "They were from Dachau."

"They were queers," said the hotelier's son from Garmisch. Besides hotelier, he planned to be a violinist. The three others—Herbert, Richard, and Johann—lay at the edge of the woods and watched him go. From terraces and open windows they heard gramophone music, jazz. American soldiers were lying and sitting around with their legs propped on the tables. Herbert the apprentice saddler, Richard from Radolfzell, and Johann lay in the bushes, looking and listening. They had never seen soldiers like these. They weren't soldiers, they were movie stars.

For a while, they were on familiar ground. They had done their training between Kreuzeck and Garmisch. When they had gotten past Garmisch, the Mindelheim boy left them.

"Take it easy, Herbert."

"You fellows take it easy, too."

Richard and Johann didn't know how long it would take them to get to Füssen. "After Füssen I know the way," said Johann. He didn't, but he hoped that if he stuck to the ridgeline from Füssen on, he could find his way to Immenstadt and, staying on the ridge, to Oberstaufen and from there, with the lake in sight, down into the foothills but keeping to the woods, to Lindenberg, Heimenkirch, and Wangen. He might even make it to Geiselharz and down through thirty-nine sweet little hamlets into the riot of cherry, pear, and apple blossoms surrounding and embracing Wasserburg.

"Stick with me, Richard, until we see how things go." But already on the third day of their trek à deux, a greenish, open vehicle occupied by four soldiers appeared in front of them on one of the forest trails; a few days later they learned that these sturdy machines built to travel cross country were called jeeps. Now they had been taken prisoner, were told to sit on the hood, and they took off down the curving trail. Johann and Richard clung to the windshield so they wouldn't be thrown off. On the paved road in the valley, they were transferred to an armored car, where they crouched—or lay more than crouched—between whipping antennas. They went roaring away and pulled up in front of a wide-open gateway where soldiers, both blacks and whites, were sitting around. It was the Garmisch hockey rink. On all the bleachers and the playing surface, prisoners sat or lay. Richard and Johann found a spot on a bench that was at least roofed over. Johann felt like crying. But then there were books. The library of Radio Munich had been evacuated here for safekeeping. Instead of lining up for work outside the camp where you could earn better rations by washing tanks, Johann became the camp librarian. And six weeks later, when a lieutenant drove him home in a jeep, his rucksack was fuller than ever. Full of books, that is, especially Stifter. He'd started right in on him. Johann came home with a library on his back.

Actually, they were afraid of this lieutenant because he always carried a whip with him. One time he had stopped beside Johann just as he was writing down a poem in his latest notebook. In the snow on the Kreuzeck, he had clearly felt that he would never write another poem. Whether he was thinking of Magda or of Lena, he would express himself in some other way. Perhaps in Zarathustra's tone. But when he discovered what being a prisoner was like, his resolution dissolved. He just had to follow his hand, which followed a mood against which he was defenseless. He felt free of second thoughts and just wrote down what came to him. And he realized that the American lieutenant everyone was afraid of because he carried a whip was standing barely a yard away from him. And he kept writing.

> Though the jumbled peaks are calling,
> Once goals of my keenest attempts,
> The valley still tugs at my heartstrings.

"Poems," said the lieutenant. Johann turned red. The lieutenant patted his shoulder approvingly with the handle of his whip. He only used it when he happened upon an SS man. These SS men, barely older than Johann, had been captured near Crailsheim. The lieutenant asked where Johann lived.

"Lake of Constance," said Johann. Suddenly the lieutenant was much more interested in Johann. His mother's people had immigrated to America from a town on Lake Constance, a place called Graubunden. Johann neglected to tell the lieutenant that Graubunden wasn't a town on Lake Constance but a Swiss canton. He pretended that Lake Constance was so big he didn't know all the towns on it.

Leave-taking from Richard. Every day Richard had volunteered for work outside the camp and had become acquainted with an American chaplain. Now he was serving at the altar on Sundays.

"So, take it easy, Richard."

"Take it easier, Johann."

And now out and over and down into the land of June.

The French wanted the lieutenant to drop off his charge at Singers' Hall in Lindau, where they housed their prisoners. But the lieutenant drove with Johann from one lakeside villa to the next until he found a Capitaine Montigny and interrupted his Sunday conversation. He was quickly persuaded to make out a laissez-passer for Johann that would supposedly protect him from further attempts to seize him. The lieutenant, who wore wire-rim glasses, dropped Johann off at the grade crossing by gatekeeper Stoiber's house. Johann thanked him in English. Although he'd had six and a half years of English in school and always gotten an A or A minus, he'd only heard real English once a year, namely, in the last period before Christmas vacation from a record on which George Bernard Shaw said that his name was George Bernard Shaw, so he understood almost nothing the lieutenant said to him.

As Johann walked along the tracks toward the setting sun, he was dissatisfied with himself for not thanking the lieutenant more profusely.

That was always the way with him. When something happened for which he should be thankful, he was so filled with what someone had done for him that he only realized much later how inadequate his thanks were compared to the favor he had received: that he was able to come home on a June Sunday evening of pure gold, his rucksack full of books—he had simply packed it with his favorites and not a soul had raised any objections—along the tracks past the fruit growers' auction hall, past the warehouse where Mother had handed Herr Witzigmann the loan guarantee, past the spot by the tracks where the blackened ground showed that for years Johann had unloaded boxcars full of coke, coal, and briquettes at that spot, past the freight depot—but by then he could already see the house, the terrace full of soldiers, a thicket of bicycles leaning against the side of the house and under the blooming chestnut trees, and in the street between the restaurant and the station and on the square where clubs and organizations had always assembled before a parade there were now soldiers riding bicycles in circles. Johann came to a stop. He was not going to get past them. He certainly couldn't interrupt what they were doing. They kept grabbing fresh bicycles from against the house wall, riding them in wild circles, and then discarding them and getting new ones. They were obviously having great fun riding around, snaking past each other, and then throwing the bikes away. In color they ranged from brown to black. Africans, probably. And Niklaus was going over to each discarded bicycle, picking it up, and adding it to the thicket of bikes that had accumulated between the wall of the house and the chestnut trees. With studied casualness, Johann turned off toward shoemaker Gierer's little house farther down the hill, walked behind it and then onto the path that led up between blooming espaliered pears to an arch of roses and onto Dorfstrasse.

He crossed it and mounted the five steps to the terrace. To his left and right were tables full of soldiers. The air was thick with the sounds of French. Only about five more strides would bring him to the two steps that led from the terrace to the open front door. Those were the five most difficult steps he had ever taken in his entire life. Luckily, the terrace was divided by planters of ivy. But he wouldn't be invisible. He was prepared to be taken into custody. Although the laissez-passer of Commander Montigny was in his pocket, if one of them was to tear it up before his eyes, they could do whatever they wanted with him. Transport him to France. To a mine. Even in Garmisch, entire truckloads of prisoners from the hockey rink were being driven off to France to work in the mines. He hadn't shaved during the whole time he was forced to sit and lie around at the skating rink. They did have faucets. You could stand in line, get some water, and shave. Johann felt that as long as he was a prisoner, he couldn't shave. So he had grown a kind of beard, and it was pleasant to rub his hand against its wiry curls. Now, in the midst of excitedly chattering French soldiers, he feared they would be more likely to let a clean-shaven man get past than one with a beard. He was glad he was wearing the farmer's jacket that was more yellow than green and had staghorn buttons. It was surely less provocative than a uniform jacket. He had tried to give the lieutenant his military service book to show to the French *capitaine*, but the American had handed it back to him with a smile, pointing to the forged birth date. In one of the lonely farms where they slept, they had heard that only soldiers born in 1927 and earlier would be taken prisoner and had used their thumbs to smudge out the sevens and then made them into eights. But of course it was obvious what they had tried to do. He did have his laissez-passer, however, with the correct information. He just had to keep that in mind and then take five firm steps, walking so confidently he would exude a sort of unapproachability. At least, that was the idea. Five steps between the ivy planters. Johann wondered who had gotten the ivy planters out of winter storage. The bright chatter of French sounds filled the universe. At any moment one of them could jump up and . . . Daniel in the lions' den, he thought. But Daniel had his God, a God who, if you believed in him, would close their jaws. All Johann had was his fear. The front door was open. The two wings of the swinging doors were also open. Then he was in the passageway. Already could see to the right of the kitchen door the framed, color print of fashionable ladies and gentlemen playing tennis on the deck of an ocean liner. Now he hoped that some other things would also be as they always had been. Just short of the kitchen door, he would turn left and then before he reached the window, turn right, up the stairs, and across the creaking floor to the door of Room 8 . . . But before he could turn left, there was Lena in the kitchen door. Dark and light purple stripes in slanting lines competed on a dress that was close-fitting and had a neckline that was a bit too deep. Johann thought of the soldiers who occupied the house.

"Your mother's in church," said the mouth beneath the eyes and the hair.

Johann said, "Thank you," ran up the stairs, threw off his rucksack, blew out the candle burning under the picture of the guardian angel, even crossed himself, but had to smile at that, ran back down, out the back door, and down into the village. He passed the Linden Tree, obviously not commandeered, but no sign of being in business, either. No need now for him to count the guests in the Linden Tree or Café Schnitzler. Even before he had reached Schnitzlers' garden, he saw a man sitting in the café window. Head Teacher Heller. He was sitting so that you saw him directly from the front. His back was straight but his head was bowed. He sat without moving. Johann was unable to look for very long. As soon as he read the sign that had been hung around the teacher's neck, he ran off. The sign said: I WAS A NAZI, and it was signed by Head Teacher Heller. Then Johann slowed down again. He didn't want to attract attention. He passed a few local people and said hello. They didn't recognize him until he spoke, and they told him so. It made him happy that they recognized his voice despite the farmer's jacket and the beard. When he reached the church-yard, he considered: should he now enter the church from the back like a grown-up, or should he enter at the side as he always had? In any case, first of all he had to gaze down at the lake through the crenellations of the churchyard wall. As in the falling snow on the Kreuzeck, he had the urge to respond to what he saw and he answered: Among your beauties, the water level in June. If it sinks half an inch, he thought, it loses one hundred sixty million cubic feet. He hoped nothing had happened to Adolf.

Then he was inside. To the front section of pews, or to where the men sat? He decided on the front section, but the last pew. As soon as he opened the door, even while he was still reaching for the handle that had always seemed too high to him, he could hear the singing. He slipped into the last pew of the front section, knelt down, crossed himself, and then slowly settled back into the pew, listening. He had never heard anything like it. He could not have imagined this. The Ave Maria, sung by . . . not a person, but a voice. The angel occurred to him. The service was already over. It was ending with this song. Of course he recognized the voice. His father had bought the record. It was the world famous meterman from Ravensburg. A sheer miracle of a voice: Karl Erb. He didn't have to turn around to know that up by the organ, Herr Grübel was standing or kneeling. Beside the singer. Cousin Anton. Herr Grübel, over sixty years old, could still hit the high C effortlessly. So you're no tenor, Johann told himself. You're no singer at all. You knew you weren't. So just listen. Ave Maria, clear and cool as water, floating into the evening light. No difference between earthly and unearthly. The Ave Maria sung this way—not anxiously or the least bit dramatically, but with complete restraint. Just allowing it to happen. The second Ave dark, but transparent, vaporous.

This strange feeling of being rich without knowing what your riches were. You're standing on a peak and have no idea what it's called. You have never seen as far as you do now.

As the voice returned to earth, it was silent in the church. Then the creaking of wood signaled that someone had gotten to his feet. The sounds of steps, the church door opening. Johann joined the exodus. Mother and Anselm were standing by the grave, Anselm almost as tall as Mother. Johann went up behind them and put his hands on their shoulders. Mother made a sound and Anselm

said quietly, "It's Johann." Then all three turned back to the grave-
stone, as was right and proper. Now Josef's name was there, too:
1925–44, Niyregyhaza. Mother's lips moved in prayer. Anselm
seemed to be praying, too. Johann couldn't. He couldn't get out the
Lord-give-him-eternal-peace-may-eternal-light-shine-upon-him-Lord-
let-him-rest-in-peace-Amen. He would have had to summon it up.

Although Mother was praying, she whispered something into
the middle of her prayer—"Say hello to Frau Brugger, too"—and
after whispering went right back to praying. A few graves away, Frau
Brugger stood praying. Her grave was the freshest one. Mother whispered, "Herr Brugger, in April, in prison."

Anselm, just as quietly, "May have been killed by the other prisoners."
Mother: "Shh!"

Johann nodded over to Frau Brugger, and she answered with a nod.
Johann didn't want to miss the singer's exit. Father's grave was located
where the singer and his entourage would pass right behind Johann.
He would stand and pretend to be praying until they came by. Between
the church door and the cemetery gate, the singer and his escort would
move and speak quite differently than all the other churchgoers. Perhaps
the singer was still speaking with the priest. If only Frau Brugger would
just leave. Then he heard the voice. Even the speaking voice was some-
what unearthly. Johann simply turned around. Anselm turned, too.
Mother kept praying. Karl Erb, beside him Herr Lohmüller, the high
school teacher who had probably accompanied him, and Kreszenz, who
might have been his accompanist, too, and two ladies about whom
there was absolutely nothing to suggest that a war of several years
had just been lost. Genteel ladies, so to speak. One was talking to the
singer insistently and in extremely loud Swabian and addressing him as
Herr Professor. In the brief moments in which Johann was able to
overhear them, she twice mentioned the name Richard Tauber and said
she had been a friend of his. The singer walked as if not walking. It had
to do with the way he lifted his chin. Perhaps he didn't even hear what
the lady was saying to him. The ancient high school teacher belonged
beside the singer, since he always wore suits from the nineteenth century

that nevertheless looked new. The presence of the high school teacher made the singer's appearance into theater. The singer smiled. Looked like a noble old Indian chief. Or a noble old squaw. Johann thought of his cousin, the great-uncle. Johann made such an obvious bow that the singer noticed and responded with a glance and a gesture. With his bow, Johann had signaled: I will never forget you or your voice. Only when they had passed beyond the cemetery was he able to tear himself away from the grave.

Frau Brugger had been waiting to say hello to Johann. It was too bad that her husband had not lived to be here. But Adolf would be happy to know that Johann was back. Adolf was in Buchloe, working for the famous livestock dealer Wechsler, Eberhard Wechsler, who was able to return from Zürich now that those brutes had abdicated. As long as Wechsler had to live in Zürich, he'd used a front man to run Wechsler and Co., and through him, her husband had kept in contact with Wechsler. Wechsler had no children and now wanted to adopt Adolf and train him to be his successor. She couldn't imagine anything better for Adolf. Thank goodness Adolf had been baptized Adolf Stefan and had already had that awful first name officially dropped. It would be nice the next time Johann saw him if he would just call him by his new name.

Johann hastened to say, "I'm very glad for Stefan. Please give him my best wishes."

Since Johann had no desire to go past Head Teacher Heller again, he said he was going to go home on the Moosweg. And he told her why.

"That poor man," said Frau Brugger. "Has to sit there like that for eight Sundays, but it serves him right. It was a terrible time." She glanced toward Mother, who nodded. As soon as Frau Brugger had taken her leave—she was going to go past the teacher again—Anselm told him that when the French tanks were entering the village, the Princess had been unable to stay put inside or at least on the terrace, but had run out to greet them, wanting a tank crew, all young guys, to lift her up onto the tank. But then she didn't quite make it, got dragged under the tank, had her legs run over, and bled to death. He could show Johann the spot between

the train station and the chestnut trees. You could still see the blood-
stain. But now Lucile was the queen of them all. If Lucile put in a
good word for you, you could even get your bicycle back. Without
Lucile's help, they would not have been allowed to stay in the house.
Downstairs, it was all an officer's mess. Lena had to play piano for them
practically day and night. Johann felt himself grimace when Anselm
said that.

As they entered the house through the back door, they could hear
the piano in the spare room. Popular hits. Probably French ones. Fairly
sentimental.

Upstairs, Anselm went right to the cabinet and took a letter out
of the drawer from the Unit APO No. 40-345-E. Beneath the date
January 16, 1945, Johann read:

> The company hereby confirms receipt of your letter
> of 21 November 1944. We are of course more than
> happy to inform you in more detail about the death
> of your son. The tank in which your son was serving
> as a gunner was deployed in the defense of the town of
> Niyregyhaza. In the course of a hard-fought defensive
> action, his tank suffered a direct hit, which immediately
> detonated its munitions and burned out the tank. Your
> son died a quick and painless death. I send you my
> very best wishes for the future and greet you with Heil
> Hitler! Signed on behalf of Lieut. . . .

The signature was illegible. *Niyregyhaza*, thought Johann, that
would have been a word for Father to spell. He pictured it in the word
tree. It hung there awaiting an equivalent: *Niyregyhaza*.

Anselm said, "Edi Fürst was also killed in action. Jim, too. And Saki.
And Trautwein Hermann. And Lange Josef. And Ellenrieder's Alois.
And Friedl's Arthur. And Frommknecht's Severin. And . . ."

"Hush now," said Mother.

"Just one more thing about Herr Hübschle, Gottfried's father in Hergensweiler," said Anselm. Because the French thought the SS man in the large framed photo in the living room was him, they dragged him out of the house and beat him to death with the butts of their rifles. His wife had been in a mental hospital ever since, Gottfried Hübschle missing in action since January.

Johann must be hungry, said Mother.

"Hungry?" said Johann. "If you say so."

So she would make something to eat now, said Mother. But she still couldn't believe that he was really home. Johann said he wanted to change his clothes. He washed up at the sink. Thinking of his grandfather in Kümmertsweiler, he first splashed cold water on the back of his neck. He cut off his beard, carefully shaved off what was left, smiled when Anselm, who was watching, said, "A shame to lose that." Then he went to the wardrobe and picked out one of his jackets, although Josef's jacket with the greenish herringbone pattern would have pleased him more. He sensed that it would be improper to come home and put on his dead brother's jacket. He needed to dress well now. Nothing wrong with that. From downstairs came the sounds of a tenor singing a sentimental song to piano accompaniment. So Lena was playing. He could ask about Magda. But he didn't. He listened to the schmaltzy tenor, listened to the accompaniment, and pictured the player to himself.

"She's got some tough-looking brothers," said Anselm. Johann looked at Anselm as if he didn't know what he was talking about. How does he know who I'm thinking of? wondered Johann.

"You're how old now?" asked Johann.

"Almost eleven," said Anselm.

"Oh yeah, right," said Johann.

Mother called them to the table. Buttered potatoes and smoked pork. "From Kümmertsweiler," she said. Johann inhaled the fragrance of smoked meat.

CHAPTER FOUR

Prose

THE WHOLE LONG, HOT SUMMER was spent reading, the intrusive heat kept at bay by elegant Venetian blinds. Venetian blinds struck him as elegant since he had read about them in novels. Reading, but always ready to hear steps on the creaking floorboards of the corridor, jump up and fling open the door, and intercept Lena, simply not let her past because three steps farther on she would disappear into Room 10 on the other side of the hall, and through that door he could not follow her. So intercept her and somehow maneuver her against the wall of the corridor and just keep her there. To bring her into Room 9 was also impossible, as impossible as following her into Room 10. So no matter what he was reading at the moment, there was nothing to do but intercept her as soon as she turned into the corridor from the stairs and keep her there and then look into her eyes so she knew she would soon have to deal with his mouth. It was still August when it happened: doing nothing but looking at each other turned into doing nothing but kissing each other. And how he hated that word! *Kissing*! Baloney, he said to himself when he heard the word. He never said it out loud. Never, not in his whole life, would the word *kissing* pass his lips. Give me a kiss. Not that word either, although since its form led much more quickly to a decisive conclusion, he had more sympathy with the noun than with the gerund. He performed the act in a way that was calculated to hurt her. She should feel that there was nothing he could do about it. He wanted to behave as if not responsible for his

actions, and he did. In August. Starting in August. Always out in the
hall. Every time he heard her steps, her heels, her high heels drumming along the corridor so the floorboards forgot their creaking. She
was the only person who walked in a way that basically never gave the
floorboards a chance to creak. That's how she walked. He jumped up,
threw down Stifter, Heine, Faulkner. Out into the hall to capture her.
He chopped at her mouth with his, as if her mouth was something
that needed to be knocked down quickly. At the very least, her mouth
should be bleeding when he was done knocking it down. He couldn't
let her get the idea that she was being kissed. Johann is kissing Lena—
horrifying.

Once he had captured and belabored her with his mouth until she
bled, made her familiar with both his lack of responsibility for his
actions and his rage at the act of kissing, he gained enough confidence
in himself so that the second, third, fourth, fifth, sixth, seventh—up
to thousandth time he captured, held, and assailed her with his mouth
he could proceed more mildly, slowly, contemplatively, gently, and
reasonably and almost allow her to guess that he might know what he
was doing.

And what could he say or not say about what was going on inside of
him? Say everything? Impossible. Although he did write down the poems
that again rose insistently to the surface, they contained almost nothing
of him. And nothing at all of Lena. They contained only themselves.
He was furious at these imperious poems. But he could not suppress
them. Not yet. He wrote down what he dreamed. What was later to be
found on the paper was not what he had dreamed but still contained
more of him than his poems did. The poems had a polished clarity he
lacked. A lucidity foreign to him. An orderliness he found laughable.
He was also annoyed by the stilted mood that writing poems inevitably
generated. What annoyed him most was that he began to hand over his
poems to Lena, too. Each time he did, she said, "Thank you, Johann."
She accepted his poems as if they were flowers. You could actually see
that she would have liked to sniff them. But she controlled herself. He
would rather have handed over the dreams he wrote down. But he didn't

dare to. He wrote down his dreams in an old purchase ledger with many blank pages. Once he dreamed that he had read in a book—half murder mystery, half science fiction (he had just read Hans Dominik's *Atomic Weight 500*)—that a woman had children who were born wearing ties. They were born with ties, congenital ties so to speak, flesh-colored and made of flesh. A stick pin, and they would have bled. He said to Josef, who was looking over his shoulder and whom he knew right away he could trust unconditionally: *Why can't I think of things like that?* And at the same time, still in the dream, he was very happy because he sensed that he was just dreaming about the congenital ties, and so the idea didn't belong to another writer, but was his own and he could use it. But then when he woke up for real, he had no idea what congenital ties would be useful for. *Just write it down, your dream.* And he did.

Beginning in the early evening, sentimental songs with piano accompaniment started drifting up from downstairs. *Bésame, bésame mucho.* The noncom who was called upon to sing every evening—yowl was more like it—would hit Lena on the fingers if she made a mistake in the accompaniment, and sometimes even if she didn't. When Johann heard that, he was unable to read or write anything once the music started up.

Of course, for the first fifty times that Lena came up the stairs and walked down the hall to Room 10 in her high heels, he made it look like their encounters were pure accident. He would just wait at the door, open it as soon as he heard the high heels, and walk toward her as if he were going downstairs and leaving the house. So then that's what he had to do. Out the back door and then up the entrance drive, for example, to where Herr Seehahn sat scribbling at a table that had been brought from the terrace and placed between the chestnut trees. Herr Seehahn spoke French. If you wanted to get back your bicycle, your radio, or anything else that had been confiscated, you had to apply to Herr Seehahn. Now every day Herr Seehahn wore the medal he had been awarded by the Holy See on the green lapel of his yellowish Tyrolean jacket. On the table before him, the lists of all confiscated items. The first time Johann walked up to him, Herr Seehahn said, "Back in town, Johann?" and then resumed his muttering and his list-keeping. Johann had heard at once that his text was still about the false serpent, miserable prick, stupid cows. But what struck Johann now was how vehemently Herr Seehahn spat out his tirade. It sounded like Herr Seehahn was responding to a particularly nasty experience he'd just had. It was just the way you'd curse if something particularly nasty happened to you. It was the way Herr Seehahn had been cursing for decades. Johann was tempted to say, like his father: You're amazing, Herr Seehahn. It was Niklaus's job to stand guard over all the bicycles, radios, and binoculars of the parish and Herr Seehahn's to administer them.

If Johann didn't feel like leaving the house after contriving one of these chance encounters with Lena, he still had to continue down the stairs but would then go down to the corner of the cellar where the highboy had ended up. He took everything out of the drawers and secret compartments and carried it all upstairs. In the process he might run into Lena a second time. He kept it up until he began to think that Lena, too, was coming upstairs and along the corridor more often than necessary to fetch something and bring it back down.

For two weeks beginning on the first of July, he even received his board from the house kitchen, now under French administration. With six other men, Johann had been ordered to paint the picket fences along the Dorfstrasse. Red, white, and blue. And why? Hermine knew, because she kept house for Lapointe, the local commandant. On July 14th, a boat with General Lattre de Tassigny was going to land in Wasserburg, and the general would then drive from the landing up into the village as far as the linden tree, and from there turn left onto the road to Reutenen to pay a visit to General Koenig in the Villa Hasselbach. On Bastille Day, all the pickets on the Dorfstrasse would be smiling a welcome to General Lattre de Tassigny in the French national colors. For as long as it took Johann and Schulze Max and Dulle and Hanse Luis and Semper's Fritz and Helmer's Franz and Herr Minn to paint pickets, they would get their meals from Lucile's fully stocked kitchen. The painters were served at Herr Seehahn's table between the chestnuts trees. It was Luise who brought them their food.

"You can get along OK with the French." That was the first sentence Johann heard from Schulze Max. Semper's Fritz, who had walked from Schleswig-Holstein to Wasserburg with a shovel on his shoulder, said he'd take French asses over their predecessors' faces any day. While they painted pickets, Semper's Fritz and Helmer's Franz debated whether a shouldered shovel or a shouldered pitchfork was the better way to get home from far away after a lost war without being taken prisoner. They couldn't reach agreement. Helmer's Franz insisted a pitchfork was better than a shovel because it was a clearer signal you were only a farmer, which was the whole point. Semper's Fritz said a shovel was better because it was plausible regardless of the season. And anyway, getting home after the first war was child's play. You came home, changed your clothes, and voilà. This time around, it only really got dangerous once you had made it home. The French had arrested him the day after he registered at the town office because he needed food stamps. He knew who had ratted on him, and he would get his someday. So they whisked him off to Lindau and stuck him in the overcrowded Singers' Hall. From there, transports were leaving every day for France, to the mines, road building, or any other such-like jobs that held no appeal for a tin-smith with his excellent qualifications. So he traded two cigarettes for four smelly foot rags from a fellow prisoner, who was ecstatic, the dope. Fritz, however, had gone to the latrine, wrapped his hands in the rags, climbed over the barbed wire, swum across the Kleiner See silent as a swan, landed on the shore at Aeschach quieter than a duck, knocked on the door of an ex-girlfriend in Aeschach, put a hand over her mouth before she could exclaim, and—his big lucky break—learned from her that a guy from Alsace was paying her a visit every other night—with marriage at some later date a distinct possibility. Fritz got a chance to tell this guy about how he'd pulled the wool over the eyes of the military district officers at his physical, and the Alsatian was amused. So that's how he came by his release papers, without which any frog who wants can collar you. Now he was going to tip off the Alsatian that Harpf didn't deserve to be locked up on the Kamelbuckel with all those died-in-the-wool Nazis. During the war, somebody had ratted

on Fritz when he told that joke about the chamber pots at the regulars'
table. He knew who it was, and he would pay him back some day and
wouldn't need the French to help him. But back then, Harpf had come
to him at night and asked through his window how long his leave still
had to go. Two days, Fritz had answered, and Harpf replied: I'll come
to pick you up on day three, then.

"Which joke was that?" Hanse Luis wanted to know.

"Why did they start painting swastikas on the bottom of chamber
pots, was the question," said Fritz, "And the answer: So the assholes can
see what they voted for."

"Oh, that one," said Schulze Max. He'd often told that one and was
surprised he hadn't ended up in Dachau.

"I'm amazed they're forcing resistance fighters the likes of you two
to paint fences," said Hanse Luis.

"Shut your trap," said Fritz. "We gotta get Harpf out." Dulle agreed.
At the end of March, the county administrator was going to hang the
Polish guy who had a thing with the Stuka, and Harpf—the Pole, an
eighteen-year-old guy, was already up on a chair with the noose around
his neck—Harpf goes and says to the county administrator: Is this really
necessary, Herr Kreisleiter? And the Kreisleiter bellows at him: I'm ordering you to kick over the chair! But Harpf refused to kick over the chair.
So Dr. Fröhlich zealously steps into the breach and does it for him. So in
May, he and the Kreisleiter were the first ones the Poles went after. They
caught them and beat them to death, both on the same day, the Kreisleiter in a ravine up in Heimersreutin and the ophthalmologist in the
ladies' room of the Lindau station.

"At least he was wearing a skirt and blouse when he went into the
ladies' room," said Schulze Max.

"And silk stockings, too, I hear tell," said Dulle.

"It's true," said Hanse Luis. "At first they couldn't figure out who was
male and who was female in all the hubbub."

When Frau Fürst passed them with her bag of newspapers, they all
said hello. She seemed not to hear them. Shortly before he got called
up, Johann had had some business with Frau Fürst, because she had

to make a list of all the hens in town so everybody who had more than two could turn over the extra eggs.

Now she was back to walking the town with her mouth stitched shut.

"Poor woman," said Herr Minn.

"Yeah, right," said Hanse Luis. "You know what the conductor said about making music. Goes for war, too: there's no trick to starting together, it's ending together that's hard. Always was a real bantam rooster in his uniform, that Edi Fürst, and then on top of it all he gets the Knight's Cross in January, went straight to his prissy little head. He bought the farm on May 13th just because he refused to believe what the Russian loudspeakers were blaring at him: War over, Throw down weapons, No more shoot. Good ol' Edi just laughs. Propaganda, nothing but a Russian trick, saw it all the time on the Eastern front, the Russkies want to round us up free of charge. But the fact that they hadn't had any radio contact with the division command post for days—you know what that means, Private Fritz, you old front-line veteran. It bothers Edi, that's for sure. Takes off with his tank in the direction of the command post. Four hours later, no Edi in sight, so the staff sergeant drives toward the woods where they had their last sight of Edi. Lead tank come in, where are you? And comes back with the news: lead tank drove over a mine, driver, chief, and gunner made it out of the tank alive but bled to death in the field. And now the radioman has contact with the division again. War's over. Has been since May 8th. All fighting to cease immediately. So they raise a raggedy white flag, the Russkies come in from every direction. They shovel graves for the chief, the gunner, and the driver and put them in, heads pointing east. That night, before they get loaded onto trucks, the staff sergeant takes off, swims across the Danube, makes it through. But our city-scene embroiderer, squad leader, first lieutenant, and Knight's Cross wearer bought the farm, that's for sure."

And Helmer's Franz called over, "Frommknecht Leo always says: The good guys buy the farm and the scum return."

"He just had to be such a big shot all the time," said Semper's Fritz. "Poached my chicks and left me the dregs. Now his chicks've come home to roost."

"What happened to his sister, Edeltraud, is much harder on poor Frau Fürst," said Herr Minn. "She killed herself and her child because she and her Sturmführer from the SS Bodyguards had sworn a pact that in case of defeat, he would kill himself and she would kill herself so no one could humiliate them. Now she's dead and her child, too, and there's been word from the Sturmführer that he's living in Spain under an alias and hopes to come back when the smoke clears a bit."

Dulle: "There ain't no limits no more." And since nobody said anything, he went on, "To what people'll do."

Semper's Fritz said nobody had died as nasty a death as the Princess, a.k.a. the Stuka. Schulze Max knew the most about it because he had it from Herr Deuerling, who saw the whole thing through the station window. She'd been standing on the terrace between the planters of ivy with Lucile and Luise, everybody glad the unpredictable SS had finally withdrawn to Bregenz because, hemmed in between Mount Pfänder and the lake, it would be easier to defend than the vulnerable Wasserburg. The French enter the town as if they were on maneuvers. And everyone's waving a welcome. The tank crews all young fellows, most likely still in their teens. Good old Stuka can't hold back, runs out, reaches for their outstretched hands and grabs one, but dangling in the air like that for a second, she should have stayed still and let them pull her up the rest of the way instead of kicking her legs. So one foot gets caught in the tank's track. She screams and the boy lets go of her hand. She falls and the big iron track rolls over both legs, and those legs she was so justly proud of get crushed. By the time they can bring the tank to a stop, she's dead.

Dulle said, "What a woman. We ain't gonna see her likes again."

Hanse Luis said that must have been what the little half-pint railroad man Deuerling meant when he said: Only one eye, but enough lip for two.

"And the beautifulest High German you're ever gonna hear," added Dulle.

"Paris is shit, London is bigger," chimed in Schulze Max.

"The expert is astonished, the layman rubs his eyes," shouted Fritz.

"O pain, be gone," said Hanse Luis.

As they were painting the fence in front of the Villa Gwinner—Dulle and Johann blue, Herr Minn and Schulze Max white, Semper's Fritz red, and Helmer's Franz in the lead, prepping the pickets with sandpaper—Hermine came out with a tray of glasses and a pitcher of cider, poured a glass for each of them, and said it was compliments of M. Lapointe. Hermine was more important than ever, having become the housekeeper for the commandant of the local occupation forces who was residing in the Villa Gwinner, where Hermine had always been in charge of cleanliness. She spent every night in a crash course in French from Herr Seehahn, because M. Lapointe was not permitted to speak German. He knew German, she said, but as commandant, he could only speak and hear French. And what a gentleman he was! And so bashful! Such a handsome fellow and yet so bashful—or rather, *timide*. And how well he went with that villa where the swans in the stained glass windows outnumbered the ones down on the lake. Our church windows looked like factory windows by comparison. "Johann," she said, "I wish I could show you the hall. I let your father have a peek once, and he said it was a marriage of tropical wood and Jugendstil!"

She thought the painters were doing a great—or rather, *chouette*—job. They all drank M. Lapointe's health.

On July 14th, General Lattre de Tassigny landed in Bad Schachen.

Johann waited for the next chance to run into Lena. He was never entirely where she wasn't. On a Sunday in June, he had finally gone to see Magda. She told him that Wolfgang and the torpedo boat in which he was serving had both been captured by the English, who were about the best captors you could ask for. Johann had steered Magda to the bench that surrounded the thick tree trunk. There they could gaze into the foliage together. He had not been able to look her in the eye. What he would have liked to say was: Let's die right now. Only so he wouldn't have to say anything else. He jumped up and looked her in the eye after all. Looked at the oval face framed by an oval of hair and was able to withstand the gaze that began at the bridge of her nose. Beneath the infinitely delicate nose, a bit of mouth, a small, noble curve. She asked about Lena as if she already knew everything. But for him to own up to everything she'd already learned via village news broadcasts (which were nothing if not instantaneous)—that he could not do. Oh, it would have done him good if he could have depicted how he lay in wait day and night for Lena signals. He could only say that sometimes he ran into Lena when she came up the stairs.

Magda: "Push her down." And because he looked at her in surprise, she added, "The stairs."

"Oh," he said, "you mean down the stairs."

He didn't bring off the parting very well. When she was gone, he knew that Magda now thought he was going to break it off with Lena at once, break it off before it had even started. He had not been able to reveal the least bit of the mood he was in. And yet, he would have liked nothing better than to let Magda feel his elation, let her participate in his rapture, in his Lena addiction. Why wasn't it possible? Why couldn't Magda feel what he was feeling? Why couldn't he draw her into his silent jubilation? Into this constant rising! rising! rising! He was flying, wasn't he? Flying to any altitude.

Johann wished for a world in which it would be possible to tell Magda about Lena's summer dresses. Only when she wore one of them did you see what Lena was like. The sleeves so short that you could look inside the dress. She had much more hair in her armpits than Anita. She moved and stood still in her dresses, but inside her dresses she was naked. He saw that. The dresses left room for her nakedness. The dresses didn't even touch Lena. They enclosed her nakedness without concealing her nakedness. Lena was naked inside her dresses. And why couldn't Magda have the same experience? Why couldn't Magda experience him? He felt himself to be a natural phenomenon. Like a sunrise, like a warm wind in winter, like hail in June. He scribbled more poems down but didn't deliver them. Lena asked him if he wasn't writing poems anymore. He wasn't, he lied. But they didn't contain him. He would rather write down what it had been like earlier, when he was feverish. In the summer. When he lay in his bed in Room 9 and outside, downstairs, there were footsteps on the gravel, in the house. It was as if the world were taking place in a huge hall that endlessly amplified all its sounds. Until they were painful. But when he thought back now, they were pleasant pains.

In the highboy he had also found the purchase ledger in which he had written his first sentence (Oh, that early in the day / I should be so lonely). If I've saved this sentence for seven years, I can save it for a few more. But it was more important to save the things of Father's that the highboy still contained. His most precious find: a booklet in land-scape format, watery green, that promoted Wasserburg with pictures and texts from an age in which Glatthars still advertised "*Delikates-sen,* linen and woolen goods, manufactures, fancy goods, and toys" but also "goose down, eiderdown, and crepe." Johann thought about Frau Glatthar, about the foreclosure auction that had frightened him more than Knecht Ruprecht's rattling chains and jangling bells. Each adver-tisement and picture in the booklet was framed by a garland of leaves he recognized from the lid of his father's inkwell. Jugendstil, Father had called it. *Wasserburg, the German Chillon* was the booklet's title. That was his father all over. He'd probably brought Chillon home from his commercial apprenticeship on Lake Geneva. And Lord Byron, whom Johann and Tell had translated together under the Gravenstein tree, had been in Chillon, too. What interconnections!

But he also read with keen interest the clippings his father had saved, "Mobilization Orders," for example:

> The German Volk today mobilizes in the battle for work.
> On the orders of the Führer, the spring offensive is to begin immediately.
> The attack on unemployment is to be carried out along the entire economic front.
> No employer may shirk his duty. All must storm forward

together.

Every business, large or small, must be a shock troop.

Two million fellow members of the Volk must be called to the colors of employment this year.

Give aid to the army of employment!

Show camaraderie and give them work!

Our goal: Germany Without Unemployment.

Sieg Heil!

Beneath it Father had written: 3/22/34. Beneath another clipping, 11/11/36. It was entitled "Seventy Years Old" and read: *At midnight on November 9, 1936, the retired senior postal inspector Ludwig Zürn, the man who has done so much to advance the cause of local history, crossed the threshold of his seventieth year. Only a modest fraction of the material on local history and traditions that Herr Zürn has collected in the course of half a century has appeared in print. Zürn's thorough and up-to-date methods were already evident many years ago, as shown by—among other things—his* Home Book of History, *setting an example which Munich, the Capital of the Movement, is now about to follow. Zürn's activities were not restricted to Wasserburg, however. In Lindau, too, he is highly regarded as a refuge for anyone experiencing difficulties with their Aryan status or similar problems. May many more years therefore be granted to him to climb the rungs of life's ladder.*

Reading such clippings, Johann felt as if he hadn't even been alive back then. Was he alive now? Certainly not in a present he shared with others. He was alive only by virtue of the fact that Lena existed. He could only perceive things that had nothing to do with her if he tried extra hard. He had to give himself reasons, tell himself why he should notice this or that, even though it had nothing to do with Lena. He had to go to the town offices to pay twenty marks for all the books left behind by Viktor Baron von Lützow after the baron, upon hearing that the war had been lost, threw himself—so people said—in front of a train. So did shoemaker Gierer. But in his case, it might have been an accident at the grade crossing. Johann was for calling it an accident in shoemaker Gierer's case. He had to accept that in the case of the baron, it hadn't been. All the written material and books in the boxes he transported home in the handcart had to do with homosexuality. Magnus Hirschfeld, *The Third Sex*. He was interested in such things. He wanted to understand Cousin Anselm, his great uncle. Who was dead. Passed away right after the liberation, and so was spared the sight of his Alpine Bee as a burned-out shell. An SS Untersturmführer had ordered an anti-tank barrier thrown up in front of the cheese factory, and although the village had run up white flags of surrender, he had shot and killed a French officer who was riding unprotected on top of his tank. The Untersturmführer was immediately blown to bits by a tank shell and the factory caught fire and burned.

The day before that, Otmar Räuchle, his great-uncle's favorite cheese maker, had been shot and killed. He was already on his way home to Amtzell, where he still resided, when it occurred to him that he had forgotten to turn off the stirring machine. So he turns around, back to Geiselharz, turns off the machine so the electric motor won't burn out, and sets off for Amtzell again. He's almost home when he runs into some French soldiers. He takes off across a field, they shoot at him, and a bullet catches him in the back of the head and exits through his mouth. That same evening, Johann's great-uncle reached home after walking six days from Rottenburg to Amtzell. In Amtzell he heard that they'd put up a tank barrier in front of his Alpine Bee, so he decided to sit on a bench in front of Otmar Räuchle's cottage and wait for him to come home from work. So he has to witness them bringing in Otmar Räuchle's body. The next morning, they find him dead in Otmar Räuchle's living room, sitting in an armchair and slid sideways a little. They said he looked like he'd just nodded off. The Alpine Bee fire also consumed the queasy piano, consumed the red upholstered chairs whose legs were so delicately curved they seemed almost not to touch the floor, consumed the grandfather clock that seemed to strike in its sleep and the glass-fronted bookcase. Not consumed, however, were the twenty-four half-leather gilt-edged volumes of *Meyers Konversationslexikon*. Cousin Great-Uncle had transported them and the six-volume edition of Schiller from Geiselharz to

Wasserburg before he was locked up; he had noticed Johann's interest in these two works and said Johann should have them. And so they were his. Whether he took out a volume of Schiller or of Meyer, he always did so reverently. He felt rich. And within himself there was room, infinite room, but only for light, or really only for brilliance, the luster of gold and the highest notes. True, he was no tenor, but he could still rise and soar. Inside himself, every note was reachable. He only needed to leave it inside. As soon as he tried to sing or just to say it, it turned out that his brilliant note wasn't that brilliant. But as long as all that was expected of it was to fill Johann up, it was the fullest, loveliest, highest note in the world. Attuned in this way, Johann was unable to take notice of anything terrible. Anything dreadful fell away as easily as it had arrived. He wouldn't deny that around him there were dreadful things going on. But he couldn't pretend. And he would have had to pretend that anything terrible could touch him. It didn't touch him. He felt himself at flood tide, in an element of pure grace and glory. Every day he could recall was the most beautiful day of his life. Any other kind of day was simply not permitted. Confirmation day, in June, he and Josef in the crowd of confirmands. A most reverend bishop, also named Joseph (although with *ph*), successor to the sainted Ulrich, had come from Augsburg to examine the confirmands, asking them in front of the entire parish what was meant by the Trinity, the mysteries of the rosary, which saints had been commemorated in the previous week and which were to be celebrated this week and next week. The girls' index fingers had competed with the boys'. After the service: gold wrist watches for Josef and Johann from their great-uncle; an excursion up the Gebhardsberg, the vista, the lake a noble blue beast with Konstanz cradled between its legs; bratwurst, lemonade, their great-uncle, a celestial concentration of inexhaustible good fellowship. The fact that the canon from Wasserburg had held the bishop's staff and the canon from Nonnenhorn had held his miter exalted those two vicars forever in Johann's eyes. Despite being clad in a festive cope, the priest, on the other hand, gained nothing of lasting value thereby. On the Gebhardsberg, his great-uncle had again taken out one of his fine white handkerchiefs and wiped—no, practically scrubbed—the tip of his tongue. He'd done the same thing when Josef and Johann had tried on worsted suits and gabardine coats at Bredl's in Wangen. Johann never had the courage to ask him why he did that. Now the Anselm of all Anselms was dead. His fine white handkerchiefs were never used for anything except dabbing at the tip of his tongue. Perhaps it was simply that their great-uncle often wanted to—or had to—touch the tip of his tongue but didn't want to do it with a bare hand occupied with everyday tasks, hence those marvelous white handkerchiefs. O Anselm, thought Johann, now you are wholly mine. His mother had told him that in the years it took his great-uncle, without a pfennig to his name, to build up his cheese-making business, he had eaten nothing but what she called *sure Bodebira* a.k.a *saure Bodenbirnen* a.k.a. sour potatoes. And in the same spirit of frugality, he always walked to Wangen to withdraw his milk money, at least seven and a half miles there and back. Once he'd made it, of course, he always drove. And hummed. Hummed at the wheel. Without that melancholy, ponderously humming man, Johann might never have discovered Schiller. And even though it had done him no good to study the half-leather gilt-edged vagina, it was one thing to know what you didn't know and quite another not to know what you didn't know. The supreme moment: all the church flags are lowered, Canon Krumbacher holds out the bowl with the chrism for the most reverend bishop, who reaches in and daubs what clings to his finger onto Johann's forehead. It feels, and seen out of the corner of Johann's eye, looks like the stuff that shoots out of his IAWIA when he crosses the finish line. And then Canon Hebel comes with two altar boys and wipes off the bright and holy smudge with a cotton ball, which he hands to Höscheler's Heini, who puts it into the bowl being held by Frommknecht's Hermann. And from every direction, a wave of song: Holy God we praise Thy name.

Perhaps Mother felt she could no longer countenance the fact that only a thin wooden partition separated Johann's sofa from Lucile's bed. They were basically lying right next to each other. He could hear her whistling, breathing, and she must have heard him, too. Johann had to move back into Room 9 and the double bed. Anselm now slept where Josef had slept. Luckily, Johann would sleep on the side next to the

window. As he lay under his blanket, engaged with himself, he thought
his way out the window and over to the first window of Room 10. On
All Saints' Day, after a mouth-on-mouth and mouth-in-mouth session
against the wall of the corridor, he said, "I'll come tonight." He said it
with as little seriousness as possible. He said it as if he was saying: No
need to fear that I'll come, Lena, I just like saying it so much, would love
to repeat it over and over a thousand times, I'll come tonight, tonight,
tonight. . . . After two hours repeating it, he would say with as much
quiet fervor as possible: No need to fear, I'm not going to come, I just
say I am because I have to say it. And then he would start in again: I'll
come tonight. . . . Against the corridor wall, of course, he only said it
a single time, and as unseriously as he could. Hopefully, it didn't need
saying that if he came, he would not come across the creaking floorboards of the corridor, because Mother would respond to that with an
immediate What-is-it-Johann? It would have been embarrassing to even
mention his mother at all in conjunction with his nocturnal plan.

Silently, he rose from his bed, slipped out the window, and pulled
it closed behind him. A dark night, the streetlight still out of service.
But the red-gold chestnut leaves almost gave off a glow. You could only
guess at the outlines of the truck scale and train station. The light yellow
exterior house wall also had a sort of glow. Grandfather had provided the
windows of his light yellow building with sills and trim of reddish sandstone, and every window also boasted a red sandstone lintel. The sill of
one window reached almost to the sill of the next. It was possible to step
from one to the other. And he could steady himself by holding on to the
sandstone lintels, which projected far enough so that it must be possible
to get a good grip on them.

Johann, barefoot and in his gym shirt and shorts, felt fairly safe as
he stood up outside his window and began to inch along the wall. The
sandstone sills provided good footing. The sandstone lintel stuck out
a good inch, rising to a low peak above each window, and his fingers
found enough purchase on its sloping sides that he could feel his way
from sill to sill with his feet. It didn't get dicey until he reached the first
window of Room 10. Had Lena correctly interpreted his throwaway

remark? Would her window be left ajar and unlocked? Either she had
felt and thought the same thing he did—then the window would be
open—or she had not felt and thought the same—then he would
grope his way back to his own window. He couldn't very well knock
on hers. She had understood him. The window opened at his push.
She was even standing next to it. Gave him a hand down, although he
didn't need it. He climbed into her room without a sound. Lena led
him to the double bed. The night between All Saints and All Souls,
the only night when Josefine would not be sleeping in the same bed,
an arm's length away from Lena, because Josefine, who had worked for
Lena's family for years and was as good as a member of the family, had
to be in the Allgäu over All Saints and All Souls to pray at her parents'
grave. But under the east-facing window stood a bed for Lena's youngest brother. Hopefully he was as tight a sleeper as Anselm. Johann had
to pretend from the beginning that he had forgotten there was a six-
year-old in the room. On the other hand, he mustn't forget it. Later,
when he was back under the blanket in his own room, he realized that
his irresponsibility on this night had been different than it was with
Luise's sister on the raincoat in the Schwandholz woods.

Lena put up no resistance, not even a show of it. Of course, she
didn't help him. That he would have taken amiss. He pretended to
know what he was doing. At first he did. Then Lena must have realized that he wasn't as experienced as he pretended. Lena let him sense
that she sympathized with his clumsiness, that she was happy to share
in it, so to speak. She gave him to understand how unimportant it
was if nothing at all happened. That was the highest, sweetest, most
beautiful thing.

It was the most complete coming together he had ever known. And
at the most crucial, fated moment of all. An unheard-of harmony.
Whatever happened, wherever they ended up on this unpredictable
night, they would survive it together, they would be one. This mood
whose inventor was Lena carried him across the finish line. Made him
more responsible than he was. And as he was hurtling across the finish line, he should also have remembered that nothing from him should

make it all the way into her. One more thing to keep track of! It seemed to him that Lena would surely think he was a complete scoundrel if he was capable of cold-bloodedly pulling out of her with total control and icy calculation. Afterwards, he hoped he had succeeded. He wasn't sure. Back in his room, under the blanket, he kept replaying over and over what had played out in Lena's bed. He felt he was lying not in bed but in bliss. He was weightless, buoyed up by something he had never felt before. He didn't call it happiness. In fact, he rejected that word. Once again, no word for what was most important. For years he'd been running uphill, running, crawling, wriggling, clambering, taking on every hardship to gain another little bit and another little bit of ground, not to be deterred from his goal by any defeat, but with next to no idea what his goal was. Perhaps it would turn out that what was most important didn't even exist. Everything—war, poetry, the mountains, physical strength, clothing, sound, talking and silence—everything interested him only to the extent that it brought him closer to his goal. And what could not bring him closer had no existence. No independent existence. He had to force himself to pay attention to it, pretend it interested him. Nothing had ever interested him that didn't lead him up and in, across the finish line of his yearning, so to speak. And now it had happened, thanks to nothing and no one except Lena. Perhaps he could call it by the name *deliverance*. Actually, he needed no more words. He was delivered now. The stretch of trouble where everything was uncertain was now behind him. There you have it. That's that. And the gratitude, so sharp and clear and urgent it almost hurt. To be delivered this way from a doubtful existence into the most pure and beautiful certainty! I really feel like I'm not swimming against the current anymore, Lena. Suddenly, it's sweeping me off and away, and I'm the lightest, happiest cork afloat.

He'd brought a little blood back with him from Room 10, a dark stain swallowed by his black gym shorts.

The next day, when Lena's high-heeled solo snatched him from his chair and he rushed into the corridor, she wouldn't let him catch her, but as she slipped from his grasp she called back, "I'll come tonight." Then she was downstairs at the piano again. Since the French were no longer living in the house, she played Mozart. When she ran away from him to play, he could hear that her playing was aimed at him.

He did feel a bit humbled when she showed up at his window, slipped inside, and acted as if it was nothing special to grope her way from sill to sill along the outside wall, holding on to the sandstone lintel with her fingers. Was Lena even tall enough to reach the lintel while standing on the sill? After all, they were tall, old-fashioned windows for high-ceilinged, old-fashioned rooms. But here she was. In a silk wrap. He played his flashlight over it: fiery red inside, outside a riot of flowers. She saw Johann's astonishment and whispered, "My mother's." Johann had bolted both doors, taking care to do it without a sound. No one could get in. If Anselm woke up, Johann would have to try an Old Shatterhand gesture. He had taken an embroidered pillowcase out of the chest and laid it on top of the sheet. It didn't even fit the pillows they used now, and must have been part of his grandmother's trousseau. The saying embroidered in Gothic script was: Sweet Dreams till the Dawn, & Troubles Begone! Afterward, when Lena returned the way she had come, she took the pillowcase with her. She said she would wash it. Johann realized that the second night had been much bloodier than the first. It was clear that he would have to wipe the blood off his member, too. He remembered that in the bottom of the night stand there was a white cover that got pulled over the blue Marine Hitlerjugend cap on special occasions. He used it to wipe himself clean. He hid the now blood-stained cover in his school bag. Tomorrow he was planning to ride his bike to school anyway. Of the four or five more or less parallel routes from Wasserburg to Lindau, he chose one that first followed a little-used field road and then ran through the Birkenried along a line of fir trees. He threw the blood-stained cap cover into the Oeschbach and hoped that it would see to carrying the bloody thing out to the lake, and it would sink out of sight forever.

On the second night, Lena had again shared everything with him. On that second, more eventful night as well, their feeling of togetherness was more important than what had produced it. More happened on the second night than on the first. Before she clambered back out the window, Lena expressed it like this: "I won't have to confess that one."

After school he returned along the same route, past Bichel Pond and through the Birkenried. He'd never run into anyone on this route. This time, he saw from a long way off that, just before the train lineman's cottage, where his field road connected to a tarred road, someone had stood a bicycle on its head and was turning the rear wheel. Even before Johann came up to him, he saw that it was Wolfgang Landsmann.

"Got a flat?" asked Johann.

"What I haven't got is a repair kit," said Wolfgang.

Johann leaned his bike against one of the little fir trees that lined the road.

"*Grüss dich*," said Wolfgang.

"*Servus*, Wolfgang," said Johann. What he really wanted to ask was if this was the balloon-tire bike Edi Fürst had thrown down the bank at the gymnasium back then. But he could see it was a balloon-tire bike, so it was the one that had been thrown down. So what he should have said was: Oh yeah, that's the bike that Edi threw down back then. But he couldn't say that. But he couldn't pretend that he'd never seen the bike before, either. Since Wolfgang had a briefcase clamped to the luggage rack, Johann could have asked if Wolfgang was on his way home from school. But if Wolfgang had been attending secondary school in Lindau, he would have been in Johann's class, so he couldn't be coming from school.

Johann fetched the repair kit from his saddlebag with over-eager solicitude, took a look at the tire, and couldn't find a nail. So he said the only thing to do was to take off the wheel, remove the tube, pump it up, and dash the few yards to the Oeschbach. They'd hold it in the water and find the hole immediately. And he thought: I hope that bloody cap cover didn't get hung up somewhere nearby.

If the rise they called a hill hadn't blocked the view, they could have seen the gymnasium from where they were standing. Luckily though, they couldn't. Johann sensed that it would have really rubbed him the wrong way if Wolfgang had started talking about Edi Fürst and about that muster back then. He would simply not know what to say. What it was possible to say. And it was inconceivable for Johann to start talking about it himself. If Wolfgang were to start, Johann would have to react. How, he didn't know. So, in any event, he should devote all his attention to repairing the flat.

When Johann saw how little experience Wolfgang had with flats, he was able to pose as an expert, and Wolfgang admired his expertise. That did Johann good. He still took all his own flats to Hotze Franz in Hege and scratched the goats' ears instead of watching Franz fix them. But he had paid attention when Crooked Hat fixed his tire in Nonnenhorn. And now he was simply the expert. His repair kit contained all the necessary items. And the way Wolfgang watched respectfully as he played bicycle mechanic, he had no choice but to succeed. And he did. At least, the tire stayed inflated until they reached the Station Restaurant. They walked their bikes, since they had a lot to talk about. That is, Wolfgang wasn't finished with what he obviously wanted to tell Johann. Every day the weather allowed, he rode his bicycle to Lindau and from there took the train to Bregenz. He'd been going to school in Bregenz since late 1943.

How little Johann knows. That's what Wolfgang is most surprised at. Wolfgang's Jewish mother and his father, Dr. Landsmann, had a *privileged mixed marriage*. Despite his name, Wolfgang's father was not Jewish. From Stuttgart, originally from Weingarten, in fact. If the wife was Aryan, then the union was called simply a *mixed marriage*. Wolfgang was baptized by Father Dillmann in 1927. Me, too, Johann wanted to say, but couldn't. So his father was what they called *jüdisch versippt*—allied to a Jew by marriage—loses his post as medical examiner and health service doctor in Stuttgart, and is lucky to be put in charge of the air raid shelter in the Schwabtunnel. They get bombed out in '43 and move back here, to their house next to the Eschigs and the Halkes. The mother and Wolfgang move to Bregenz where he's admitted to a school. The principal knew he was breaking the law: pupils with a Jewish mother were only permitted to attend school through grade nine. In '44 Wolfgang volunteers for reserve officer training in Innsbruck without telling his parents. All that's left is the

Home Guard, under Commander Halke. At night they take down the tank barriers they had built during the day. Wolfgang's mother lived in constant fear of getting arrested. Head Teacher Heller had intended to see that she did. That's why she asked that the teacher be forced to sit in that window eight Sundays in a row with the sign around his neck: Iᴄʜ ᴡᴀʀ ᴇɪɴ Nᴀᴢɪ. Wolfgang's father had laughed and said it was misleading. It should have said: Iᴄʜ ʙɪɴ ᴇɪɴ Nᴀᴢɪ.

Wolfgang could see he was telling Johann things he'd never heard. "So you don't know that Rudolf Hess paid a visit to Frau Haensel in 1934 either?" No, Johann doesn't know that. He doesn't know that Frau Haensel is Jewish. Wolfgang is amazed. She was being protected by someone in Munich, said Wolfgang. Johann wanted to interject that Frau Haensel had always been a good coal customer of theirs. But he couldn't. He couldn't say anything. At the moment, the anti-fascist working group that had always existed in the town was putting together a documentation of the Nazi persecution of anti-fascists in Wasserburg from 1933 to 1945. Springe the lawyer, who'd already left town for Berlin in 1937, was chairing the group. Johann knew him only by sight, since he bought his coal from the competition. Frau Prestele, Dr. Rütten, Professor Bestenhofer, Hajek-Halke all belonged to the circle, all people who lived in the villas. Except for Frau Prestele and Herr Hajek-Halke, they weren't Johann's customers.

When they reached the chestnut trees, they could hear someone playing piano in the spare room. "Lena," said Wolfgang. Johann was nonplussed. But acted as if he was only vaguely familiar with the name. Wolfgang said, "A student of Frau Prestele's." Of course, Johann knew that. But since he was already the one who knew next to nothing, he nodded at this piece of information as if it were also news to him. "Prestele says she's very talented," said Wolfgang. And that was something Johann really hadn't heard before. "You know who she is," said Wolfgang. "She's the daughter of the family leasing your restaurant." Johann nodded but also shrugged his shoulders as if it were a matter of indifference whether he knew the lessee's daughter or not. But there was still more that Wolfgang knew. Her father Georg had always been an anti-fascist, and even in the darkest times, he and Wolfgang's father had discussed everything together. Lena and her whole family had lived through the terrible bombing raid in April of last year. At which point Johann could have said that Lena had told him the worst thing about that night was that when she scrambled out of the bomb shelter, there was no place to go to the bathroom in the smoldering ruins of Ludwigshafen. But he didn't say it. Wolfgang mastered the details of Lena and her family so thoroughly that Johann felt left out. Wolfgang had called Lena's father Georg. He was obviously on familiar terms with the whole family.

Then Wolfgang went up to one of the spare room's windows and rapped on the pane, but Lena was playing so loudly she didn't her him knocking. "She doesn't hear me," said Wolfgang. "When you see her, give her my best," he said. He hoped they would see each other more often now. Johann nodded. Wolfgang got on his bike, waved, and rode off toward the western grade crossing. Johann knew the way to the villas of the Eschigs and the Hajek-Halkes and to the Landsmanns' house.

He entered his house by the back door. He didn't want to see Lena yet. Mother had waited with his food. Anselm had already taken off again.

Afterward Johann sat and resisted the urge to write a poem. His inside was bubbling with the words Lena had whispered in his ear the last two nights. They had to whisper everything they wanted to say into each other's ear. That alone created a warmth that penetrated him through and through. And the words themselves were penetrating. Lena was a fanatic of diminutives. Instead of making what they diminished smaller, her diminutives duplicated and triplicated it, made it infinite, world-filling. Words and phrases didn't stream out of Lena's mouth, they were summoned. That was perhaps what made them so penetrating, that she summoned them so softly. Next to no consonants. Lena was a language macerator. The words that pressed in upon him could not have been softer or more vehement.

Till now he had had to be constantly on guard when he had anything to do with other people, careful that there were no mistakes he would have to make up for. And all the people he had to do with had also been on their guard not to make any mistakes. Mother had never been able to do anything about the fact that he was alone. She didn't even know he was alone. She was just as alone as he was. When Lena spoke into his ear, he had to think of his father, of the Eskimo language, of rubbing noses in greeting, and of the word tree. All at once, his whole word tree was a-rustle with Lena words. They didn't belong in his mouth. He would have to find his own words. Including for what Wolfgang had told him about himself and his mother and father. The fear in which Wolfgang's mother had lived because the teacher was going to have her arrested. Johann had to fend off the fear in which Frau Landsmann had lived. He had felt sorry for Wolfgang when Edi Fürst threw his bicycle down the bank. Then he had forgotten Wolfgang and forgot that he had forgotten him. Why didn't he say that he recognized his bicycle? He could have shown that he recognized it. Then Wolfgang would have known what Johann meant by it! Why didn't he say that? He is constrained by the fear Frau Landsmann had lived in. He wants nothing to do with it. Once or twice he had seen Frau Landsmann when he delivered Herr Hajek-Halke's coke to his ground floor storage shed, a kind of lean-to built onto his greenhouse. Frau Landsmann had stood at the fence, chatting with the permanently tanned Herr Hajek-Halke. Landsmanns were not their clients. Johann hardly glanced at the two of them while carrying the full coal hod into the greenhouse addition and the empty hod back to the cart where Niklaus or Dusan had the next full hod ready. Every year he had carried a hundred and twenty hundredweights of coke into Hajek-Halke's storage shed. Frau Landsmann's face: eyes that wanted to escape their sockets but were held back by her lower lids. Her eyes lay heavily on her lower lids. And her lips were also heavy. Wide and heavy. Her chin kept them from slipping off her face. Johann sensed that Wolfgang had told him what he told him because Johann needed to know it. Maybe Wolfgang thought Johann was at fault because he hadn't known all those things, hadn't noticed them. Johann resisted the assumed reproach. How was he supposed to know that Frau Haensel was Jewish? He didn't want to be told that something was expected of him. He wanted to decide what his own feelings should be. No one should require him to have a feeling he didn't have on his own. He wanted to live and not be afraid. Frau Landsmann would pass on her fear to him, he could sense it. He had to turn his thoughts away from her and her fear. One fear gives birth to another. Nothing was as certain as that. He was afraid of encountering Frau Landsmann. Since he knew about the fear she had lived in, he didn't know what he would do if he met her. How would he greet her, look at her, look away from her? Express more than he felt at that moment? He did not want to be forced. By anybody to do anything. The dead awaited him. He could not imagine Josef dead. In his mind's eye, he always saw him alive. Perhaps in the winter he would imagine the dead as dead. Not now. Not in the glow of this summer. He had volunteered in order to choose his branch of the service. And he had not volunteered for the flak because he didn't want to be branded a coward. He wanted to boast like ten naked niggers. The language he had learned after 1933 was his second foreign language after the language of the church. He had not embraced it any more than he embraced the language of the church. He had grappled with both languages. He needed to find his own language. For that, he had to be free.

Once, in the schoolyard in Lindau, on the last day of school, the flag was to be lowered and the principal had assigned Johann to uncleat the rope and slowly bring down the flag. The principal himself stood with outstretched arm right next to the flagpole. Because this principal had once sent Johann home with an insulting message for his mother—to the effect that, as he said to Johann, she would have to decide whether she wanted Johann to be a secondary school student or a coal shoveler—Johann first pretended that the line was tangled in the upper pulley, thereby forcing the principal to hold his arm out even longer. Then he pretended the line had unexpectedly let go and the flag came swooshing down and half buried the principal, who struggled free and said, "'The head idiot, who else.'" Johann would never forget his look of contempt and fury. The only other person who'd looked at him like that was the corporal with the MG 42 on the Kreuzeck when Johann said he thought the snow was white.

Johann never wanted to be subjected again, neither to power nor to fear. No one should have any claim on him. He wanted to be freer than anyone had ever been before.

Then he heard Lena's steps coming up the stairs and along the hall. He had to jump up and get out there in a flash, blocking her way and asking the question, "Was there anything between you and Wolfgang Landsmann? Is there still something?" He grabbed a fistful of her hair as if to indicate how well Wolfgang's fabulous, beautiful black hair, reaching smooth and shiny down to his collar in back—how well it went with her unruly and equally black, upsurging waves.

"Oh you," she said, "come here." And pulled his head to her in order to whisper more words full of weighty diminution and macerating power into his ear. Obviously she was not about to run out of words.

"And she's only sixteen," said the eighteen-year-old and furiously covered her mouth with his. That is, he was not furious at all; he just wanted to rage. Rage furiously on and in her mouth.

The next day it rained heavily. Johann took the train to school. On the way home, he recalled what he had dreamed the previous night. He worked himself into a kind of state free of volition. The dream should not have to obey him. He and Lena in a double bed. They are alone in the room. Lena is Josef's wife. Josef joins them. Johann and Lena ought to have known that they couldn't do such a thing here in Josef's realm, and Johann had asked Lena ahead of time if it wasn't too much—his brother's wife. Josef stood in the door and said only two words: scruffy clothes. Johann had stood in front of the mirror in Josef's jacket. But he had also lain in bed next to Lena with no clothes on.

When Johann woke from this dream, he felt ashamed.

Never again would he wear one of the lovely jackets that had been Josef's. He couldn't get rid of that dream. He could avoid the details, but the mood remained and colored everything. He tried to read. The dream intruded.

Luckily, he heard Lena's steps approaching and was in the hallway to intercept her, but she did not cuddle into his arm as usual. "Herr Krohn from Friedrichshafen is sitting at the regulars' table," she said. "He's weeping and telling how in April he was supposed to blow up the bridge across the Argen near Giessen. But he went out of his way to wait until five young French soldiers were crossing the bridge and then he pushed the plunger."

"What's he doing now?" asked Johann.

"Selling pants again," said Lena, "from a shack, since his shop is kaput."

"Lights out, knives out, three men to stir the blood," said Johann.

"Yes, Herr Seehahn," said Lena.

When Johann was alone in his room again, listening to the sounds the wind and rain made against the shutters on the four windows, he had to admit that he could not bring himself to tell Lena the dream in which she was Josef's wife. He should have told her the dream. She told him everything about herself. He could not tell her everything. Every day there was something he couldn't tell her. Write what he couldn't say to her? Write down the dream, then let Lena read the written words? A kind of hope that he could appease the dream by writing it down. Or that its power to shame him would lessen. He had to write down the dream. He had to defend himself.

Writing down the dream felt like something he shouldn't do. But he did it. He had to. Simply entrust yourself to language. Perhaps it can do something you can't.

When he had written down the dream, he saw that he had not written down the dream but what he thought the dream meant. There was nothing left of the dream's overflow. As long as he dreamt it, he had understood everything. Now, awake, he understands only its meaning. He had destroyed the dream by writing it down. He had not trusted language but had written what he wanted to write. He had wanted to deprive the dream of its power to shame by writing it down. He had aimed at something rather than entrusting himself. He would have to lose the habit of calculation, entrust himself to the sentences, to language. He imagined crossing the sea on a raft of sentences, even if the raft dissolved in the very act of being built and needed to be constantly rebuilt out of new sentences if he was not to drown.

When he begins to write, what he would like to write should already be there on the page. What reached the page through language, and thus on its own, would need only to be read by him. Language, thought Johann, is a gushing fountain.

Foreword as Afterword

"*IHR WERDET EUCH WUNDERN, Vater, wie es Euch da ring wird um die Brust.*"—"You'll be surprised how much it clears up your chest, Father," says Johann's father to his father. A more literal translation would be " . . . how light (or: easy) it becomes around your chest." Contemporary German would use *leicht* (light, easy) instead of the dialect word *ring*. But *ring* is more than "light"; it also encompasses "open," "comfortable," "at ease." First, one's chest is constricted; then it is *ring*. Which has nothing to do with *Ring* (ring) or *gering* (small, scant, limited). As a positive adjective, *ring* has died out in standard written German. *Grimms Deutsches Wörterbuch*, begun in the nineteenth century by the great philologists and folklorists Jakob and Wilhelm Grimm, is the German counterpart to the *Oxford English Dictionary*. It needs four closely-printed columns for its definitions and citations of *ring* in its various senses of "light," "easy," "small," "little," "meager," "cheap." Although according to Grimm, the use of the word begins to decline in the seventeenth century, "it continues a robust existence as an adjective and adverb in many dialects." If only that were still true. It is hard to understand why High German allowed this word to die out without having one of equal value to replace it. The High German word *gering* accounts for only a fraction of what *ring* was once able to express: only "small," "little," but not "light," and "easy." A sixteenth-century verse by Hans Sachs cited in Grimm demonstrates that *leicht* is not a synonym for *ring*:

nun diese pflicht
daucht sie gar leicht und ring.
Now this duty
seems to her quite light and easy.

If *leicht* was the equivalent of *ring*, a poet as concrete and precise as
Hans Sachs would never have written *leicht und ring*. In short, we've
lost *ring*. "Light" plus "open" plus "comfortable" equals *ring*. And the
fact that Johann's father, who insisted on speaking his Royal Bavarian
Middle School German in the village's thicket of dialects, couldn't get
by without the word *ring* shows me that there is no substitute for it.
So I must run the risk that most readers will either take no cognizance
of the word or will regard it as a meaningless syllable and hold it against
the book or its author.

Another example: on Christmas Eve in the restaurant, Hanse Luis
says, "*da fällt der Rotzglonker, wie sich's gehört, wenn er wieder eine Zeit
lang gelampt hat, regelmäßig in den Abgrund.*"—"When the glob o' snot
has hung there long enough, it finally drops—as is right and proper—
down into the abyss." At issue is the word *gelampt*. Because several people not native to the village are present, Hanse Luis is speaking High
German here, every word of which "sounded like he was standing on
a pedestal to say it." And yet he must say about the thing described as
temporarily suspended from his nose that it has *gelampt*. High German
gehangen (past participle of *hängen*, to hang) simply won't do; *hängen*
doesn't convey the swaying, the imminence of a fall already inherent
in the hanging, the way *lampen* does. It comes from the noun *Lampe*
(lamp), derived from Greek and Latin via French. I think German is
the only language that developed a verb from the noun, but it was a
verb not destined to enjoy the imprimatur of High German. So it just
hangs around in dialect and will eventually fall into oblivion.

Another example: *losen*. This is how Semper's Fritz has to talk: "*Also,
Kameraden aller Jahrgänge, loset, was einem eingerückten, das Ehrenkleid
der Nation tragenden ehemaligen Spenglergesellen hat zugefügt werden
dürfen.*"—"OK, OK, comrades of all ages, listen up to what an enlisted

former apprentice tinsmith wearing the honorable uniform of his nation had to swallow." Since out-of-towners are among his auditors at the regulars' table, he, too, speaks High German. But when he requests their attention, he can't say *Hört mir zu!* (Listen to me) or *Horcht her!* (Hearken here), and certainly not *Spitzt eure Ohren!* (Perk up your ears). He has to say *loset*.

Grimm's dictionary notes that in all its uses, the verb *losen* expresses an appeal for attention and calls it "a word completely unknown to the modern written language." There's nothing to be done about that. Johann Peter Hebel (1760–1826), who wrote in both standard German and Alemannic dialect, makes it into Grimm as a source for *losen*:

> *loset, was i euch will sage!*
> *d'glocke het zehni gschlage.*
> Listen to what I have to tell you!
> The clock has struck ten.

Why does High German forget a word for which it has no replacement, or merely a replacement instead of an equivalent?

One more example, the noun *Masen*: "*Einen rotglänzenden Prinz-Ludwig-Apfel nach dem anderen brach er und ließ ihn vorsichtig, daß der Apfel keine Masen bekomme, in den umgehängten Rupfensack gleiten.*"—"He picked the shiny red Prince Ludwig apples one after another and slid them carefully, so they wouldn't get bruised, into the picking bag slung over his shoulder." *Masen* does not appear in Duden, the standard dictionary of contemporary German from the publisher of the same name. But Kaltschmitt's *Gesammt-Wörterbuch der Deutschen Sprache* of 1850 still includes *Mase* with the meaning "bruise," "blemish." In Grimm, it is linked to the verb *masen*, to taint, stain, blemish. Kaltschmitt also revealingly includes the alternative spelling *Mose*. In fact, in dialect, the *a* in *Mase* is pronounced like the *a* in English "wall" or "fall" or "tall." Neither a standard German *a* nor an *o* but an open vowel somewhere between the two. High German has forgotten the word since 1850, and offers in its place: *Fleck* (spot, stain), *Mal* (mark, stigma), and *Makel* (flaw, taint, blemish, macula), but none of these represent what a *Mase* is. A *Fleck* contrasts too much with its immediate environment. The precise and therefore beautiful thing about a *Mase* is that it concentrates and only slightly darkens all the color values around it. *Mal* is too abstract, too stilted and filled with pathos. *Makel* is too moralistic. But *Mase* gets forgotten and there is nothing to replace it.

A word about names: like many regional German dialects, the one spoken in Wasserburg and its surroundings puts the family name first and then the given name. But when a family name crops up in too many houses, the names of the houses themselves (names they have inherited from their original inhabitants) become important. Gierer's Hermine and Hagen's Fritz are not enough; one needs Helmer Gierer's Hermine and Semper Hagen's Fritz, who then come to rely entirely on the house names: Helmer's Hermine and Semper's Fritz. It's the same with Hanse Luis, whose real name is Alois Hotz. Because of a plethora of Hotzes, the house name Hans comes to his aid. He's the Luis from Hans's. If a name has only one syllable and ends in a consonant, however, then an extra *e* gets attached to it. This final *e* is just barely voiced, as in French *trente* or *pente* or *quarante* in the south of France, or in the first person singular inflection in German: *ich gehe, halte, hauche* (I go, stop, whisper), which is also barely voiced. This is how the names Schnelle Paul and Hanse Luis come to be. If there hadn't been so many Hotzes, Hanse Luis would have been Hotze Luis. A Georg Schmitt, however, wasn't called Schmitte Georg but rather Schmitt's Georg. The hardness of the double *t* permitted the *–s* inflection. Polysyllabic family names, on the other hand, always get a genitive *–s* no matter how they end, cf. Helmer's Hermine, etc.

These are linguistic processes. No one organizes them, to say nothing of regulating them. And yet they occur with a regularity that one can formulate as a law. It is a refreshing realization. Languages that have written traditions, languages that are registered and monitored and brought to our consciousness by all the disciplines of linguistics—such languages are rather overburdened with rules telling us what is correct and what is incorrect. Oral dialects take care of all that with perfect precision and without the aid of academies or even of a written tradition. That is, the dialect doesn't take care of it, the people do—for example, the people in the village. Like all natural things, however, the dialect dies when conditions no longer favor its continued existence or, to express it in the language of today, when its logotope is destroyed. Then the time is at hand to prepare a eulogy. And gradually, such a time is becoming imaginable.

Glossary

Ankerkette	anchor chain
Ata	a brand of scouring powder
Beatrijs	The eponymous heroine of a fourteenth-century Dutch poem recording the legend of a nun who leaves the convent for the man she loves. After seven years, he deserts her. She spends the next seven years as a prostitute to support her children. When she asks outside the convent what became of the nun Beatrijs, she learns that she is still at the convent. The Virgin Mary has taken her place for fourteen years and she can now return, her absence unnoticed.
Bienenstich	"bee sting" cake
Brennabor	German manufacturer of automobiles, motorcycles, and bicycles from 1871 to 1945
"Dein ist mein ganzes Herz"	"My Whole Heart Is Thine," an aria from Franz Lehár's operetta *The Land of Smiles* (1923)
Dominik, Hans	German science fiction author, 1872–1945

Erb, Karl	German tenor, 1877–1958
Flaggleine	flag halyard
Heesters, Johannes	Dutch-German actor, 1903–2011
Henkel	a brand of German sparkling wine
Horney, Brigitte	German-American actress, 1911–1988
"Jägerlied"	"Hunter's Song" by Franz Schubert (D. 204)
Jungvolk	Nazi organization for boys ten to fourteen years old
KDF	*Kraft durch Freude* (Strength through Joy), Nazi organization for leisure and vacation activities such as group tours
Knoteck, Hansi	Austrian actress, born 1914
Kommerzienrat	"councilor of commerce," an antiquated honorific conferred on a businessman
"Kommet ihr Hirten, ihr Männer und Frau'n"	"Come, Ye Shepherds, Men and Women," Bohemian-German Christmas carol
"Komm zurück"	"Come Back," hit song from 1939
Krahl, Hilde	Austrian actress, 1917–1999
Kreisleiter	National Socialist county administrator
Kyffhäuser Bund	Kyffhäuser Association, an umbrella organization for veterans' and reservists' groups
Leuchtturm	lighthouse
NSKK	*Nationalsozialistisches Kraftfahrerkorps* (National Socialist Motor Vehicle Drivers Corps), provided instruction in the operation and repair of motorcycles and automobiles, especially to young people

NSV	*Nationalsozialistische Volkswohlfahrt* (National Socialist Public Welfare Service)
Obersturmführer	"Senior assault leader," SS rank equivalent to a first lieutenant
"Oh du fröhliche, oh du selige"	"Oh You Joyful, Oh You Blessed" *(grace-bestowing Christmas time)*, German Christmas carol
Ordensburg	Originally a fortress built by a medieval German military order; during the Third Reich a training school for Nazi and SS leaders
Persil	a brand of laundry detergent
Regenbogen	rainbow
Röhm, Ernst	(1887–1934) leader of the SA, the paramilitary wing of the National Socialist Party, homosexual, assassinated on Heinrich Himmler's orders
Rökk, Marika	German-Austrian actress, 1913–2004
"Sag beim Abschied leise Servus"	"When Parting Just Whisper 'So Long,'" hit song from 1936
Schlageter, Albert	Nazi martyr, court-martialed and executed by the French in 1923
Section 11	A Nazi law making it illegal to christen a child with a Jewish name
Section 175	An 1871 law, repealed in 1994, criminalizing homosexual relations between men
Signalgast	signalman
Steuerbord	starboard
Steuermann	helmsman

Stifter, Adalbert | Austrian novelist, 1805–1868

Sturmführer | See *Obersturmführer, Untersturmführer.*

Tauber, Richard | Austrian tenor, 1891–1948

Untersturmführer | "Junior assault leader," SS rank equivalent to a second lieutenant

"Von Apfelblüten einen Kranz" | "A Wreath of Apple Blossoms," an aria from Franz Lehár's operetta *The Land of Smiles* (1923)

Wer hat dich du schöner Wald | *Who [raised you up], you lovely forest,* opening lines of "The Hunter's Farewell" by Joseph von Eichendorff, set to music by Felix Mendelssohn-Bartholdy and others

Werner, Ilse | German actress, 1921–2005

Wer nie sein Brot mit Tränen ass | *Who never ate his bread in tears,* opening lines of a poem, often called "Song of the Harp Player," from Goethe's novel *Wilhelm Meister's Apprenticeship,* set to music by Franz Schubert (opus 12, no. 2) and others

Werwolf | Werewolf, a member of a group of irregular fighters organized in 1944 to resist the Allied invasion of Germany

Winnetou | Wild West novel by Karl May (1842–1912). The eponymous hero is an Apache chief and the friend of the first-person narrator, a German immigrant nicknamed Old Shatterhand.

WHW | *Winterhilfswerk* (Winter Relief Organization), collected donations of money, clothes, and food for needy citizens

Zürnewible | name of a local bogeyman